THE
SHAAR
PRESS

THE JUDAICA IMPRINT
FOR THOUGHTFUL PEOPLE

THE RUN

A novel by

CHAIM ELIAV

Translated from the Hebrew *Kesones Passim*
by Libby Lazewnik

AWAY

A frightening disappearance,
a cult, and a desperate search

A
SHAAR
PRESS
PUBLICATION

Published by **SHAAR PRESS**
Distributed by MESORAH PUBLICATIONS, LTD.
4401 Second Avenue / Brooklyn, New York 11232 / (718) 921-9000

Distributed in Israel by SIFRIATI / A. GITLER BOOKS
10 Hashomer Street / Bnei Brak 51361

Distributed in Europe by J. LEHMANN HEBREW BOOKSELLERS
20 Cambridge Terrace / Gateshead, Tyne and Wear / England NE8 1RP

Distributed in Australia and New Zealand by GOLDS BOOK & GIFT SHOP
36 William Street / Balaclava 3183, Vic., Australia

Distributed in South Africa by KOLLEL BOOKSHOP
Shop 8A Norwood Hypermarket / Norwood 2196 / Johannesburg, South Africa

ISBN: 1-57819-148-3 Hard Cover
ISBN: 1-57819-149-1 Paperback

Printed in the United States of America by Noble Book Press Corp.
Custom bound by Sefercraft, Inc. / 4401 Second Avenue / Brooklyn, N.Y. 11232

1

As sudden as a bolt of lightning, the thought flashed into Zevulun Kimmerman's mind: "I haven't heard from Yossi in four days!"

He stood at his office window, hands clasped behind his back as he gazed out at the endless blue of the Mediterranean Sea. Dusk was falling gently over the darkening water, changing the hue of the sky. The setting sun painted the quiet waves shades of silver. It was the hour when Zevulun allowed his thoughts free rein. Today they tumbled about in admirable abandon: from thoughts of work to those of home; from today's triumphs to tomorrow's agenda. They wandered from last night's satisfying *daf yomi* class in his neighborhood shul to the warmth of pleasant conversations and new ties forged that day. From there, his thoughts passed into more vexing channels, dwelling on the various problems that faithfully accompanied each day.

And that was when, without warning, he remembered Yossi.

His right hand moved up to his head, adjusting the black yarmulke. The gesture, for him, was a clear sign of tension, though its source was still unclear. Why, he wondered uneasily, was he so troubled by the fact that Yossi had not called?

He returned to his paper-strewn desk, sat down, and picked up the phone to call his wife.

"Hello, Tzipporah?"

"Hi! What's new, Zevulun?"

"Nothing special." He forced a casual tone. "I just thought I'd call to see how things are going at home. Everything all right? … Yes? Good!"

"And what's new at your end?" she asked again.

Zevulun was quiet for a moment. "Everything's fine here. Nothing special. You know — business here, business there. Ilan managed to conclude that deal in Hadera. Those 300 dunams were sold for a good price — $5000 per dunam … Who bought them? A young Canadian. He's going into business here in Israel. He's planning to build a community for young couples on that land … True, it's still zoned for agriculture, but there's going to be a change soon. Somebody over there — you know where — has promised to help … "

"Wonderful!"

"Yes. Wonderful. But this isn't something to discuss over the phone."

A brief silence descended. Tzipporah's keen antennae were receiving signals that her husband had something on his mind. Her imagination groped rapidly, but failed to come up with even a glimmering of an idea about what Zevulun wanted. Simply to break the silence, she asked, "When will you be home?"

"I think I'll come right after *Ma'ariv*. I'm a little tired tonight, so I'll skip the *shiur* … No, no, it's nothing. Just a headache."

"Did something happen to trouble you today?"

"No. Just the usual work-related stresses … All right, I'll say good-bye now."

"Good-bye, Zevulun."

Just before she hung up, Zevulun hastily — and, he hoped, casually — tossed the question at his wife: "By the way, did Yossi happen to call home today?"

"Yossi? No."

Silence.

Tzipporah hesitated, then asked, "Why do you ask? Are you worried about something?"

"No special reason. Worried? Not at all. I just wanted to know."

"All right," Tzipporah said reluctantly. "No, he hasn't called." She paused, then burst out with, "What's the matter, Zevulun?"

His tone sharpened. "I told you — nothing."

"All right then. Come home and we'll talk."

Slowly, Zevulun hung up the receiver. Swiveling in his chair, he stared out the window at the darkening sky. His eyes rested on the strip of purple the sun had left on the horizon, where sky meets sea — a farewell gift before complete night descended. In the distance, a lone light shone on the dark water. A fishing craft, most likely.

So he hasn't called home, either, Zevulun thought. *What's going on?*

He was forced to admit to himself that this was not the first time his son had seen fit to act as if his parents did not exist — sometimes for days on end. No, it was not a new phenomenon. But this time, the father felt a powerful, though inexplicable, pang of worry. His chest felt constricted, his breathing slightly labored. Why hadn't Yossi called in all this time? What was he trying to tell them?

With an abrupt motion, Zevulun swung back around to face the desk. Both hands rearranged the files lying there, as his thoughts stampeded on. Was it because of what had happened between them last Friday, just minutes before Yossi returned to yeshivah?

No. It couldn't be that. Yossi himself had realized that his father was right. And yet, if that was the case, why had Zevulun dredged up that memory now? He had no idea. All he knew was that, because of what had happened last Friday, he would feel immensely reassured to hear his son's voice.

His right hand reached for the phone again, seemingly powered by a will of its own. He had dialed the number of the yeshivah's public telephone and was listening to the first ring, when he hastily slammed down the receiver. No! After what had happened, he could not be the one to do the phoning. Yossi must be the one to call *him*!

Zevulun stood up. He stretched his cramped limbs and switched on the light. Most of the offices in "Hero House" on Kaufman Street were already closed for the night, though he could still discern sounds of movement in the building. He enjoyed these quiet hours at the start of the evening. It was a good time to think — to clear his desk and his mind. Most days he found the time to murmur a few *mishnayos* from the small *sefer* he always kept in his pocket. That had been the deathbed wish — more, the command — of his own father, who had been distressed by the way Zevulun was immersing himself so completely in his business affairs.

To be honest, these were also the hours when Zevulun did not especially relish being at home. It was the nerve-wracking time of putting the children to bed, a time of noise and tumult when he preferred peace and quiet. This was truer than ever tonight, with his thoughts turning constantly to the yeshivah — to Yossi.

He never had much patience with the children after a full day's work. They all made him nervous — but no one as much as Yossi. Why was it that Yossi always drove him to the point of distraction? Not Pinny, not Elazar or any of the others. Just Yossi!

Returning to his chair, Zevulun closed his eyes and tried the relaxation exercises he had recently learned. For a moment he toyed with the tempting plan of driving down to the yeshivah on some pretext. He would be satisfied with a glimpse of his son from the distance, without approaching him. Just to ease his conscience and make certain that everything was all right. He would decide afterwards what to do next.

But, on second thought, the idea seemed illogical — even dangerous. Yossi was no fool. He might notice Zevulun's presence and take it as a sign that his father had relented, or even regretted what had happened. Yossi could turn this knowledge to his own benefit. Zevulun shook his head. No! He must not go to the yeshivah tonight.

After an internal struggle, he gave in and dialed the yeshivah's number again.

"Hello? Is this Yeshivat Sha'ar L'Banim?"

"Yes." A student's young voice answered.

"Can you call Yossi Kimmerman for me, please?"

"Sure."

Zevulun waited long minutes, the silent receiver pressed to his ear. He intended to hang up the instant he heard his son's voice. He would not speak to Yossi tonight. The time was not yet ripe for a dialogue between them — not after what had occurred on Friday ...

"Hello?" It was the same young student. He sounded breathless.

"Yes, I'm still here."

"I'm sorry, I couldn't find him. He wasn't in the *beis medrash* or the dining room or his own room."

Zevulun gripped the phone tighter. "Then where could he be?"

"I don't know, sir. Are you his father?"

"No." All he needed was for Yossi to hear that his father had phoned. "But please answer one more thing for me."

"Yes?"

"Have you seen Yossi at all today?"

The boy fell silent. Then, hesitantly, he said, "I ... think I did ... " Another brief silence, followed by a more decisive answer. "No. No, I didn't see him today. I'm sorry."

Zevulun answered weakly, "Thank you. Good-bye."

The line went dead. Zevulun did not hurry to replace the receiver at his own end. Instead, he stared at it blindly, while his other hand twisted the cord around and around his fingers. Dimly he heard the monotonous buzz of the dial tone. It sounded vaguely like the wail of a siren ...

"So what if that boy didn't happen to see him?" he said aloud in the empty office. "Just because some kid who happened to pick up the public phone didn't run into Yossi today, does that mean Yossi isn't at the yeshivah?"

How many times in the past had the father tried to reach his son by phone, only to be told that Yossi could not be found? On the second or third try, they would find him. It might happen that way again tonight. Perhaps Yossi had stepped out of the yeshivah building to buy something at the kiosk across the street? In the end, after Friday's monumental battle, Zevulun had thrown his sons a few shekalim — as opposed to the other times when Yossi had left without his allowance. No, there was no cause for worry.

Then why were his nerves twisted into such an anxious knot?

He had no recollection of replacing the receiver, but its shrill signal jerked him abruptly from his tangled musings. In the course of two seconds he mentally reviewed all the people who might possibly be phoning him at this hour. "Hello, Regev Investments."

"Zevulun! How are you?"

"Ah, it's you, Ilan! How did you know I was still at the office?"

"I called your home. Your wife told me." Curiously, Ilan asked, "What *are* you doing there so late, anyway?"

"And here's a question for you," Zevulun countered mildly. "Why don't you mind your own business?"

Ilan was his chief clerk. Though he himself was nonobservant, he got along well with the rest of the office staff, all of them religious. Still, there were some things about the younger man that Zevulun disliked — such as the earring Ilan chose to wear to the office. Zevulun tried to accept it, telling himself that this was merely another sign of the times in which they were living. He certainly never voiced his feelings aloud. It was enough that Ilan was a faithful employee, dedicated to the job. Ilan was well versed in property investment and Zevulun often sought his opinion.

On the personal level, they were on friendly terms; Ilan had enjoyed the hospitality of Zevulun's home a number of times already. Living in the neighborhood, he sometimes dropped in on a Shabbos to partake of the family cholent. Ilan was accustomed to Zevulun's bantering, and took no offense.

"Okay, boss. You're right," Ilan laughed. "Actually, I'm calling about my own business — that is, the business I've been involved in. The

Hadera land deal that I thought I closed with the Canadian this morning." He paused, his voice growing somber. "I'm afraid the deal is on the rocks."

"Yes?"

Sharply, Ilan asked, "What do you mean, 'yes'? Why are you so apathetic, Zevulun? Do you have any idea how much money we're talking about here? Not to mention two months of running around, planning, negotiating — all about to go up in a puff of smoke! What's the matter with you?"

Zevulun realized he had made a mistake. Normally, Ilan's news would have elicited a spate of anxious questions from him. And here he was, reacting with nothing but a distant, and oh-so-polite, "Yes?"

"Ilan, calm down. My mind was somewhere else. That's why I answered you that way. Let's talk about this matter sensibly during work hours tomorrow. All right?"

"That would be fine — except that the Canadian is leaving the country first thing tomorrow morning!"

Zevulun took a deep breath. "Okay. In that case, we'll discuss it right now."

"I'm coming over."

"*No.* Let's deal with this over the phone."

Ilan did not answer. Zevulun's reaction astonished him but, sensing that his boss meant what he had said, Ilan did not press the point. The truth was, the Canadian was not leaving tomorrow, but the day after. Their talk could easily be put off until the morning. Ilan had a special interest in meeting privately with Zevulun this evening, on another matter entirely, but he had a feeling he was not wanted around the Regev offices just then.

"You know what, Zevulun?"

"What?"

"You're right. We'll talk about it tomorrow."

"I thought you said the Canadian fellow is leaving first thing in the morning!"

"I'll speak to him tonight. I'll hold out some vague promises that will get him hoping for a better deal, and I'll try to keep him here another day at least. Trust me."

"Be careful, Ilan. Don't tell him anything we can't back up."

"Do you know me to be a liar?"

"Of course not! But you do have a habit of prettying up the facts from time to time … "

"Thanks for the compliment," Ilan said dryly. "I gather you're nervous about something this evening."

"Hmm … Where do you get that idea?"

"Haven't a clue." Ilan waited a beat, then asked, "Does it have anything to do with your son, Yossi?"

Zevulun was taken aback. "What? What did you say?"

But Ilan had already hung up.

Anger suffused Zevulun — anger at this invasion of his most private thoughts. What was Ilan doing, accusing him of being nervous, and bringing up Yossi's name? Tzipporah must have let something slip. When he asked her earlier whether Yossi had called home, he had noticed that she found the question strange. Still, did that give her the right to divulge her concern to Ilan? Never!

Besides, he wasn't at all sure that he really *was* nervous about Yossi. A little worried, maybe. He wanted to know where his son was. But nervous?

With trembling hands, Zevulun pulled a pack of cigarettes from his desk drawer and lit one. He had almost succeeded in breaking the smoking habit. But at the moment he needed a cigarette to alleviate the tension. The rising smoke seemed to screen him from himself. His eyes followed the smoke rings as they floated ceilingward. It would be hard to go home now, to face his wife's scrutiny with a semblance of calm. She would doubtless want to interrogate him the moment he walked through the door. Before he did, he had to be sure that all was well with Yossi — to rid himself of the nagging anxiety that was disrupting his peace. But what to do? How to find out?'

He picked up the phone again.

"Hello — Yeshivat Nachal Kedumim?"

"Yes, this is the office. There's no one here right now."

"Who are you?"

"The janitor."

Zevulun grunted in annoyance. The voice at the other end said, "Excuse me? What did you say?"

"Nothing, nothing. Do you happen to have the number of the yeshivah's public telephone?"

The number was supplied. Zevulun jotted it down, thanked the man, and hung up. An instant later, he was dialing again.

"Good evening. I'd like to speak to Elazar Kimmerman, please."

"Just a second."

"Thank you."

Moments later, he heard the welcome sound of his oldest son's voice. "Elazar? Hello, it's Abba. What's new?"

"Everything's fine, Abba. We're learning, and that's about it. Why are you calling?"

"First of all, isn't it possible that I might just be calling to see how you are? And apart from that … I want to know how things are going with Yossi."

With Yeshivat Nachal Kedumim located only a short distance from Yeshivat Sha'ar L'Banim, Zevulun had appointed Elazar to keep a watchful eye on Yossi. Elazar was 21 years old; Yossi, 16. The brothers learned together three times a week, each of their sessions lasting an hour and a half. The father had wanted them to learn every evening, but Elazar had claimed that that would put too much pressure on Yossi. Now, with this phone call, Zevulun hoped in a roundabout way to learn more about his younger son.

To his disappointment, Elazar answered, "I don't know. He hasn't been over to learn for several nights already."

Zevulun caught his breath. "What do you mean, he hasn't been over?"

"Exactly that, Abba. For the past few days Yossi hasn't come here to learn with me. I'm not about to run after him!"

"Has he come at least once since Shabbos? Just once?" To his own ears, the words sounded like a plea.

"No. The last time we learned was last Thursday … Why are you interested in exactly when he stopped coming?"

Zevulun groped for words that would not reveal his inner turmoil. "Oh, no special reason. But why didn't you check up on him, to find out why he hasn't been coming?"

"I told you, Abba! I don't think I have to be the one to run after him. But if you want, I'll go over there right now."

"No, no," Zevulun said hastily. "Don't do that!" The words burst from him almost in a scream.

Something is not right, Elazar thought. He pressed, "But Abba, why not? I'll tell him you're worried about him."

"Elazar, I forbid you to do that! Do you hear me?"

His father's stern and very forceful tone took Elazar by surprise. After a moment's silence, he asked quietly, "Abba, has something happened?"

Zevulun replied hurriedly, making a monumental effort to restore a measure of calm to his voice. "What in the world are you talking about? Whatever makes you think that?"

Elazar fell silent again. Finally, with a feeling of deep unease, he said, "All right, Abba, don't worry. If you don't want me to go, I won't. What I don't understand is this: A minute ago you asked me why I didn't try to find out where he is, and now you're not letting me do exactly that."

He heard his father sigh. "I've decided that you're right, Elazar. We must not make him think we're begging. You know what Yossi's like — he'll turn that to his advantage. Do you understand?"

Zevulun believed he'd managed to divert Elazar from the concerns he preferred to keep to himself. The knowledge that Yossi had not come to learn with his brother since last Shabbos only increased his worry.

"Yes, I understand," Elazar answered softly.

The first thing Elazar did after hanging up with his father was call his mother at home.

Once again, Zevulun was left alone in his office, to try to ward off the demons of anxiety that threatened to consume him. There was little else he could do about Yossi tonight. He was convinced that nothing terrible had happened to his son — at least, intellectually he was convinced. But there was a growing inner conviction that told him otherwise ...

Right now, his job was to go home and allay his wife's fears. He locked his office and went out into the empty parking lot, where his silver Mitsubishi awaited him in lone splendor. Zevulun began the drive through the traffic-laden Tel Aviv streets, toward his home on HaNevi'im Street.

2

evulun Kimmerman rose at 6:30, as he did every morning.

"I won't be coming back home after *davening*," he announced to his wife, who was barely awake.

"Why?" she asked drowsily.

"I have to go somewhere. The matter is urgent."

Tzipporah was quiet for a moment. When she spoke, all she said was, "At least drink something hot before you go."

He tossed a vague, "Maybe," over his shoulder as he left the room.

Zevulun walked out of shul before *davening* was finished. He left the velvet bag containing his *tallis* and *tefillin* on a table as though he planned to return momentarily. A short drive down Ibn Gabirol Street brought his silver Mitsubishi to Shaul HaMelech Avenue, where the early-morning traffic was still light. At the railway station near the Ayalon junction he turned right onto the road to Jerusalem.

As he drove, his eyes darted repeatedly to the rear-view mirror to check the traffic behind him, and his nervous hand adjusted the mirror needlessly time and again. During one of these adjustments, he suddenly caught sight of his own reflection in the mirror. It was a frightening spectacle, dominated by eyes sunken with sleeplessness and radiating a nebulous fear. His cheeks were drawn and pale. Zevulun bit his lip in vexation: He did not like what he was seeing. Angrily, he increased the pressure of his foot on the gas pedal. He was angry because he sensed — without quite knowing why — that he and his son Yossi stood at the brink of a yawning chasm....

At this stage, he had no reason to suspect a tragedy, Heaven forbid. There was no reason to call in the police. All that had happened so far was that his "gem" had decided to do a vanishing act for a few days — for the express purpose of enraging his father. Just another in a long chain of such behavior on Yossi's part.

Only this time, he had gone too far. Yossi's action had been calculated to elicit maximum worry and trepidation. That boy would certainly hear from his father when he came home!

Why, then, did anxiety continue to burrow its way into Zevulun's innards, like a snake into its hole?

Traffic thickened as the road wound its way up past Telz Stone. Zevulun's car crept along at a maddeningly slow pace. He resented every minute's delay that kept him from Yeshivat Nachal Kedumim, where his son Elazar learned. He wanted to arrive before the boys began their morning *seder,* having no desire to summon his son out of the *beis medrash;* that would only serve to alert the other students to his unexpected visit. At all cost, Zevulun wanted to avoid attracting undue attention and the rumors that would circulate afterward. He hoped that a talk with Elazar would help him arrive at a solution to Yossi's mysterious disappearance.

And he must do so before word spread among those who devoured such stories with relish — before his family's good name was affected. He could already hear the kind of talk that would be generated.

"Have you heard what happened to the Kimmermans?"

"No. Who are they?"

"You know, the wealthy real-estate magnate from Tel Aviv. Didn't he learn with you in Chevron?"

"No, I don't recall..."

"Never mind, that's not important. His son ran away!"

"What? Are you serious? And what do you mean, 'ran away'?"

"Just that! I don't know the details yet, but he's run away, and believe me, it's not pretty..."

Gnashing his teeth, Zevulun rammed his foot hard on the gas, and just barely succeeded in hitting the squealing brakes in time to avoid crashing into the car ahead of him. With both hands gripping the wheel, he leaned back, trembling. He had not lost control in this way for a long time.

Once in Jerusalem, not far from the Central Bus Station, Zevulun parked near a bank of public telephones and dialed the number of his office in Tel Aviv.

"Varda? Listen, I'm out of town at the moment. I hope to be back in the office by this afternoon. Is everything under control there? Good... Now, I want you to tell Ilan — what? He's there now? No, no, I don't want to speak to him. *I don't want to speak to him now, understand?* Just give him a message from me. Tell him not to run after the Canadian — you know who I mean, the one who's interested in that property in Hadera. Tell Ilan that if the fellow's not interested in buying, he doesn't have to buy. With Hashem's help, we'll find another buyer. The important thing is, Ilan must not lower our price — the price the Canadian has already agreed to. Got that? Good. Thank you, Varda. Good-bye."

Zevulun was satisfied. He had managed to intercept his son before he entered the yeshivah's *beis medrash.* Elazar understood, from the jerk of his father's head, that he was to follow him. Without a word, he trailed Zevulun out of the yeshivah and into the car. They sat in silence during the quick drive to the neighborhood of Rechavia. There, on a narrow side street, Zevulun killed the motor and turned to face his son. Fixing Elazar with a long, penetrating and suffering look, he asked, "Well? What do you think is happening?"

Elazar knew what he was referring to. He flexed his fingers nervously. "I don't know."

"You didn't see this coming?"

"No."

"How is that possible? You see him a few times a week, don't you?"

"That's true, Abba. But I didn't suspect anything."

"Nothing?"

Elazar hesitated. "Well... Yossi seemed — nervous lately."

"Did he say anything? Hint at anything?"

Silence.

"Why don't you answer, Elazar?"

"Because... This conversation is hard for me."

"Why?"

Elazar shrugged. "It just is. It's hard for me to talk."

"Do it anyway!"

"Maybe some other time."

Zevulun's voice grew steely — the tone Elazar hated. "Now! Talk now! Don't you realize we have a real problem? Our whole family is standing on a precipice — and all because of that rascal!"

Elazar was decidedly uncomfortable. On the one hand, he was afraid of his father. Zevulun was dominating, strong willed. He did not know how to yield or how to lose. Many of the problems their family experienced derived from this trait.

On the other hand, Elazar respected his father very much. Though Zevulun no longer belonged strictly to the yeshivah world, he had studied in some of the great yeshivahs, including Chevron and Ponovizh. His entry into the world of business had changed him a little, it was true. Still, Zevulun's home was a place where words of Torah were heard and love for the Torah was paramount. He sent his sons away to yeshivah despite the fact that many of the family's friends in Tel Aviv did not do so. Zevulun had earned Elazar's respect in many different ways. That was why the last thing Elazar wanted to do now was deliver the blow his father was asking for.

"Abba, have pity on me. I just can't!"

Zevulun stared at his son. It was a frightening stare, beginning in blazing anger and quickly growing cold as ice.

"Leave my car this instant!" Zevulun hissed, very low. "Go now!"

Elazar was dumbfounded. He stared uncomprehendingly at his father, unable to remember the last time he had spoken to him in such a hurtful way. For a full minute he sat frozen, uncertain how to react. Should he actually get up and walk away from the car, or sit tight and see what happened next?

There was no question that Zevulun was furious — but why? Elazar had sensed the tension last night when his father had phoned him unexpectedly, asking about Yossi. Out of the blue, Zevulun had been interested in hearing about Elazar's learning sessions with his brother. When had he ever asked about that before? A few months earlier, Zevulun had informed Elazar that he was to learn with Yossi, and that was that. Zevulun had never followed up on it in any way.

This was not very surprising, considering the many demands on Zevulun's time. Apart from his business affairs, Zevulun was deeply interested in politics — the Oslo Accords, Rabin, Peres, Beilin and the rest. The progress of Elazar and Yossi's learning partnership was definitely not in the forefront of his consciousness.

And now, this sudden outburst. What was going on?

Elazar fingered the handle of the passenger door while his eyes remained riveted to the windshield. He could feel his father's burning gaze on him, unwavering.

"I believe I just asked you something."

Elazar caught the inflexible tone in his father's voice. Still, he did not budge. He was convinced that the entire episode stemmed from something more than Yossi's simple disappearance from yeshivah for a few days. So what if Yossi had decided to take a short vacation? The boy had been under a lot of stress lately. He had taken a breather of sorts — not the proper thing to do, but understandable nonetheless.

The fact that Yossi had not told anyone that he was going was slightly suspicious... or at least a cause for wonder. Still, when a boy was feeling stressed and under pressure, you really could not blame him. Elazar was positive that Yossi would be back soon. After all, what choice did he have?

So why was their father reacting so hysterically? What was he afraid of?

Elazar gripped the door handle and turned to watch the pedestrians passing his window.

"I asked you something, didn't I?" His father's voice was quiet but very firm. Elazar was accustomed to obeying him. Slowly, he opened the door and set one foot on the curb.

"Get in!"

Elazar swiveled around in surprise, his foot still outside the car. Hoarsely his father barked, "Get in and close the door!"

The youth complied. Zevulun repeated, "I asked you something. Speak!"

Zevulun eyed Elazar's suffering face. It pained him to behave so harshly toward his son. But his intuition was very insistent, whispering to him that the information that Elazar was concealing from him might contain the solution to the riddle of Yossi's mysterious disappearance.

He could not blind himself from the knowledge that he was anxious — deeply anxious. It was an anxiety whose source was unclear to him, but strong enough to squeeze his heart with red-hot pincers. Nothing he tried to tell himself, no appeal to logic, had any effect. That was why he was so adamant now.

"Speak!"

Elazar said softly, "It's hard for me, Abba. It...it's something that has to do with you."

Zevulun's curiosity grew to almost overwhelming proportions. The pressure in his chest made it difficult to breathe. Elazar, noticing this, became apprehensive. What was all this doing to his father's blood pressure? And if he felt this way now, how would he feel after hearing what Elazar had to say?

The son hesitated again, but at his father's commanding, "Tell me!" he knew he had no choice. Without thinking, Elazar took off his hat and twisted the brim in his fingers. Very low, as though to soften the blow of his words, he said, "By forcing me to tell you, Abba, you're harming both of us."

"Speak!"

"This will hurt you very much. Your health..."

"*Speak! I said.*"

Elazar felt tears stinging his eyes. The words emerged almost involuntarily, in a near-whisper:

"He hates you, Abba. Really hates you. I don't want to repeat what he's said about you...."

Elazar buried his face in his hands. The tears that had threatened to flow from his eyes did not materialize, but he felt dizzy from the effort to contain his emotions. When he dared look up, he peeked at his father. Zevulun was immobile, seemingly paralyzed.

His son's words had struck him with the force of a blow to the face. He closed his eyes for an instant, then immediately opened them again. His hands held tightly to the steering wheel to contain their trembling.

At last, he croaked, "How do you know?"

"He told me."

"When? This week? After...Friday?"

"No, Abba. Last week."

"Did he also tell you why?"

"No. He didn't."

The last question surprised Elazar. Didn't his father have any idea what was going on? Didn't he realize how Yossi felt under Zevulun's treatment? Didn't he remember the way things were at home, how infractions that were forgiven in the other children were harshly punished in Yossi? Strange!

Zevulun asked, almost inaudibly, "Do you understand the way he feels?"

Elazar stirred uncomfortably in his seat. "The question is not whether or not I understand him, Abba. What's important now is that it's reality!"

Zevulun studied his son's shuttered face, trying to guess what he was thinking. The words Elazar had thrown at him echoed through the car. They seemed to Zevulun unjustified. He would be the first to admit he had a problem with Yossi, but even the boy was sufficiently intelligent and self-aware to know that he himself was the cause of the friction between them. Had he honestly believed that his father would give in to him? That Zevulun would let him destroy their home? He was prepared to accept the fact that Yossi was angry at him — but hatred? That seemed to him an exaggerated claim. It was insulting... and painful. Very painful.

He asked Elazar, "And you think that's the reason he's disappeared?"

"I think so, Abba."

Silence.

"Where do you think he could be?"

"I don't know. Maybe he's gone on a trip to the Galil? The Golan? Maybe the Negev?" Elazar thought another moment, then shrugged. "I really don't know."

Another silence descended, a heavier one this time. Tentatively, Elazar added, "But I don't think there's any reason to worry. He'll be back in a day or two."

Zevulun did not respond, except to ask, "Did he say anything else — about me?"

A negative shake of the head was Elazar's reply.

Rolling down his window to catch a breath of fresh air, Zevulun inclined his head toward his son and said softly, "Please don't hold anything back, Elazar. Tell me everything. Because I *am* worried. Every word you say may help me to better understand what happened... And maybe to discover where Yossi went." He paused, then repeated with emphasis, "I'm worried, Elazar."

"But Abba, I really don't know anything else. I could never pry anything out of Yossi that he didn't want to tell me. He's very close mouthed. He doesn't usually talk to me about you, or about home. What he told me that one time just burst out of him, I don't know why... Lately I've sensed that Yossi's been very nervous. He's been behaving strangely. And — "

"Strangely? How?"

"I can't put my finger on it. He's been talking about all sorts of strange things — subjects I've never heard him speak about before." Elazar made a helpless gesture, and repeated, "Strange things."

"Give me an example!"

"Well, one day he suddenly started talking about other worlds. About the universe, and reincarnation, and freeing the soul from the body. I don't know what else. I didn't manage to get him to tell me what was bothering him. But I'm convinced it wasn't only because of what happened between the two of you, Abba. He wouldn't have run away just because of that. After all, Ima always takes his side, and he does love her."

Zevulun waved a hand in a weary, dismissive gesture. "That's the whole source of the problem. Ima protects Yossi and thwarts all my efforts to teach him. You can see the result for yourself."

Elazar chose to remain silent. He had no desire to engage in an argument with his father just then. The moment was tense enough already.

Varda, Zevulun Kimmerman's loyal secretary, made her usual morning stop at the fax machine. It was her job to deal with the bank statements, contracts and price quotes that streamed into the office daily. At the moment, she was alone. Ilan was working outside the office and Yael was home tending a sick child.

Varda pulled the fax paper from the machine, tore it off carefully and carried it back to her desk. Quickly she scanned its contents.

Suddenly, she emitted a gasp that was almost a shriek. Covering her mouth with her hand, she stared at the fax. She must reach Zevulun! How could she find him in Jerusalem? It was urgent — urgent!

4

arda reread the fax message. The words seemed to swim before her eyes. In a departure from his usual practice, Zevulun had not left a number where he could be reached. She stared at the fax, nonplused. What to do now?

All at once, her spinning thoughts came to a halt. She tore her eyes from the printed words as she tested a new idea. Might Zevulun's sudden trip this morning — a trip of which he had given the office no advance warning — be somehow connected to the message on this fax?

A feeling of deep compassion spread through her. "Poor things," she murmured as her imagination painted a picture of Zevulun and his wife's faces as they read the awful message. "Poor, poor things..."

Zevulun lifted his head from the steering wheel, where it had rested for several long minutes. For Elazar's benefit he tried to produce a smile. "Do you want me to drive you back to the yeshivah now?" His voice was soft, and somehow defeated.

Elazar hesitated. "What are you planning to do now?"

"I don't know yet." Zevulun paused, then added, "But the first thing to do is to find the boy."

Elazar caught the new note in his father's voice. This was the first time he could remember hearing Zevulun refer to Yossi as "the boy." Always, it was "this kid," or "your son" or "that wild man." Now, it was "the boy." Elazar felt like crying.

"But how will you find him? And anyway, Abba, I think you're panicking over nothing. I'm sure he'll be back. Another two, three days, tops."

His father's eyes were sad. "I'm not so sure," he whispered. His hand crept up to his chest. "My heart tells me otherwise."

Elazar did not know what to say. He, too, was beginning to feel that this time was different. This was no childish show of protest on Yossi's part. There was no logical basis for the conviction, except the memory of Yossi's strange behavior of late. Elazar was forced to make the private, and painful, admission that he had not really been all that interested in his younger brother's life.

But he *had* noticed Yossi's increasing tension lately — a tension that had erupted in odd behavior and sudden outbursts.

He sat upright. "Abba!"

"What is it, Elazar?"

"Let's drive over to the *kollel* in Givat Shaul. I want you to meet Reb Yaakov."

"Who?"

"Reb Yaakov Frankel."

Zevulun stared. "What connection does he have with all this?"

"He comes to Yossi's yeshivah in the evenings. I know that Yossi would often speak with him."

"Well, what do you want from him now?"

"I'm not sure, exactly," Elazar said slowly. "Let's go talk to him. Maybe he'll be able to supply some details that will help us understand what's happened to Yossi — maybe even where he's gone."

Without another word, Zevulun started the engine.

❦

They stood near the *kollel's* front entrance, listening to the subdued roar of voices engaged in Torah study. Zevulun's heart lurched with fresh sorrow. *Why isn't Yossi sitting and learning?*

Elazar slipped through the door into the study hall. Minutes later, he reappeared in the company of a young man in a dark suit and large yarmulke. Yaakov Frankel was very thin. His beard was short and scrawny. Catching sight of his eyes, Zevulun was surprised to find a calm self-confidence radiating from them. This man seemed to know just what he was doing.

Elazar introduced the two men. They shook hands. Yaakov Frankel inclined his head politely, but it was Zevulun who spoke first.

"Pleased to meet you." He came right to the point. "I hope that Elazar had time to fill you in."

"Yes." Yaakov's voice was soft as velvet.

Zevulun breathed deeply, tension filling him again. "Perhaps you can explain to me what happened? Elazar says that Yossi was in the habit of speaking with you. I'm afraid I can't say the same thing."

Yaakov gazed at him searchingly. "Yossi was certainly laboring under emotional stress lately. I tried to talk to him about it..."

Impatiently, Zevulun prompted, "And?"

"It wasn't easy to get him to look at his situation more objectively," Yaakov said gently. "A pity."

"But how do you explain his sudden disappearance? Where do you think he's gone?"

"I have no way of knowing where he is. It was news to me that *you* don't know. I thought he'd gone home."

Zevulun's nerves were jangling. He forced himself to speak calmly. "Okay, so he's not at home. What can you tell me about him?"

Yaakov was silent. His eyes traveled from Zevulun's face to Elazar's and back again, searching for words. Other young men passed them going in and out of the building, and throwing them what Zevulun imagined to be appraising looks.

"I think," Yaakov said, "that you both know what Yossi's like. He hasn't been able to concentrate on his learning for some time now. He wanders around the *beis medrash,* sleeps a lot in his room and even goes out to roam through town."

"Well?" Zevulun snapped.

"He doesn't feel good about himself. I don't want to interfere... but I think you know better than I what's bothering him." He paused. "The problem is, I have the impression that he's been keeping the wrong kind of company lately."

"What do you mean?"

"In our last few conversations, Yossi spoke about things that I'm sure he didn't pick up inside the four walls of his yeshivah."

"Do you suspect someone or something specific?"

"Yes. But until I'm sure, I won't say a word. What worries me is that recently he stopped confiding in me."

"Why is that worrying?"

"Because it's a sign either that Yossi has given up, or that he's found someone else to talk to. My instinct tells me he's found someone else."

"Do you think that's connected to the fact that we don't know where he is?"

"Possibly. I'm not sure... but very possibly."

Zevulun became conscious of a keen disappointment. This talk had not done much to further his search for his son. Yaakov was clearly determined to withhold at least a portion of what he knew. It seemed to him that in the young man's manner, too, there was a silent accusation. And for no good reason!

Zevulun said good-bye and made his way back to his car. His whole body ached as though he'd undergone a severe beating. Where could Yossi be? And who was the stranger he'd been meeting?

At the car, he waited for Elazar, who had lingered to exchange a few more words with Yaakov Frankel.

"Call me tonight," Yaakov whispered. "I have a few things to tell you."

An hour later, Zevulun was back in his office in Tel Aviv.

Varda approached, holding the fax that had arrived in his absence.

"Better go into your private office, Zevulun," she suggested soberly as she handed him the fax. "This is something you'll want to read alone.

5

Zevulun took the fax from Varda. Something in her expression made him uneasy. It was as if she were trying, with her eyes, to prepare him for whatever message the fax held.

It had the opposite effect.

Noticing his scrutiny, Varda quickly dropped her eyes. Her fingertips found her computer keyboard and began typing at a furious pace. Zevulun, observing her ill-masked agitation, asked no questions. Varda was someone he deeply respected. In fact, his nickname for her was "my *talmid chacham.*" Not only was she married to a prestigious Bnei Brak Torah scholar, but she herself was well versed in halachah and exuded a profoundly genuine awe of Heaven that exerted a very beneficial influence on their clientele and on him, personally.

After a moment, he followed her advice and took the fax into his own inner office. Slowly he turned the lock in the door. His hands were trembling slightly. What had there been in Varda's manner to create this mounting tension? What was it about the fax that had made her look that way?

Sinking into his executive chair, he carefully unrolled the fax. The words leaped up to meet him:

To Abba,

Please don't worry about me — that is, if you ever worried about me in your life. I've decided to make things easier for you, and to simply disappear. That way, you won't have to bear with my annoying presence and can just enjoy nachas from your other children.

At first, I planned not to write at all. I planned to just disappear without a word. But I have some pity on Ima — not a whole lot, but some. I want her to know that I'm still alive. Please don't search for me — you won't find me. I'm all right.

The fax was signed: *Yossi.*

Zevulun sat paralyzed. The hands that clutched the fax did not move. It seemed to him that even the blood had concealed in his veins. Slowly, with motions stiff and uneven, he folded the fax, fold after fold. Without any conscious volition he tucked the wad into his pocket and stared sightlessly at the locked door.

"I knew it," he thought, when he could think again. His intuition — the nagging feeling he had had last night, and again this morning, that something was wrong with Yossi — had proven to be accurate.

He jabbed at the intercom on his desk. "Varda."

"Yes."

"What time did this fax arrive?"

His voice sounded miraculously calm, almost indifferent. Zevulun wondered how he managed such a feat when his innards were torn to shreds.

"It came this morning, at about 10."

Varda was amazed at her boss's even tone. How could he be unmoved by what he had just read? Tears sprang into her eyes as Zevulun's voice came again.

"Was anyone else in the office when it came? Has anyone else seen the fax?"

"No." Her answer was muffled. "No one."

There was a moment's silence. Zevulun broke it. "Varda!"

"Yes?"

"I must ask you to tell no one about the fax, all right? Thank you!"

His voice broke on the last word. He disconnected hastily, before she could answer. As for Varda, she heard the catch in his tone, and oddly enough, it relieved her.

Zevulun's hand crept into his pocket and touched the dreadful fax. It burned his fingers like hot coals. Against his will, he drew out the fax and carefully unfolded it so that he could reread the message it contained. He closed his eyes — and instantly, his wife's face appeared before him.

Tzipporah. Yossi's mother.

How to tell her?

He rose to his feet. With trembling hands he arranged the scattered papers into neat piles on his desk. Gently, he locked the various desk drawers and left the room. Varda lifted her eyes as he passed. They looked red. Had she been crying, Zevulun wondered — because of the fax? He tried to smile. Varda responded with a feeble smile of her own.

"I'm going out for a while," he said quietly.

Varda hesitated, then said, just as quietly, "Why don't you go home and rest a little?"

Zevulun shook his head. "Home? How can I go home?"

"Why not?"

He gripped the fax more tightly, nearly crushing it. "You ask why not? What do I tell Tzipporah? How will I break this news to her?"

Varda didn't answer. Her eyes were anguished as she thought of Zevulun's wife, a woman who was far from strong. How would she endure this blow?

Zevulun sank into the nearest chair and closed his eyes.

"I don't know what to do," he whispered. "I just don't know. You know the secret. Do you have any ideas? Tell me what I can do!"

In her five years at the office, she had never seen her employer so broken. Zevulun always radiated a vast sense of self-confidence, the decisive manner of one who knew something about everything — an attitude of "Don't tell me what to do!" Varda had never liked his complacency; to her, it smacked too much of *"kochi v'otzem yadi,"* of a less-than-perfect reliance on the Almighty.

Right now, however, she was finding his new helplessness jarring. He was waiting for her answer, but she had no idea what to say.

"But — but you have to tell Tzipporah. There's no way you can hide it from her."

"True."

"I think that the faster you do it, the better."

He looked up. "Why?"

Varda searched for the right words. "It's like... like..."

"Like what?" he prompted.

Tears seeped from the corners of her eyes. Zevulun asked again, "Like what?"

Through her tears, she said, "It's like when someone dies suddenly, Heaven forbid. The sooner the news is told to the people closest to him, the sooner they can all share their pain and support each other." She broke off, then added quickly, "I know, it's not exactly the same thing, but I couldn't find another analogy. Anyway, the sooner Tzipporah knows, the better it will be for her. You can deal with it together. Don't you agree?"

Zevulun said heavily, "To my sorrow, this case is exactly the same thing."

"Excuse me, Zevulun, but you're wrong. The dead will not rise until the end of days. While there's life, there's hope."

Zevulun made no attempt to answer. He leaned his cheek on his palm and closed his eyes. It seemed to Varda that he'd fallen asleep. Softly, she said, "Go home, Zevulun. Hashem's salvation can come in the blink of an eye. You'll see!"

Yaakov Frankel heard the telephone ring. It was nearly midnight, an hour when he usually disconnected his phone. Tonight he had been waiting for Elazar's call. He hurried to lift the receiver.

"Good evening, Reb Yaakov."

"Good evening? It's nearly morning!"

"Please forgive me for calling so late. I've got a lot on my mind..."

"That's all right. I understand. It happens."

"No, you don't understand."

Yaakov stiffened, then whispered into the receiver, "What do you mean?"

"The reason I'm calling so late is because of Yossi."

"*Nu*, do you have good news about him?"

"No. *Bad* news!"

At once, Yaakov's imagination paraded a host of ghastly possibilities before his inner eye. Cautiously, he probed, "Has something happened?"

"Yes."

"What is it?"

"Yossi sent a fax."

Yaakov was bewildered. "A fax? What do you mean?"

"Exactly what I just said! A fax came to Abba's office, written in Yossi's handwriting. There can be no question as to who sent it."

Yaakov had stopped breathing. "And what did the fax say?"

"Yossi wrote that he's decided to disappear. He doesn't want anyone coming to look for him."

"From where was the fax sent?"

"We don't know."

Yaakov Frankel struggled to absorb the shocking news. "What about Yossi's yeshivah? Weren't they concerned when he didn't show up for three days?"

"As soon as they realized Yossi was missing, they tried to call my parents. But when we moved into a new apartment this year, nobody remembered to give the yeshivah our new phone number. It seems they were calling the old number for three days now, and getting no answer. They finally tracked us down tonight — just after Abba had broken the news to Ima." Elazar emitted a bitter laugh. "As you can imagine, there wasn't much time for a real conversation."

"How did your mother take it?"

"Ima was hysterical. Abba had to call a doctor, who gave her a tranquilizer. It's like Tishah B'Av in our house. Abba told me the news over the phone a few hours ago, but I just didn't have the strength to call you till now."

Abruptly, Elazar fell silent. There was no response. He was afraid that the line had been disconnected and that he'd vented his feelings to the empty air.

"Reb Yaakov, are you there? Can you hear me?"

"I'm listening, Elazar. You don't have to shout."

"Oh, sorry. It's just that I didn't hear any reaction from your end. I thought maybe the line was dead."

"What kind of reaction did you expect to hear? I'm in shock! Can't you understand that?"

"Well, I guess so."

A silence fell between them. Finally, Yaakov straightened his yarmulke with a distracted hand and spoke into the phone, "Elazar?"

"Yes."

"Where are you now?"

"In yeshivah. Why do you ask?"

"How long would it take you to get here?"

"*Now?* In the middle of the night?"

"Yes, now! In the middle of the night!"

"But — why?"

Yaakov drew a deep breath. "Because I think I know exactly what's happened. I think that I have the key to all of this. Call a cab and come down at once."

6

Zevulun sat in an armchair in his living room, staring up at the crystal chandelier suspended from the ceiling. Despite the relatively early hour, his wife had already retreated to her bed. Silence roosted on the house like a brooding hen. There was none of the peace that he expected to find here each evening after a hard day's work. Zevulun felt as though something was at his throat, slowly strangling him.

He went to the window and flung it open, but the choking sensation did not go away. Impatiently, he returned to his chair. Breaking the silence at intervals was the sound of Tzipporah's muffled weeping. The sound reached his ears through the closed bedroom door, grating on his nerves and his heart. At one point, he found himself wondering whether he really heard the sobs at all, or was just imagining them. At the moment it was hard for him to tell what was real and what was not.

He had told her about Yossi's fax only an hour ago, though he had returned home from the office nearly one hour earlier. With a self-control he had not known he possessed, he had managed to keep from blurting the news while the younger children were still up. At all cost, he must preserve a calm atmosphere in his home. There was no need for the children to witness their mother's reaction to the terrible news — or even to know about it at all, at least for now.

And tonight of all nights, his youngest, two-year-old Avi, refused to fall asleep. He had played around in his bed, deaf to all parental threats. Zevulun had thought he would explode from the tension as the fax sat in his pocket like an undetonated bomb. With quick, impatient strides he had approached Avi's bed, hand upraised to administer a few sound spanks where it would do the most good.

But just as he reached the bed, his hand had dropped. A strange lassitude enveloped him. Instead of hitting, he reached out and stroked the little boy's tousled head. Avi fell silent, gaping at his father in astonishment. Perhaps he could feel the current of love passing to him from his father's fingers …

Zevulun did not understand what happened to him at that moment. Why had he refrained from giving little Avi the spanking he had so definitely deserved? For the space of a minute he searched the child's eyes. Then, with halting steps and sagging shoulders, he left the room.

In the hall, he stopped and listened. To his surprise, all sounds of activity from Avi's room had ceased. He heard only the child's soft steady breathing. Avi was asleep.

Slowly, he had made his way to the kitchen to break the news about Yossi to his wife. Her reaction had been just what he'd expected: shock, casting of blame, escape, shutting herself up in her room, tears...

Recalling the scene, Zevulun shifted in his chair. Tzipporah had not been interested in hearing any details — not about Zevulun's trip to Jerusalem, nor about his meeting with Yaakov Frankel. He interlocked his fingers until they hurt. Where could Yossi be? Where had he sent the fax from? For the hundredth time he drew the page from his pocket and smoothed its folds.

There were no identifying marks to tell him its point of origin. It was clear that Yossi had not sent it from any post office branch, or it would have borne some sort of phone number or other identification. The implication of his thoughts made him sit up straight. The fax must have been sent from a private home! That way, it was possible for the sender to leave out his name and phone number.

So Yossi was not wandering the streets, alone and destitute. Someone had taken him in, at least to the extent of allowing him to send a fax from his home. Who could it be?

Questions tumbled through his mind with chaotic urgency. Where was Yossi now? What to do? And could it be true that he, Zevulun, was to blame for what had happened — as his wife had accused him before running off to her room?

He stood up, went to the bookcase and took down a volume. Whenever he could, he tried to end the day with a *perek* of *mishnayos*. He opened the *sefer* to the last *perek* of *Maseches Kelaim,* the section dealing with the prohibition of *sha'atnez.* But after a minute he put the *sefer* down. Concentration completely eluded him.

༺❀༻

Elazar arrived at Yaakov Frankel's house in the Ramot section of Jerusalem at 1 a.m. The streets were deserted and nearly all the windows of the surrounding buildings were dark. Yaakov was waiting for him by his open door.

"Sit down," he whispered, after leading Elazar inside.

Elazar sat gingerly at the edge of the couch. Yaakov took an armchair facing him. They regarded each other in silence. For an instant their eyes met, then wandered on. Finally, they met again, and Yaakov smiled sadly. Neither of them had yet spoken a word.

"Your father," Yaakov whispered, "actually made a good impression on me."

Elazar's eyes opened wider. "What do you mean, 'actually'? What did you expect?"

Uncomfortably, Yaakov shrugged, as though to say, "Who knows?" But Elazar would not let the matter lie. "Yossi's stories?" he persisted.

Yaakov began to finger his skimpy beard. After a moment, he admitted, "Well, yes, you're right. Yossi's stories."

"Well?"

Yaakov heard the rebuke in the youth's voice. "I confess, I didn't act properly. I'm probably guilty of having listened to *lashon hara.*" He paused. "But I did it with the best of intentions. I wanted to calm your brother down. I thought that if I listened to him and showed him I believed him, he would return to a normal yeshivah life." He raised a hand to prevent Elazar from responding. "What is important — and this is also linked to the reason I asked you to come here tonight — is that I have a different view of your father now."

Elazar longed to know what Yossi had told Yaakov about their father, but he didn't dare ask. Instead, he said, "On the phone before, you said something about having the key to the whole business."

"That's right."

"What did you mean?"

"I mean that now that you've told me about the fax, I think I know which direction to pursue, to explain what happened to Yossi."

"In other words, you think you know where he is?" Elazar's eyes shone with excitement.

Yaakov chuckled. "You're getting carried away, Elazar."

"So what did you mean?"

"Exactly what I said. I have an explanation. It's certainly possible that it will also help us track him down."

Elazar was growing impatient. He leaned toward Yaakov and demanded, "Can you give me some details?"

"I'll try."

At that moment, the telephone rang.

Its shrill peal shattered the quiet of the night. Yaakov started. Who could be calling at such an hour? His first instinct was to ignore the phone, as anyone who had the nerve to call at this late hour deserved. But the ringing did not stop. Though he knew it was not possible, it seemed to him that each succeeding ring was louder and more urgent than the one before.

At last, he got up and went over to the phone. Cautiously, he lifted the receiver and murmured, "Hello?"

Elazar saw Yaakov's eyes widen in astonishment and heard the words burst from him:

"Yossi, is that you? Where are you?"

7

Varda burst out, "Why did that have to happen to him?"

Her husband, Rabbi Shaul Egozi, sat opposite her at the small kitchen table, which was still cluttered with the remains of their supper. He had noticed that his wife was preoccupied all evening.

"I still don't know exactly what happened, and to whom," he pointed out. "I can't answer your 'why' until I know the 'what.' Now, can I?"

Varda smiled sadly. "I don't really expect you to be able to tell me why. The question sort of exploded from me... Besides, you're right. I haven't even told you what happened yet."

And she proceeded to tell him.

Shaul Egozi listened attentively. When she was done, he put down the slice of bread he had been holding and sighed deeply. "And now you want to know why your boss's son has run away?"

"Not really. It just hurts me to see such a thing happening to him. Zevulun and his family are fine people. And Yossi, the missing boy, made a good impression on me. He dropped in at the office more than once."

"And so?"

"So I just can't understand why such a thing should happen to them!"

The rabbi, like most Torah scholars, did not hasten to answer at once, but sat mulling over what he had just heard. He knew the Kimmermans only through his wife's stories — that is, only superficially. He had never had more than a casual conversation with Zevulun Kimmerman. However, as a *maggid shiur* in a small yeshivah, he had met many parents and spoken with innumerable students, both separately and together. He was well versed in the complexities of parent-child relationships, and especially between fathers and their sons. What he felt now, at hearing about Yossi Kimmerman, was sadness but not surprise. Though he had not been personally involved up till now with an actual case of a runaway student, it did not surprise him to hear that such a situation had occurred.

Varda wanted to hear her husband's response. She prompted emotionally, "Don't you think it's awful? A boy runs away so easily, and then sends a fax from wherever he's hiding — a fax that causes his parents such pain!"

Rabbi Egozi maintained his impassive mien. Varda was not sure he had even heard her impassioned outburst. He seemed miles away.

Suddenly, like a man aroused from a dream, he asked, "Do you think he would agree to talk to me?"

"Would who agree?" Varda was startled.

"What do you mean, who? Zevulun, of course. Zevulun Kimmerman! Do you think he would agree?"

Varda was in a quandary. The fax was supposed to be a secret. She had promised Zevulun that she would divulge its contents to no one. Unable to keep it to herself, she had shared the news with her husband. It was clear that she could not consent to her husband's plan. Miserably, she asked, "What do you want to talk to him about?"

"Leave that to me."

"But Shaul, you *can't* talk to him! He mustn't find out that I told you about it! I promised him I wouldn't tell. He'll never trust me again!"

"Maybe," her husband said. "But we're talking about a human life here, aren't we?"

Numbly, Varda nodded. She felt like crying.

"In that case, we have an obligation to try to save that life, don't we?"

Again, Varda nodded.

"And I, Shaul Egozi, believe that I can help. I believe I can save him. Don't you think I'm required to try?"

His wife lifted her head and looked at him directly. "You're right. We have to try. But how can we? Yossi's gone! What can you possibly want from his poor father?"

"Nothing. Just to save him."

"Save who? Zevulun? Yossi?"

An understanding smile softened the rabbi's features. "Both of them," he replied gently.

"Of course Yossi has to be saved — but why are you talking about saving Zevulun? What kind of help does he need?"

But her husband would only repeat, "I want to save them both."

Looking into her husband's eyes, it seemed to Varda that they held a secret. Her consent was implicit in her next words. "And how will you do it?"

"I told you — leave that to me."

An anguished sigh escaped her. "And what about me? What will he think of me?"

"Is that the main problem right now, Varda?"

Varda bowed her head.

Elazar rose from his seat, trembling. With quick strides he crossed the room to Yaakov Frankel, whose ear was still pressed to the telephone receiver. Yaakov was in constant motion, shifting his weight from one foot to the other, brows furrowed and eyes blinking repeatedly in his intense effort not to miss a single word being whispered to him from the other end of the line. Elazar came close and grasped his host's hand. "Let me talk to him!"

With suppressed anger, Yaakov shook his hand off and pressed his ear to the receiver again.

"Yossi, listen," he said, low and urgent. "I can hardly hear you. Where are you?"

He listened closely, then said, "But Yossi, why didn't you speak to me first? Why did you disappear without saying a word?"

Again, he listened. Elazar waited with mounting frustration, then renewed his efforts to wrest the phone from Yaakov's grasp. Yaakov forcefully repudiated each attempt. Elazar finally desisted, and tried to glean what information he could from Yaakov's responses.

"I understand, Yossi. But still, it's important to talk! Will you come see me? You don't have to tell me where you're staying. Just come."

After listening for a few seconds, Yaakov exclaimed, "What do you mean, you can't come? Why can't you come? I won't tell anyone you were here. Do you hear me? Yossi, you have to talk about this! Maybe there's something we can do. Do you hear me?"

Suddenly, Yaakov held the receiver away from his ear and stared at it in astonishment.

"We've been disconnected," he said. "The line went dead. I'm not even sure he heard my last words."

"Maybe someone cut him off?"

"Maybe." Yaakov replaced the receiver. He gazed at Elazar thoughtfully. "You know something? Without knowing why, something tells me you're right. They disconnected us."

"They? Who's 'they'?"

"I wish I knew."

"So how do you know there is a 'they'?"

Yaakov threw him a veiled glance. "Just before this call came, I was about to tell you what I know — or what I think I know — about your brother."

A powerful curiosity struggled with terror in Elazar's heart — terror at hearing what Yaakov might reveal about Yossi. Yaakov's reference to some mysterious figures — the unknown "they" who might have cut short Yossi's phone conversation with Yaakov — made Elazar afraid. And his fear led to a feeling of overwhelming tension. He changed direction: "Why didn't you let me talk to him?"

"Maybe in time I will let you."

"What do you mean?"

"You'll find out."

"Do you think he'll call again?"

"I'm assuming he will."

"Why?"

"When you hear the whole story, you'll understand."

Once again, Elazar was aware of a strong desire not to know. He was afraid the truth might be too hard to bear.

He swallowed hard. "What did he tell you?"

"It was a difficult conversation," Yaakov answered with a sigh.

"But what did Yossi say?" Elazar persisted.

"He said that he does not want to come home. Ever. That he's chosen a new lifestyle, far away from the yeshivah and from everything else."

"But why didn't you let me have the phone for a minute? I just wanted to tell him how upset he has made Ima and Abba!"

"You are obviously not aware of the true situation, Elazar. Yossi just doesn't care. He doesn't care about any of you. He wouldn't believe you if you told him how much pain he has caused your parents. He's convinced that none of you care about him — and that whatever distress you may feel is only because of what this might do to the good name of the Kimmerman family. He says he's not prepared to suffer all his life just to protect his family's image. Do you understand me?"

Elazar didn't answer. With dragging feet he made his way to the window, and without asking his host's permission opened it wide. A blast of cold air struck his face and took away his breath for a moment. The buildings lining the street outside were almost uniformly dark. A few isolated lights twinkled in the distance. By Elazar's calculation, they belonged to residents of Har Nof, nestled serenely on the far-off hill opposite.

He sensed that Yaakov had come up behind him. Both stood silently, looking out.

Elazar was still vexed by the fact that Yaakov had not let him exchange a word with his own brother. He was not ready to accept Yaakov's contention that Yossi hated them all — Abba, Ima, even himself. It just was not possible!

Anger, yes. He could believe that his brother was very angry. And in some respects, Yossi was probably even justified. But that was beside the point right now. Elazar was convinced that if he had only had a chance to talk to Yossi, he would have succeeded far better than Yaakov. With all due respect, Yaakov was not Yossi's brother. Blood was always thicker than water. If only he had been able to tell Yossi about their mother, Elazar was certain something would have happened. He did not know what would have happened, because he had no idea where Yossi was, but something would have happened. And the conversation would not have been cut off the way it had been.

"What are you thinking about, Elazar?"

Elazar shrugged. "It's not important."

After a moment, he added, "What interests me right now is to know where he was calling from."

Yaakov stepped decisively over to the phone and dialed. "Hello — Information? Good evening." He cast a fleeting glance at his watch. The hands stood at 3 a.m. Dryly, he amended, "Actually, it would be more accurate to say 'Good morning.' I want to know this: My phone number is 586-4000. Somebody called this number about a quarter of an hour ago, and I'd like to know where he called from. I'll wait, thanks."

Yaakov listened intently as the operator returned. His face registered chagrin. He mumbled a hasty "thank you" and hung up.

"What did they tell you?" Elazar asked eagerly.

"It didn't work. They're not allowed to give out that kind of information unless so instructed by the police."

Elazar ground his teeth.

8

Yaakov Frankel left the window and crossed back to the center of the living room. Elazar did the same. Without a word, both sank into armchairs, facing one another. Elazar caught his host in the act of trying to stifle a yawn. He wondered if he should leave.

Tentatively, he asked, "Are you tired?"

Yaakov smiled. "Yes. At 3 o'clock in the morning, I think one is entitled to be a little tired."

"I'm sorry — but you're the one who asked me to come here after midnight."

Another smile. "Guilty as charged."

Abruptly, Elazar leaned forward. He moved directly to the heart of the matter. "You asked me to come because you wanted to tell me something about Yossi, I believe."

"Yes."

"Well, tell me — at least a brief synopsis — and then I'll go."

Yaakov rose suddenly to his full height, and stretched. "No! We will speak as long as necessary. I asked you to come and I'll keep my promise."

It seemed to Elazar that Yaakov was now fully alert. He clasped his hands tightly together as Yaakov began to speak.

"I've sensed the changes in your brother for some time," Yaakov began. "When I first met Yossi, our relationship was very superficial. He didn't talk much. He would ask me what he wanted to know about the Gemara he was learning, and that was that. He didn't seem to want any closer tie. Yet, I could see — very clearly — that his eyes were sad.

"I like to solve puzzles. They pose a challenge for me. With Yossi, I didn't go about it directly. From time to time, when we met, I'd try to start some sort of conversation. I showed him that I was very sympathetic. I wanted to win his trust."

"And did you?"

Yaakov considered. "I think so. Gradually, we began talking. I asked him — very cautiously — to tell me about his family. I remember asking him what his father does for a living. At first, he answered only with a shrug, as if to say, 'Do I know?' That was when I first began to sense some sort of complex in Yossi.

"I pressed him for a real answer. 'At least you must know what sort of work your father does.' Yossi's answer surprised me."

Elazar's face tightened. "What did he answer?"

"He said, 'I know what my father does. But I'm not interested in him or his work.'"

"How did you react?"

"At first I wanted to continue the discussion. But I had a different idea. I let the matter drop."

"Why?"

"I wanted time to think about what he had said — and to give Yossi time to understand the significance of his own outburst, made to someone who was essentially a stranger to him. After all, I'm only a *kollelnik* who comes to learn briefly with the boys during their night *seder*."

Elazar's expression registered discouragement. "Yes, I know Yossi's way of answering. Didn't you think it disrespectful?"

"Even if I did think so, what difference would it have made?"

"I think that such an answer deserves a reaction! Yossi has to be put in his place, doesn't he?"

Yaakov smiled, even as his hand rose to hide another yawn. "You see, Elazar, that's precisely your problem! You focus on your brother's words without looking to see what lies behind them. I am not anyone's policeman or judge. As a stranger, I was simply curious to understand what brought on his response, what led him to say those things to me. Do you understand?"

"I guess so. What did you do next?"

"Nothing. I waited. I didn't answer him, and we went our separate ways. That's all!" Yaakov looked into Elazar's eyes, which were also fighting the urge to close. "I can see that you really don't go along with what I'm saying. Hm?"

Elazar said, "The truth? I don't. Yossi is a kid who needs to be put in his place when he's disrespectful. And that's apart from the complaints he has against our father. Believe me, I just can't understand the depths of his hatred."

The wind rattled the window. Yaakov listened to it absently as he rose again to stretch his limbs in an effort to remain alert. He crossed to Elazar and stood over him as he continued.

"Listen. Over time, Yossi told me a great deal about his life at home. About how harshly his father treats him in comparison to his brothers. He especially recalls the time his father made him stay behind, with an uncle, when the rest of the family went up to the Galil for a week's vacation. That incident left a deep scar."

Elazar cut him off. "That's not true! It didn't happen that way!"

Touching Elazar's shoulder lightly, Yaakov said, "Relax, my friend. That's not the important thing. In my opinion, what's important is the way Yossi felt. He felt discriminated against for no good reason."

Elazar snorted. Ignoring him, Yaakov continued, "It's important for you to know that he felt that way. And that's the reason behind everything that's happened with Yossi. Today, after meeting your father, I have a clearer understanding of why Yossi did what he did. Still, you must admit that the solution to the problem — and Yossi's eventual return home — depends on this point."

"Do you think you can get him to come home?"

"I have some ideas about that." Yaakov smiled.

"Really?" Elazar asked eagerly.

Yaakov nodded.

Elazar's next question was cut off by the sudden shrilling of the telephone. He and Yaakov stared at each other. It was 4 in the morning. The ringing didn't stop. Who was it now?

Yaakov picked up the receiver.

9

"ello?" Yaakov said.

After a moment he repeated loudly, "Hello?"

Elazar saw the impatience in Yaakov's face. "Hello — who is this — Yossi? Why aren't you saying anything? Talk to me!"

After a few more fruitless attempts, Yaakov held the receiver away from his ear and slowly replaced it.

"Who was it?" Elazar asked.

"Very strange." Yaakov seemed to be speaking to himself.

"Yes — but who was it?"

Yaakov returned to his seat and slumped into it. "No one."

"What do you mean, no one?"

"Just what I said. No one!"

"I don't understand."

"Neither do I. I heard a sound, as though someone was trying to say something. I'm not sure, but it seemed to me that I heard my name: Yaakov. But what I'm positive I heard was a strong voice saying, '*Nein*' — that is, 'no,' in German."

"'*Nein*'? Elazar gripped his hands tightly together.

"That's right — '*nein*'! I heard that German word clearly. And then the line went dead."

Elazar's head began to pound. "Do you think the call is somehow connected to Yossi?"

"That's what I'm afraid of. But I'm not sure. On the other hand, who else would be calling me at this hour of the night? It's never happened to me before. It certainly wasn't my *rosh kollel* calling!"

Silence blanketed the living room. The first faint light of approaching dawn touched the edges of the eastern sky. From the next room came the quiet, even breathing of the Frankel children. Elazar sat slumped over, head on his knees and his arms wrapped around it. His eyes shut of their own accord — yet even through closed eyes he saw his brother Yossi standing before him.

In a voice thick with fatigue, he asked Yaakov, "How would you explain that German '*nein*'? Can it be linked to Yossi?"

Yaakov's reply was a sober, "I wish I knew."

"Aren't you curious?"

"Of course I am!"

"Well?"

When several moments passed without an answer, Elazar lifted his head in surprise to look at his host. Then Yaakov did speak, and his words frightened Elazar. "I never got around to telling you the most important thing tonight."

Elazar waited, unconsciously holding his breath.

"I believe that Yossi's run away to join a cult."

Elazar gasped. "Wh-why do you think that?"

Yaakov's fingers raked his thin beard. "Not now, Elazar. I can't talk anymore. I must get some sleep. I'll tell you the rest tomorrow."

He phoned for a taxi and escorted the youth to the door. At the head of the stairs, Yaakov spoke again. "After that second strange call tonight," he said in a tone of quiet resolution, "I've decided that I must find Yossi no matter what. I have a few ideas."

Elazar didn't answer. He was too tired to talk, and he heard the the taxi honking. But how in the world would Yaakov find his brother?

Elazar had no idea of the adventures that lay ahead of both of them, from the moment Yaakov made his decision.

⚜

At 8 a.m. Zevulun was ready to leave home. He had endured a restless night, sleeping only fitfully. Not a word had passed that morning between him and his wife. Ever since he had delivered the dreadful news about Yossi, Tzipporah had been wrapped in a cocoon of silence.

Was she angry at him? Or was her behavior a reaction to the severe shock she had received? In his heart, Zevulun was convinced that his wife *was* angry at him. Apparently, she blamed him for what had happened.

He had been turning over these bitter thoughts all night, and they rushed to the forefront of his mind now, as he stood at the front door to the apartment. He hesitated, waiting with faint hope for the sound of his wife's customary good-bye before he left for the office.

But there was only silence — a deep, painful silence that emanated from the living room and the kitchen, between which Tzipporah had raced all morning, in an effort to escape her pain or dispel some of her anger.

Suddenly, the telephone rang. He felt disinclined to answer; then his curiosity got the better of him.

"Hello?"

He listened stony-faced to the voice on the other end. The only word he spoke was a quiet "Thank you." He added, "I'll call if I need you," then he hung up and crossed back to the front door.

Mechanically, he pushed the button that summoned the elevator. When it arrived at his floor, he watched the doors open — then abruptly swiveled around and returned to his apartment. Opening the front door, he called, "Tzipporah, Elazar just called."

There was no answer. Zevulun continued loudly, "He tells me that last night, at about 2 or 3 in the morning, the young *kollel* man Yossi used to speak to received a call from him." He paused. "Are you listening?"

Still no answer from his wife. Zevulun ground his teeth and left the apartment again, slamming the door behind him. The elevator carried him downstairs. Despite his simmering anger at the way his wife was treating him, he was glad he had passed on the news Elazar had given him. It cast a faint ray of hope, even though Zevulun had no idea what Yossi's call meant or what it portended.

Tzipporah stood at the kitchen sink scouring the dishes that her husband had used for his breakfast. He had eaten alone, after years in which Tzipporah had made certain to join him for the meal each morning before he left for work. She had heard his sorrowful "good-bye" at the door. She had paid close attention to the message he had returned to relay, about Yossi's call. But her anger — a fury that filled her heart completely — did not allow her to respond, to ask a single question, to betray the slightest interest.

Still, the knowledge that Yossi had called — it did not matter whom he had called — gave her a small measure of comfort. Deep down, she was grateful to her husband for giving her the cheering news despite her fuming silence this morning. Maybe he was reeling under the blow just as she was. The blow that had descended upon them so unexpectedly — out of the blue …

She straightened up, the dishes momentarily forgotten. Out of the blue? Had it really happened like that? Had there been no warning?

She and her husband had often discussed Yossi. Tzipporah had bewailed the difficult relationship between Zevulun and Yossi, regarding it as a thundercloud on the horizon of their family life. Whenever she attempted to take Yossi's side, her reward was a cold and cynical, "What do I care?" from her husband.

"Don't you care what happens to him?" she would demand.

And the answer would come — a scornful, "No!"

Yossi, she remembered, would be taking refuge in the living room or his bedroom, keeping a close ear tuned to his parents' conversation, hearing every awful word his father said to his mother about him. Afterward, Tzipporah would catch the wounded look in Yossi's eyes.

Standing alone in her empty kitchen, she wiped a tear from the corner of her eye. Tzipporah had never been able to understand just what it was about Yossi that so infuriated her husband. What had Yossi done to alienate his father to such a degree? Her shoulders sagged. She had no strength for this.

Her thoughts were constantly with Yossi. Where was her poor boy? Was he alone or with people — young people like him who felt they had no real home? Or maybe he was with bad people who had attracted him to their own bad ways... She did not want to think of it. She let her tears flow unchecked, down her cheeks and into the sink, where they mixed with the steady stream of water that flowed from the faucet. She knew her Yossi was alive — thank G–d! But where? *Where?* And what were they to do now?

Tzipporah turned off the water. Total silence descended on the kitchen. She dabbed at her face with a corner of her apron, then removed it and went into the living room. Sinking into an armchair, she once again gave herself up to her bleak thoughts.

Her heart felt shattered into tiny fragments. An overwhelming exhaustion made it hard for her to move. She felt a longing to call her widowed mother, then dismissed the idea as foolish. Maybe she had been wrong to be so hard on Zevulun. Maybe she should have spoken to him. Yossi's disappearance seemed to have had an impact on him at last. Something in his own heart seemed to have broken, too. He was hurting, just as she was.

She recalled the way he had looked and sounded last night as he broke the news. He had sat slightly hunched in his chair, the words coming slowly and haltingly. An air of defeat had enveloped Zevulun, as though he were suffering from an inner crisis. She was not sure how deep it went, or whether her husband knew how he had wronged their son by his continual rejection. A prayer arose in her, that Zevulun would prove to have genuinely changed, and that things would be different in the future if… when …

Tzipporah could not finish the sentence, even in her thoughts. She breathed deeply, fighting the tension that threatened to overpower her, until the words came. When… Yossi… came… home…

She lifted her eyes. They sought the antique clock that hung on the wall opposite. It was 8:20. Her husband had left home just 10 minutes ago. Most likely he had not yet reached his office. There was still time.

She went to the telephone and, with quivering fingers, began to dial.

10

Varda came to the office early. Yesterday, in the turmoil of emotion after Yossi's fax came, she hadn't completed her allotted work. It had been impossible to concentrate. She wanted to clear her desk before Zevulun arrived.

She lifted the plastic cover from the computer monitor and switched it on. She made her selections from the main menu quickly and was soon facing an accounting program on the screen. Concentration still eluded her. Bank deposits, bank withdrawals and bank charges all danced senselessly before her eyes. Finally, with an impatient frown, she rose from her desk and went into the tiny office kitchen to make herself a cup of coffee.

Sipping the scalding brew, she acknowledged to herself that she was a little nervous. Her husband had instructed her to tell Zevulun he was interested in speaking with him about what had happened. Last night, hearing the suggestion from her husband's lips, Varda had agreed. In the cold, clear light of morning in the office, she wasn't so sure. How to raise the subject without wounding her boss?

Zevulun was a naturally suspicious man. It was likely that, in these tense days, his threshold of suspicion, of sensitivity, would be at its peak. The mere mention that her husband, a rabbi and Torah scholar, wished to speak to him, might give Zevulun the impression that somehow he was being blamed for Yossi's disappearance. Varda was fearful of insulting her boss.

She put down her empty mug. Instead of returning to her desk, she crossed the room to the window overlooking the Mediterranean. Blue water stretched to the horizon. It looked tranquil, untouchable. Varda felt some of the tension leaving her. Maybe this question — how to approach Zevulun with her husband's request — was not the real problem right now. The important thing was to find Yossi and to bring him home. Then, and only then, could an attempt be made to rectify what was wrong. That would be the time for heart-to-heart talks and introspection, if they should prove necessary....

The phone rang. Varda went to her desk and picked it up there.

"Regev Investments, good morning."

The voice at the other end was very familiar to her.

"Varda? It's me — Tzipporah. Tzipporah Kimmerman."

Varda's breath caught in her throat. She babbled, "Oh, Tzipporah, is it you? I hardly recognized your voice! How are you? You're calling very early this morning. Is there a problem?"

She heard a deep sigh at the other end of the line. "You're asking if there's a problem? Yes, there definitely *is* a problem! And who would know about that more than you?"

"Is that why you're calling?"

"You could say that." Tzipporah sounded bitter. After a moment, she continued, "Tell me, is Zevulun there?"

Depression settled over Varda's heart like a heavy iron ball. *What's going on between them?* she wondered. Aloud, she said, "No, he hasn't come in yet."

"So I can speak to you freely?"

Varda paled. What did Tzipporah want from her? "Y-y-yes... Of course."

"Then listen to me, Varda. I want you to tell me the truth — and *all* the truth! Okay?"

"What do you want me to tell you? You're making me very curious." Varda tried for a nonchalant note.

The line went quiet, except for the sound of Tzipporah's labored breathing. "Varda, is it true that you were the one to receive the fax?"

Varda hesitated only an instant. "Yes."

"All right. Is it true that you gave the fax to my husband? That's what he told me."

"Yes, it's true."

"How did he react?"

"React?" Varda echoed stupidly.

"Yes — react! What did he say after he read it?"

Varda spun back and forth on her swivel chair. "I don't understand you. What do you mean, how did he react? He reacted the way any father would in such a situation!"

"Meaning what, exactly?" Tzipporah's voice had suddenly turned cold as the north wind.

Varda found herself growing annoyed. "I don't know what you want from me."

"Nothing! I only want to know whether Zevulun was upset when he read the fax! Did he scream, did he laugh, did he cry? Or — or was he totally apathetic? I need to know, Varda. It's very important to me. Why can't you understand that?"

Varda relented. Her feminine intuition gave her a clear view of Tzipporah's great distress. "I'm sorry," she said quietly. "I didn't mean to hurt you. I understand you now. And I can tell you that he was very broken up."

"Meaning?"

"He read the fax in his own office. Then he came out to where I was sitting. At first he was quiet — in total shock. He kept staring at the fax, which he was holding with both hands. Then he looked at me, and his eyes were bewildered, as though he didn't understand what was happening to him. I felt sorry for him. Really sorry. I've never seen him like that before. It was hard to believe that such a strong person could look so crushed."

After a moment, Varda asked, "Is that what you wanted to know?"

"Yes, that's it. I wanted to know whether the indifference he's shown toward Yossi all these years — the indifference that used to drive me crazy — was genuine or not. I wanted to know whether or not his uncaring attitude was only an outward show; to know if, in his heart, he loves Yossi as much as our other children. I don't know if I'll ever see Yossi again" — Tzipporah's voice broke — "but at least I'll know that his father did love him, in spite of the way he would criticize and humiliate him."

Varda felt an overwhelming pity for the other woman. "Please forgive me if I've hurt you, Tzipporah."

"You didn't hurt me. On the contrary — you've given me peace of mind! You've told me that Zevulun is not the cold, uncaring father he made Yossi and me believe he was. If only Yossi would have known that, he might not have run away." Tzipporah sighed. "Anyway, thank you, Varda. You don't know how grateful I am."

A heavy tread sounded outside the office door. "Tzipporah," Varda whispered hastily, "I think Zevulun's coming in. Let's say good-bye. And believe me — Hashem will help."

She replaced the receiver. She lifted her head — and froze. Zevulun was standing beside her desk. Had he heard her last words to Tzipporah?

His opening words provided the answer she sought.

"Who were you talking to about me?" Zevulun demanded.

Yaakov Frankel rose abruptly from his bed. It was 6 a.m. When he had flung himself onto his bed, after parting from Elazar, it had been 5 o'clock. The single hour's sleep had done much to refresh him.

The resolution he had made — to go out and search for Yossi — suddenly frightened him. Why in the world had he made that decision? He thought about it as he dressed. Perhaps it was because Yossi had chosen to call *him*. He had even called twice. The second time, it had seemed to Yaakov that the boy was trying to cry for help. Could all this be a sign from Heaven that this was a burden he was meant to take upon himself?

But — what to do? Where to go? Yaakov did not have a clue. Obviously he was not a detective. In essence, he was a man who enjoyed nothing more than immersing himself in Torah study, a man who had never been involved in public affairs. Even his *rosh yeshivah,* who encouraged the other young men in the *kollel* to engage in *kiruv* work in the community, had ordered Yaakov to stay in the *beis medrash.* And now — a decision like this.

He was not in any manner of speaking an adventurer. He had no experience in such matters. Where to begin?

Without waking his family he left the apartment, heading for the shul near his building. As he walked, his thoughts raced madly. Should he take back what he had said? The decision had been made impulsively, goaded by some strong inner compulsion. There had been no careful reasoning upon which to base his action. No one would ever know if he backed out now. Even Elazar would understand, and would forgive. This was a job for professionals, for the police....

Yaakov grimaced. Why was he trying to convince himself that no one would ever know? Hashem would know! His fingers raked his beard as he thought: There's no choice. I have to do this! This was a quest he was required to undertake, though he grieved for the hours it would steal away from the study of his beloved Torah.

Later, on his way home from shul he was once again seized with panic. He had never interested himself in the workings of the various cults that infiltrated Israel from such places as India and China. It was only when Yossi had begun to speak of them, in half-sentences and unfinished paragraphs, that Yaakov had done some research into the matter. It was important to know how to respond. Maybe, if he learned enough about cults, he would know how to influence Yossi to stay away from them.

Now, with Yossi apparently in the clutches of one of these groups, fear overcame Yaakov. Included in the sparse knowledge he had gleaned about cults was one chilling fact: They could be very dangerous. They did not brook interference by outsiders. They also did not easily relinquish their grasp on their prey. He vaguely remembered reading somewhere about people who attempted to disrupt these cults and had been severely injured as a result. Yaakov apprehensively thought of his wife and children....

As he climbed the stairs to his apartment, he was gripped by a strange new sensation, something he had never felt before. He had decided — and that was that! Feeling infinitely calmer, he opened the door and stepped inside.

"Who were you entertaining here last night?" his wife called from the kitchen.

Yaakov was startled. She was usually still asleep at this hour.

"Just someone from the yeshivah I went to."

"Okay, but what about all those strange phone calls? Do you have any idea how scared I was?"

Yaakov did not reply. With all his heart he longed to confide in her, to tell her how frightened he had been by those phone calls, too. But he kept still. And after a moment, to his relief, his wife changed the subject.

Yaakov allowed himself a grim inward smile. She had no inkling, his wife, how many more times she would probably be feeling scared in the not-too-distant future.

11

Zevulun's gaze was stern. Varda knew that look: It meant that her boss was not prepared to back down.

It was clear to him that she was hiding something — but what? And why? And did it have anything to do with what had happened to Yossi?

The fingers of Zevulun's left hand beat a light tattoo on the desk. There was a faintly menacing undertone to his quiet voice as he said, "I'll repeat my request. I want to know who you were talking to — about me! That is my right, don't you think?"

Varda was at a loss. She didn't like the look in his eye, or the cold, commanding tone he had adopted when speaking to her. The phone shrilled suddenly at her elbow, shattering the tense silence. Neither Varda nor her employer moved to answer it. The ringing continued for several long moments, then stopped.

"I didn't say anything bad about you," she ventured. "Why are you so suspicious?"

"Right now, I'm not concerned with whether you spoke good or bad about me. I just want to know who you were talking to!"

She did not answer at once. Frankly, she did not know what to say. How to avoid the need to reply without actually lying? All that was needed now, to round out the dismal picture, was for her to fill Zevulun in on her conversation with his Tzipporah! Telling him the truth could lead, Heaven forbid, to a quarrel between husband and wife. Her fingers moved restlessly on the computer keyboard without actually striking any letters.

Zevulun spoke again. "You should know that I'm very angry at you. I don't think I deserve this kind of treatment."

The words pierced her like white-hot needles. Tears prickled her eyelids. "Mr. Kimmerman," she said stiffly, "I don't think it's fair to pressure me this way. You have to try to understand my side."

Her boss took a seat nearby and set his attache case on the floor by his feet. He was visibly struggling to maintain his composure. "Why?" he snapped.

Varda was perplexed. "Why — what?"

"Why must I understand you in this matter?"

"I — I — Because — "

She lifted her hands and dropped them into her lap in a gesture of despair. "I — I don't really know why..."

Her anguish made Zevulun soften slightly. He leaned forward, asking, "Why won't *you* understand *me*? I don't want the tragedy that happened yesterday to spread all through town. That's why I haven't gone to the police — especially since I know that Yossi left voluntarily and is alive, *baruch Hashem*. What matters to me right now is to know whom you've already managed to tell about my problems. This is very important to me! I'd like you to ask them to keep what happened a secret. I know that's practically impossible... But still... "

He spoke with great feeling. Varda sensed his pain.

"Yes, yes," she hastened to assure him. "Of course I understand." Inwardly she was relieved: At any rate, Zevulun did not suspect her of talking to his wife.

"Well, do I deserve an answer now?" he demanded.

Varda hesitated. She had just thought of an idea, a way out of her difficulties. But it was hard to lie. She did not want to lie. Surely, she knew it was halachically permissible — and possibly even mandatory — to stray from the truth in a case like this, for the cause of domestic peace.

At last, she said, "I was talking to my husband." She held her breath. Would he believe her?

His eyes narrowed in open suspicion.

"Are you trying to tell me that you only told your husband about it now? You went home yesterday and said nothing all evening about what had happened? That's a little hard for me to believe!"

The final words exploded from him in real anger. Zevulun sprang up and began stalking toward his inner office. Varda saw that he was wounded. She called, "Mr. Kimmerman, please don't misunderstand me!" As he neared the office door, her voice rose. "Of *course* I told him about it last night! Don't you know how devastated I was by what happened? But this morning, my husband called to remind me to do something he'd asked, in connection with all this."

Zevulun halted and spun around in one fluid motion. Anger was replaced by curiosity. "I don't understand."

"You know my husband. After I told him about the fax, he was quiet for a long time. He was thinking. For him, everything is like a *sugya* in Gemara. He thinks and thinks, until he reaches a conclusion."

She paused. Zevulun waited expectantly for her to go on.

"In the end," she said, "he asked that you come speak to him about it."

Zevulun's astonishment was total. She had succeeded, both in diverting his suspicions and in transmitting her husband's request. It was as though a great burden had been lifted from her shoulders.

"What does he want to talk to me about? What could he possibly have to tell me that I don't already know? Is he a private investigator or a police officer? Has he thought up some brilliant scheme for getting my son back?"

Breathing deeply, Varda gathered her courage. "Maybe he has. If you don't talk to him, how will you know?"

"Hmm. You've got a point there."

"Mr. Kimmerman, I don't know what he wants to say to you. What I do know is that my husband is a serious *talmid chacham* and a very solid

Jew. Talking to him can never hurt. Please don't be angry, but I think that if he has offered you his time, it's a sign that he has a plan for you."

Zevulun heard the slight acerbity in her tone. She was defending her husband's honor against Zevulun's sarcasm. Privately, he admitted that she was right: He had not behaved as he should. He resolved to take the next opportunity to appease Varda by showering praise on her husband.

At the same time, with all due respect, he could not really believe that Shaul Egozi, astute as he might be, could help him with Yossi. What ideas could he possibly have on the subject? Rabbi Egozi didn't know Yossi. He had never even been inside the Kimmerman home. He was a Torah scholar, not a detective.

Was the rabbi's intention simply to preach at Zevulun, to give him *mussar,* to offer tips on child-rearing and the proper relationship between parents and children? In that case, he was decidedly not interested.

"Tell your husband I have no desire to speak to him about this. All right?" His voice was frosty.

Varda was still struggling to frame an answer when the office door burst open and a stormy wind seemed to blow in.

It was Ilan.

Yaakov Frankel skipped *kollel* that morning. His wife, a teacher, left for school, and their young children had been duly dispensed to their own pre-school and early elementary grades in *cheder* and the local Beis Yaakov. Yaakov needed a few hours of solitude in which to think of possible ways to fulfill the strange promise he had made to himself in an emotional moment.

So far, his thinking had produced no results.

He filled the electric kettle and waited while it came to a boil, both hands cupping the kettle for warmth. When the water was ready he made himself a cup of instant coffee, his second that morning. He sat in an armchair and took small sips of coffee as he urged his mind to work.

How to begin his journey? Where to take the first step in the search for Yossi?

12

Yaakov Frankel left his apartment in Jerusalem's Ramot neighborhood without any specific destination in mind.

For 10 long minutes he stood irresolute beside the bus stop near his home. A bus arrived, came to a halt beside the stop, and then, at a wave from Yaakov, drove on. At last, he decided against traveling by bus at all. He would walk toward the center of town on foot. That would give him plenty of time for thinking — time to continue groping after a plan of action.

His self-imposed quest had become a burning goal. He was filled with a powerful compulsion to accomplish what he had set out to do, though the source of that compulsion remained a mystery to him. Was it the confusing phone call he had received in the early hours of the morning — or simply the human need to rescue a fellow Jew from danger? At that moment, he had no ready explanation for his own illogical involvement in the problem of Yossi Kimmerman.

His walk took him along the side of the Ramot road. Time and again, neighbors and acquaintances, roaring past in their cars, signaled their offer of a ride; each time, he smiled and shook his head "no." In the back of his mind, as he started out, was a vague plan to visit one of his former *rebbeim,* a man of formidable intellect, to relate the story, pour out his heart, and ask for advice. But as the walk lengthened, he debated the usefulness of such a move at this time. Perhaps it would be better for him to first devise some sort of plan of action, and then to ask for the rabbi's opinion of it.

Yaakov had no idea how long he had been walking — an hour, or possibly longer — when he found himself standing in the courtyard of Yeshivat Nachal Kedumim. Yossi's yeshivah.

He hesitated. Though accustomed to visiting the yeshivah during the evening hours, when he learned with some of the boys, he had never been there in the morning. Why had his feet carried him here? His appearance would attract attention — something he was anxious to avoid. He did not want to be placed in a position where he would be forced to answer unwanted questions.

He was about to turn and leave when, with a sudden change of heart, he entered the building.

Yaakov had no idea whether or not Yossi's friends were aware that he had disappeared. He would have to be careful. He stopped a student in the entrance hall and asked, "Tell me, where can I find Yossi Kimmerman's room?"

The student stopped and looked at him in surprise. Yaakov evaded the youth's eyes.

"You're looking for Yossi? I don't think he's in yeshivah right now."

"Never mind. Where is his room?"

"I don't think he's in his room. He hasn't been around the past few days."

"Why?"

The student shrugged. "I don't know."

"A friend is gone and you aren't even interested?"

The words were delivered in a tone of only mild rebuke, but the youth seemed distressed. "Rabbi," he said apologetically, "I'm not really a close friend of his."

Yaakov was silent for a moment. Then he asked, "Which boys in the yeshivah *are* his close friends?"

"Has something happened to Yossi?" The student was beginning to suspect something. His voice held a mixture of curiosity and concern.

Yaakov decided to beat a hasty retreat. The last thing he wanted to do was draw attention to Yossi. Quickly, he answered, "No. Nothing special. Just tell me where I can find his room."

The boy clearly longed to ask further questions, to understand Reb Yaakov's sudden interest in Yossi Kimmerman. "Up those stairs, second floor, second door on the left."

"Thank you!"

Yaakov climbed the steps. Within seconds he was standing outside the door of the room he sought. He knocked, though he was certain the room was empty at this hour. All the boys would be in the *beis medrash* for their first *seder*.

As he had expected, his knock elicited no reply. Yaakov opened the door cautiously and regarded the room from the threshold.

It was a typical dormitory room, with a bed against each of the four walls and a medium-sized table in the center, piled high with assorted Torah volumes. An unlocked clothes closet stood in one corner.

Yaakov advanced tentatively. He tried to guess which bed was Yossi's. Intuition told him it was the one on the left wall, beneath the window. It was neatly made, as though no one had slept in it the night before.

He walked over to the bed, uncertain what he was searching for or what he hoped to find. Just like a police detective, he thought wryly, beginning his search for clues at the scene of the crime.

Carefully, he lifted the mattress. There was nothing there but some old newspapers.

After considering his next move, Yaakov went over to the closet in the corner. The door squeaked slightly as he opened it. He stood very still, praying that no passing student had heard. Only when a few seconds elapsed without incident did he breathe freely again.

The closet was made up of a deeply recessed hanging section and four roomy drawers. A rapid search of the former brought to light nothing suspicious or out of the ordinary. He directed his attention to the drawers.

Each bore the name of one of the room's inhabitants. Three of the drawers had a gaping hole where the lock should have been. Only Yossi's drawer was locked.

Yaakov's shoulders tensed. What was inside that drawer? For all he knew, it might contain any number of secrets about the boy he sought!

A foolish thought. Before he left, Yossi had almost certainly cleared out anything that might offer a clue to his whereabouts. Still, there was a chance that he'd forgotten something — something that Yaakov could use.

He tried to force the drawer open, to no avail. Next, he slipped the entire drawer out of its slot and tried — unsuccessfully — to break the lock. The more the drawer resisted his efforts, the more determined he became to learn its secrets.

All at once, he froze. Turning around seemed to take an eternity.

Two of Yossi's roommates were standing in the doorway, staring open mouthed at the sight of the respected scholar crouched over the drawer, and struggling with its lock like a common thief …

Zevulun stepped into his office and motioned for Ilan to follow. He sat behind the desk in his large swivel chair and waited while Ilan took the small chair facing him. Ilan was the first to break the silence.

"What's happened to you, Zevulun?"

Zevulun's glance was weary, his smile sad. "Who told you that anything happened?"

"It's not exactly easy to hide, my friend!"

Despite the cordial relationship they enjoyed, Zevulun had no desire to involve his employee in his personal affairs. "Never mind, Ilan. Everyone has to cope with his own problems."

Ilan spread his hands as though to indicate that he respected his boss's right to privacy. Zevulun hastened to change the subject: "Well, what's the status of the Hadera deal?"

Before answering, Ilan subjected his boss to a long, level gaze. This enraged Zevulun. "What are you staring at?"

Ilan realized he had stepped out of bounds. "I'm sorry. I didn't mean anything."

Zevulun had no patience, either for Ilan or for the property in Hadera. At the same time, he knew it was imperative that he should not betray any sign of weakness. Life and business must go on.

He leaned slightly forward and spoke in a conciliatory tone. "Let's meet tomorrow morning. The truth is, I'm a little stressed right now. It doesn't matter why. A man has to relax sometime, doesn't he?"

Ilan watched him a moment longer, then said, "All right. But tomorrow I'm bringing along the Canadian who wanted to invest with us and then changed his mind." The young man paused, then added, "It would be a good idea for you to meet him."

Zevulun did not have a clue, but the last sentence resounded suspiciously in his ears.

The two yeshivah boys stood stupefied in the doorway of their room. They knew what they were seeing, but were at a complete loss to make any sense of it.

Yaakov Frankel recovered first. He stood up, dusted off his pants and faced the students. He smiled at them — a smile that did not quite manage to mask the confusion he felt. His eyes looked apologetic. The boys exchanged a quick glance.

Yaakov spoke pleasantly. "I hope you boys remember the Gemara in Shabbos, *daf* 128?

The boys' bewilderment intensified. What did Reb Yaakov want from them?

"Well, the Gemara relates several episodes in which students of Torah scholars might have suspected their teacher of sinning. The rebbe asked them, 'When you saw me do so-and-so, what did you suspect me of?' Do you remember?"

One of the boys, the older of the two, nodded in assent. The second student glanced at him questioningly, and listened while the first whispered something in his ear. Bravely, Yaakov forged ahead: "And if you remember the Gemara, you undoubtedly also remember that the students gave their teacher the benefit of the doubt. Right?"

This time, both boys nodded.

"In that case, I'd be interested in hearing what you think about finding me just now crouching on the floor, trying to open one of the closet drawers. What do you suspect me of?"

The students looked extremely uncomfortable. Neither answered.

Yaakov breathed deeply. He looked penetratingly into each boy's eyes, noting how they attempted to avoid his gaze. The younger one fixed his eyes on a portrait of the Chazon Ish, *zt"l*, hanging on the wall to his left. The older one stared vacantly into the center of the room. Both gave the impression of longing to flee. Yaakov felt a small stab of triumph. He had taken a situation in which he had been forced to defend himself, and managed to put *them* on the defensive instead.

He moved the room's single chair over and sat down behind the table. With an elbow on the table and a broad smile on his face, he waited.

"Well?" he prompted. "I asked you a question. Why don't you answer?"

The boys were at a loss. They could come up with no reasonable explanation for their discovery of Reb Yaakov rooting through their closet this morning. If a perverse suspicion did enter their minds, they did not venture to express it. On the contrary, they made every effort to banish it utterly.

Yaakov rose from his seat and approached them. It was time to take advantage of this unexpected encounter. He would put it to good use as a first step in his quest.

"Well?" he repeated, more strongly. "Tell me already! What am I doing in your room?"

Avraham Blum, the older boy, stammered, "I — I really don't know. But of course we don't suspect anything wrong."

Yaakov burst into laughter. "Whatever you say." Then, quickly sobering, he said, "Tell me, do just the two of you sleep in this room?"

"No."

"Who else?"

Though they did not understand the meaning of this interrogation, politeness prompted them to answer, "A boy named Amiram Dotan. He went home for a few days."

"Is that all? I see four beds here!"

"Right, we have another roommate. His name is Yossi. Yossi Kimmerman."

"Why didn't you mention him right away?"

The question surprised them. The boys exchanged another hasty look. One of them offered, "I don't really know why we didn't mention him. Maybe because he's been away from yeshivah for the past few days."

It was clear to the boys that their unexpected guest was deeply interested in what they had to say. "Do you happen to know where he is?" Reb Yaakov asked.

"No. We don't."

Slowly, Yaakov returned to his seat.

"I don't understand you," he scolded. "A roommate of yours doesn't show up in his room or the *beis medrash* for days on end, and you don't even care to find out what happened to him? Maybe he's lying sick in bed at home! Maybe he's waiting for his own roommates to show some interest in his welfare! How can it be that none of you bothered calling his house to find out what was happening? What if something worse had happened, Heaven forbid? Haven't you learned what the Torah says about sharing your friend's burden?"

The boys knew that Reb Yaakov was right, but they did not wish to tell him the whole truth about Yossi's bizarre behavior of late — behavior that had jarred their nerves and the equilibrium of their room. It had actually been a relief to have him gone these past few days. That was why no one had phoned Yossi's home or inquired after him. Reb Yaakov's lecture made them uneasy. Was this the reason he had visited their room during morning *seder?* To check out their closets and give them a scolding?

Yaakov noted their irritation. It would not do to stretch the rope too taut.

"I've come here about Yossi," he said.

No reaction.

"You might have noticed me spending a lot of time talking with him during evening *seder* these past weeks," he continued.

Silence.

"Well... Yossi has disappeared."

Shock stamped itself on both boys' faces.

"What do you mean, disappeared?" Avraham Blum challenged.

"Exactly what I just said."

"He's not at home?"

"No. I told you, he's disappeared."

"But — but where could he be?"

Yaakov sighed. "It seems — though I can't be certain — that he's left the country."

"Left? But why? What is he looking for?"

Yaakov only shook his head. After a moment, Avraham Blum said in real distress, "I don't understand. Why did he run away?"

Yaakov took his hand. "Ah, that's exactly it! That is the reason I came here today. I hoped to find some clue, a letter or something else, that might help me solve this riddle. I want to understand Yossi's reason for leaving the yeshivah and the country. After all, a boy doesn't just wake up one morning and decide to leave for no good reason. True?

"So now, before I ask you to help me break open the lock of Yossi's drawer, I'm going to use this opportunity to ask you a few questions. Maybe you boys can help me find the reason for his disappearance."

"Us?"

"Yes. You."

They stared at him dubiously. With quiet authority, Yaakov ordered: "Sit down."

Obediently, each boy crossed to his own bed and sat on it. Their nervousness at the upcoming interrogation was palpable.

14

Zevulun remained alone in his office. The drawn window blinds kept out the morning sunshine, and the resultant gloom suited his mood perfectly. His desk was piled high with matters requiring his attention, but — after one fruitless attempt to concentrate — he ignored them. He was not in the mood for work. Over and over, his mind kept reverting to his refusal to meet with Varda's husband.

As his fingers stroked his chin in a characteristic nervous gesture, he became aware of a gathering fury. What nerve that couple had, suggesting that he needed counseling — as though *he* were the one with the problems, and not his runaway son!

After a moment, Zevulun reached for the phone and punched in a number.

"Hello — can I speak to Elazar Kimmerman? ...Yes, yes, it's urgent."

He knew he was dancing at the edge of rudeness, omitting even a "please" and "thank you." For an instant, the thought disturbed him — but only for an instant. Then all pangs of conscience vanished in a rush of renewed anger. He was furious at the whole world. It was as though he held every member of humanity, and the very heavens and earth, to blame for what had happened to him.

Right now, however, his anger was focused primarily on his secretary, Varda, and her husband.

The telephone came to life.

"Is that Elazar? Good morning. Is there any news? Have you heard anything about him?"

"No, Abba. I'm sorry, I haven't had a chance to hear anything yet."

Zevulun was silent a moment. There was a strange sensation in the pit of his stomach. "So what happens now?"

"I don't know."

"What should we do?"

"I don't know that, either."

Zevulun breathed deeply — a long, tortured breath that his son, at the other end of the line, picked up clearly.

"All right," Zevulun said heavily. "Then I'll say good-bye."

"Good-bye …Oh, just a minute, Abba. Actually," Elazar remembered, "I do have some news for you. Reb Yaakov — Reb Yaakov Frankel, the man we met at the entrance to the *kollel* — has decided to do his best to try to find Yossi. And he's a conscientious person."

Zevulun uttered a short, bitter laugh. "So he's conscientious! How is that going to help him find Yossi? Is he a police detective?"

"I don't really know. But detectives aren't the only ones with any wisdom. There's also *siyata di'shemaya* — help from Above. Have we never seen cases where that was true? Hashem can help Reb Yaakov locate Yossi's trail. Anyway, he told me he's planning to dedicate time to the search. A lot of time. I don't know why; maybe the story touched his heart. And I'll say again, Abba — from the little I know of him, he's a conscientious man. He's also stubborn, and very persistent when he sets his mind to something."

In his heart, Zevulun mocked his son's words. But a drowning man will clutch at any straw.

"And the rabbis agree to his involvement?"

"Well, don't you think he'd have consulted with his rabbi?"

Impatiently, the father said, "Oh, all right. Just tell that detective of yours *not* to go to the police or the press. I'd never be able to live it down if this thing became public. Understand? And he'd better not hand it over to any private investigators without consulting me first!"

"I understand. I'll tell him. Good-bye, Abba."

"Good-bye."

Zevulun hung up, thinking about what his son had just told him. What a ludicrous idea!

Then again, who knew? Perhaps Yaakov Frankel would succeed in his self-appointed quest. Maybe he would actually manage to trace Yossi to his hiding place...

A sudden thought startled him into rigidity. He flung his head back and stared sightlessly at the prints of Switzerland on his office wall. Could it be — was it possible — that this was a plot conjured up by the two of them, by Frankel and Yossi, to teach him a lesson? To force him to back down?

He shook his head. The notion was absurd — outrageous. ...And yet, it wouldn't let go of him. Suspicion continued to tug at him for several minutes after his conversation with Elazar. At last, he picked up the phone again and dialed his home number.

"Tzipporah?"

"Yes."

"What's new?"

A tense silence came to him over the phone line. Then Tzipporah said, "Nothing."

"Did — did he call?"

"Who?"

"Come on. Your son!"

The ensuing silence was like the uneasy calm before a storm. She snapped, "What do you mean, 'your son'? You're going on as though nothing happened! Don't you have a heart? Haven't you even stopped to think for a minute whether you behaved right toward Yossi?"

Tzipporah broke off. Zevulun heard the sound of her anguished breathing before she continued, "I ...I'm not trying to justify what he did. I know Yossi wasn't perfect. He was disrespectful, he acted silly — I know all that. But you're the adult here! You're the father! It was up to you to try to teach him, not just treat him with contempt. And then you'd get angry at me when I tried to explain that to you.

"Even now, Zevulun, don't you realize what's happened? Are you still so sure you're right in what you did? You think Yossi ran away because he's afraid of you. Because of the way you'd hit him. No! He's running away from your contempt! From your lack of willingness to try to understand him. I think ...I think he ran away because ...because he wants you to notice him! To pay attention! Do you hear me, Zevulun?"

Zevulun listened to her tirade with his eyes closed, a faint tremor running through the hand that held the telephone. His silence made Tzipporah ask again, with a touch of anxiety, "Do you hear me, Zevulun?"

"Yes." Faintly.

Her next words were laced with tears. "Where could he be? My Yossi! Look what you've done to him..."

Zevulun gently placed the receiver back in its cradle.

Accusing fingers were being pointed at him on all sides. First his secretary, Varda, and her scholarly husband; now Tzipporah, his own wife. This infuriated him. Why was *he* to blame? Doesn't the Torah obligate a father to raise his son to know right from wrong? Had he ever intended any harm to Yossi? He personally knew hundreds of men who gave short shrift to their disrespectful or unruly sons, and saw that approach bear rich fruit! Didn't Tzipporah remember the Finkelsteins, close friends of theirs at one time, whose son had been a real wild animal? His father had dealt with him firmly and harshly, and brought the boy around for the better! Zevulun paced his office in a state of simmering resentment. What did everyone want from him?

He grabbed the phone and punched in the number of Elazar's yeshivah again.

"Hello, I'd like to speak to Elazar at once ...Who's speaking? His father! What kind of question is that?"

His nerves were ragged, his patience nonexistent. He was angry at himself for his short fuse, but could not seem to control it.

"Hello, Abba. What happened? Why are you calling again so soon?"

"To be honest, Elazar ...I don't really know. But as long as I'm on the line, I thought I'd ask you if you also think..."

He fell silent. His self-respect did not permit him to go on.

"What, Abba? If I think what?" Elazar sounded frightened.

"Never mind. It doesn't matter."

Elazar's voice hardened. "No, I won't let it go. Please tell me what you wanted to ask!"

"Very well." Zevulun suddenly had no strength to argue. "I wanted to know if you also believe that I'm to blame — that I'm the reason Yossi ran away."

The question was met with an abrupt silence. Zevulun pressed, "You wanted me to ask. Why won't you answer?"

"Uh ...Who thinks you're to blame, Abba?"

"Everybody!"

"What does that mean?"

"Everyone. Your mother, my secretary — who, I might add, accepts a salary from me! She and her husband have banded together and decided that I need some pep talks!"

"That's two. That's not everyone."

"Never mind that. I want to know if you agree with them."

"Abba ...I'm not comfortable."

There was a sudden constriction in Zevulun's chest. "In other words, your attempt to avoid answering has already given me your answer. But I still want to hear it clearly, from your own lips."

"What do you need that for?" Elazar protested miserably. "Just to further aggravate yourself?"

"Elazar, do as I say!"

"All right! If you insist, I have no choice. Yes, I think that you're to blame." He paused, then blurted, "I know it's not respectful of me to speak to you this way, but you forced me."

"Don't worry about that. Thank you very, very much, Elazar. Goodbye."

Without another word, Zevulun hung up.

He went over to the window and yanked viciously at the blind cord. The full light of day burst in on the room. Zevulun stared for many long minutes at the gentle swell of the waves in their endless rush to the shore. But the view failed to restore his peace of mind.

15

Yaakov Frankel sat behind the table in the center of the dormitory room, eyes boring into the two students. They were seated on their beds, facing him with ill-concealed impatience. He let them stew for a while, his fingers idly stroking his chin, as if he were trying to understand a difficult concept in the Gemara. The boys squirmed.

Suddenly, his voice broke the tense silence. "I want to explain something important to you. I came here, to Yossi's room, to search for a clue as to his whereabouts. I know that he's been suffering lately. Maybe you two didn't notice. I'm not blaming you. You're too young to catch what we adults might grasp a bit faster.

"I want you to consider the questions I'm going to ask you very, very seriously. Try to answer as precisely as you can. That way, with Hashem's help, we may make some progress. It is possible — and I only say 'possible' — that Yossi's life will depend on the answers you give me here today. In any case, I have a feeling that the beginning of the solution to the riddle will be found here, in the room where Yossi's downfall began."

The two straightened their backs and looked alert. Reb Yaakov's opening words had turned the occasion into something significant, almost solemn.

The interrogation began.

"Tell me," Yaakov asked, "how long has Yossi been your roommate?"

Avraham Blum answered: "About half a year, I think."

His younger friend, Shimon Pollack, was eager to be a part of the proceedings. He corrected Avraham: "Longer! At least seven months."

Yaakov was anxious to prevent time-consuming debates. He said mildly, "Never mind. Let's say approximately half a year. Now let me ask you something else. Did you boys in this room talk among yourselves?"

"Yes, of course we talked. Why does the rabbi ask?"

Ignoring the question, Yaakov plowed on, "What did you talk about? Try to remember."

The question clearly struck the students as odd.

"We just talked," Avraham said with a shrug. "We talked about the kinds of things all yeshivah boys talk about. The yeshivah — what we're learning — our friends — politics. All kinds of things!"

"Very good. I understand. Now, another question: Was Yossi, in your opinion, a normal boy?"

"Of course he was normal!" Avraham asserted. He paused, then added doubtfully, "At least, I think he was."

Shimon Pollack made an involuntary motion, which did not escape Yaakov's eye. He turned to the boy. "Yes? What do you think?"

A sense of the importance of the occasion made Shimon stammer slightly. "L-lately he's been acting strange." He turned to Avraham. "Didn't you notice it?"

Yaakov demanded, "Details. Give me details."

Shimon threw a hesitant glance at the older boy, as though debating whether or not to speak further. Yaakov urged, "This is very interesting. What do you mean, acting strange? I'd like to hear everything. All the details!"

"Won't it be *lashon hara* if I tell you everything?"

"No!" The word shot out impatiently, in a near-shout.

Shimon stirred uneasily in his place. "I don't know exactly how to explain it. Lately, Yossi's been away from yeshivah a lot. Sometimes he would miss an entire *seder*. Sometimes I'd come into this room and find him flat on his back in bed, staring up at the ceiling. I'd ask him what was wrong, but he wouldn't answer. If I repeated the question, he would usually turn over onto his side, as if he wasn't interested in talking."

The stream of Shimon's confidences broke off for a moment. His eyes were fixed on Avraham's, as though seeking confirmation. Then, realizing that the others were waiting for him to continue, he did.

"Sometimes he would be missing from yeshivah for hours at a time. That's why I wasn't especially worried when I didn't see Yossi around lately." The boy paused. "But... that's not all."

With an effort, Yaakov kept the suspense from his face. He said blandly, "Go on."

"That's not all," Shimon repeated. "A few times in these last few weeks, I saw Yossi pacing back and forth in the room, head down, staring at the floor."

"What's the meaning of that?"

Shimon shrugged. "I don't know. I didn't know what was happening to him, but I was afraid to say anything. He would go from the window to the door and back again. The only one I told was Avraham. Right?"

Avraham nodded his head.

"But that," Shimon stated, "*still* isn't all."

He drew some air into his lungs and met Reb Yaakov's eyes.

"Sometimes, while he was pacing the room, he would do something very strange. He would put his two hands together and bring both up to his chest. Then he would lift his eyes up to the ceiling. After that he would start walking again with his head down, looking at the floor. From the window to the door and the door to the window." The boy shook his head. "Crazy."

Yaakov had been listening intently. "Crazy?"

Shimon quickly backtracked. "Actually, I don't know. But it didn't seem like perfectly normal behavior to me."

Yaakov didn't answer. Closing his eyes, he considered what he had just heard. His nebulous suspicions, never far away since the two strange phone calls he had received in the middle of the night, were beginning to take shape. It seemed to him that he knew what had happened. But it would not do to jump to conclusions. It was still early for that.

"Tell me, Shimon and Avraham — did you ever have a chance to discuss this with him? To ask him why he paced the room like that?"

Shimon answered first. "No."

"Why not?"

"I don't know. We were afraid."

"Afraid — of what?"

"It seemed like Yossi had gone a little crazy."

"Did you tell anyone?"

"No."

"I ask again: Why not?"

"Actually, we wanted to tell the *mashgiach,* but there wasn't time."

"What do you mean?"

"The whole thing started only two weeks ago. We didn't think it was necessary to tell anyone. Maybe that was wrong of us."

Avraham Blum decided to speak up. "I did ask Yossi what was going on. His answer was very unclear. He started babbling about some kind of a third eye that we can't see, but that sees us in some sort of magical way. I didn't understand a word he was saying."

Yaakov sank into a profound silence. His heart churned within him and his fingers plucked at his beard. He was certain now that his surmise was correct: Yossi had fallen into the clutches of one of the cults that riddled the country. But how to discover which cult? What was this "third eye" Yossi had spoken of? Yaakov had never heard of such a thing. Though, to be honest, how much did he really know about any cult?

The important question was: What to do now? Yaakov stood up and began crossing and recrossing the room, immersed in his thoughts. Soon, however, he forced himself to stop. This was the way Yossi himself had paced. *These boys will think that I'm also....*

"Tell me," he commanded abruptly. "Who did Yossi meet outside the yeshivah? Did any stranger visit him here?"

"No," Shimon said. "No one."

Avraham disagreed. "There *was* someone. A man. Sometimes he came after lunch, and they would go out together."

"Where to?"

"I don't know. The man came with a car."

"What did he look like?"

"He didn't look religious, though he did wear a *kipah* on his head." Avraham spread his hands. "I don't know why; he just didn't seem religious."

"Can you describe him to me?"

Avraham hesitated. "Well, he wasn't especially tall, but he wasn't short, either. About this high." He held his hand up in the air, palm down.

"What was his hair like?"

"Very curly. As far as I can recall, it was brown. But I only saw him once close up."

"Did he actually enter the yeshivah building?"

"Usually he would wait outside, near the entrance. He would ask someone to get Yossi."

"What do you mean by 'usually'?"

"Sometimes he did go inside."

"When, for example?"

"A few times. For instance, last Thursday."

"Are you talking about the day Yossi disappeared for good?"

"Yes. That time he even came into this room."

Yaakov muttered something under his breath, then continued grilling the boy. "What kind of car did he drive?"

"I think it was a Mitsubishi. A red Mitsubishi."

"Was he fat?"

"No."

"Skinny?"

"No."

"Then what was he?"

"I don't know. Normal."

"About how old?"

"Around 30-something."

"How was he dressed?"

"It's hard to remember. I think he wore a plaid shirt and jeans. And Reeboks."

Shimon started. "I just realized how it connects! How could I have missed it?"

"Missed what?" Yaakov asked sharply.

"Avraham, didn't you notice? He wore a bracelet on his left arm..."

"So?"

"There was a charm hanging from the bracelet — *in the shape of a big eye!* A silver charm, I think. How could I have forgotten? I just connected it to the stuff Yossi used to babble about the 'third eye'!"

Yaakov followed this exchange carefully. He was still at the beginning of the road. He still didn't know where to look, and for what. However, Yossi's roommates had provided some valuable information. It was clear to Yaakov that his search must begin with Yossi's mysterious friend, the man with the silver charm in the shape of an eye...

He turned to the boys. "And you never asked him who the man was who came to visit him?

"Oh, sure, we asked. But Yossi avoiding answering. Once, when he pressed him, Yossi said that the man was a secular cousin and that he was trying to teach him about *Yiddishkeit*. He said his 'cousin' was very interested."

Yaakov laughed grimly. "And you believed him?"

"Not really."

"Then how do you explain these meetings?"

The two friends exchanged glances, each seeking the answer to Reb Yaakov's question in the other's face.

"Honestly, we have no idea," Avraham said at last.

After a moment, Yaakov said, "Another question."

The boys waited.

"Did you ever see him reading something that goes against our beliefs? A magazine, or maybe a book?"

"Yes. Sometimes, when we'd come into the room suddenly, we noticed Yossi trying to hide something from us. We're not stupid. We saw him very well. He'd be reading in bed, and when we came in he'd turn over fast and pretend to be asleep. We saw him stuff what he was reading under his pillow. I'll admit," Avraham said, "that I was very curious to see what he was reading. One day, when Yossi was out of the room, I looked under his mattress."

"And what did you find?"

"Nothing! I was frustrated. Then I thought of checking his closet drawer — and found that he'd put a lock on it! I don't know when he put it on. The rest of our drawers are open. We don't hide things from each other. And now — a lock! That looks suspicious, doesn't it?"

"Apparently," Yaakov replied.

"One day," Shimon volunteered suddenly, "the drawer was open."

"Well?"

"I didn't see anything. The drawer was completely empty. But once I definitely saw him hide a package inside — or rather, a bulging brown paper bag. I couldn't even guess what was inside it."

Yaakov's eyes flew to the drawer he had been trying, some half hour earlier, to break open. He stood up again and went over to the closet, two intensely curious boys on his heels.

16

Zevulun stood motionless before his large office window. The window, sealed and slightly tinted, muffled the street noises — the roar of cars and the honking of their irritable drivers as they passed to and fro along Kaufman Street. He gazed out at the golden beach and the waves that broke incessantly over it. The sight calmed him in some measure, though it also brought to mind a very painful analogy: his son, Elazar, had joined the ranks of those who believed that he, Zevulun, was to blame for what had happened to Yossi.

He gnawed his lip, well aware of the churning anger inside. With each passing moment, he felt the burden increasingly his, alone, to bear. There was no one with whom he could truly share how he felt about the tragedy. His wife accused him, his son found him likewise guilty and he, Zevulun, refused to even discuss the matter with Yossi's *rosh yeshivah*. On the phone last night, he had indicated that Yossi had come home for some unspecified reason and hinted that he would prefer in this instance to deal with his son without the yeshivah's intervention. The shame of sharing the truth with the *rosh yeshivah* was too daunting. He would keep it within the family, if at all possible.

Which brought him back to his frustration. He simply could not understand why everyone insisted on regarding him as the sole guilty party here — as though the boy himself had been a *tzaddik!* How would they have suggested that he behave toward Yossi, when the boy was always acting wild and unruly? Would they have wanted him to back down, to have his son understand that he could do pretty much as he pleased? Tzipporah had always been an emotional woman. But Elazar — why was he drawn into this view?

With an effort, Zevulun uprooted himself from his place by the window and stood with his back to it instead. Once again his eyes raked the pile of papers and files covering his desk: mountains of paperwork, randomly tossed about. He could not summon his usual desire to plunge into work. Almost automatically, he reached for a cigarette; but even the slow, seemingly soothing puffs did not repair his mood.

Could it be — was it possible — that they were right? Did they see the situation more clearly than he did? Were they right and he completely wrong? Perhaps he should have embraced a different method of child-rearing. After all, here was the best proof one could ask for: The child had not turned out the way his father had wanted. He had actually taken the audacious step of running away, Heaven alone knew to where...

With a sudden, abrupt motion, he squashed the burning cigarette in the nearest ashtray, fingers kneading the cigarette until they ached. Ruthlessly, he pushed aside these treacherous thoughts. A few determined strides brought him around the desk to his big executive's chair. No! He would not give in to this nonsensical accusation — the baseless, dangerous notions that others were trying to plant in his mind. He would not be sucked in! He would go back to work with all his accustomed energy, as though it were business as usual.

As for Yossi, Zevulun was certain he would find a way to make the boy return. It would require much patience and nerves of steel — not a spirit of whining surrender! Zevulun felt that he was beginning to come back to himself. He began tidying the mess that was on his desk.

The phone rang.

Reluctantly, he picked up the receiver.

"Reb Zevulun?" It was a soft voice, and an unfamiliar one.

"Hello," he answered briskly. "Who is this, please?"

"This is Avraham Leizer Josekovich, your son's *rosh yeshivah*."

"My son's...?"

"Elazar."

Zevulun straightened in his seat. "Ah, hello, Rabbi. I didn't recognize the rav's voice at first. To what do I owe the pleasure of this call?"

Zevulun respected Rabbi Josekovich highly. The older man bore himself with the humility and dignity of the Torah scholars of yesteryear. He had been a student of Rav Boruch Ber of Kamenitz. Whenever Zevulun had occasion to speak with him, he was always left with a feeling of elevation that one derives from the company of a true *talmid chacham*.

"I wanted to know," the *rosh yeshivah* said softly, "if I may suggest a *shidduch* for your son?"

The *rosh yeshivah's* words took Zevulun completely by surprise. The topic was certainly not attuned to his mood of the moment. His head was not clear enough to deal with such things now. But it was impossible to refuse the *rosh yeshivah*.

"Of course, certainly," he replied. "But to what do I owe the honor of having the *rosh yeshivah* himself pick up the phone to me about this?"

The rabbi laughed. "*Nu*, why not? First of all, do you think I'm exempt from the mitzvah of *hachnasas kallah?* And, apart from that, I want you to know how highly I think of your son. Elazar is a real *talmid chacham*. Hashem should only grant you the same *nachas* from all your children."

The seemingly innocuous blessing struck like a pointed spear in Zevulun's chest. Almost silently, he whispered, "Amen."

"Do you understand, Reb Zevulun? It is an honor for me to suggest a *shidduch* for such a beloved student."

"Yes, of course. I'm — I'm not feeling quite myself right now. A bit... overwhelmed."

The *rosh yeshivah* chuckled. "You will overcome whatever troubles you, Reb Zevulun. Surely you have dealt with greater crises in your life?"

Zevulun breathed deeply. For the second time, albeit unwittingly, the *rosh yeshivah* had pierced him painfully. To his relief, there was no need to answer. The *rosh yeshivah* was speaking again:

"Well, to business. I'm talking about the daughter of Reb Yaakov Hirschenson. Do you know him?"

"No."

"He is a very fine Jew — a serious *talmid chacham* and a very pious one. As for his daughter, she is bright and will make a perfect wife. Really perfect. What more can I say than tell you that if I had a son, I'd do something to bring about this *shidduch* for him. A veritable pearl of a girl!"

Zevulun was silent. This suggestion had come at the most inopportune time, a time when his thoughts could not focus for long on anything but Yossi's mysterious disappearance and his possible whereabouts.

"I'm listening," he said.

"It would be worth your while to investigate her, Reb Zevulun."

"If the *rosh yeshivah* suggests it, then it is certainly a good *shidduch*. I have no doubt of that. I will, of course, take your advice and ask about her. Thank you very much for the suggestion."

He was about to hang up when he caught something in the *rosh yeshivah's* manner than seemed to indicate he wasn't through yet.

"I had wanted to add something, Reb Zevulun — if you have the time and the patience."

Zevulun chewed on his lip, but the words he spoke were calm enough. "Of course," he said courteously. "*Baruch Hashem,* I have plenty of patience."

"I don't know exactly how to put this. The girl's family does have a...small problem." A pause. "*Nu,* it's not actually a problem, but I feel an obligation to pass it on to you anyway." Again, the *rosh yeshivah* fell silent.

Tension gripped Zevulun. Inside, he was screaming, "Tell me already!"

"Reb Zevulun, we both know the maxim that one should investigate the brothers of a woman he wishes to marry. But I don't think that rule applies here, and I will explain why."

"I'm afraid I don't understand what the rav is getting at." Zevulun hoped his impatience didn't show.

"I will tell you. The brother of the girl we're talking about is — how shall I put it? — a bit wild. How does that religious newspaper put it? Oh, yes — the "fifth son.""

Zevulun stopped breathing for an instant. "What does the rav mean?"

"What do I mean? Nothing very good, I'm afraid. This boy learned in yeshivah, and at the age of 16 left the ways of the Torah. You know it occasionally happens in this day and age."

Another spear lanced Zevulun's heart. Through a pounding in his head, he heard the *rosh yeshivah* continue:

"But you should know, Reb Zevulun, he's a good boy. His character is not a bad one. In this case, we know that the father was to blame. He came down a little too hard on the boy — with the best of intentions, you understand — but it turns out that he didn't really know his son well at all. And... well, you see what happened. Does it really make a difference? Of course, it's important to know about these things before entering into a *shidduch*. But you know how people are, Reb Zevulun. They enjoy talking, and who knows what kind of stories they'll tell you!

"In the case of a rebellious son, the Torah tells us that the father's and mother's voices must be equal. Only then is it possible to punish the boy. In a case where the parents disagree, the commentaries tell us, punishment becomes out of the question. In this case, too, I think it would be worthwhile for you to check into the matter of the son. Because the girl, his sister, is truly excellent, as I've told you. And the family is a respected one."

Zevulun felt like bellowing, "Enough!" and slamming down the phone. Instead he remained silent, mentally plucking out, one by one, the white-hot needles embedded in his psychic skin....

The soft voice reached his ear again. "Reb Zevulun, when shall I call you?"

"That won't be necessary. I will call the rav."

"When?"

"I can't know that yet. I'll need a few days to check out the family."

"All right. I will try to call you back in two days."

Zevulun felt as if he would explode. "But, *Rosh Yeshivah,* I just said that I would call."

"Very well. But remember that we're talking about a very good *shidduch,* and I will be very happy if something comes of it."

"Okay, thank you very much."

"One more thing, Reb Zevulun. Don't pay too much attention to the girl's brother. I only told you the story so that it wouldn't come as a surprise."

"Yes, I understand. Thanks again. Good-bye."

"Good-bye."

Only when he had heard the definite click from the other end of the line did Zevulun permit himself the luxury of banging down the receiver as hard as he could. Then he slumped in his big chair and buried his head in his hands.

What had that call been all about? Should he suspect Elazar of telling his *rosh yeshivah* about Yossi? Was that righteous man himself interested in spreading yet more salt on his wounds?

Impossible.

Then what? Was it just a coincidence that the *rosh yeshivah* had phoned him at this specific time? Was Heaven itself fighting him, sending him signs? Now the *rosh yeshivah,* too, was talking about guilty fathers. What was going on?

His hand reached out for the telephone. He must speak to his son at once.

"Hello — Elazar? Forgive me for disturbing you again this morning, but I need to ask you something. Please tell me the truth: Did you say anything to anyone about what happened?"

"No. Why do you think so? Anyway, who would I tell?"

"The *rosh yeshivah,* for example."

"Abba, why do you suddenly suspect that? Do you think your shame is not mine also, or all of ours? Why do you ask?"

"No special reason. You understand, I'm just very nervous. I wanted to be sure... Is there any news?"

"What news could there be since the last time we spoke, half an hour ago?"

"It was only half an hour?" Zevulun felt as if he were losing his perception of time.

Elazar sounded bewildered, and a little wary. "Okay, Abba. 'Bye."

For the first time, Zevulun became conscious of an overwhelming desire to weep. Biting his lower lip, he turned resolutely to the pile of paperwork on his desk, picked up a file and began with a mighty effort to read it.

The attempt lasted a little more than a minute. Almost without volition, his hand put down the file and reached again for the phone. He dialed the number of Rabbi Yitzchak Abramson, an old friend from his younger days. To his good fortune, Yitzchak was home.

"Yitzchak, I need to speak to you urgently!"

"What happened?"

"Not over the telephone."

"You're making me curious."

"When can I come over?"

An instant's hesitation preceded the answer. "Come right after *Ma'ariv.* But at least give me a hint — what is it about?"

"Never mind. I'll tell you everything when I see you. Good-bye."

Zevulun replaced the receiver even before his friend had returned his parting greeting.

Yitzchak had been his learning partner for many years, both in yeshivah and in *kollel.* Whereas Zevulun later went into business, Yitzchak had remained in *kollel* and had become an accomplished scholar. Zevulun greatly respected his friend. More than once, he had relied on Yitzchak's sound advice and leaned on him for support. The thought of spilling his heart out to Varda's husband only enraged him; confiding in his old friend was another thing. Zevulun needed to talk to somebody, to relieve himself of the terrible burden he was carrying.

The hours until evening crawled. Contrary to his usual habit, he left the office two hours early. Two hours of driving aimlessly through the streets of Tel Aviv, trying to impose some order on his thoughts before it was time to head for his friend's home in nearby Petach Tikvah. On the way, he stopped at a small shul on a side street in northern Tel Aviv to *daven Minchah.*

It was neither a large shul nor an impressive one, with no more than two *minyanim* of men *davening* there that afternoon. The service was over quickly, and Zevulun would have been on his way at once — if not for a sight that halted him in his tracks.

The sight of a father slapping his 6-year-old son.

The boy, apparently, had displeased his father by some childish inattention during *davening.* The ring of the first slap was clearly audible in the small shul. Heads turned. Immediately, eyes returned to *siddurim* — but not for long. A second slap rang out, and then a third, echoing in the shul even over the whimpering of the child.

Irresistibly, the worshipers' attention was caught by the scene. It was not a pleasant one. The father, gripping his son firmly by the arm, was using his free hand to rain more slaps on the child's reddened cheek. The hand rose and fell, rose and fell, to the tune of the boy's sobs. Several of the worshipers could not bear the spectacle a moment longer, and went over to try to stop the beating. It was to no avail. The father was in no mood to listen.

An elderly man of eminently respectable appearance, sporting a long white beard, began shouting at the father: "What are you doing? Murderer! Stop it at once, do you hear?!"

The old man — by his look, a *talmid chacham* or even a practicing rabbi — left his place and walked quickly over to the father, who was still raining slaps upon his son. He seized the father's beating arm and screamed again, directly into his face: "What are you doing? You are a murderer!"

The father's face was purple with rage. He tried to wrest his arm free of the old man's grip, then screamed back, "He's my son! What do you care?"

"I care! As a Jew, it's my duty to save a victim from one who would kill him. Even a father can be a murderer!"

"This is ridiculous! It's my duty to educate my son! He wasn't *davening*, do you understand?!"

By this time, a number of other men had joined the white-bearded one. They tried to calm the father, while the old man continued berating him. "This is not called education! With your own hands, you are turning him into a hater of our religion! Do we beat a child over prayer — and such a beating? You're humiliating the child. That's forbidden, do you hear me? You are a madman!"

The old man seemed on the point of striking the father himself. Twisting aside, the father — with some effort — managed to break through the circle of spectators and flee the shul, dragging his young son after him...

Zevulun stood frozen in his place. Only his eyes had moved throughout the dismal scene, taking it in. No, he had never hit his Yossi like that. No. He had never punished him like that other father did. No. No. NO!

He squeezed his eyes shut, to banish the image of himself beating Yossi. Opening them again, he saw to his surprise that several of his fellow worshipers were watching him with interest. The words, "No. No. NO!" had, it seemed, been spoken aloud.

On trembling legs he walked to the exit. Automatically, as he went, he mumbled the appropriate responses to the *chazan's* "Kaddish" along with the rest of the *minyan*. A few minutes later, he was seated in the driver's seat of his car.

But he didn't start the engine. Lassitude enveloped him completely. He could not summon enough energy to move a muscle.

Avraham Blum took the initiative. He bent over Yossi's locked drawer, handling the lock and scrutinizing it from every angle. Lifting his head, he said, "I don't know why, but until now I never paid attention to the type of lock Yossi used here. I mean, I saw that he locked it, but this is really something."

Yaakov Frankel and Shimon Pollack bent also, to see what Avraham meant. "It's an expensive lock!" Avraham exclaimed. "See, you set it with a combination. You have to know the code in order to open it."

Yaakov murmured, "It seems the boy knew how to guard his secrets..."

Avraham continued examining the lock, searching for some way he could break it open. "How can we ever find out the combination? You know, this is starting to interest me, too."

The younger boy said eagerly, "How about trying the *gematria* of the words 'the third eye'?"

The other two burst into laughter.

"A nice idea," Yaakov said. "But I wouldn't recommend wasting time now on *gematrias.*"

"Then what should we do?"

All three fell silent in thought.

"Okay. I have another idea," Shimon whispered.

"Well?"

"Instead of trying to force open the lock, why don't we unscrew the two parts of the drawer that the lock is holding together?"

"You're right!" Avraham exclaimed.

Encouraged, Shimon continued, "All we need is a simple screwdriver, and the problem is solved!"

The words had scarcely left his mouth before he was out the door, seeking a screwdriver. Not many minutes passed before he was back, bearing triumphantly aloft that very tool. Hastily he shut the door, leaning against it to discourage the entry of another student who had followed him to the room out of curiosity, interested in discovering why Shimon needed a screwdriver.

"No, Avi," Shimon called. "You can't come in now. Do me a favor and go away."

The pressure on the door abated at once. The boy had apparently decided to humor him. The sound of his receding footsteps echoed clearly to those in the room. Yaakov Frankel exhaled in relief. All he needed now was for other students to see him in one of the dormitory rooms under such suspicious circumstances...

Avraham Blum set to work. Several minutes' work succeeded in separating the two halves of the drawer. All three leaned forward eagerly to see what it contained.

The drawer was empty.

All the work had been for nothing. They looked at each other, the same keen disappointment reflected in each of their faces. Yossi's roommates began to harbor a tiny doubt about Reb Yaakov. Was he leading them on a wild-goose chase? Was there something he was concealing from them?

They had no way of knowing.

Yaakov gathered the drift of their thoughts. Moving slowly, he returned to the chair behind the table and lowered himself into it. With a smile that held a trace of embarrassment, he admitted, "I see it's not easy being a detective. Interesting, maybe. But not easy."

There was apology in his tone.

After a moment, he added, "I confess, I had hoped to find something in the drawer that would help me make some progress. All I want is to save a yeshivah boy — a boy who, apparently, has fallen into the hands of strangers who are using his vulnerability to lead him astray. I believed that Yossi would have inadvertently left behind some clue that would have helped me in my investigation." He shrugged ruefully. "It seems that Heaven wants me to work a little harder."

"What did you hope to find in the drawer?" Avraham asked.

"I don't know. Some sort of note or letter, perhaps, or maybe a book he'd been reading lately. I can't state specifically what I was looking for — but I'd hoped to find something! Something that would set me on Yossi's trail..."

"Just like the police," Shimon said.

"Yes. Like the police. Criminals never perpetrate the perfect crime. They always make some mistake that helps the police track them down." Rising, Yaakov continued, "All right, boys. I'm very grateful to you for your help. I'll search for Yossi some other way. I'm positive that Hashem will help me. The information you've given me today is invaluable. Meanwhile" — he fixed the boys with a hard stare — "I have to ask both of you to keep everything that happened in this room today a solemn secret. Do you understand? Spreading the story could be very dangerous. A Jewish boy's life is hanging in the balance!"

Both students nodded to signal their comprehension. Their eyes followed Reb Yaakov as he left the room. When he was gone, they remained seated on their beds, talking.

"Reb Yaakov likes playing detective, huh?"

"I don't think it's a question of playing. It seemed to me that he's really worried about Yossi."

"Maybe."

"Why 'maybe'?"

"How do I know? Something is fishy here. It's hard for me to believe him."

"I think you're making a mistake. The two of them became very close these last few weeks. They talked a lot together. Don't you remember? Sometimes Reb Yaakov would stand with Yossi for a whole hour during third *seder,* both of them talking nonstop. I think Reb Yaakov feels responsible for him in a way."

Shimon did not reply at once. Finally, he said with apparent nonchalance, "Maybe you're right." He paused, then added, "I'm still in shock over the story he told us about Yossi. I also feel a little guilty."

"Why? What happened?"

"Just the fact that we didn't notice that something was happening to him."

Avraham got up and went to sit in the chair Reb Yaakov had used. Leaning back in it, he asked, "What would you have done if you had noticed?"

Shimon shrugged. "I don't know. All I know is, if I had noticed, I would have done something. It feels like we did the sin of '*al ta'amod al dam rei'echa*' — don't stand on your brother's blood."

"Come on, Shimon. You're exaggerating."

"Why?"

"What do you mean, 'why?' I tell you, there was nothing we could have done. How could you have known that Yossi had a problem? Was it written on his forehead?"

"No, not on his forehead. Looking back, I can see now that it was written all over him! You can tell."

"How?" Avraham challenged. "Can you go into his soul and see what was happening there? If you can, I have news for you: There are other candidates in this place, just like Yossi, who could use some help. Maybe you want to start digging into everyone's 'kishkes' to see whether anything is happening? Come on, Shimon!"

A small silence filled the room. Shimon broke it first.

"Maybe you're right," he conceded. "About Yossi, anyway."

All this time, without realizing it, Avraham had been clutching the empty drawer in his lap. He suddenly became aware of this. Muttering, "Why am I still holding this thing?" he got up and went to return it to the closet.

Trying to slip the drawer into its groove, he felt something blocking its smooth passage. He tried again, and then again, without success. Finally, he yanked out the drawer and bent over to see what was impeding his progress.

Almost before his hand reached into the dark slot, he cried out, "Shimon, come! I think I found something!"

Shimon sprang up and ran over to the closet. "What is it?"

"I don't know yet." Carefully, Avraham pulled out a small bundle of folded pages, ripped in places. "It looks like a letter."

With a fluid motion, Avraham straightened up. He ran an eye over the letter. It was written in Hebrew, but the torn spots prevented either boy from making out its meaning.

Shimon grabbed Avraham's arm. "Come on!"

"Where to?" The words burst from Avraham as he allowed himself to be dragged along after his roommate.

"Let's run and catch up with Reb Yaakov! Here's some real *hashgachah pratis!* Maybe this letter can help him find Yossi!"

Yaakov Frankel left the yeshivah building a disappointed man, and proceeded to the nearest Egged bus stop. He wanted to return home as quickly as possible, to immure himself in his tiny study and think over the meager information he'd gleaned from Yossi's roommates.

He was frankly discouraged. He had practically nothing to work with. Right now, his only hope rested with the strange words, "the third eye." Was it the name of some new cult to sprout within the borders of Israel?

How had these people contacted Yossi? That was something worth finding out.

He glanced at his watch. It was past noon already. He had spent much longer than he had expected at the yeshivah, though he hadn't been conscious of the passage of time. As he waited for the bus, he kept rotating the questions in his mind. What was the 'third eye'? Where to begin looking?

A bus arrived. Although it was not the one he had been waiting for, he climbed aboard anyway. He would alight at the Central Bus Station and switch there. Flashing his bus card at the driver, he moved toward the rear in search of a place where he could sit and think. The bus began slowly moving away from the stop.

Suddenly, the passengers were startled by a commotion just outside. Fists pounded frantically on the side of the bus nearest the curb. The driver, acting instinctively, pressed his foot harder on the gas pedal, and the bus zoomed forward. Through the roar of the accelerating engine, Yaakov heard the cry, "Reb Yaakov! Yaakov Frankel!"

He twisted his head to stare out the window. There were Yossi's two roommates, running with all their might after the bus. Avraham Blum held a sheaf of papers in his hand and was waving it above his head as he ran.

"Reb Yaakov, we found something for you. It's Yossi's, we're sure it's Yossi's!"

Yaakov was stunned. He stood up and made his way rapidly toward the driver. "Stop here, please. I need to get off."

The driver did not even deign to glance at him. He continued driving.

"Do me a favor — it's a matter of life and death!" Yaakov pleaded.

"You want a cop to catch me and give me a ticket? Will you pay the fine? Don't you see it's dangerous to stop here? What's the matter with you?"

Yaakov breathed deeply, as though preparing to battle for his life. "You're right. But this is a question of life and death, of saving a Jewish child from missionaries. You must let me get off!"

The driver glanced at him indifferently, a look that held his contempt for the illegal request.

"You'll get off at the next stop, sir. Save the Jewish kid from missionaries 10 minutes later!"

Yaakov stole another look out the back window. He saw the two boys standing desolately in the center of the sidewalk far behind, uncertain of their next move. Yaakov was intensely curious to know what they had found that had brought them pounding after the bus in such a hurry.

Yaakov jumped off the bus at the next stop. He crossed the street and waited impatiently for a bus going in the other direction — the one that would get him back to the yeshivah.

18

A slow drive of three-quarters of an hour brought Zevulun to the outskirts of Petach Tikvah. The entrance to the city was slightly congested at this early evening hour. With dogged persistence, he wound his way along Rothschild Avenue, turned left on Herzl and finally parked on Chafetz Chaim Street, not far from the home of his friend, Reb Yitzchak Abramson.

His progress up the narrow stairway of the old building was weary. The stairwell smelled musty and its walls revealed patches of flaked paint. The place had clearly seen better days. It was a sad reminder of the old Petach Tikvah, which had not kept pace with the beautiful modern homes that fill the city today. Zevulun reached his friend's door and rapped lightly. After a short delay, it was opened by Reb Yitzchak himself.

"He-e-e-llo!"

His old friend's welcome was warm and heartfelt. Reb Yitzchak's eyes glowed like a pair of lanterns, and the radiance of his broad smile lit up the gloomy corridor.

Zevulun tried to smile back, but the effort felt stiff and artificial. Reb Yitzchak seemed to discern his friend's mood at once. He had always had this ability, and seemed to retain it still, though it had been two years since the two had met face-to-face. Though it consisted these days of only sporadic phone calls, each knew that their friendship had stood the test of time. There was no need to nourish it through regular meetings. The friendship, born in the yeshivah hall where they had learned together as youths, had endured into their adult lives though their paths had diverged. Even after long years of separation, the two could pick up instantly where they had left off, enjoying hours of stimulating conversation which Reb Yitzchak always made sure to leaven with words of Torah.

Now, as they stood facing one another in the doorway, Reb Yitzchak did not allow his friend's diffidence to dampen his own mood. He threw an arm around Zevulun's shoulder and led him kindly but firmly into the living room.

One sweeping glance at the room told Zevulun that nothing here had changed since his last visit, some two years earlier. There were the ancient bookcases, groaning under the weight of numerous heavy Torah volumes that covered the entire eastern wall. A large, colored portrait of the Chazon Ish adorned the wall opposite. On the table lay an open Gemara — *Maseches Bava Kama* — along with two books of commentary. "He was probably in the middle of preparing a *shiur*," Zevulun thought. The thought was accompanied by a small stab of envy. "His lifestyle allows him to learn a great deal. Maybe... Maybe... if I would have learned like him, I would not have had all those problems with Yossi?"

Zevulun chased the question out of his mind the way one might swat at an irritating fly. He was not in any condition to deal with it at the moment. Exhaustion washed over him — a feeling that was much more than mere physical fatigue.

"Can I offer you something to drink?" His host's voice penetrated his tangled thoughts.

Zevulun lifted a hand in a negative gesture. "No, thanks."

"Maybe just a little one?" Reb Yitzchak persisted.

There was an impatient edge to Zevulun's voice as he said sharply, "No! Maybe afterwards!"

If anything had been needed to convince Reb Yitzchak that his friend was suffering from a surfeit of tension, this was it. It took no great leap of logic to decide that the source of the tension was the reason which had brought Zevulun here this evening.

The two sat facing each other in silence. Finally, Reb Yitzchak smiled again, and asked gently, "So, Zevulun, what brings you here so unexpectedly?"

Zevulun did not hurry to answer. He tried for a time to organize his thoughts so that he could present a coherent story. In the end he simply blurted, "Yossi's gone!"

Reb Yitzchak started. He reached up and straightened his large yarmulke, which had nearly slipped off his head in his shock, and asked, "Who? Who's gone?"

"Yossi! My Yossi!"

Reb Yitzchak took a deep breath. With an effort at calm, he asked, "What do you mean, he's gone?"

"Simply that! One morning I get a fax — Heaven only knows from where — and in it my son informs me that he has decided to leave home for good. That's all!"

A silence descended on the room like the blow of a powerful fist. Reb Yitzchak toyed with a pen that had somehow found its way into his hand, while Zevulun sat motionless. Reb Yitzchak simply did not know how to react to the news. What should he — and shouldn't he — say at a moment like this?

"Can you give me any more details?"

"There's not much to tell. He disappeared from his yeshivah at the end of last week, without a word to anyone."

"I understand that. What I'm asking about is the reason he might have left. What might have led to such a move?"

A bitter smile tugged at Zevulun's lips. "How should I know? Yossi, to my sorrow, is not a very well-behaved boy. A little wild and unpredictable. And now — he's gone!"

He rubbed his chin nervously, evading his friend's eyes. The search for Yossi's motive would undoubtedly lead back to him. It would be hard indeed if his friend, Reb Yitzchak, joined the chorus accusing him of causing Yossi's flight. The mere thought of this possibility sent a flicker of anger through Zevulun.

But Reb Yitzchak pressed on: "My friend, things don't just happen. There has to be a reason — even with a boy you call unpredictable. I find it hard to accept the label 'wild.'"

"What?" Zevulun's face became suffused with red. "Are you like all the others? Are you blaming me?!"

Reb Yitzchak was taken aback. He had never heard Zevulun shout like that. His wife peeked through the kitchen door, then hastily withdrew. He understood suddenly that a ferocious storm — an emotional storm — was raging inside his friend, though Zevulun was trying to hide it. Even more, it seemed to him that Zevulun was afraid of some sort of exposure, and that this was the reason for his rage. He was using anger to protect himself from...from what? All Reb Yitzchak had done was ask an innocent question. Yossi was gone, but what lay behind his disappearance? It was this, apparently, that Zevulun was trying to conceal.

He stood up and went to the kitchen. At the door, he turned and asked, "Coffee or tea?"

A pause. "Coffee."

Reb Yitzchak vanished into the kitchen, where he filled the electric kettle. His wife whispered, "I'll bring in the drinks. Don't leave him alone."

Reb Yitzchak smiled. "I left deliberately. I wanted him to be alone for a few minutes, to give him a chance to cool down — and especially, to regret his outburst. I know he wants me to help him. But right now he's all locked up inside. If he can start to feel ashamed over what he did, he might open up a little. Then we'll see what we can do to help...."

He returned presently with a laden tray. Various baked goods flanked two steaming mugs. "Here, please, make a *berachah* in my house."

In silence they sipped their coffee and nibbled at the cakes. After a few minutes, Reb Yitzchak put down his mug and faced his guest squarely.

"Listen, Zevulun. I don't know what happened. You don't have to tell me unless you want to. But I'd just like you to remember one thing, no matter how upset you are or what crisis you're dealing with. And that's this: Nothing 'just happens' to people. Everything is a test; and the test, in practical terms, serves as a mirror. A mirror from Above, to help a person see himself more clearly...."

"But —"

"Just a minute, Zevulun, I'm not finished. Please be patient for a few more seconds. Life sails along in its quiet, routine stream, and it seems to a man that he's honest, upright, pious, filled with all sorts of good qualities. Then comes the testing hour. Hashem sends him a challenge — usually, an unexpected one — and all at once his boat overturns. At that moment, the person senses exactly who and what he really is. He finds out from his spontaneous reaction to the test."

"But —"

"Zevulun, do me a favor. Another minute and I'm done. After that, you can answer however you want. All right?

"I'll give you an example: I have a friend who, in the years when his business was prospering, often spoke about his faith in Hashem. He really believed that he was a 'man of faith.' Then, one fine day, one of his employees suddenly left and starting a competing business of his own. My friend was devastated, terribly afraid that his own firm would fold. His wife reminded him, 'Haven't you always talked about your faith in Hashem? Whenever anyone would come to you with a tale of hardship, you would comfort him with words of faith and tell them that everything would be all right. What's happened to you now?'

"I remember asking him the same question: 'What's happened to you?' My friend answered, 'It's true. Until today I really thought I was a man of faith. Hashem has just proved to me that I was only deluding myself.' Do you understand, Zevulun? When my friend looked at himself honestly in the mirror, he was able to admit the truth."

Zevulun managed only with great effort to restrain his anger. "What does all this have to do with me, with what I'm telling you about Yossi?"

Reb Yitzchak smiled patiently. "You're right. I don't know how it applies to you. Or, more accurately, I don't know *yet* how it applies to you. Maybe, if you don't get angry, we'll be able to talk it over calmly and peacefully, and we'll find out how it applies to you. In the meantime, the point is this: Remember, everything that happens to a person is a mirror

— a mirror that strips the mask away and shows him his true face."

Reb Yitzchak allowed a moment to pass in silence, then said, "I am prepared to help you, Zevulun. We're close enough friends for me to see that you need help, and that's why you've come to me. Do you deny it?"

Zevulun shook his head: No.

"In that case, tell me the truth. Why did Yossi run away?"

Zevulun raised his mug and sipped lingeringly at his coffee, which had cooled a little by this time.

"Yossi and I," he said slowly, "have not been getting along for a long time now. I can't remember when it started, but it must have been a few years ago — before he left to yeshivah. I think it was sometime in the later years of elementary school, sixth, or seventh, or possibly the eighth grade. It's hard to remember exactly."

"What happened to him?"

"I don't know. I don't remember. Yossi started acting wild suddenly, behaving disruptively every chance he had. He rebelled against my authority. I don't know why."

"You never thought about why it happened so suddenly, out of the blue?"

Zevulun betrayed impatience. "Of course I've thought about it."

He fell into a reverie, reviewing the past. Finally, he said in a low voice, "Actually, I didn't think about it very much. I'm a working man. I'm busy all day. I'd come home tired in the evening, and my wife would tell me about Yossi's antics that day, and I'd lose control...."

Zevulun broke off. His breathing became ragged and uneven, his eyes wide and staring. Reb Yitzchak rose in alarm and crossed over to his friend. "What's the matter, Zevulun?"

Zevulun closed his eyes and covered them with his right hand. His head drooped.

"Do you feel ill? Zevulun, answer me!"

Zevulun did not answer. He couldn't speak. Before his mind's eye the memory had sprung up, full blown, of the time he had beaten his Yossi mercilessly. The child had pleaded with him to stop, but Zevulun had not listened. He could not remember, now, what the beating had been about. The image merged with the one he had carried with him this evening from the small shul: the small child being slapped over and over by his father. What was the connection? Was he that man? Was the scene he had witnessed tonight in that unfamiliar shul a mirror, the kind Yitzchak had just described?

A black confusion overwhelmed him. Through it, he heard his friend's anxious voice, demanding, "What's happening to you, Zevulun?"

This time, he heard. But he could not find the strength to answer. Instead, after a few minutes, he got unsteadily to his feet.

"I'm going home now. I'll be back tomorrow night, if that's all right with you. I — I think I really do need your help."

Reb Yitzchak was not comfortable about allowing Zevulun to leave, but the situation did not offer him many options. He inclined his head. "Very well."

He escorted Zevulun to the door. They parted with subdued good-nights. Then Zevulun turned away and was swallowed up by the gloomy stairwell. The hour was approaching midnight.

The apartment was quiet and dark when he turned the key in his own lock.

Zevulun made his way to the kitchen and switched on a light. He wanted a last cup of coffee before bed. His hands moved mechanically to prepare the drink, while his thoughts flew in disordered fashion through his heavy head.

Suddenly, the phone rang.

A quick glance at the clock on the kitchen wall showed him that it was already 1 a.m. Who could be calling? Moving slowly, almost sluggishly, Zevulun picked up the receiver and uttered a low, "Hello?"

From the other end, he distinctly heard the click of the receiver being replaced.

Startled, Zevulun hung up. A sudden thought struck him: "Could that have been Yossi? Maybe he called here, just like he did with that other man, that *kollelnik*, Frankel? Maybe he hung up because he heard my voice, when he had hoped his mother would answer the phone?"

He paced the kitchen in extreme agitation. This might have been a unique opportunity to try to re-establish some sort of bond with his son, and now it was gone! He could not bring himself to leave the kitchen, hoping against hope that the phone would ring again. If it did, he planned to start talking right away, before Yossi could hang up...

And then, it did ring.

Zevulun lunged for the phone and said breathlessly, "Yossi, listen, it's Abba. Please don't hang up! I know that you're very angry at me. But I still think we can talk. It's very possible that I've also made mistakes. Come home. Let's talk. After all, I'm your father who loves you! Yossi, tell me where you are. I'll come to you anywhere. You'll see, it can be good between us again."

"Abba, what's the matter with you?"

Zevulun reeled and nearly dropped the phone. The voice was that of his son, Elazar.

Anger coursed through him at the realization that he had betrayed his weakness to Elazar. He slammed down the receiver.

In Jerusalem, Elazar stood dumbfounded, still clutching the dead receiver in his hand. He felt embarrassed and worried in equal measure. Had Yossi's disappearance made something snap in his father? The stream of sentences Zevulun had babbled so hurriedly had made no sense to Elazar.

Why had his father hung up so abruptly? All he'd wanted to do was tell him that Yaakov Frankel was pursuing the matter with zeal. Maybe that would help calm his father a little ...

19

This time, for some reason, the bus was late. Yaakov Frankel stood at the stop in an agony of impatience. Curiosity tormented him: Why had the boys pursued him like that? He had seen Avraham Blum wave a sheaf of papers in the air. What could they contain? He recalled vividly the way the boy had shouted, "It's Yossi's! I'm sure it's Yossi's!" What might those pages be? And where had the boys found them? When they checked, Yossi's drawer had been empty.

Ten nerve-wracking minutes later, the bus rolled up to the stop, crammed to the gills. As he opened the doors to let passengers descend, the driver bellowed, "No more room! No one gets on!" Heedless, Yaakov pushed his way aboard anyway.

Moments later he flew out again, at the stop nearest the yeshivah.

To his great good fortune, he caught sight of the boys he sought just as they were crossing the threshold into the yeshivah building. He ran after them as fast as he could, and caught them on the point of entering the *beis midrash*.

Breathless and unable to speak, he motioned urgently for them to follow him. The three left the building. Outside, in the building's courtyard, they searched for a quiet place to talk.

In a shaded corner that afforded a measure of privacy, Yaakov gasped, "Show me what you found!"

"Here. It looks like a letter to Yossi." Avraham Blum held out the tattered pages.

Yaakov took them. He studied the torn papers, turned them over and examined the envelope they had been mailed in. It was a standard airmail envelope. The letter had been sent from somewhere outside the country.

After his initial scrutiny, Yaakov raised his eyes to the boys. "Where did you find this? And who told you it belongs to Yossi?"

"We tried to put the drawer back in its place, but it kept sticking. Something was blocking its way. We bent down and looked inside the closet — and saw the letter. It didn't fall out of our drawers, that much we know for sure."

Yaakov studied the letter again, and especially the envelope. The place where the return address should have been was torn; the stamp, too, had been ripped off. As Yaakov smoothed the creases on the envelope, his eye caught something. It was a portion of a circle.

"This must be where the post office stamped it," he mused. There was only one single clear letter that he could read. It was an "H." He began thinking furiously. The letter H? What country could the letter have come from? Smoothing the envelope still more, he thought he saw the top portion of another letter. He could not be sure, but it looked like a "T."

He looked up, to see the two students watching him avidly. "Tell me, has Yossi spoken of any particular country lately?"

Neither of the boys recalled any discussion of that sort.

Next, Yaakov turned his attention to the letter itself. He tried to make out the words scrawled on the torn pages. They were written in Hebrew, in a rounded hand. (Might it be worthwhile, he wondered, to consult a handwriting expert?) He read aloud:

"Don't worry... It's all right... Stream of consciousn... Telling of the...

Body, temple of the sou... blessed light... true happines... of the reincarnat... differences in..."

Yaakov grew weary of reading the senseless fragments. Discouragement settled on his shoulders with an unwelcome thud. He had no idea how to proceed from here. There was nothing to hold onto.

"Okay, boys. I'm very grateful to you for finding this. I'll take it home now. Maybe I'll be able to piece together a picture from everything you've told me."

Shimon Pollack spoke up: "I hope, if something interesting happens, that the rabbi will let us know. We're very curious."

And Avraham Blum added, "We deserve it, don't we? We helped."

Yaakov smiled. "Certainly you deserve it. But don't say, 'We helped,' in the past tense. I suspect that you'll be helping me again in the future."

They parted amiably, and Yaakov left to catch the bus for home.

Rabbi Yitzchak Abramson stood motionless in the doorway of his apartment, in his mind's eye following his friend Zevulun down the stairs and into his car. He heard the engine's ignition shatter the stillness of the night, and remained standing there, listening, until the last echo had died away.

He returned to the well-lit living room. Sitting at the table, he lost himself in thought. Finally, he shook himself and opened the Gemara that lay in front of him. He must finish preparing his *shiur* for tomorrow.

Less than five minutes later, however, he closed it again. The letters had bounced around crazily without forming coherent words or sensible sentences. His thoughts persisted in reverting to Zevulun and his vanished Yossi.

The news continued to stun him. He had heard of boys like this in recent years, boys from fine Orthodox families who had gone astray. *Baruch Hashem*, nothing like that had happened in his own yeshivah, so he hadn't devoted much thought to it until now. He was forced to admit, in his heart of hearts, that because this phenomenon was far from the public eye, it had also remained distant from his concern.

Now, abstract knowledge had been exchanged for hard fact. It was Yossi Kimmerman who was involved here. There was a living, breathing boy involved, and a grieving family. This time, Reb Yitzchak reflected, the situation was close to him. Very close.

Reb Yitzchak was especially disturbed by the fact that his conversation with Zevulun had been prematurely cut off — exactly, in his opinion — at the crucial point. Zevulun had been about to open up. He had already begun to confess his feelings, and then — he got up and left. It was possible, very possible, that, had Zevulun continued to pour out his heart, Reb Yitzchak would have been able to determine the root of the problem — the circumstances that had led to such a grievous occurrence.

He felt parched. Going into the kitchen, he poured himself a glass of cold soda, which did much to alleviate his thirst. As he stood there, glass in hand, he remembered that Zevulun's first outburst had occurred when he, Yitzchak, had mentioned the mirroring effect of life's challenges, the way they force a person to face himself honestly and see his true face. Afterwards, Zevulun had apparently felt troubled, recalling how he used to lose control when dealing with his son. What had happened inside Zevulun at that moment? Was he thinking of specific episodes in which he had wronged Yossi? And, if so, when and how?

Reb Yitzchak placed the empty glass on the countertop and returned to the living room, still sunk in thought. He had known Zevulun for many years, since their youth in yeshivah. A lively boy, but never one to lose control or explode. And yet here in this very room, not long before, Zevulun had forgotten himself and exploded with real anger.

To Yitzchak, the most interesting point was still the fact that, after he had told how he would often lose control with Yossi, Zevulun had found it impossible to remain in his friend's home a moment longer. What did it mean?

He made another attempt to open his Gemara and concentrate. This trial, too, resulted in failure. He could not stop dwelling on the fascinating question he had heard an angry Zevulun cry out. "Are you like all the others? Are you blaming me?!"

For some reason, Zevulun had felt persecuted. Yitzchak could not understand why. He had not accused his friend of a thing. Why had the question burst from Zevulun — and straight from his heart? Apparently — this was just a guess — those close to him, his wife, children, perhaps others as well, were holding Zevulun accountable.

Or was that only in Zevulun's imagination? Maybe he only thought they were blaming him. Was it because — in his innermost heart — he believed he was to blame, that he imagined others felt the same?

But this was precisely what Yitzchak had been saying! The crisis had acted upon Zevulun as a mirror. And his angry outburst was an attempt at concealing his guilt — especially from himself!

Reb Yitzchak frowned. Was Zevulun really at fault in what had happened? As an educator, he himself had worked extensively with children and their parents (though never a case as harrowing as this one). In some of the problems or crises he had come across, the fault did lie with the parents. But not all. No, definitely not all. The subject was a difficult and complex one. In most cases, the crisis was precipitated by both sides.

But in Zevulun's case, he was sorry to have to admit to himself that all signs pointed in a different direction. It seemed that Zevulun really did have something to regret.

Reb Yitzchak threw a weary glance at his wristwatch. The hands stood at 2:30 a.m. He might as well face the fact that there would not be a well-prepared *shiur* to deliver in the yeshivah tomorrow. He might not even go to yeshivah at all, but visit Zevulun instead, at home or in his office. It seemed to him that this was a matter of life and death, and that took precedence over many things...

Yaakov felt infused with renewed energy. Apart from the mitzvah of saving a life, the matter had become a fascinating puzzle for him. The challenge was enormous.

If he still lacked the definitive clue that would bring the solution to this riddle, there was no question that he did hold the ends of various strings that might help lead to it.

He went to the telephone, and paused. His first move would be to try and get to the bottom of the mystery of Yossi's unknown friend. Whom to call first?

Elazar, he decided. It was possible that from Yaakov's description he would recognize some business acquaintance of his father's. A good idea... His fingers were already punching in the number he wanted.

"Hello, is this Yeshivat Nachal Kedumim? Good. Elazar Kimmerman, please!"

After a short pause, "Elazar? Hello. How are you?"

Elazar groaned. "How well could I be? I'm worried sick about my father and mother — especially my mother."

"What happened?"

"What do you mean, what happened? Do you think what already happened has passed over them lightly? I don't know how my mother will hold up."

There was nothing to say. Yaakov waited a few seconds, then said gently, "I understand. But listen, Elazar. I have some news for you."

"You found out where he is?!" Elazar sounded jubilant and disbelieving at the same time.

"Not quite. What I meant to say is that I have a few new pieces of information. If we can figure out how to interpret them the right way, we should be able — with Hashem's help — to reach our goal."

"Well, tell me!"

"All right. Do you know of any nonreligious friends of Yossi's?"

Elazar's reply came after a delay, and it sounded strained. "No... But what do you mean, exactly, when you say 'nonreligious friends'?"

"Do you want a composite I've put together?"

"A composite of whom?"

"A young man who, if we manage to track him down, should help us make considerable progress in finding our runaway. Ready?"

"What kind of question is that? Of course!"

"Okay. We're talking about a man of medium height — not too tall and not too short. Very curly hair. From what I've been able to learn, the hair is brown, but this is still uncertain."

There was a moment's silence. "Is he fat?" Elazar asked.

"No."

"Thin?"

"No."

"Then what is he?"

"His build was described as 'normal.'"

"How old does he look?"

"Thirty-something. Elazar, can you picture anyone you know?"

"At the moment, no. But give me a chance to think.... Wait a second. How does this not-too-tall, not-too-short, not-too-fat and not-too-thin guy fit into Yossi's story?"

"A good question. Not yet. Hear me out first, to the end. This man apparently visited Yossi at yeshivah more than once."

"V-visited the yeshivah? What for?" Elazar was stunned.

"That's exactly what I'd like to know."

At this stage, Yaakov did not want to bring in the "third eye" business. The first order of the day was finding out just whom they were dealing with. But there was one other unpleasant bit of information he felt obligated to pass on.

"Sometimes Yossi would go away with the man in his car for several hours."

"What? I don't believe it!"

"So don't believe it. But if you won't believe, we'll get nowhere. Oh, and Elazar, maybe this will help you identify the fellow. He drives a red Mitsubishi. Does that remind you of anyone?"

"At the moment, no."

Yaakov sucked in his breath and let it out in a long sigh.

"Elazar, try to think. This is important. For the time being, I'd like to leave your father out of this. I'm afraid he might react too emotionally and slow down the investigation."

"I understand. But no one pops into my head yet."

"Look, Elazar. Your father works with secular Jews. There must be all sorts of them coming and going in that real-estate office of his. Maybe this is one of them?"

"Why are you thinking in that direction?"

"I'm simply trying to figure out where Yossi might have met a non-religious man, much older than he, who has the audacity to visit him at his yeshivah." He paused. "Did Yossi ever visit your father at work?"

"Of course."

"Maybe someone came in just when Yossi was there and struck up a friendship with him?"

"It's possible. But I don't see why you're thinking only of my father's office. Yossi could have met the guy anywhere."

"True. Still, I'm looking there first. We'll see what happens. If we don't find what we want there, we'll keep looking."

Elazar's voice was suddenly electrified. He had remembered someone. In a choked voice, he said, "You know, I think I know who we're talking about. What did you say — curly hair, dark brown?"

"Yes. Not too thin and not too fat, etc."

"Listen, it must be him!"

"What's his name? Tell me!"

"No. Not now. I want to check it out myself first."

Zevulun waited tensely for the meeting. Ilan was expected in the office momentarily, accompanied by the Canadian investor who had backed out of the Hadera deal at the last minute. From the office's perspective it was a good deal, even a very good deal. In Zevulun's opinion, the investor had been offered good terms, and the chances of that land being zoned for building were good. There was a real prospect of raking in a quick, substantial profit. Why had he backed out?

He glanced at his watch: 9:30 in the morning. The meeting had been scheduled for 9:15; Ilan was a little late. Zevulun prowled his office restlessly; his mood had not improved since the day before. He found it especially hard to forgive himself for leaving his friend's house so abruptly last night. That had been very disrespectful. And what was worse, he had exposed a piece of his heart. A small piece, but enough for Reb Yitzchak, a shrewd judge who needed few words, to learn what lay behind them.

On the other hand, Zevulun thought, had he really had any choice? His friend had angered him right at the onset with his talk of reality mirroring a man's true, inner being. That analogy had irritated him to no end. It did not allow him to deal with Yossi without getting personally involved. And was he the only guilty party here?

Zevulun recoiled from his own thoughts. This was the first time he had admitted, even to himself, the possibility that he was also to blame, even if he shared that honor with others. What was happening to him? Had they all succeeded in brainwashing him? Where was all this leading? Where …?

There was a knock at the door.

Hastily, Zevulun straightened his tie and smoothed his lapels. "Come in!"

The door opened and Ilan stood there, cheerful as ever. The Canadian was close behind.

Zevulun shook Ilan's hand and then listened courteously as Ilan introduced him to their guest. "Meet Robert Clancy, from Winnipeg, Canada."

Zevulun and Clancy shook hands. Even as he led them to their seats, alarm bells were ringing inside Zevulun's head. There was something he did not like very much about the Canadian.

21

Yaakov was content. Elazar's readiness to do his bit in the investigation — specifically, to try to identify the mysterious, curly-haired man who had apparently lured Yossi off the beaten track — aroused hope in him. It was good for Elazar to become involved in the search. A person grows attached to the things he invests himself in, and Yaakov very much wanted Elazar's investment. Yaakov needed his help. He could not do it all alone.

Accordingly, before they hung up, he decided to release an additional piece of information.

"Elazar, I have something else for you. Are you listening?"

"Of course!"

"I'll give you an identifying mark that might help you."

"Well?"

"The man wears a bracelet on his wrist."

"A bracelet?" Elazar was surprised. "Why a bracelet? Is he some kind of hippy? If that's the case, I think I've made a mistake. It can't be the man I'm thinking of."

Yaakov sighed in open frustration. "Did I say he was a hippy?" He raised his voice. "The bracelet is a symbol of the cult he — and, apparently, Yossi too — is involved with. It has an engraving of a large eye."

When Elazar spoke, it was slowly, as though he was weighing each word: "So you're certain that Yossi has fallen in with a cult? It's still possible that he's just run away, isn't it? If my father hears about this..."

"Elazar, are you *listening* to me? I've already learned a number of things about Yossi. There are still a good many details missing, but that doesn't concern me at this moment. Right now, our job is to learn the identity of the man with the curly hair and the bracelet. Understand?"

"What does the big eye stand for?"

"I don't know that yet. I can make a few guesses, though — but for the moment, I'll keep those to myself. Just accept this, Elazar: Your brother is linked with them in some form or another. About a week before his disappearance, he babbled something to one of his roommates about a magical, all-seeing, third eye. That remark ties in very nicely with the other things I've found out."

"Are you telling me you questioned Yossi's roommates?"

"Let's leave that for now. What's important is for you to check out — discreetly — the man you suspect. He mustn't guess that we're interested in him. We don't want the cult to get wind of our investigation."

Elazar had the sensation of having left the secure boundaries of the world he knew and entered a strange new one — a dangerous world. Already, he was beginning to regret the suspicions he had voiced. Now it was up to him to pursue the lead for Yaakov. What was the purpose of this? It would not help anyway. They would never find Yossi this way!

"Reb Yaakov?"

"Yes?"

"Maybe you should drop the whole thing."

"What? Why?"

"It's not for me, and it's not for you."

Yaakov was aghast. "Are you suggesting that we abandon your brother?"

"G–d forbid!"

"Then why drop it? What are you trying to say?"

A confused silence answered him. Then Elazar asked, hesitantly, "Maybe we should contact the police after all?"

Yaakov was growing impatient. "My dear Elazar, you know your father's dead set against that! Sparing his family embarrassment is paramount to him right now. What can we do?"

Another silence. "Well, how about hiring a private investigator?"

"A good idea. Now, do you have another good idea, such as where to find the money to pay for it?"

"Maybe Abba..."

The last shreds of Yaakov's patience were fast disintegrating. "You know that — at this stage anyway — your father will never agree. Maybe later, if we reach a dead end, we can try to persuade him. Okay?"

Elazar did not answer. Yaakov had not left him with many options. He heard Yaakov's ringing command over the telephone wire: "And now — to work!"

Weakly, he replied, "Okay."

"Good luck."

Yaakov replaced the receiver. "We're moving," he murmured to himself, rubbing his hands together with satisfaction. The next step was to figure out where the letter had come from. Its contents were, at this point, less important. In what country had the letter originated? To know that, he must solve the riddle of the torn postage stamp. How to go about that?

The Unger children, on the first floor of his apartment building — they collected stamps. Not very useful for him, though. How could he, after never once evincing the slightest interest in stamps as a hobby, suddenly knock on their door asking about their collection?

It was 5 in the afternoon when inspiration struck. He glanced at his watch; there might be enough time. He stood up, donned his jacket and hat, and ordered a cab.

"Where to?" the driver asked as Yaakov got in moments later.

"To Geulah."

The driver had already turned his cab in that neighborhood's general direction, when he heard his passenger speak again.

"No, I'm sorry, I made a mistake. I'd like you to drive to King George Street and let me off in front of the Mashbir, please."

It was not long before he was crossing the busy avenue in front of the Mashbir department store. The Ben-Yehuda pedestrian mall stretched before him, lined on both sides with tourist-attracting gift shops and cafes. Yaakov scrutinized each window display as he passed, finally stopping in front of one. The store was dimly lit and empty at this hour. The elderly proprietor, resting comfortably behind his counter, seemed slightly put out at being disturbed.

"Excuse me," Yaakov said. "Do you sell postage stamps for collectors?"

"Certainly. I have packages of 50 stamps. I also carry packages of 100, and larger ones containing 250 stamps. Which one are you interested in?" He leaned forward confidentially. "Let me tell you, the larger package comes out cheaper than the one of 50 or 100." Having delivered this piece of advice, the shopkeeper fixed his eyes expectantly on his customer.

Yaakov was unmoved. "Give me the 50, please."

Before the man's stupefied gaze, Yaakov took the packet, ripped it open and scattered its contents onto the glass counter. Carefully, without a word, he inspected each stamp. A few he brought up close to his eyes, removing his glasses to see better. But none of the stamps contained the letter "H."

"Can I have another fifty, please?"

The proprietor brought his odd customer another packet of stamps. The ritual was repeated. Yaakov scattered the stamps, studied them one by one... and was again disappointed.

The older man was beginning to lose patience. "What is this? An instant lottery ticket that you scratch off and then ask for a new one?"

Yaakov hardly heard. Tension was building inside him, sharpening his tone as he said, "Give me the package of 100!"

The shopkeeper hesitated.

"Don't worry," Yaakov said. "I'll pay for them all."

"Yes, but tell me what you're trying to find."

"Never mind. I'll find what I'm looking for."

Yaakov rummaged among the stamps in the new pile. And... yes! He'd found it! He held the stamp up to the light. It was not very large. Along the bottom of the stamp appeared the mysterious letter "H." He read the whole word: HELVETIA.

He frowned. He had never heard of that country. On which continent was it located? And how had Yossi established a link to that place?

Where was this Helvetia?

He was at the point of solving the riddle by the simplest route possible: asking the shopkeeper. But he resisted the impulse. He did not want the shopkeeper to view the ultrareligious as ignorant. He contented himself, therefore, with showing the old man the stamp, and saying, "See? I was looking for this!"

The proprietor glanced at the stamp in Yaakov's hand. "What's so special about a simple Swiss stamp? I could show you many that are much more beautiful!"

With an effort, Yaakov swallowed a smile. He had succeeded in obtaining the information he wanted, in an indirect way that took nothing away from *kavod haTorah*.

Even as he offered some lame excuse for his behavior, the wheels in his mind were spinning furiously with new questions. If Yossi had received a letter from Switzerland, did that mean that he had fled to that country? Some cults, he knew, had branches in many parts of the world.

In other words, the mystery was far from solved. He still had a long way to go.

"Sit down," Zevulun invited courteously.

Ilan and the Canadian sank slowly into the pair of armchairs facing Zevulun's desk. Zevulun's eyes remained glued to the Canadian. The man was very tall and thin, dressed with no particular sense of fashion or style. Zevulun was not at all certain that his visitor was really from Canada.

He turned to Ilan and said, in Hebrew, "Well, how can I help?"

Ilan glanced at the Canadian before answering. "It's a question of the price."

"Do you agree with him that it's too high?"

Ilan considered, then answered, "I don't know. The important thing is that the client believes it's too high. He's not prepared to pay it."

Zevulun fell silent, making his calculations. The sense of unease he had felt upon meeting Ilan's prospective buyer remained with him. For some reason, it seemed to him that the Canadian understood Hebrew. It was only a feeling, and one that he could not test directly. But neither could he ignore it.

At length, he said, "Then let him not buy. I don't think we should lower our price. It won't be long before the building permits come through. You know and he knows that the land will be worth 10 times as much."

Ilan bristled. "Then maybe it's not worth our while to sell it altogether?"

"We're only agents. The owner of the land, Kibbutz H -, is interested in selling." Zevulun shrugged. "That's the price. Period."

Ilan passed his boss's message on to the Canadian, in English. Zevulun saw the client nod occasionally as he listened, but it seemed to him that Ilan was not telling him anything he did not already know. When Ilan stopped speaking, the man from Canada sat mute, as though waiting for the two agents to confer again. Zevulun was at a loss to understand this lack of reaction.

An uncomfortable silence reigned, a silence that none of the three knew how to break. Ilan perceived Zevulun's inexplicable hostility toward his client. In the man's presence, however, it was impossible to question his boss about it. With an effort, he tried to break the ice that had formed in the room.

"Then what are you saying, exactly? Is that it? We're not selling?"

"At the price you're asking for, in your client's name," Zevulun said evenly, "we're not selling. Don't worry, the value of that property will rise as we move closer to the date when the land is zoned for building."

"I know. But he has cash in hand."

Zevulun raised a skeptical brow. "We're talking six figures! I find that very surprising."

Ilan threw up his hands in surrender. "Okay, so you don't believe him. There's nothing I can do."

"Excuse me, Ilan. I didn't say I don't believe. I said it's a little unusual to come forward with such a large sum in cash. The matter calls for caution and careful authentication. I'm sure you agree."

Throughout, the Canadian sat impassive. But he was not completely indifferent. Zevulun noticed the way the man's eyelids twitched in reaction to what he and Ilan were discussing. Though that might have been nothing more than a trick of his own imagination....

Suddenly, the door opened. Elazar stood in the doorway.

His father rose in astonishment.

"Elazar, what are you doing here?"

"A friend of mine is getting married nearby this evening, so I came from Yerushalayim. I decided to pop in here and see you before going home."

Elazar shook Zevulun's hand, then that of Ilan, whom he knew, and the Canadian stranger. Zevulun watched these proceedings in silence, then asked his son, "How are you?"

"*Baruch Hashem,* I'm fine!"

"Nothing... new?"

"Nothing new."

"I mean, in relation to Yossi."

"That's what I meant, too."

Ilan and the Canadian exchanged a glance, swift as lightning. But it did not escape either Zevulun or Elazar — both of whom became convinced, in that instant, that these two knew something about Yossi's disappearance.

The sudden silence that had descended on Zevulun's office thickened. Without thinking about what he was doing, Zevulun yanked the curtain cord and opened the window a few inches. Additional light poured into the room. This, however, had no visible effect on the tension in the room. If anything, it increased slightly.

An unpleasant moment.

Elazar was particularly confused. The lightning glance that Ilan and his client had exchanged aroused his deepest suspicions. Something within insisted that Ilan had played a hand in Yossi's disappearance. How and why, Elazar had no way of knowing. He faced his father's employee with what he hoped was a friendly smile. "What happened to you, Ilan? Where are the curls?"

Ilan waved a hand. "Here today, gone tomorrow."

"Why'd you cut them off?"

The instant he asked, Elazar knew he had made a mistake. Ilan regarded him suspiciously and countered with a question of his own. "Why do you ask?"

Elazar shrugged. "Just curious. I remembered you differently. Has it been long since you got the new hairstyle?"

Ilan lifted his palms in a nonchalant gesture that seemed forced. "Oh, it must be a year now." He accompanied the words with an empty smile.

Elazar knew he was lying. It had surely been less than a year since they had last met. And at that time, if his memory was not playing tricks on him, Ilan's head had been a riot of curls.

He glanced at his father, who smiled lightly. "Ilan's exaggerating a little, Elazar. It hasn't been a year since he cut his hair — more like half a year. Or maybe just a few days! What difference does it make? Why are you asking?"

"I told you. Just curious."

Elazar thought hard. He must have been mistaken. Yaakov's description had made him suspect that Ilan was the one they were looking for. All the way from Jerusalem today, he had been mulling over the possibility that it had been Ilan who introduced Yossi to a cult and brought about his vanishing act. But without the curls, his suspicions were groundless.

Then Elazar remembered something else. The bracelet. His eyes moved to Ilan's wrist. Seeing this, Ilan raised both hands in a gesture of innocence. "See, they're clean! Are you looking for something?" When Elazar didn't answer, Ilan pressed, "What's the matter with you today?"

Elazar said nothing. He had not seen any sign of a bracelet on Ilan's arm... And yet, something in the other's reaction triggered a strong sense of danger. He glared at Ilan, saying, "I don't know what you're talking about! What do you think I accused you of?"

Ilan hesitated, then turned away with a shrug. "Whatever you say." To Zevulun, he said, in a businesslike manner, "I think we're passing up a good deal here. The Canadian has cash."

Zevulun was obstinate. "I've made my decision, and it's final."

Ilan rose, and the Canadian followed suit. Without a word, the young agent and his would-be buyer shook Zevulun's hand. Ilan clasped Elazar's hand as well, with a wink. "Relax, kid!"

Outside, as the two stood blinking in the sun outside the office building, Ilan murmured as if to himself, "Well, we got nowhere today."

And the "Canadian," in fluent, native-born Hebrew, answered, "I think he suspected something."

"Who — the kid?"

"No. The father. Your boss."

Ilan sighed. "Maybe. But Elazar, his son, worries me more. I didn't like the way he was acting in there."

The two were quiet for a moment, each lost in his own thoughts. Then, above the continuous hiss of the sea as it broke into waves not far away, Ilan's voice came again.

"The boss's son knows something. I would be extremely interested in knowing what it is."

Upstairs in the office, Zevulun and Elazar were left alone. Elazar found his way to one of the armchairs that had been recently vacated, and watched his father. Zevulun appeared to be deep in thoughts of his own, apparently oblivious to his son's presence. Elazar decided not to disturb him.

The stretch of silence was broken at last. Zevulun said, "Now that it's just the two of us, tell me: Why did you really come to Tel Aviv?"

Elazar looked at him. "Abba, have you forgotten that you have a son who has disappeared?"

At once, Zevulun's face grew brick-red. Elazar had gone too far. The younger man squared his shoulders, determined to endure the coming tongue-lashing stoically.

"Would you like to explain what kind of question that is? *And* your behavior!"

"I'm sorry, Abba. I didn't mean to make you angry."

Zevulun wasn't mollified. "Then what *did* you mean?"

"I don't know. I wasn't thinking."

"Words don't just say themselves."

Elazar knew his father was right. Glaring, Zevulun ordered, "Well? Speak!"

"Look, Abba, I didn't put it right. But — Yossi *has* disappeared. *Your* son, and also *my* brother. I suddenly felt the urge to be with you and Ima, at home. It's hard for me alone. Hard to concentrate on my learning."

His father regarded him in silence, one hand toying with a pen on his desk while Elazar tried to avoid his gaze. He saw Zevulun shoot out of his chair in one abrupt motion and stride over to the window. With his back to his son, he stared out at the Mediterranean.

Elazar, internally, was coiled tight as a spring. He had no idea what to expect next.

Presently, Zevulun turned and said, "I believe you when you say it's hard to concentrate. Still, I don't believe that that's the real reason you left the yeshivah and came down to Tel Aviv." He broke off. Moving closer to Elazar's chair, he bent over until their faces were just inches apart. "And especially," he added softly, "to come here, to the office, instead of straight home the way you always do!"

Elazar shrank back slightly. "I just felt like it."

"Ah, I understand." Zevulun straightened up. "At this difficult moment, you preferred to be with me instead of your mother. Why?"

Elazar bit his lip. With all his heart he longed to share with his father the information Yaakov Frankel had succeeded in uncovering about Yossi. He wanted his father to know that they were doing something about it. But he knew he must keep silent. He had promised Yaakov not to tell anyone about the progress of the private investigation, and that included his father. Yaakov had his reasons for keeping it quiet.

And so — though inside he was as worked up as a volcano in mid-explosion — Elazar sat mute.

He watched every move his father made: the slow walk back to his executive's chair, the bitter smile that touched the corners of Zevulun's mouth.

"I think I'm beginning to understand," Zevulun said wearily. "You've apparently joined forces with that comic detective — what's his name again? Yaakov. *Reb* Yaakov. He must have sent you here to my office to sniff out something or other." He peered at his son. "Am I mistaken?"

Elazar raised his palms in a gesture of surrender. "No, Abba, you're not mistaken! How did you know?"

Zevulun broke into laughter, and the tension dissipated at once.

"How did I know? If you could only have seen yourself — the way you entered this room, your confusion at seeing Ilan and that Canadian here with me, the way you inspected Ilan from head to foot as though meeting him for the first time. Then your tasteless question about his curls. That made me suspect that there was more here than met the eye. I think Ilan suspected something, too. And now" — Zevulun fixed his son with a steely stare — "I'm asking you: Can you tell me what's been going on?"

Elazar was vastly relieved to find his father taking it so well. Still, he did not feel at liberty to accede to Zevulun's request. Softly, he answered, "I'm sorry, Abba. I can't tell you."

Zevulun was startled by the blunt refusal. He could only blurt out, "Why?"

The word was spoken quietly, but Elazar sensed in it his father's mounting annoyance. Forcing himself not to cringe, he replied in the only way he could. "I promised Reb Yaakov to keep it secret."

"Even from your father?"

"Even from you." At the last instant, Elazar stopped himself from adding what had been on the tip of his tongue: "Especially from you."

Zevulun maintained his calm. "And what about the mitzvah of honoring your father and mother?"

"That doesn't apply here." Elazar dropped his eyes to the floor, tensed as though for flight.

The expected explosion finally came. "What do you mean, it doesn't apply? What kind of Torah are they teaching in that yeshivah of yours? Where did you pick up such chutzpah? A father orders you to tell him something, and you say it doesn't apply?! A direct commandment from the Torah means nothing to you?" Zevulun leaned forward, knuckles white where they gripped the arms of his chair. "I'm ordering you again to tell me everything! I'm your father and you are required to answer me! You hear?"

Elazar breathed in deeply, preparing himself for what was to come. He answered with a gentle serenity whose source was a mystery to him: "In this case, I can't."

His manner was as quietly unyielding as the relentless waves that broke upon the shore. His father sensed it.

"What do you mean, in this case you can't?"

"It's a clear halachah in the Rambam."

"What are you saying?" Zevulun demanded furiously. "Does the Rambam say that a son should not listen to his father? What's happening to you today?"

"The Rambam, in the laws pertaining to honoring one's parents, sets out the cases in which one is required to listen to his father, and those in which he's not required. For example, he doesn't have to obey if his father tells him to cook for him on Shabbos."

"I need you to tell me that? Besides, what does that have to do with what I'm asking you here?"

"You're asking me to trespass on the laws of the Torah!"

"*What?!*"

This was not easy for Elazar. He collected his wits, then said slowly, "You're asking me to break my promise. The Rambam's opinion applies here. I don't mean to behave disrespectfully to you, Abba, but this falls into the category of things I'm not required to do."

Zevulun was stunned. For the first time Elazar, his "good" son, had refused a direct order from his father. He had declined to tell Zevulun what he wanted to know, to fill him in on Yaakov's investigation and why he had fixed his interest on Ilan.

For the first time, the father understood that he did not have complete dominion over his son. He did not have the authority to order Elazar to obey him. A man could not say to his son, "Obey me because I am your father and I wish it." Rather, he could insist that his son obey him only because the Torah requires it of him. In a case where a father demands that his son break the Torah's laws, the son must refuse.

It was a novel idea. It had never entered Zevulun's head that the Torah did not make him master over his son. Rather, his son stood opposite him as his own being, required to honor his father within the parameters the Torah had set down.

The sudden influx of these startling thoughts threw Zevulun off balance. He lifted his eyes to his son, who was staring at him in astonishment. It was clear that something was happening to his father, but the nature of that something was hidden from him.

Zevulun felt powerless to enlighten him. The force of the revelation clamored and reverberated in his mind. He knew that something deep had stirred within him, and that he must pursue it and study it. Was Yossi's disappearance the catalyst that had permitted him to grasp what he had just understood?

He did not know. Again, his eyes strayed to Elazar, the son who had emerged victorious from their present encounter. In his refusal to obey, he had taught Zevulun something new and important about the laws governing the behavior of father and son. Did he, Zevulun, truly understand the nature of the lesson he had just learned? And if he had learned it earlier, might the tragedy of Yossi have been preventable? He was not sure about that, either.

Zevulun rose from his seat and went around his desk to where Elazar sat. Without a word, he reached out and placed a hand on his son's shoulder, gripping it tightly.

23

lazar didn't move. His father's hand, resting on his shoulder, felt heavy as a boulder. He lowered his eyes, feeling unequal to the task of meeting Zevulun's eyes directly. A powerful current of pity — a compassion laden with pain — moved over him in waves. It was not easy witnessing his father in surrender.

Stealing an upward glance, he noticed the way softness had crept in to replace the unyielding sternness that had marked his father's face since Yossi disappeared. Elazar wasn't sure how his father really felt about his own refusal to obey. It had certainly been uncharacteristic of him, and so all the more unexpected. But the softness in Zevulun's expression told Elazar that his father was not angry — in itself a cause for wonder.

He felt the urge to speak, if only to dispel the silence that had fallen between them.

"Abba, I hope you understand me...and aren't angry."

Zevulun's chest rose and fell as he tried to absorb the import of what he had just learned. On the one hand, he felt compelled to admit that Elazar was right; and on the other, a powerful contradictory force urged him not to give in, especially to his own son. Feelings of anger battled his sense of justice. For a time justice prevailed, but it was quickly followed by an irrepressible annoyance:

"Yes, I understand you. But I'm still not sure if I agree with you."

For Elazar, it was enough for now. Enough that his father understood.

Then, as he recalled his mission in coming here today, his contentment vanished. His suspicion of Ilan had been groundless. He had traveled all the way from Jerusalem for no reason. Ilan did not answer to the description of the man described by Yossi's yeshivah roommates.

And yet, he could not shake off the feeling that he had seen Ilan with his former hairstyle fairly recently. Was he so far off? He leaned forward and asked urgently, "Still, Abba, tell me — when *did* Ilan cut off those curls?"

Zevulun threw him a shrewd glance. He had not been mistaken when he had suspected that Elazar had not come to Tel Aviv merely because he missed his parents. He smiled wryly: "And if I tell you, Yossi will instantly reappear?"

Elazar ignored the barb. "Just tell me when it was. Please."

Zevulun rounded the desk to his own chair. His first impulse was to pay his son back in kind: to withhold the information for which Elazar was so anxious. Then his good sense reasserted itself.

"Ilan got a haircut just yesterday. The day before that he still had the curls."

Elazar was appalled. "But when he said he'd cut them off a year ago, all you said was that it had been half a year!"

Hearty laughter was Zevulun's response. "Apparently, you misunderstood me. What I said was, 'Maybe half a year, maybe a few days, what difference does it make?' I was being deliberately vague. I could see that you had something on your mind."

Elazar sat sunk in thought. Then, rousing himself, he said decisively, "I need to talk to Ilan, Abba. Where can I find him now?"

Zevulun's face grew serious. "I don't like it. Tell me what happened. Oh, don't tell me everything — I agree with you that a promise is a promise. Just about Ilan."

Elazar shook his head. "Just help me find him, and then things will become clearer to you." He paused, then added, "If, that is, my guess turns out to be right...."

A fresh surge of anger swept through Zevulun. "If I knew what you wanted from him, I might be able to help. Call your Reb Yaakov and ask him if, in a case like this, you are permitted to tell your father something about what's going on." He watched his son's face for a minute. "I understand that your friend, this *kollelnik*, is afraid that I'll spoil his little detective act. That's why he's sworn you to secrecy. But in the case of your own 'police investigation' into Ilan, I'm the one who can help. Is that acceptable to you, Inspector Kimmerman?"

"Don't make fun of us."

"Believe me, I'm not making fun. But I do have to say that I think that the two of you are either wasting your time — or playing with fire."

"What do you mean?"

"Simply this. If your investigation is nothing more than the fruit of an overactive imagination — and I don't know what you're basing it on — then it seems to me you're just playing cops and robbers, like kids... But if not — if there really *is* something to all this — then you have no idea how much danger you're putting yourself into. In any case, you won't be bringing Yossi home."

Elazar lifted his eyes. "That's it? You don't believe that Yossi will be coming back?"

"I didn't say that! I only said that *you* won't be bringing him back, that's all."

Elazar considered this. "Then maybe you should consider going to the police?"

"No!" Zevulun smacked a fist down on his desk. "Under no circumstances!"

"Why not?"

His father leaped to his feet and began prowling his office, restless as a tiger. "Why not? You're asking me why not? Because, apart from getting the scandal splashed over the pages of all the newspapers, the police won't do a thing. Let's not talk about it anymore. I've already had bitter experiences with them."

Elazar shot his father a questioning glance. "Then maybe a private investigator?"

"Are you looking to destroy me? Do you have any idea how much these people charge? Have you even thought of that?" He stopped, then added, "If I thought there was a chance that someone like that could get results, I'd think about it. But I'm convinced he couldn't. I just don't see success down that route."

The rumble of traffic down on Kaufman Street filtered into the office. Elazar broke the silence to revert to his original topic.

"Well, about Ilan. Where can I find him?"

Zevulun clenched his fists. "So, you insist on being stubborn, hey?"

"It's not stubbornness, Abba. I just want to be sure... that I was wrong."

"Oh, is that it?"

"Yes. I'll be thrilled to find out that Ilan has absolutely no connection with Yossi's disappearance. You have no idea what I'm even referring to..."

The phone rang.

Zevulun made no move to lift the receiver. It rang again, and then twice more. Elazar was the first to succumb. He picked up the phone. "Hello?"

He heard a familiar voice. "Elazar, is that you?"

"Yes.

"Wonderful! It's me: Ilan. What a lucky chance that you answered. I wanted to talk to you."

Elazar broke into a smile. "And I want to talk to you!"

"Great! Let's meet somewhere."

"Where?"

Ilan thought. "How about in front of the Central Post Office, on Allenby. Okay?"

Elazar hesitated only briefly. "Okay. What time?"

"Hmm... Let's say, in...in two hours. At 5. All right with you?"

"Fine."

"Okay, then. See you later."

Elazar replaced the receiver, a triumphant light illuminating his face.

"Who was that?" Zevulun asked in surprise. Who would be calling his office to speak with his son? When Elazar didn't answer immediately, he pressed, "Well? Who?"

Elazar would have been happier not having to answer at all. By the most amazing good fortune he had a meeting set up with Ilan this very day. He had no desire to deal with his father's qualms. Reluctantly, he answered, "It was Ilan."

In his astonishment, Zevulun sat bolt upright. "Ilan?!"

"Yes."

"What did he want from *you*?"

"He said he wants to talk to me. I agreed."

Zevulun's face darkened. Every one of his senses went on alert. If, until this moment, he had made light of Elazar's fantastic suspicions, he found he had some of his own now. He faced his son grimly. "And you intend to go?"

"Yes. Why not?"

Zevulun was silent, thinking. Elazar did not want to let him think too long or too hard. Quickly, he asked, "What's the problem with my meeting him? You seem troubled."

"I am. I don't think you should meet. Something smells fishy to me."

"Why?"

"Look, Elazar. Something obviously bothered Ilan about the questions you asked him. He wants to clear it up with you. Again, I have no idea why you're suddenly so interested in Ilan's hairstyle, but I could tell that it made Ilan suspect something. Elazar, don't go."

Elazar chewed his lip. Here was a real problem. He knew he must meet with Ilan. It would help advance Reb Yaakov's investigation. Even if he learned that he had been wrong in his suspicions, it was important that they meet. But how could he refuse to obey his father? After their discussion about the limits and parameters of the Torah's commandment to honor one's parents, he could not pretend to be ignorant. He knew very well that this case warranted his obedience. What was he to do?

He turned to face Zevulun.

"All right, Abba. If you insist that I don't meet him, I won't. It's just a pity. It might have helped answer a few questions for us."

Zevulun regarded his son with grudging approval. Elazar had very cleverly deposited the responsibility for this decision squarely in his father's lap. If the search for Yossi failed, *he* would be the one to blame! That, at any rate, was the message implicit in Elazar's answer.

And was Zevulun prepared to leave unturned even a single stone that might bring Yossi back?

He nodded heavily. "All right, I understand. If you want to go, go. But I do ask one thing, Elazar. Be careful. Very careful!"

"With Hashem's help, I'll try, Abba. I really will."

Elazar lingered in his father's office for a short time before taking his leave. He started off on foot toward the corner of Allenby and Ben-Yehuda Streets.

It had been a long time since he had last walked in this area. Everything — the people, the shops, the very atmosphere — felt alien to him. After such a long time studying Torah within the four walls of his yeshivah, it was hard to get used to Tel Aviv. It was not long before he changed his mind about going all the way to the Central Post Office on foot. He boarded a number four bus.

He got off a stop early, deciding after all to walk the rest of the way. That would give him a chance to approach the rendezvous point gradually and check out the area as he went. It was possible that there was something to the danger his father had sensed. And he had promised he would be careful....

He reached the post office at 5 o'clock on the dot. There was no sign of Ilan. As he paced back and forth, waiting, various moneychangers converged on him. "Something to buy? Want to sell? Dollars? Swiss francs? Deutsche marks?" Elazar waved them off, eyes darting constantly in search of Ilan.

Ilan did not come.

It was already a quarter past 5 when Elazar, seething with impatience, decided to call his father's office from a public phone nearby. He wanted to find out how punctual Ilan was as a rule. But before he could reach the phone, a short, balding man tugged — none too gently — at his sleeve.

"What's the time, mister?"

Irritated, Elazar spun around, glanced at his wristwatch, and said, "It's 5:20."

He was about to turn away when something caught his eye about the hand that had pulled at his sleeve. On the wrist was a bracelet. A silver bracelet, featuring a large, green, staring eye!

As though he had not heard Elazar's answer, the man stayed where he was. This gave Elazar a chance to study the bracelet more closely. It was the very one Reb Yaakov had told him about! Could this fellow belong to that strange cult? A slew of questions leaped to mind. With difficulty, Elazar swallowed them all. He must not betray a suspicious interest in this man or his bracelet.

A second later, the man turned and walked away, without so much as a "thank you." Impulsively, Elazar decided to follow him. Maybe this fellow would lead to some of the answers he and Reb Yaakov were seeking.

He stayed well behind the squat figure as it crossed Jaffa Road. On and on the man walked, with Elazar discreetly following. Never once did the man turn. He did not suspect a thing. At one point, as he was climbing a few steps to reach the upper level of a small side street, the man turned without warning and looked back. Startled, Elazar ducked quickly behind a pillar, hoping that the man had not noticed his sudden agitation.

The man faced forward and continued walking. Near Emek Yizrael Street, he turned again. Elazar feigned a great interest in the window display of a liquor store. Out of the corner of his eye, he saw the man continue until he nearly reached the corner of Selma Street, before turning abruptly into a narrow side street. Cautiously, Elazar followed.

The man he was trailing vanished behind a rusted iron gate. Elazar went to the gate and looked over his shoulder. There was no one watching him. He reached out to the gate and carefully pushed it open.

From that instant, he remembered nothing at all.

24

For some time after his son had left the office, Zevulun remained seated in his large executive's chair, swiveling aimlessly to and fro. He heard Elazar speak to Varda, his secretary, and then the sound of the door closing. In his mind's eye he followed Elazar out of the office and down to the street.

He turned his chair to face the window, and the calming view of the sea. For a moment he rested his head in his hands. It had been a long time since he had last felt so overwhelmed by events and his own emotional responses to them. Elazar's words, and the revelation they had wrought in Zevulun's own heart, echoed in his consciousness with a sense of wonder.

Elazar had been right on one point, he reflected. There are times when a son is not required to heed his parents. That much was clear. Zevulun had been acquainted with that particular halachah even before his *"yeshivah bachur"* had brought it up. He himself had learned in yeshivos once, too; and even today, despite his many business concerns, he tried to devote a certain amount of time each day to the learning of Torah — though it was never quite enough.

But he had never linked that halachah with his own authority as a father in his home. Elazar had been the one to tie them together. Was he right?

Questions rose up in him, and doubts. *Was* the connection valid? Of course a son would be called upon to refuse if his father asked him to desecrate the Shabbos, for instance. But this was another matter entirely! They were talking about two different halachos. Here was a case of a son who simply refused to obey. It was forbidden to be disrespectful to a parent! A son had to do what his father told him to do!

Zevulun sprang to his feet and began nervously pacing around the room. Why had he been so convinced, before, that Elazar was right? He was wrong — dead wrong! A father was in charge of his children. That, in his opinion, was what the Torah demanded of him. Without absolute authority, how could a man educate and bring up his offspring? If children subscribed to the kind of notions Elazar had been spouting just now, no one would listen to his father at all!

Conflicting thoughts chased one another through his mind with all the force of Niagara Falls. He reached for a cigarette, then let his arm drop. "Interesting," he thought. "Elazar has always been my 'good' child. Interesting that he should be the one to behave this way now."

The ringing of the phone broke into his inner turmoil. He snatched up the receiver. "Yes?"

"Zevulun? It's me — Yitzchak."

Zevulun relaxed into a smile. There was no voice he wanted to hear now as much as that of his friend, Reb Yitzchak Abramson of Petach Tikvah. "Oh, is it you? How are you?"

"*Baruch Hashem,* I'm fine."

Before his friend could say another word, Zevulun burst out, "Listen, Yitzchak, I have to apologize for what happened last night. It wasn't very nice."

"Oh, it doesn't matter. It's not important."

"But it really wasn't nice — the way I left your apartment so abruptly like that. I hope you'll forgive me. I'm a little...uh, not really myself these days."

"Did you think I wouldn't understand? Forget it! I wasn't insulted."

"Good. I'm glad to hear it. Well, to what do I owe the honor of this call?"

"I happen to be in Tel Aviv; I came in to take care of a few things. I'm on Allenby Street right now, not far from you. Can I drop in?"

A laser-beam of suspicion streaked through Zevulun. It came through clearly in his voice as he answered, "Sure, why not? But what exactly do you want from me?"

Yitzchak laughed. "I told you, I just happen to be in the neighborhood. I'd just like to drop in and see you. If it's a bad time, just tell me. Feel free to say no."

"No, no, it's fine." Zevulun felt his resistance melting. "Come right up. I'll be happy to see you."

"Good. I should be there in about 10 minutes."

In truth, Yitzchak Abramson had come to Tel Aviv for the express purpose of seeing Zevulun. He had found himself unable to relax for hours after his friend had left his apartment so unexpectedly the night before. He had never seen Zevulun in such a state. If Zevulun had made the effort to travel from Tel Aviv to see him, Reb Yitzchak reasoned, Heaven was clearly directing him to do his best to help.

Despite his long years as an educator, Yitzchak was at a loss as to how to proceed. How to proceed in the strange and tragic case of the runaway yeshivah boy? This was more than a simple case of teenage rebellion. It would be necessary to dig deep, in order to uncover the secrets that would explain why this had happened to the Kimmermans. The prospect fascinated him even as it hurt. He was determined to stand staunchly by his old friend and learning partner through this terrible ordeal.

The office door opened and Yitzchak walked in. In the reception area, he was surprised to see Varda, wife of one of his fellow *kollel* members. Shaul Egozi and he had learned together for years.

"You work here?"

She nodded affirmatively.

He glanced at the closed door of Zevulun's inner office and, in a lowered voice, asked, "How is he?"

Varda sighed. "Not good."

"What do you mean?"

"He's taken it very hard, this business with Yossi —"

She stopped short in confusion. This was supposed to be a secret! Zevulun had warned her repeatedly not to discuss it with anyone. She hastened to ask, "Do you know what I'm talking about?"

"Yes. Zevulun told me."

She felt relieved. Yitzchak asked, "Is he blaming himself for what happened?"

"It doesn't seem that way. He gets furious at anyone who even suggests such a thing, or tries to give him advice." She remembered how he had refused to speak with her husband.

Yitzchak said nothing. He knew his friend well from the old days — a man who found it difficult, if not impossible, to admit that he had been wrong and to revise the principles to which he stubbornly clung. That was why Yitzchak had been so astonished at the way Zevulun had begun to open up to him the previous night. It seemed to run completely counter to the personality he knew.

The uncharacteristic surrender to self-doubt signaled the approach of a real crisis in his friend, Yitzchak believed. Which was why he decided to drop everything and come to Tel Aviv this very day....

He turned back to Varda. "Tell him I'm here, please. He's expecting me."

They met with smiles. Zevulun led his friend to a comfortable armchair at one side of his desk, ordering, "Sit!"

"Thank you!"

Zevulun seated himself in his own chair and leaned back, trying to appear unconcerned despite the hammering of his heart. "So, what do you say about this story of mine?"

"I don't know your story yet. You haven't told it to me."

After a moment, Yitzchak added, "The only thing I've been able to gather so far is your state of mind."

He studied the new lines in Zevulun's face as he waited for his answer. When it came, the force of the words startled him.

"They're all blaming me!"

Yitzchak looked at him penetratingly, and waited for more.

With shaking hands, Zevulun lit a cigarette. He was aware of a powerful emotion surging through him in a way he could not control. All his concentration went into maintaining a calm exterior. "And now, my son Elazar was just here. He also, apparently, belongs to the camp that is pointing a finger at me and laying all the blame at my door. But Elazar goes one further. He knows how to learn. He quotes Rambams at me, no less. All he does is spout halachah. Do you see what we've come to?"

Yitzchak tried to grasp the import of his friend's words. "Which Rambams?"

"The laws of honoring one's parents." Zevulun waved a dismissive hand.

Yitzchak ignored Zevulun's obvious impatience with the subject. "Could you possibly specify which halachah he was referring to?"

"The well-known one that says a son is not obligated to obey his father if the father tells him to desecrate the Shabbos."

"Ah! I see. 'You and he are obligated to honor Me.'"

"Exactly."

Yitzchak stirred in his chair. "Well, what's your problem with that halachah?"

"I have no problem with the halachah, Heaven forbid. It's Elazar's interpretation that's bothering me a little. For a minute or two I thought he was right — but then I decided that he wasn't. He's dead wrong."

Cautiously, Yitzchak asked, "Can I ask what it is he told you?"

Zevulun's lips shaped themselves into a cynical smile. "Elazar has concluded that the Torah does not mandate a man complete control over his children."

"Meaning?"

"Meaning that a son is not obligated to obey his father in certain circumstances."

Yitzchak was confused. "And therefore...?"

"Then Elazar went on to explain that, even when he *is* obligated to obey me, it's because the Torah commanded him to do so and not because I'm his father. Understand?"

Yitzchak sat back and chuckled. "*I* understand. But I'm not sure if *you* do."

Zevulun blanched. "What do you mean?"

"If you really understood, you'd react differently."

"Really?"

"Yes."

"Well, I think you're mistaken!"

Yitzchak was undeterred. "I'll repeat: You do not understand what we're talking about here. It's that simple."

Zevulun did not like what he was hearing. For a moment he entertained the idea of ordering his friend out of his office. He managed to swallow the words, but his eyes darkened with fury.

Those eyes frightened Yitzchak a little. He recalled Varda's words in the outer office just now: Zevulun was standing firm in his resistance to accepting blame of any kind. It was important, Yitzchak felt, not to back down now. Instinctively, he knew he must try to dislodge his old friend from the notions he clung to so tenaciously. Somehow he knew that would help.

"Zevulun, don't look at me with those stranger's eyes. I haven't done anything to you. I'm allowed to disagree with you. We're talking about a halachah in the Rambam right now, and it doesn't make any difference if that particular Rambam has a personal bearing on your own life. Try to calm down so we can discuss the question logically and objectively, all right?"

The words, spoken with an unaccustomed forcefulness, had a calming effect on Zevulun. He was silent. With downcast eyes, he listened as Yitzchak continued.

"Listen, I don't know what went on between you and Yossi. The whole thing fell on me like a bombshell last night. I'll admit that I haven't rested easy since then. I'm an educator, and I'm well aware of the complexities of adolescence, of the endless tensions that exist between parents and children. Tensions that come along with so much pain, so much energy wasted in fighting and arguing, instead of being harnessed to constructive goals. You have no idea how much time I spend helping my students work things out with their parents or teachers."

He paused, face set in grim lines. Then, all at once, he relaxed into a smile: "And this very Rambam you're talking about — if we, as parents, understood it correctly, we would believe that it contains the solution to our problems. I don't know if it's the solution to your situation, but it certainly has a powerful, built-in deterrent for a very widespread problem: the relationship between parents and children. Seems strange, eh?"

Zevulun threw him a sardonic look. "Don't make me laugh!"

"Okay, okay," Yitzchak answered, allowing a semblance of anger to show. "But I tell you there's a nugget of truth hidden in here. It would be well worth your while to be a little more humble and to listen to a differing point of view. Remember, not only is this my field, but I've also spent a lot of time thinking about it. You have no right to mock me." He looked, if anything, even angrier as he added, "Is this the person you know me to be — someone who doesn't know what he's talking about? All those years we learned together in yeshivah, was I just talking through my hat?"

Zevulun looked contrite. "Look, I'm sorry. I didn't mean —"

Yitzchak didn't let him finish. "I tell you, I *am* insulted. You're the one with the problem here, not me. You can see for yourself that I'm interested in helping. But, out of sheer arrogance, you're ready to push away the hand I'm stretching out to you. Believe me, I find it hard to understand you!"

He sank back, sensing that his artificially induced tantrum had had its effect. He had made Zevulun uncomfortable enough to soften his attitude a little. Yitzchak had won this round.

This conclusion was bolstered by Zevulun's low voice as he said, "You're right. I'm ready to listen."

Rapidly, Yitzchak marshaled his thoughts. His plan was to aim a few crushing blows at his friend's entrenched opinions about the Torah's true educational approach. Deep in thought, he hardly heard the phone ring.

Zevulun picked it up.

"Zevulun!" came his wife's overwrought voice. "Zevulun, come to Ichilov Hospital right away!"

Zevulun sat bolt upright, electrified by a sudden fear. "What happened?"

"I don't know exactly. They told me that Elazar's been injured. They found him unconscious in some alley. Come quickly. I'm leaving for the hospital right now."

Zevulun remembered the meeting with Ilan. "I *told* him not to go!"

"Where?" Tzipporah asked in rising panic.

"Never mind. I'm leaving immediately!"

Almost before he had hung up the phone he was on his feet, slamming shut his attache case and getting ready to leave the office. Bitterly, he told his friend, "You see, Yitzchak? When the troubles start coming, they come in bunches."

"Don't tempt Satan," Yitzchak murmured automatically, too startled by the sudden turn of events to think clearly. He watched Zevulun hurry out of the office, feeling an uncharacteristic discouragement. He had had Zevulun at the point of relenting — at least to the extent of being willing to listen. And then this incident with the hospital had intervened.

What next?

25

Zevulun reached Ichilov Hospital in record-breaking time. The information desk on the ground floor directed him to the emergency room, where he found Tzipporah soaking a handkerchief with her tears.

"Tell me what happened!" he said urgently.

She gulped. "I d-don't know."

"What do the doctors say? *Tell me!*"

His wife made an effort to control her sobbing. "Th-they're not saying. They're just walking around with their noses in the air and not saying a word. One doctor did me a favor and told me it looks like Elazar was attacked with a heavy, sharp instrument. He's been wounded in the head. Apparently, the — the brain wasn't touched. Maybe a c-concussion."

Zevulun took a deep, steadying breath. It took every ounce of willpower he possessed to speak calmly. "Is he conscious?"

"Not all the time. The doctor says Elazar keeps drifting in and out..."

"Where is he?"

Tzipporah pointed a trembling finger to the left. "There, at the end of the hall."

As Zevulun began striding in that direction, his wife called after him, "They won't let you in!"

Paying no heed to the warning, Zevulun continued to the end of the corridor. His son, he calculated, must be lying behind that curtain. A policeman, talking into his cell-phone, stopped to bark, "Mister, where are you going?"

"I am Zevulun Kimmerman! The injured boy is my son!"

He spoke with confidence and authority, waving his identity card. The police officer did not seem impressed. As Zevulun tried to move forward, the officer said firmly, "No one is allowed to go in there right now. Understand?"

"But — why not?"

"The police are questioning the patient."

Zevulun glanced at him sharply. "Do they suspect a criminal motive?"

"It's a possibility, anyway."

Zevulun was panic stricken, frustrated and furious with Elazar for not listening to him, for obstinately going off to meet Ilan against his father's better judgment. Now, as he paced to and fro like a caged tiger, he berated himself for not insisting that his son do as he wished. *This* was the final result of all the babble about loopholes in the halachah! Elazar had succeeded in sowing a seed of doubt in his father's heart, if only for a brief moment. That seed had been responsible for Zevulun's temporary weakness — the weakness that had led him merely to request, and not to command, that Elazar refrain from keeping the rendezvous with Ilan.

"Can I peek at him around the curtain at least?" Zevulun asked the officer on duty.

"Sir, that's not allowed," replied the upholder of the law. "The questioning should end in a few minutes, and then it will be up to the doctors to make a decision. Wait patiently — and don't worry. His life is not in danger. His injuries were light."

This information — tossed at him almost incidentally, — did wonders for Zevulun's morale. Light injuries — thank G-d! And in a few minutes he saw two police officers emerge from the curtained-off area. They departed quickly and silently. The moment they had gone, Zevulun burst through the curtain to see his son.

Elazar lay on his back, head swathed in bloodstained bandages. He was very pale, but he managed a weak smile when he saw his father.

Zevulun grasped his son's hand. "Tell me, was it Ilan? I have to know!"

Feebly, Elazar shook his head from side to side, in the negative.

"Did you meet him?"

Again, the negative shake.

Zevulun stroked the hand he held. "But he was involved in what happened to you?"

Elazar's face assumed a surprised expression, as if to say, "How should I know? Maybe he was, and maybe he wasn't."

A moment passed in silence, a moment during which Zevulun gazed with compassion on his oldest son. Softly, he asked, "Did they ask you a lot of questions?"

Elazar's head bobbed once.

Suddenly, Zevulun was seized with impatience. Pulling his hand away, he demanded, "Then why can't you talk to *me*? All you're doing is shaking your head! I want to know everything you told them."

But Elazar didn't hear. He had fallen asleep, and was sunk in oblivion once again.

Some time elapsed before Yitzchak Abramson made a move to leave Zevulun's office. He was confused, angry and disappointed. For the second time in as many days, Zevulun had abruptly departed just when he had been on the brink of making some real progress. Yitzchak had succeeded in piercing the armor plating of his friend's heart — when one ring of the telephone had snatched away his victory.

Finally, reminding himself that everything his Creator caused to happen was undoubtedly for the best, Yitzchak rose and left the room.

In the outer office, Varda was still at work. Yitzchak said his farewells and passed through the door. Then, on second thought, he turned and retraced his steps. He stopped in front of her desk.

"You've been working here for some time now, haven't you?"

"Five years."

"So you know your boss pretty well, I'd imagine."

She nodded. "I think so. Over the years our families have become friendly."

"Does that mean that your husband also knows him?"

"Yes. Why do you ask?"

He evaded the question. "You know that your husband and I learned in *kollel* together."

"Of course I know. But why do you ask if we know Zevulun?"

"Because Zevulun is an old friend of mine from our yeshivah days, and I want to help him through this crisis."

"So...?"

"So, maybe your husband can help me. In the final analysis, the two of you know more about what's been going on in the Kimmerman home in recent years than I do."

"But how can that help?"

He shrugged. "I'm not sure. Maybe to supply additional information, or perhaps to help figure out the best course of action to pursue. I'll talk to him and we'll see. Do they speak to each other now and then?"

"Sometimes, yes, certainly. There was even a period of time when the two of them would meet once every two weeks to learn together."

"Good. This will help us make progress."

She shook her head grimly. "No. It's not good."

"What do you mean?"

"Right now... Right now he's angry at me and at my husband. The mere mention of Shaul's name is liable to make him blow up."

"Why?"

"I told my husband what happened with Yossi. We were both very broken up about it. We like the Kimmermans. The next morning, I told Zevulun that my husband was interested in speaking to him about it. You should have seen his reaction — how angrily he rejected the idea! He has the notion that my husband intends to give him either advice or *mussar*. He was deeply wounded. 'Am *I* a person who needs to ask others for advice?'" She sighed. "A stubborn man, Zevulun."

Yitzchak chuckled, saying, "That's one thing you don't have to tell me!"

He threw a hasty glance at his watch. "I have to get home. Maybe I'll stop in at Ichilov on my way, to see how Elazar is. I'd be very happy if I could speak with your husband on this matter."

"With pleasure."

Late that night, the phone rang in the Egozi household. Reb Shaul answered it. Yitzchak Abramson was on the line.

"Ah, Reb Yitzchak! Yes, my wife told me that you were in the office today."

"I was, and I wasn't."

"Meaning — what?"

"I was present, but I didn't accomplish what I'd set out to do."

"Yes, I know."

"Reb Shaul, to the point. What do you think about him?"

"What are you referring to?"

"Exactly what I just said. I want to help him. In order to do that, I need as much information as possible."

Shaul Egozi shot back a question. "How does that matter? The problem is with Yossi, not with him."

"What do you mean?"

"Look, we've gotten pretty close to them over the past few years. My wife probably told you that. We had plenty of opportunities to observe that Yossi was a difficult child, undisciplined and wild. A boy who could easily drive any sane adult crazy. Do you have any idea how he behaved?"

Yitzchak breathed deeply. "I can imagine. I agree with everything you've just said. Nevertheless..."

"Nevertheless?"

"I know my old friend's personality from our yeshivah days. I want to know whether that personality manifested itself in relation to this son."

"Which part of his personality are you talking about?"

"The part that is obstinate, arrogant, contemptuous. The part that can lead him to use derogatory language and to act cold and distant. Have I made myself clear enough?"

Shaul persisted in asking, "Are you referring to physical abuse? Zevulun tended to hit Yossi a lot."

Yitzchak was finding it hard to hold onto his patience. "Reb Shaul, I think you know exactly what I mean. The problem is not the hitting. Sometimes a father has to smack his son. The halachah permits this. 'Spare the rod,' etcetera. I'm talking about Zevulun's overall attitude toward Yossi, apart from the occasional smack which I'm sure the boy sometimes deserved."

He was answered by a long silence. At last, he asked, "Reb Shaul, do you hear what I'm saying??"

"Yes, of course I hear. I'm just thinking how to answer you."

"Well?"

"In my opinion, I think that he went overboard in the hitting department as well — especially when you compare it to the treatment he dispensed to the other children. They were afraid of their father, and generally obeyed him without a word. But it seems to me that Zevulun had a different attitude toward Yossi. He would treat the boy with scorn, as though Yossi disgusted him in some way."

"That's it!"

"What do you mean?"

"*That's* the point that interests me! What was Zevulun's overall attitude toward the boy? Apart from the fact that I don't think he really understands what a father's true obligation is in educating his son."

"Reb Yitzchak, explain that, please."

"I know Zevulun very well. He's a stubborn man, a hard man and one who can be very blunt in his dealings with others. The main problem, though, is that he has a definite streak of arrogance. Even back in our yeshivah days, things had to be done the way *he* wanted them done. In yeshivah, he wasn't the 'boss.' But at home... who knows?"

"It's still not all that clear to me."

"I just mean that the approach, 'I'm your father and you must obey me,' can be very dangerous if not linked precisely to the Torah's guidelines. I have a feeling that this may have played a large role in Zevulun's problems with Yossi." He paused. "It definitely seems that Yossi was no ordinary young troublemaker. But if the traits his father displayed in yeshivah are still part of him, they must surely have exacerbated the problem. Don't you think so?"

Yitzchak heard a wry chuckle down the line. "Not only do I think so — I *know* so!"

"Really? Then it seems my diagnosis was on the mark!"

"On the other hand," Shaul cautioned, "agree with me that not every child can be the judge of how his father must raise him."

"Of course not! My point is, if the child knows that his father is bringing him up according to the principles laid down in the Torah, then their relationship is different."

"You keep saying 'according to the Torah,'" Shaul remarked. "There's the mitzvah to honor one's parents, and there's the mitzvah to educate one's children. Both are mandated by the Torah. What exactly do you mean?"

"That," Yitzchak said, "was just what I was on the point of explaining to Zevulun when the phone rang and he rushed away."

"Well, what's your explanation?"

Yitzchak said, "I won't keep you long, Reb Shaul. It's very simple. There's a big difference between a child who knows that his father is required to educate him, and that he himself is obligated in the mitzvah of *'kibbud av v'em'* — honoring one's parents — and a child who fears his father, who is told, 'You must obey me because I am your father.' Do you see the difference?"

"Tell me."

"Listen, it's really amazing. A child, whose father demands respect just because he's the father, can be disappointed with his father one day. None of us is perfect. In little ways, in ways we all know about, the child can see his father's faults."

"How true!"

"Well, think about what happens when this child gets angry at his father for one reason or another. I'm prepared to admit that, in the majority of cases, the child — objectively speaking — is in the wrong. But that's the moment when he will rebel against the 'I'm your father' approach. Without a doubt, the child may not behave in this way. Nevertheless, such behavior on the part of the father risks having the child react this way. Right?"

"Right."

"Now, let's picture what happens if the father succeeds in transmitting the true value to his child: that the child is obligated by the Torah to honor him, regardless of the kind of personality the father may or may not have. The Torah has commanded the child in this area, just as it commands the father in others. This gives the son the status of a free individual in relation to his father. And that, in turn, liberates him to fulfill his obligation without resentment, and in any situation. Understand?"

"Yes. But how does that apply to Zevulun?"

"It applies to all of us, and it applies to Zevulun — especially now."

"Why?"

"It's really so simple. I don't know what went on in their home, but let's imagine that for years — at least the years since Yossi's bar mitzvah — the boy had known that he was obligated by the Torah to honor his father, and that this obligation has nothing to do with his father's conduct toward him. Such a realization would make it easier to bear whatever his father did to him, even if he himself judged it wrong or unfair. But I think this information was missing — and that's why what happened, happened."

There was a thoughtful pause at the other end. Then Shaul asked, "Well, what do you think ought to be done?"

"I don't know.... Wait a minute. I do have an idea."

"Tell me."

"I want to think about it. Let's speak again tomorrow!"

⚜

Every morning, as he left his building on his way to shul, Yaakov Frankel would glance quickly at the headlines of the newspaper that had been tucked into his mailbox. A rapid perusal of the first page gave him the outline of events that had transpired in the world while he slept.

This morning his eye was caught almost at once by the left-column headline.

YESHIVAH STUDENT ATTACKED IN SOUTH TEL AVIV

His interest snagged, Yaakov read on. And as he did, he became almost dizzy with shock.

> "... reports that E.K., a 21-year-old yeshivah student, was stabbed yesterday on Aliyah Street, not far from Selma Street. He was found bleeding and unconscious on a dusty side street, near a locked metal gate set into the stone wall of a courtyard. Passers-by called an ambulance, which arrived within minutes and bore the wounded youth to Ichilov Hospital.
>
> When he regained consciousness, police attempted to question the student, but were not able to make sense of his ramblings. The youth did mention following a member of a cult called the "Third Magical Eye." Police have no knowledge of such a cult, and have determined to question the victim further when his condition stabilizes."

Yaakov read through the account a second time, and then a third. Almost in a trance, he refolded the newspaper and slipped it back into his mailbox. He had no doubt that the victim of the attack was Elazar. The initials fit: E.K... Elazar Kimmerman. No doubt at all.

What had Elazar been doing on Aliyah Street? Who had stabbed him? Had he actually managed to identify the curly-haired man he had suspected, and had that man attacked him? If that was the case, the matter had become very dangerous. It was necessary to act with caution — but also with determination.

On his way to shul, Yaakov decided on his course of action. Immediately after *Shacharis* he would travel into Tel Aviv, to Aliyah Street. He wanted to see for himself the spot where Elazar had been attacked.

That done, he would find out whether he could obtain permission to visit Elazar in the hospital.

Z evulun was shaken to the depths of his being. As he stood by, helplessly watching his oldest child sink into unconsciousness, a voice screamed inside him, "Am I going to lose a second son? Please, Hashem, help me!"

For a moment, he was taken aback by a fresh realization: This was the first time he had viewed Yossi's disappearance as a loss.... Without realizing what he was doing, he seized Elazar's hand and shook it hysterically. "For goodness sake, wake up! Elazar, do you hear me? Enough! Wake up, Elazar! *Elazar!*"

Two nurses thrust aside the curtain to look in. Apparently, the words he thought he was whispering had been audible outside the alcove in which he stood. An emergency-room physician, young and stern, stepped around the nurses to confront Zevulun.

"Excuse me, sir. What are you doing here?"

"This is my son!"

"I understand. But you are requested to leave at once!" The order was issued in a raised, commanding tone.

Zevulun glared. "I'm not disturbing anyone!"

The doctor had reached the end of his patience. "You *are* disturbing!"

Zevulun looked at the doctor, then at the nurses standing on either side. Anger and fear battled in his heart. At that moment, he despised himself for dropping the bland mask behind which he was accustomed to hiding his face. Seeing him so, the doctor relented. More gently now, he said, "Sir, your son needs rest. A lot of rest! You want him to get well, don't you? If you do as I tell you now, there's a very good chance that he'll be released by tomorrow evening. Don't be so anxious."

"Yes, but — what's wrong with him?"

"A gash in his skull. The cut has already been stitched up, and X-rays show no damage to the brain. Probably a light concussion. A few solid hours of total rest should go a long way toward reviving him." The doctor gazed at Zevulun gravely. "Do you understand, sir? A miracle happened to your son. A centimeter higher, and we'd have some real trouble. And now — " he half-turned away — "let him have the rest he needs."

Inwardly grateful to the young doctor, Zevulun still felt reluctant to leave. "Please give me just a few more minutes, to collect myself. My wife is out there, and I don't want her to see me looking like this."

The physician hesitated. "Very well." He and the nurses passed through the curtain, once again leaving Zevulun alone with his unconscious son, and his thoughts.

It was midnight before Zevulun and his wife arrived home that night.

All that evening, Tzipporah had found her husband gentler, more open to listen and to engage in conversation than he had been in a long time. Suffering could change a man the way nothing else could, she had once heard a lecturing rabbi say. It could straighten out the crooked parts of his soul and give him a whole new perspective on life — and thus, lead to full repentance for his old ways.

Had this happened to Zevulun? Tzipporah could not know. She woke suddenly at 4 in the morning, and saw a light under the crack of her husband's study door. She hesitated, then threw on a robe and went toward the light.

She found Zevulun bent over a small book. Coming closer, Tzipporah saw that it was a *Tehillim*. Startled by her footsteps, Zevulun swung around. It seemed to his wife that there was a moistness around his eyes.

Quietly, she retreated and closed the door. Back in the bedroom, she looked upward with a silent, hopeful prayer: "Please, Hashem. Let it last...."

On that same day, Yitzchak Abramson closed his Gemara at an earlier hour than usual. He left his seat in the *beis midrash* and went out to catch the bus. Contrary to his usual routine, he was traveling out of the city today. Destination: Jerusalem.

And the cause was Zevulun Kimmerman. Yitzchak wanted to discuss the matter with their old *rosh yeshivah* — a man who, Yitzchak knew, Zevulun revered to this day. He might be obdurate in the face of his old friend and reject the overtures of a Shaul Egozi, but he would not, could not, turn his back on the *rosh yeshivah*. Maybe this was the key to helping Zevulun change his approach to the problem of Yossi.

Yitzchak reached the *rosh yeshivah's* house as dusk was falling. The elderly man received him with joyous warmth. Inviting him to sit, he focused his full attention on the story Yitzchak had come to tell.

"I've come about Zevulun. Zevulun Kimmerman. Does the rav remember him?"

For a moment, the *rosh yeshivah* was silent. It was clear that he was trying to sort out that name from among the thousands of students who had passed through the halls of his yeshivah over the years.

Then his face brightened. He sat up straighter, saying, "Yes, I remember Zevulun. What has happened to him?"

Yaakov Frankel reached Tel Aviv in midafternoon. Riding the number 480 bus, he realized that its last stop was near the train station — and Ichilov Hospital. This led to a change in his plans. First he would visit Elazar, listen to the details of his escapade the day before, and then go see the scene of the crime.

At the hospital, he was directed to the ward and the room he sought. He found Elazar in good spirits, though still weak. He was newly returned from his first venture out of bed: a brief stroll around the ward.

Yaakov whispered, "Are you sure it was one of 'them'?"

"Yes."

A pause, then: "Was it the man you suspected?"

Elazar shook his head. "No."

"How do you know?"

"Know — what?"

"That the one who stabbed you was one of them? It wasn't a good idea to tell the police that."

"What else could I do? They grilled me. All I'd need was for the police to suspect that I was hiding something from them. Do you know what would have happened then?"

"All right. But why did you say what you said?"

"Because it was true! The man wore the bracelet you told me about. He did everything he could to make sure I would notice him. Then he walked off. For some reason, I decided to follow him."

"What happened next?"

"He turned around two or three times, to see whether I was following."

"So you think he was leading you into a trap?"

Elazar grinned wryly and lifted a hand to touch the bandage on his head. "From the results, I'd say he was."

Yaakov sat on the edge of the bed, lost in thought. One foot, suspended in the air, wagged aimlessly back and forth. At last, he roused himself to ask, "Did you recognize the man who attacked you?"

"No."

"You had never seen him before?"

"No."

"But it's clear, from what you tell me, that he recognized *you*."

"Apparently."

"And he also seems to know that you're interested in this."

"Why?"

"Otherwise, why would he try to lure you to a deserted alley and try to bash your head in?"

"You've got a point there."

Yaakov tugged at his sparse beard. "Well, think for yourself. What did he want from you?"

With another feeble grin, Elazar complained, "My head, as you just mentioned, was nearly bashed in. It's hard for me to think. You do it for me."

Yaakov smiled. "All right. I'll try to form a hypothesis. Let's take it step by step. The man wanted to attack you; that much is clear. The proof of that? The fact that he *did!* Also, he must have known that the attack would bring about a certain result. The most obvious one, I think, is to prevent you from probing any further into their activities. The blow was a warning to you — to forget about your brother."

"Let's say you're right," Elazar said slowly. "How did they know?"

"That's a good question — the question of a *talmid chacham*," Yaakov joked. "It tells us that the person you suspect, or possibly someone else, suspected that you were on to them. You see the problem?"

"What?"

"I wanted to investigate these people quietly, without them being wise to us. That way, I could have uncovered one detail after another without arousing suspicion. But somehow, they found out what we're doing — and now, *they're* interested in *us*. Or at least, in you." He sighed lightly. "This business is getting more and more complicated."

"It's my fault. I'm sorry."

"Why do you think it's your fault?"

"Maybe I talked too much with the man I suspect."

"What do you mean?"

"I asked him some direct questions. Too direct. I saw that he was getting suspicious. And he — *he* was the one who asked me to meet him at the Central Post Office. In his place, the other guy showed up, and ended up stabbing me!"

Yaakov listened intently, but his only comment at the end was, "Interesting. Very interesting...."

"What's so interesting?"

"How heaven is helping us. It will be easier to uncover our hidden enemy now."

Elazar's lip curled. "Glad to be of service."

"You'll see. They cracked open your head, but this may help us to crack open the case! With Hashem's help, some good will come out of this, you'll see."

"What do you mean?"

"Simple. I have a confession to make. I didn't know which way to turn in this investigation of ours. I have a letter that Yossi received from someone in Switzerland. So what? Can that tell me where he is now? I have no information about that cult, and don't know how to check it out without arousing suspicion. But now — thanks to you — we may be able to track them down."

Elazar looked intrigued. "How?"

"I don't know that yet. Right now, I want to use the fact that they're after you as bait."

Seeing the expression on the younger man's face, Yaakov punched him playfully on the arm. "Elazar, a little self-sacrifice would be in order here! We're talking about the mitzvah of *pidyon shevuyim* — rescuing a prisoner. And not just any prisoner, but your own brother. Courage, my friend!"

Elazar stirred restlessly on the high bed. He felt warm in the overheated room. Tossing the covers off, he said, "You're scaring me. What do you have in mind?"

"I don't know that myself. But I do know that I want to take advantage of what happened yesterday, to lead us to Yossi." He held up a hand to forestall the obvious question. "How? I don't know — yet."

Elazar closed his eyes, opened them and closed them again, as Yaakov watched. At last, in a voice of doom, he said resignedly, "Okay. I'm game."

Yaakov stood up. "First of all, you have to get well. I wish you a speedy recovery. And now, I'm going to pay a visit to Aliyah Street. Where, exactly, did our mystery man attack you?"

"On a small side street right off Aliyah Street, before you get to the corner of Selma." Elazar eyed Yaakov curiously. "What do you expect to find there?"

"I haven't a clue. Where exactly did he strike you?"

"I followed him into the narrow street. He must have been hiding behind a rusted metal gate there. I carefully opened the gate — and after that, I don't remember anything."

⚜

Yaakov caught a taxi outside the hospital. "Aliyah Street, please."

Then, as the cab began moving forward, he changed his mind. "No. Drop me on Kikar HaMoshavot, on the corner of Allenby."

The driver glanced at him in the rear-view mirror, as though desirous of a closer look at this religious fellow who had changed his mind about his destination within seconds of getting into his cab. Encountering Yaakov's placid but firm gaze, he shrugged, shifted gears, and set off.

Getting out at Kikar HaMoshavot, Yaakov stood still for a moment to accustom himself to the roar and bustle that was Tel Aviv. How different from the peace of Jerusalem! Though he had grown up in this city, the years away had made him forget how noisy it was.

He must adjust to it, he knew, and quickly. All his senses must be fully alert for this venture. He must pay attention to every detail, especially those that stood out as unusual in any way. He began walking down Aliyah Street, in the direction of Selma. The further he went, the slower he walked. His eyes were peeled for a glimpse of the narrow side street Elazar had described.

It was not long before he saw it. And there, at the end, stood the rusted metal gate, just as Elazar had said.

Yaakov stood still. Behind the high stone wall into which the gate was set were signs of a garden. He looked up and down the street, but all appeared normal. Cautiously, he advanced, until he was standing directly in front of the gate. After a pause of several minutes, during which his heartbeats drummed loudly in his ears, he lifted one hand and slowly touched the gate-latch. Another pause, as he listened for any sound within. Then he lifted the latch with agonizing slowness. The gate creaked open a few inches, then stopped.

Yaakov tried to peek through the opening to see what lay beyond. He pushed the gate open another inch or two. Now he could make out the courtyard on the other side. It was filled with building materials, discarded lumber and assorted rubbish of every description. A cat streaked past him, intent on business of its own. Behind it all stood a two-story building, painted entirely in green....

Then, without warning, the gate swung open to its fullest extent. A coarse voice demanded, "What are you looking for here?"

Yaakov stood stunned. The utter unexpectedness froze his limbs and his vocal cords. Before him stood a short, squat man, staring at him with expressionless eyes that were somehow infinitely menacing. And on his hand, Yaakov saw, was a bracelet. A bracelet featuring the magical third eye....

27

Keeping one wary eye on the short, angry figure before him, Yaakov's eyes darted swift glances up and down the narrow street. Not a soul in sight. His mind worked at lightning speed. *That's him! The man who attacked Elazar yesterday!* It was ridiculously easy to identify him from Elazar's description — especially the most blatant identifying mark of all: the mysterious bracelet on his wrist!

Despite his real and natural fear, Yaakov felt euphoric. He had found the right street and, apparently, the right gate. Why, for all he knew, Yossi himself might be behind those rusted metal bars, in the green building he'd just glimpsed! Was the boy being held prisoner by the shadowy group Yaakov had been trying to learn more about?

He was, he knew, still very much in the dark. This sudden encounter excited him, though its very unexpectedness left him temporarily bereft of the power of logical thought. One thing, though, only was clear in his mind: He must not leave this place. Hashem had brought him here sooner than he had dared to hope. It was up to him to discover the next step.

Yaakov was groping for the right words to say to the man, who continued to face him with a glowering look of menace, when the stranger spoke again. He repeated roughly, "Are you ready to explain to me exactly what you're looking for here?"

Yaakov smiled. "Nothing special. A friend of mine was attacked here yesterday, and I wanted to see the place for myself."

The man squinted up at him. "What are you — some kind of detective?"

Still smiling, Yaakov said, "Maybe."

The other's face darkened. Abruptly, one well-muscled arm flashed out in an attempt to slam the gate in Yaakov's face. Yaakov pushed back at the gate with both hands. For a few moments they struggled for mastery, eyes fiercely locked. Yaakov inserted a foot in the narrowing gap between gate and wall.

"You — asked — what I'm — doing here," Yaakov gasped, not relinquishing his grip on the gate. His face was crimson and his chest heaved with the effort of straining to keep the gate open against the other man's more powerful attempts to shut it. "Now I — want to know — if you can give me — a little information — about what happened here — yesterday." He filled his lungs. "It's very — important to me. As I heard it — the man who struck him — came out of this gate."

The squat man bellowed, "Get out of here! I don't know what you're talking about!" He heaved furiously at the gate.

Yaakov pushed back. "Why are you shouting? Is something making you nervous?"

"Yes — *you* are!" The man's eyes blazed. "I don't know anything about any attack!"

"You don't read the newspapers?"

"No, I don't. They poison a man's soul, they take a man's peace of mind away."

"You're right. You have no idea how right. But you don't look like a man who gets peace of mind simply by avoiding newspapers."

"That's not your problem," the man growled.

Yaakov decided on a frontal attack. "You're right, it's not. But the fact that *you* struck down my friend — that *is* my problem!"

His words galvanized the swarthy stranger. Letting go of his grip on the gate, he advanced slowly and menacingly on Yaakov. It was all Yaakov could do to maintain an outwardly unruffled appearance, and to stand his ground when every instinct was screaming at him to run.

The man thrust a steely fist at Yaakov's face, stopping just short of touching him. "*I* attacked your friend? Are you insane, or dreaming? Now, *get out of here!*"

Yaakov neither answered nor moved a muscle. Watching his opponent's every move, it seemed to him that the other was quickly losing what little self-control he possessed. The man was literally shaking with rage. Yaakov gave himself encouragement by reflecting that, with a little patience, he might achieve his goal in a very few minutes. He whispered, "Be happy I didn't go to the police!"

"You can go to the police, the General Security Service, or the U.N., for all I care. No one will believe you!"

Yaakov persisted softly, "I'm prepared to leave, if that's what you want. But I suggest that you hear me out before I go."

The man did not react. Yaakov continued, in the same calm tone, "My friend first saw you near the Central Post Office on Allenby Street. It was at about 5 o'clock yesterday, right?"

"*Not* right. Go on, let's have some more of your lies!"

"You asked him what time it was. Right?"

"Wrong!"

"He followed you. Do you know why? You won't believe it."

He could see a spark of curiosity in the man. Though still angry, he muttered with visible interest, "Why?"

Yaakov was elated. The short stranger had fallen neatly into the trap he had prepared. Instead of reiterating, "Wrong," to Yaakov's every question, he was asking "Why?" It was an accomplishment. Yaakov decided to try to take it one step further. Observing the other man closely to gauge his reaction, he stated:

"He was attracted by the bracelet you're wearing."

A look — startled and confused — flashed into the man's eyes. Yaakov was careful to conceal his triumph. "He knows that the bracelet's given him away!" he thought exultantly.

The fellow rallied rapidly. Shrugging an indifferent shoulder, he said coolly, "You're mistaken. Maybe your friend saw someone else with this type of bracelet."

Two could play at this game. Yaakov patted back a yawn and said, "Maybe so. But aren't you curious to know why he was so drawn to the bracelet?"

When there was no answer, he drew cautiously closer. "Aren't you curious? Don't you know that the eye in the center of the bracelet is the symbol of one of the cults that operate in this country?"

The squat stranger was clearly taken aback by this frontal attack. Yaakov pressed his advantage: "After my friend was injured, he confided in me that he was attracted to this cult. He'd found some material about it in his younger brother's possession, and what he read moved him. So when he saw you wearing that bracelet..."

The sudden shout startled him. "He didn't see me! Stop saying that!"

"Okay, so he didn't see you. He was following a different man who looked like you and wore a similar bracelet. Have it your way... Well, this other man came out of a house on this street and struck the back of my friend's head with a sharp weapon." Yaakov peered at him. "Now do you understand what I'm looking for in this place?"

"Not yet."

Yaakov took a deep breath. "I'm a yeshivah man, and so is my friend. I'd like to prevent him from getting caught up in the nonsense he's been reading about. I want to save him! I came here to see if I could find the members of this cult — to warn them to leave my friend alone. That's all."

With a frigid look, the other answered only, "I repeat: You've got the wrong place. I have no connection, either to what happened to your friend yesterday or to this imaginary cult of yours." He glanced down at his wrist. "I bought this bracelet in a bazaar in Nachalat Chaim. This whole cult business exists only in your own head!"

There was a brief silence. The short man broke it by saying, with a sneer, "And now, will your honor permit me to close the gate, in the hopes of never laying eyes on you again?"

The gate slammed shut. The echo seemed to linger in the deserted street....

Yaakov was moving almost before the last echo faded. He made his way back to the hospital, and Elazar's room.

"Elazar, now it's your turn to do something for your brother Yossi."

"What happened?"

"Oh, nothing special. I just had an interesting conversation with the man who attacked you."

Elazar bolted upright in his bed. "*What?* I don't believe it!"

"You don't have to believe it. But when he or one of his cronies contacts you, you'll believe."

"What do you mean?"

"He'll be in touch. I planted the idea that you're interested in the cult, and that was why you followed him."

"But — why would he contact me?"

"I'm convinced that he believed me. They'll try to persuade you to join them. And you, of course, will agree."

Elazar was conscious of a feeling of panic. "What have you done? Why should I agree?"

"Because it's the only way — maybe! — for us to find out where Yossi is. You'll have to infiltrate them, Elazar. This is a question of rescuing a Jewish soul! And your own brother, to boot. Can you just walk away from that?"

Elazar buried his face in his hands. The idea of infiltrating the cult frankly terrified him, but he could not fault Yaakov's logic. Through his fingers he moaned, "I can't!"

Yaakov answered sharply, "You must!"

Yitzchak Abramson hitched his chair a little closer to the table where the *rosh yeshivah* sat. The old rabbi's cheek rested on the palm of one hand as he waited attentively for Yitzchak to speak. It was easy to read the thought processes that were taking place within Yitzchak, as he struggled to frame his story in clear and comprehensible terms.

"Zevulun has problems with his son."

The old man sighed. "*Nu, nu.* It is *tza'ar gidul banim* — the pain of raising children."

Hesitating, Yitzchak said, "This is much more serious."

"What do you mean?"

"The boy has run away from home."

The *rosh yeshivah* paled. "Where did he go?"

"That's just what we don't know."

They both fell silent. Finally, Yitzchak ventured, "He was learning in Yeshivat Nachal Kedumim, and ran away from there."

The *rosh yeshivah* looked at him sharply. "What exactly do you mean by 'ran away'?"

"If — If the rav remembers Zevulun, it's not so difficult to understand..."

Slowly, the old man nodded. His wise eyes transmitted his understanding to Yitzchak. He remembered, and he understood.

Encouraged, Yitzchak continued, "Zevulun is a stubborn, headstrong man. Nothing can budge him from what he believes or what he decides. The rav must remember, he was like this back in our yeshivah days. I think it's safe to assume that he hasn't changed, and that he behaves in the same way in his own home."

"Did he beat his son?"

"By all accounts — yes."

"Tell me this. After he hit the boy, at the proper moment did he try to comfort him?"

Yitzchak thought a moment. "Apparently not. He's a stubborn man. Also, he has a proud streak that makes it hard for Zevulun to express his feelings."

"That's not good." The *rosh yeshivah* heaved a sorrowful sigh. "We're supposed to follow the example of Hashem, who disciplines when necessary, and then embraces. A father is permitted, and sometimes even obligated, to take his son in hand. But it's not enough for the mother to step in with words of comfort. That job belongs to the father who chastised. Otherwise, he's only performing half of his task, which should be to 'push away with his left' and draw his son close with his right." Another sigh. "A pity. A very great pity."

Silence hung heavily in the room. The *rosh yeshivah* presently broke it to say, with a smile, "But I'm sure you didn't come here simply to make me sad. What do you want from me, Yitzchak?"

Yitzchak cleared his throat. "Reb Shaul Egozi and I — both of us friends of the Kimmerman family — decided to ask the rav if he would speak with Zevulun. Despite the fact that Zevulun left the yeshivah world to go into business, he's still a pious man with a deep reverence for the *rosh yeshivah*. We're convinced that the rav's words can have a profound effect on him."

The *rosh yeshivah* registered surprise. "In what way can I influence him?"

"First of all, to help Zevulun see that he hasn't always been correct in his dealings with his son. To help him recognize that he has a problem. He gets angry at anyone who tries to discuss these things with him. If he can change, there's still a chance that the boy will come home again."

The *rosh yeshivah* considered this at length, while Yitzchak sat and waited impatiently for his answer. When it came, he was shocked.

"I'm sorry," the *rosh yeshivah* said softly. "But — no. I won't ask him to come here."

"Why not?" The cry burst from Yitzchak's throat.

With a smile, the old rabbi said, "King David said in *Tehillim*, 'Go, my children, and listen to me, and I will teach you to be G-d fearing. Who is the man who desires life?... Guard your tongue against evil and your lips from twisted speech; avoid evil and do good.' Now, the middle phrase would seem unnecessary. King David should have said, 'Go, my children, and listen to me, and I will teach you to be G-d fearing: Guard your tongue, etc.' Why does he insert the words, 'Who is the man who desires life?'

"I think he is trying to teach us an important principle. If a person does not desire life of his own choice, all the words of *mussar* in the world won't touch him. Therefore, David is only prepared to teach a person to avoid speaking evil, if that person asserts first that he indeed desires life — true life."

The *rosh yeshivah* patted Yitzchak's shoulder affectionately. "You know very well, my young friend, that speaking to a person who doesn't want to hear is never successful. And from what you have told me, I understand that Zevulun is not now in a receptive mood. In fact, his problems with his son happened because he never helped the boy become receptive to his teachings, to *want* to listen. Do you want me to make the same mistake with Zevulun?"

Yitzchak was conscious of a sense of disappointment. "Then what does the rav suggest that we do?"

"It is necessary to come up with a way to help Zevulun want to come to me on his own. Then, maybe — maybe! — I will be able to influence him."

When Yitzchak stepped out of the *rosh yeshivah's* house a few minutes later, night had already spread a cloak of darkness over Jerusalem. It was a dark night, with no stars.

28

Elazar covered his head with the pillow, as though to escape from reality. Fears beset him on every side. The images that passed before his closed eyes were heavy ropes that fell on him the way a fisherman's net ensnares a large fish, imprisoning him so that he cannot move. A scream rose up in his throat, only to be swallowed. At last he fell into a fitful, troubled sleep.

He had no idea how long he had been sleeping when he woke with a start, heart hammering. The total darkness outside the square window by his bed told him it was nighttime. Turning his head, he saw his father standing there, smiling. His mother, he remembered, had already visited him that morning.

Zevulun moved closer. "How do you feel?"

Elazar smiled back weakly and drew himself into a half-sitting position. "*Baruch Hashem*, better."

"Good. Please get up now. We're going home."

These words had the effect of banishing the last shreds of sleep. "The doctors were in here before I fell asleep," Elazar said in some confusion. "I heard them talking. They said I need a lot of rest and medical attention."

"Maybe so. But I just spoke to them, and asked them to discharge you."

Elazar's eyes widened as he tried to understand. "Why?"

"Because your mother and I want you home now."

"Yes, but — but why?"

"I don't know... I'm afraid."

"Afraid of what?"

Zevulun sat gingerly at the edge of the hospital bed, inhaled deeply, and whispered, "I wish I knew. I would have been glad to leave you here for another couple of days of rest..."

"You mean, you're afraid something will happen to me here?"

Zevulun hesitated. In an instinctive gesture, he took Elazar's hand and stroked it lightly. Elazar was at once startled and moved. He could not remember when his father, even when Elazar had been a young child, had caressed him in such a gentle way. Without words, it told of the love that was stored, largely unexpressed, deep in his father's heart. Elazar was profoundly touched.

In the face of Zevulun's continuing silence, he finally ventured, "I want to understand, Abba. Are you afraid that something might happen to me, specifically?"

Zevulun's smile was sheepish. "Maybe... That is, yes... You're right, I *am* afraid of something like that."

"But, Abba — why?"

"I don't know. Call it a father's intuition."

After a moment, Zevulun added, "Come on, get up now. I'll help you get dressed. The doctors say you're all right, and you can rest just as well at home for the next few days. All this will pass as if it never happened, *b'ezras Hashem.*"

Inwardly, Elazar had to smile at this. *As if it never happened!* If his father only knew what was awaiting him now because of that blow on the head, he would understand that a lot more had happened than he knew...

Bending over to put on his shoes made Elazar's head swim. Another thought came to him: If Abba knew, he would be absolutely right in being afraid. Oy, how right he would be! He felt the same impotent anger at the memory of Yaakov's request — and the same realization that he couldn't say no…

They were home an hour later. As they walked into the apartment, the phone was ringing. Zevulun hurried to answer.

It was Ilan.

Yaakov did not return to Jerusalem that night.

He had not planned it that way. Upon leaving Ichilov Hospital for the second time, he had walked up Shaul HaMelech Street toward the train station, intending to catch the number 400 bus to Jerusalem. But before he got there, he stopped walking and stood as motionless as an island amid the swirling sea of pedestrians. Several people stared at him curiously, but Yaakov did not notice. He was immersed in thought.

He could not get the swarthy man with the mysterious bracelet out of his mind. He pictured the scene of the crime, and believed with powerful intuition that the solution to the riddle of Yossi's disappearance somehow lay there, behind the rusted metal gate the man had so zealously guarded. At the thought, a surge of renewed energy washed through his veins. This was war — a true battle of wits between himself and Yossi's captors, be they physical or spiritual.

The challenge drew him irresistibly. His goal stood out clearly and sharply before him: to save a Jewish soul. What could possibly be more important?

He decided, accordingly, to return to South Tel Aviv, to the place where he had confronted the man with the bracelet several hours earlier. What he would do when he got there, he had no idea. Maybe he would manage to glean a few additional details, to help shed light on his search for the missing boy. Until he discovered where Yossi was actually located, he was still very much at the beginning of the trail.

He entered a small shul to *daven Minchah,* one of the last to exude genuine *Yiddishkeit* in this run-down area. There were few religious people left in this part of the city these days. Yaakov adapted his lengthier *davening* style to the *minyan's* quick pace. When the service was over, he turned to his fellow worshipers and inquired: "Do any of you happen to live on Aliyah Street, at the beginning of the street, near Selma?"

The congregants of the small shul were mostly pensioners, slow of movement but alert enough as they studied Yaakov. Why, their tired eyes asked, was this young yeshivah man interested in someone who lived on Aliyah Street? The question, and the curiosity it aroused, imparted a certain excitement to otherwise drab and routine lives.

"What are you looking for there?" one of the old men wanted to know.

Yaakov did not know what to answer, so he remained silent. It was his hope that someone would respond to his question without posing one of his own, as Jews tend to do.

Another man tugged at the questioner's sleeve. "Reb Efraim, I'll tell you what he's looking for. Maybe he's looking for the wild men who hide out in the green house!"

The first man gave him a scornful look. "What kind of nonsense are you talking? Can't you see that this is a fine yeshivah man?"

"It was only a joke," the second muttered.

Yaakov listened to this exchange in growing excitement. His first impulse was to ask them what they knew about the green house, concealed behind wall and gate. Then, on second thought, he decided that it would be imprudent to betray too much interest.

He now knew one thing, however: The neighbors knew what was going on there. This knowledge encouraged him. All he had to do now was find someone who lived close by. Someone who was Torah observant and responsible, to whom Yaakov might entrust his secret.

"Just a minute," another pensioner announced, wrinkling his brow. "You want to know who lives there? I know someone!"

The others looked at him with a certain amount of envy, because he had managed to remember what they themselves had forgotten.

"There, right on the corner, lives a man — what's his name again? Ah, yes — Mordechai Koselovitch. He's a very observant Jew, about 50 years old. Not young, but not old, either. Not too tall, but not very short; not fat, but also not skinny." The pensioner was vastly pleased to find himself the center of attention. He smiled, revealing large, yellow teeth. "I'll tell you one thing: He's got money." He winked. "Do you have a daughter you're looking to marry off?" Moving closer, he whispered loudly, "If you stand firm, you can get a lot out of him!"

Yaakov maintained an impassive face, merely thanking the man for the address before hurrying out of the shul. He found Koselovitch's house without difficulty, an old place at the corner of Aliyah and Selma. He climbed a flight of dark, narrow stairs to the second floor, still unsure how to introduce himself. The building had obviously not seen a painter in years, not even on a courtesy visit. Yaakov reached the apartment he wanted and rang the bell.

There was no answer. He rang again, straining every nerve to pick up a sign, any sign, of life on the other side of the door. Only total silence met his ears.

A third, almost hopeless ring, however, brought a reaction. An old woman opened the door of the apartment next door and screeched into the dim corridor, "Why are you ringing and ringing? Can't you see they're not home!"

Yaakov apologized. "Sorry about that. But they told me someone should be home at this hour. Do you happen to know where they went?"

"How do I know? I think they went to a wedding in Haifa. I don't think they'll be back until tomorrow or the next day."

"Thank you, and good-bye. I apologize again for the noise."

The old woman slammed her door before the last words were out of his mouth.

Yaakov descended slowly to the street, and stepped into a dark night — a night crisscrossed by cars' headlamps in constant motion. For a moment he stood still, downcast. Then, aloud, he said, "Everything Hashem does is for the best," and began walking again.

Yitzchak Abramson returned home from the *rosh yeshivah's* house troubled in spirit. His interview had failed to bring about the desired results. Even in the midst of his disappointment, he knew that the *rosh yeshivah* had been correct in his assessment of Zevulun. Still, it did nothing to further the objective that had brought him to Jerusalem.

He would have been happy knowing that Zevulun would be sitting with his former *rosh yeshivah* in the course of the next day or two, listening to sage counsel. Instead, the work was now Yitzchak's, to persuade his friend to take the initiative in seeking that counsel. He had no idea how to go about this persuasion, or how long it would take.

It was near midnight when he finally arrived home. He decided to phone Shaul Egozi anyway. Chances were good that Reb Shaul was still awake, poring over his Gemara.

"Reb Shaul, excuse me for calling so late."

"Forgiven!"

"I hope I'm not disturbing you."

Shaul chuckled. "If you'd thought you were disturbing me, you wouldn't have called at all. I know you well enough to know that." Reb Yitzchak was known in his circle as a man who took scrupulous care in the way he treated others.

Shaul continued, "In any case, what brings you to call at such an hour? No, let me guess. Zevulun!"

"Correct. How did you know?"

"Simple. We've hardly spoken for the past five years. Now, since this thing happened to Zevulun, we've been exchanging phone calls practically every few hours. Am I right?"

Yitzchak laughed, "You're right!"

"So… to business."

"All right. I visited the *rosh yeshivah* in Yerushalayim today."

"Great! What did you ask him?"

"Remember, the last time we spoke, I said I had an idea for Zevulun? My idea was to get the *rosh yeshivah* involved."

"Sounds good to me. And what did the *rosh yeshivah* say?"

"That he doesn't want to ask Zevulun to come to him."

"What? Why not?"

"He has his reasons. Believe me, they're good ones, but not for now."

"Well, what next?"

"The *rosh yeshivah* wants us to try to persuade Zevulun to take the initiative and call *him*."

Shaul said doubtfully, "That won't be easy."

"Agreed. Unless we try convincing him by force."

"Meaning…?"

"We visit him tomorrow night, without warning, and 'sit on him' until he agrees."

"You're apparently not taking into account what's liable to happen, if you know him as well as you claim you do."

"I'm taking everything into account. All I know is that it's a mitzvah to save Zevulun from himself. And you're the one to do it!"

"Well… we'll see."

"*We won't see.* You're closer to him than I am these days. I'll be along to help you."

After a few seconds, Shaul Egozi was heard to say softly, "*Nu* — all right."

29

Zevulun's mellow mood upon entering the house with the recently discharged Elazar evaporated instantly at the sound of Ilan's hearty voice over the phone.

"Hello, good evening, this is Ilan speaking!"

Zevulun's voice, by contrast, was cold as ice. "Yes, I hear. What do you want?"

At the other end of the line, Ilan was dumbfounded at his boss's blatant hostility. Hesitantly, he said, "I'd like to talk to Elazar." Immediately, he added, "I want to apologize to him for not showing up where we had arranged to meet."

Zevulun was in no hurry to hand the phone over to his son. "What interests me, Ilan," he said, "is why you arranged to meet him in the first place."

Elazar, who was already lying down on the sofa, sat up, electrified.

Zevulun heard Ilan say, "I wanted to discuss something with him, face to face."

"Very interesting. Maybe, as his father, I might also be permitted to know what you wanted from him?"

Ilan was gripped by tension. He had made a quick recovery from Zevulun's cold reception, but was in the dark as to its source. He decided to stand his ground.

"What I need to speak to you about, I'll tell you. This is for Elazar."

Zevulun fought down an urge to bellow. Ignoring his boiling blood, he said, "Hm… I'm standing in your way, aren't I? It seems you've not yet given up on the notion of dragging my son into the trap you prepared for him."

Alarm bells rang clangorously in Ilan's head. "Zevulun, I don't know what you're talking about! What trap?"

"Don't play the innocent with me, Ilan! Don't you read the newspapers?"

"Now and then. Why?"

"You don't know that Elazar was injured because of you?"

"Because of *me?* What's the matter with you today?"

Zevulun plowed on. "Yes. Because of you!"

Impatiently, Zevulun waited for Ilan to respond to his open accusation. He did not believe a word of Ilan's protests that denied any knowledge. It infuriated him to think of his own employee trying to make a fool of him. What *had* Ilan wanted from Elazar?

Ilan burst out: "I'm in shock! I don't understand what you're talking about. Why are you suddenly attacking me?"

"I don't believe that you don't understand," Zevulun said, with enforced calm. "I'm very angry at you, Ilan."

"But — "

"I don't deserve this kind of treatment from you. In fact, *I'm* also shocked — by your behavior."

"But believe me, I told you the truth. I don't know anything. Even now, I don't know what you're referring to."

"If you didn't know anything, how did you know Elazar was here at home?"

"I didn't know. I called the house as my first step in finding out how to reach him."

"Oh, really? So that's why your first words were, 'I want to talk to Elazar'? You didn't say, 'Does Elazar happen to be home?'" Zevulun breathed deeply. "Ilan, there are limits!"

Ilan felt trapped. Any way he turned, he would only draw more fire. He decided to retreat.

"All right, I can see that something's happened, something I can't begin to understand. I can sense your mood and it's no use trying to fight it. So have a good night, Zevulun. I'm sorry I made you so angry."

"Just a minute! You said you wanted Elazar. Well, he's here! I just brought him home from the hospital."

"Hospital?" Ilan sounded dumbfounded.

Without answering, Zevulun passed the receiver to Elazar. His son's sudden movement, in reaching for it, caused him to wince — mute testimony to the lingering ache in his head. In a low voice, he said, "Ilan, I waited for you by the Central Post Office!"

"I'm sorry, I really am. Strange as it may sound, I forgot all about our appointment. That Canadian distracted me... But tell me, Elazar, what's this *intifada* your father's suddenly waging against me? What does he want from me?"

"First ask me whom I met in your place near the Central Post Office. Then you'll understand what my father's feeling."

"What do you mean?"

"The man I met there instead of you ended up sending me to the hospital."

Ilan was silent a moment, then asked, "Well, are you prepared to explain? I want to know what's going on!"

"That's all. I waited for you. You didn't come, so I went to phone you. Somebody tugged at my sleeve and asked me for the time, I answered him, and then..."

"And then — what?"

"Wait, I'm getting to it."

"Excuse me… Go on."

"And then I noticed a bracelet on his wrist that attracted my interest. I decided to follow him."

"What kind of bracelet was it?"

Elazar gripped the receiver tightly. He was well aware that his father was listening intently to every syllable he uttered.

"A very interesting bracelet. It resembled a large, green eye. Have you ever seen anything like that?"

Ilan hesitated. "No, I can't say that I have."

"Really, Ilan. You've never seen a bracelet like that?"

There was anger in Ilan's voice as he demanded, "What's going on in the Kimmerman house? Doesn't anyone believe a word I say?"

Elazar's suspicions grew stronger. By now he was almost certain that Ilan had some sort of connection to the cult that was responsible, apparently, for Yossi's disappearance. He felt an urgent wish to press on with some direct and very uncomfortable questions, but he was afraid to stretch the rope too taut, lest Ilan cut it and run. His goal was to get closer to the mystery cult, as Yaakov had ordered. That called for extreme caution.

Elazar's manner grew conciliatory. "Okay, okay, don't get mad. If you don't know, I'll tell you. The eye in the bracelet is the symbol used by a cult that calls itself the Third Magical Eye. Have you ever heard of it?"

Again, he caught the infinitesimal pause before Ilan answered, "I must be very ignorant. I haven't heard of it." Elazar heard Ilan's breath come short and quick.

"I don't know why, but I had the impression that you had heard of it."

"Well, you were mistaken. Just explain to me why you followed that man."

The moment of truth had arrived. It was time to convince Ilan that he was interested in getting closer to the cult. Covering his mouth with his hand to muffle his voice, he whispered into the phone, "Listen, Ilan, I don't want my father to hear this. I'm a little interested in this cult. It doesn't matter how right now, but recently I came across some of their literature. There are some interesting ideas there. I thought I might be able to find out more by following that man — and look what happened."

"What did happen?"

Elazar laughed. "Something hard and sharp on the back of my head — that's what happened."

"Oh! I'm sorry."

"And I'm frustrated. Instead of talking to me, that guy gave it to me over the head!"

Ilan said nothing for several long moments. Then he whispered, "In any case, I want to meet and talk."

Elazar was satisfied. Ilan, it seemed, had gotten the message. Ilan's desire to talk to him only served to confirm Elazar's initial suspicions. He said, "I'll be here at home for the next few days. You can come by."

"No, that's no good. It has to be outdoors. I'll come pick you up in my car and we'll go somewhere."

"I still haven't fully recovered from the attack. I have to rest for a few days."

"All right, we'll meet in a few days. Maybe I'll have something important to tell you."

Zevulun had dogged the conversation intently. He was displeased. It seemed to him that Elazar was hiding something from him. His whisperings with Ilan — of which Zevulun was only able to pick up a word or two — sharpened his curiosity as well as his apprehension. He sank into a black leather armchair, not far from the sofa where Elazar reclined, and waited.

He saw Elazar lean back and close his eyes as though exhausted. *Or maybe*, Zevulun thought, *only pretending to be exhausted.*

"Elazar?"

His son opened his eyes. "Yes?"

"Tell me something."

"Believe me Abba, it's all a lot of nonsense."

"I don't mind listening to nonsense." Zevulun paused. "Besides, from what I managed to overhear, it didn't seem like nonsense to me."

Elazar smiled. "Abba, you're right. The truth is that it's a long story, and I have an awful headache."

Anger shot up instantaneously. Elazar saw the flaring of his father's nostrils and the gradual reddening of his neck and cheeks. He had no desire to irritate his father just now, but neither did he want to share Yaakov's plan with him. There was no way to predict how Zevulun would react.

Zevulun witnessed his son's dilemma with a sardonic smile. "So, your Reb Yaakov has once again forbidden you to speak?"

"No, Abba. Actually, he wants me to talk to you."

"Oh, what happened? Why am I suddenly back in the fold?"

"You're my father. It would be impossible to keep the truth hidden from you indefinitely."

"Well, thank you very much!"

Elazar ignored the sarcasm. "Abba, what do you want to know?"

"I heard something about a magical eye. What is it? You have to realize that it scares me!"

"The Third Magical Eye is a cult — one we don't know too much about yet."

Zevulun sprang to his feet and moved closer to the sofa where Elazar lay. "What do you have to do with cults?"

"Nothing."

"Do you honestly believe I didn't hear what you and Ilan were talking about just now? Come on, put your cards on the table!"

Elazar struggled into an upright position on the sofa. His expression, half sad, half smiling, did much to dispel some of the tension between them. Softly, he said, "Do you know where Yossi is?"

Zevulun's breath caught in his throat. The way Elazar had put the question told him that his son had the answer. He was overcome with a strange weakness as he whispered, "No, no, I don't know."

"Abba, Yossi ran away, apparently, into the arms of the group we're talking about — the cult of the 'Third Magical Eye.'"

Zevulun's mouth opened, but no sound came out. His hands moved in futile gestures, as though asking wordlessly, "How?" "Why?"

In the end, he managed to blurt a single word. "Cult?"

Elazar nodded.

With great effort, he rose from the sofa and went over to perch on the arm of his father's armchair. An immense feeling of pity flooded him, pity for his father. The man who was usually so confident sat beside him now like a broken shell.

"Abba!" Elazar said urgently. "Abba, please. You've got to be strong!"

Zevulun did not answer. He rested his face between his hands for a long moment, then shook his head and looked up at his son.

"I'm okay now. I just need you to explain. A full explanation, with all the details."

Elazar told him everything.

30

Zevulun heard Elazar out in silence. He did not interrupt once as he listened to the account of Yossi's odd behavior in yeshivah; of his strange mutterings; of the letter found wedged behind his drawer in his dormitory room; of the young man with the curly hair who had visited Yossi at yeshivah ("That's why I suspected Ilan, Abba!"). He heard about the mysterious cult of the Third Magical Eye, and of Yaakov Frankel's determination to have Elazar penetrate the cult to learn of Yossi's whereabouts.

Elazar finished speaking, but kept his eyes trained on his father. Zevulun had not moved a muscle or uttered a sound all through the long presentation. His thoughts were as jumbled as motes of dust in a windstorm.

Then, suddenly, things clicked into place. He understood everything: why Elazar had acted so strangely in his office when Ilan and the Canadian were there; why he had been so insistent on keeping his rendezvous with Ilan despite his father's warnings.

As for Elazar, he felt drained and spent. A deep sorrow filled him. "Abba, I'm sorry. I've hurt you."

Zevulun regarded his son expressionlessly. When he spoke, it was only to say, "It's a good thing your mother decided to leave the two of us alone for a while. This way, she spared herself the pain of hearing the story you just told me."

"Yes."

"Has Yaakov agreed to have you tell me everything?"

"Yes!"

"Why?"

Elazar hesitated. "Because…because I explained to him that you're suffering even more from not knowing. That you could sense the presence of secrets swirling all around you, secrets that were making you suspect the worst. I told him that this was very painful for me, and also limited my ability to act. That you might stand in my way and not let me do what I have to do."

Zevulun smiled a twisted smile. "And now that I know exactly what you're planning to do, I won't stand in your way? Elazar, I forbid you to have anything to do with that cult! I'm afraid!"

Elazar took a long, calming breath. As he lifted one hand to adjust the bandage that was wound around his head, he said, "If you forbid it, naturally I won't do anything. You're my father, and I'll obey you. But I have to tell you that my conscience will bother me for the rest of my life. If I had the chance to save my brother from a cult and did nothing…" He paused, gazing earnestly at his father. "And because of that, Abba, you *will* give me permission. You wouldn't be able to forgive yourself, either. You would always wonder if there had been a chance to rescue Yossi, and you had prevented it from happening."

Elazar was a little shocked at his own daring in speaking so openly to his father. He had never done so before. Zevulun did not encourage others to express their opinions, and particularly not his own children. The speech had burst from Elazar almost without his volition. To soften its effects, he added in a pleading tone, "It's *piku'ach nefesh*, Abba! The saving of a Jewish life!"

Zevulun said nothing. After a moment he stood up, led Elazar back to the sofa, and helped him lie down again. One hand reached out to smooth his son's hair. Then he turned and left without a word.

But there was no need to say anything. Elazar knew.

His father would not stand in his way.

Zevulun entered his study. Without turning on the lights, he sat in his chair. It was more comfortable sitting in the dark.

After a while he got up to open a window. The moist night air of Tel Aviv blew in. Along with the unpleasant humidity came the street sounds: music from adjoining apartment buildings, the loud voices of wandering groups of teenagers below, and the distant but ever present roar of traffic on the main thoroughfares.

Zevulun heard none of it. His mind was busy replaying, word for word, the story Elazar had just told him. "These past few months," Elazar had said, "Yossi's been acting like a fish caught in a net. He wanted something, but we didn't hear and didn't understand." Zevulun tried to picture where his son was right now, at this moment, and what he might be doing there. It was not long before, shuddering, he stopped trying. The images his mind conjured up were too frightening.

He felt as though his heart was being squeezed in a vise. Had he really been wrong in the way he'd tried to discipline his unruly son? *Had* he been too hard on Yossi?

But the Torah teaches that a man who spares the rod hates his son! A father is obligated to raise his child and to discipline him. Had his approach been wrong, especially in light of Yossi's strange behavior — especially at home? How could he have acted differently?

With all his other children, it was more or less smooth sailing. What had happened with Yossi? And why did he, Zevulun, feel that everyone was blaming him for what had happened? He still did not know. A feeling of black despair began to creep over him.

He closed the window and turned on the air conditioner. Absently, he stood listening to its low hum for a while, before returning to his armchair, the darkness and the bleak companionship of his thoughts.

Those thoughts turned presently to Ilan.

Anger coursed through him. "*He's* the problem! He's the one who led Yossi off the right path. I'm not to blame! It's Yossi's friendship with the wonderful Ilan. What a snake… He fooled me, and lured Yossi away…"

All at once, Zevulun sprang from his chair and crossed the small study in a few quick strides. Flinging open the door, he raced to Elazar's supine figure. His son was dozing lightly, but Zevulun could not wait.

"Listen to me, Elazar! I'm firing him — tomorrow!"

Elazar had been rubbing the sleep from his eyes, but at these words he was suddenly fully awake. "Who are you firing?"

"Ilan, of course!"

"But why?"

Zevulun snorted. "What a question! Have you forgotten what you told me about him only half an hour ago? About him, and that cult, and his meetings with Yossi?"

Elazar's hand shot out as though to stop his father. "Abba, no!"

"Why not?" Zevulun demanded.

"It's only suspicion at this point! Nothing is certain. We don't know if Ilan was the man who lured Yossi out of the yeshivah. And even if we did, it's crucial that he doesn't get suspicious. We have to keep him close to us, to follow him. Yaakov has a plan. I don't know if he'll succeed, but it's worth a try. Fire Ilan if you want, only not now. Wait a while!"

There was a constricted feeling in Zevulun's chest. It was hard for him to breathe. He waited a moment, until the feeling eased. Nothing was certain. Ilan might not be involved at all. He felt conscious of a certain shame. A minute ago, he had been floating on a cloud of liberation at the thought that it was all Ilan's fault. He had been thrilled at the speed with which he had found someone else to bear the blame for what had happened to Yossi.

To his relief, this uncomfortable train of thought was interrupted by a long and insistent peal of the front doorbell. He went to the door and opened it.

Facing him were Rabbi Shaul Egozi from Bnei Brak and Rabbi Yitzchak Abramson from Petach Tikvah.

Surprise battled with alarm. As Zevulun stood hesitating, his unexpected visitors smiled at him with affection. Reb Yitzchak said, "May we come in?"

⁂

Yaakov Frankel returned to his home in Ramot, Jerusalem, with a certain dread of tomorrow.

At the first light of day, he hurried out to an early *minyan*. Back home again, he took down the heavy telephone directory and looked up a number in the Gush Dan neighborhood of Tel Aviv. It took just minutes to find the name he was seeking: Mordechai Koselovitch.

He glanced at his watch and thought: "Seven a.m. I'll try to catch him at home, before he leaves for work or any place else." He dialed.

"Hello, is this the Koselovitch family?"

A child's voice — sounding somewhere between 3 and 5 years old — answered, "Yes."

"Can you get your Abba?"

"Yes." There was a slight clatter, and a childish voice called, "Abba! It's a phone call for you!"

"Hello?"

"Am I speaking to Mordechai Koselovitch?"

Cautiously, the other man confirmed this.

"Good morning. This is Yaakov Frankel, from Yerushalayim. I stopped by your apartment and rang the bell last night."

"My apartment?" Koselovitch was taken aback. "What did you want? I don't know you."

"True. But I wanted to talk to you about a very important matter. Only you can help me."

"That sounds a little strange. Only I can help you? What exactly are you talking about?"

"You live on Selma, at the corner of Aliyah, right?"

"Right. You said you were here!"

"Yes. What I'm interested in is the house opposite yours. It's a green house. You can probably see it from your balcony. Do you know who lives there? What do they do? I want to know everything."

The suspicion in Koselovitch's voice, present from the beginning of the conversation, sharpened dramatically. "Are you a detective? Do you work for the police — or the tax people, maybe? What did you say your name was?"

Yaakov chuckled. "The name is Yaakov Frankel. I live in Yerushalayim and learn in a *kollel* here. I am neither a detective nor a police officer. But I am searching for a yeshivah boy who, if I'm reading the signs correctly, has become involved with the cult that is, apparently, connected to the green house." He waited a beat. "Am I correct in assuming that a cult does operate out of that house?"

Grudgingly, Mordechai Koselovitch answered, "Yes, it does."

"What do you know about the cult?"

"Hm… Not much. Maybe not anything."

"Tell me anyway."

Koselovitch was silent for a moment. Then he said gruffly, "Listen, very ugly things go on there. I can't go into detail, especially not over the phone. All kinds of strange characters come to that house at night. Sometimes I hear strange, quiet music coming from there, and at other times there are screams that you can hear a block away. The neighbors are afraid of getting involved, and the police don't seem to care very much."

Yaakov thought fast. "Can you describe any of their members that you've seen? How are they dressed?"

"From what I can see by the light of the street lamps at night, they dress fairly normally."

"Anything else?"

Silence.

"Please try to remember more details! For example, have you ever noticed young people dressed as observant Jews?"

"Look, I don't think about them all day. I've gotten used to living near these crazy people. I have other things to do with my time."

Yaakov summoned all his reserves of patience. "Of course you do. Still, maybe you happened to notice a boy with them, dressed in the clothes of a yeshivah student? I'm just asking."

Seconds later, Koselovitch suddenly exclaimed, "You know what? You're right! A few weeks ago, I did see a boy, dressed like someone from our circles, walking at the edge of a large group of believers in this cult. Yes, yes. I'm sure now."

Yaakov's heart began to hammer painfully against his ribs. "Can you describe him to me?"

"Yes. I can."

31

After his initial surprise of finding the two unexpected visitors at his door, Zevulun made a rapid recovery.

"Yes, of course. Please come in." The words were more gracious than the manner that accompanied them.

His rabbinical guests had not expected anything different. All three knew that this was no friendly visit, to be spent in inconsequential chitchat. The moment of truth was fast approaching. It was up to them to catch Zevulun off guard.

Yitzchak Abramson and Shaul Egozi entered the apartment and, at a gesture from Zevulun, took seats on the sofa adjacent to the broad coffee table in the living room. Politely, they waited for their host to be seated. Instead, Zevulun disappeared into the kitchen. In an attempt to regain his equilibrium through a flurry of activity, he prepared drinks for his guests, and bought himself a little time to gather his wits for the impending, un-looked-for confrontation.

Presently, he reappeared in the living room, carrying a tray. It held an array of glasses, bottles of mineral water, Coke and club soda; his face held a fixed smile.

"He's recovered a bit from the shock," Yitzchak thought, amused.

"Will you have a cold drink?" Zevulun asked, his tone still coldly formal. "Or would you prefer something hot?"

"Thank you very much, Zevulun," Yitzchak Abramson said gently. "Don't worry about us. We'll take something to drink while we talk."

Zevulun responded with a wry smile. "I wanted you to make a *berachah* in my home first — before you start in on me!"

His two guests exchanged a quick glance.

"On the contrary, Zevulun," Yitzchak said evenly. "We're only here with a *berachah* for you."

Zevulun sat down near the table. "Interesting."

Yitzchak chose to ignore the ironical inflection. "I take it you know what we're here about."

Zevulun nodded without speaking.

"Well, we've decided — Reb Shaul and myself — that you have to go to Yerushalayim to discuss the situation with the *rosh yeshivah*."

Zevulun did not react.

"You have to go," Yitzchak continued, "because you're obviously not prepared to listen to anything *we* might tell you."

Zevulun struggled to maintain his composure. "For what purpose should I travel to see the *rosh yeshivah?* Is this a holiday? Is Rosh Hashanah coming up — time to wish him a good year?!"

Yitzchak looked away from him, down at the tray. Deliberately, he selected a glass and poured himself some club soda, saying almost nonchalantly, "No, no. Just to tell him what's been happening, and to ask for his advice in finding a solution to this difficult problem of yours."

The words were like an arrow in Zevulun's heart. Shaul Egozi gazed at the pretty crystal light fixture dangling from the ceiling. Yitzchak Abramson closed his eyes, murmured a blessing and began sipping his soda. Both of them knew how Zevulun's pride and obstinacy could be triggered when his authority was called into question. They tensed for the coming attack.

Zevulun leaned forward to rest an elbow on the table and covered his face with his hand. At all cost, he must avoid looking at his two "friends." If he did, he was liable to explode with the fury of a pent-up volcano.

He was already simmering with all the rage of a man humiliated. They were being so condescending! They were judging him — deciding that he had problems! They had even decided on his course of action and expected him to docilely conform to the script they had written. Suddenly, he had two masters!

He hardly knew how to respond to such gall. If he had any real courage, he knew, he would order them from his home at once. Still, he kept quiet. Sitting up, he reached out to grasp one of the glasses on the tray. Without a word, he filled it to the brim with Coke. As he sipped slowly, his mind continued to spin with outrage. The nerve of those two, telling him what to do! Who were they, anyway? They had made up his mind for him, without even the courtesy of discussing it with him first. On what basis had they decided that he had problems — that he was to blame for what had happened to Yossi?

In one abrupt motion, he straightened up in his chair, both hands gripping the armrests. He faced Yitzchak squarely and said, in ringing tones, "No, my honored friends! I don't have problems, and I'm not going to see anybody! As for you two — with all due respect — you're not my guardians and won't tell me what to do!"

Neither of his guests hurried to respond. To abandon their mission never entered either of their heads. Neither were they taken aback by Zevulun's explosive reaction. They knew him too well.

"Interesting," Yitzchak drawled cynically, in unconscious imitation of Zevulun. "You're speaking and behaving exactly like your runaway son. *He* also said, 'No one will decide for me! No one will tell me what to do!'"

Zevulun cut him off. "Do you really think we're talking about the same thing? Are either of you my father? Do you think that just as Yossi has to listen to me because of his obligation to respect his father, I'm required to obey you? Is that how you understand the situation?" The questions emerged like a series of hammer blows.

Yitzchak took a deep breath. "Relax, my friend. Otherwise, you won't be able to really hear what I'm saying. I know I'm being a little hard on you, but I don't have any choice."

Zevulun rolled his eyes. "A *little* hard...?"

"All right." Yitzchak permitted himself a small smile. "Very hard. We won't argue about that. Just concentrate on the essentials! What I was trying to point out just now are the similarities between your personality and your son's. Yours is the personality of a man who's unprepared to listen to anyone else. A man who takes any criticism as a declaration of war. There's a little — how shall I put it — a little arrogance here. I think Yossi has some of those same traits.

"But, for all that, there *is* a difference between you and your son. Yossi is obligated to listen to you, and you are not obligated to listen to us. But" — Yitzchak pointed a stern finger at Zevulun — "for that very reason, it would be worth your while to listen to what we, and many of those who know you, are saying. True, you're not obligated to listen. But you are a man of good sense. Your own logic must tell you, 'If they're all coming to me with the same complaint, I must look into myself.'" He paused. "What did you want from Yossi, and what do you want now?"

"I have nothing to say to my son. Let him do what he wants."

Shaul Egozi bit back a comment. Yitzchak must be allowed to speak without his interference. He well remembered how Zevulun had reacted to his wife's suggestion that they meet and talk. So, while his eyes followed the action intently, he uttered not a word.

Reb Yitzchak leaned forward, eyes keen and probing.

"Really?" he asked. "You don't care what your son is doing? That's not what your face told me when you showed up at my apartment the other day!"

The direct attack threw Zevulun off balance, but only momentarily. Recovering quickly, he shot back, "No, I don't care. I really don't!"

Yitzchak would not yield. "Really? Don't try to make a different impression on me now. That night, you were a washed-out rag! A broken man! I could hardly recognize the Zevulun Kimmerman I knew — Zevulun the strong, Zevulun the successful, Zevulun the confident, the one who always talks and acts with such authority. No, it wasn't the Zevulun I knew. Someone else was sitting in my living room that night. Someone who, without words, was crying out with all his might for help! Everything about you that night pleaded with me, Yitzchak Abramson, to help you get through this crisis. So what's this new act of yours?"

Zevulun sat shell shocked. At that moment, he felt as if he hated his old friend. Yitzchak was twisting a knife in his wounds, the wounds Zevulun had let him see that night in Petach Tikvah — and pouring salt on them besides. The suddenness of it stole the breath from his throat and robbed him of speech. Without knowing what he was doing, he raised his glass to his lips and sipped his soft drink.

There flashed into his mind the words Elazar had spoken half an hour previously. *Yossi…wanted something, but we didn't hear and didn't understand.* His brother's wild and rebellious behavior, Elazar had gone on to say, had been nothing more than a ploy to draw attention — a cry for help. Like a young child sobbing hysterically, Yossi had been trying to elicit a reaction from his parents. Here was a young yeshivah student, acting in an unruly fashion at home and at school, all for the sake of that longed-for attention!

Once again, it became difficult for Zevulun to breathe. It was too much. He could not bear any more. Was Yitzchak right? Had his own visit to Petach Tikvah been a cry for help? The same thing that — according to Elazar — Yossi had been asking for? If that were so, then he, Zevulun, had not been called upon to discipline Yossi and put him in his place. Rather, instead of reacting at once, he should have observed his behavior, and listened to him, and sought to understand what was driving the boy.

Should he have acted differently?

Right now, seated opposite his two friends, should he admit that he had, indeed, come to Yitzchak Abramson for help? It was true. He had wanted someone to listen to what he was going through, though unable to express that need in so many words. Had Yossi needed the same thing? Was it possible? Zevulun's head began to pound.

Through the pain, Yitzchak continued to bombard him.

"Zevulun, sometimes a person has to be saved from himself. There are times when he must be forcibly committed to a hospital that will heal him. A man isn't always able to help himself. He needs an outside person, someone objective, to show him what needs to be done. Right now, you are not responsible for your actions. You came to me, begging for help. For a moment, you were able to put aside your pride. It had no power over you just then. And do you know why? Because you *do* care what happens to Yossi! You felt totally helpless — not like the front you've been putting on, the strong man who doesn't care about anything."

Zevulun lifted a hand in a self-protective gesture. "Yitzchak, do you realize how much you're insulting me with every word?"

"Believe me, I'm not. I'm only peeling away the mask you're hiding behind. Look at yourself, Zevulun. This is the moment of truth!"

Never before had Zevulun felt so powerless, so bereft of authority, so vulnerable in the presence of another.

"But what do you want from me?" he asked plaintively. "Yossi ran away. How am I to blame?"

"I think the very fact that you believe they're all blaming you is the best proof that you yourself, deep down, know that you *are* to blame. Do you remember what I told you about the mirror, about looking at yourself long and hard and seeing who you really are?" When Zevulun did not answer, Yitzchak pressed, "It was a couple of days ago, when you were at my house. *Do you remember?*"

Zevulun's nod was almost imperceptible.

"Then stop playing the hero," Yitzchak said quietly. "Stop pretending to be Mister Perfect. A person is allowed to be imperfect. There's no one in this world who *is* perfect. That's no tragedy! The real tragedy is when the imperfect person is not able to admit that he's made a mistake, that he must search for ways to improve himself. The tragedy is when — to justify himself — he is prepared to heap endless new mistakes on top of the initial one. In his effort to preserve his image as the man who's always right, he causes immeasurable harm to those around him." Yitzchak paused, studying the silent Zevulun. "In your misguided pride, you've been shutting your ears to what your heart is trying to tell you. Zevulun, I'm only translating into words what your own heart is saying."

It seemed to Yitzchak that he detected a gleam of pain and sorrow in the depths of his friend's eyes. He moved closer and grasped Zevulun's hand gently.

"Believe me, that's the power of *teshuvah*. It seems to a person that giving up means losing — losing a part of himself, of who he is. Not true! Just the opposite. When a man who had been clinging to a lie stops, and faces the truth — only then does he become truly content. Why? Because at that moment he is his true self and not an impostor. At that moment, his soul awakens in him.

"Zevulun, go up to Yerushalayim and talk to the *rosh yeshivah*. Stop this pretense. Tell the truth about yourself and Yossi. Believe me, you'll feel a lot better after you humble yourself in front of that great man. Believe me!"

In a sudden burst of rage, Zevulun lunged to his feet.

Enough!" he bellowed. "You've spilled my blood — enough! I'm not going to see anyone! And no one is going to lecture me, understand?"

He did not accompany his two friends to the door when they left.

It was 1 a.m.

32

Yaakov Frankel tensed with excitement. Pressing the receiver closer to his ear, he closed his eyes for better concentration. "How did he look, that yeshivah student?"

Mordechai Koselovitch, at the other end of the line in Tel Aviv, did not answer immediately. He groped for the best words with which to describe the youth he had seen marching alongside the other cult members. To Yaakov, the wait seemed endless.

"Look," Koselovitch said finally. "I don't think I remember any special signs that would identify him. He looked like any normal yeshivah *bachur*."

It was necessary, Yaakov saw, to break his interrogation into small, specific questions. Subduing his impatience, he asked, "Was he a tall boy?"

"Hmm... No."

"Short?"

"Also not."

"Fat?"

"No."

"Thin?"

"No."

Tension had Yaakov well in its grip. "Then what *was* he?" The question emerged almost as a shout.

Koselovitch answered calmly, "Like I told you, a plain yeshivah boy: black pants, a white shirt with long sleeves and a *kipah* on his head."

Yaakov seized on this last detail: "Tell me, maybe you noticed the *kipah*. What kind was it?"

"Yes, I did happen to notice it. It was not the kind usually worn by yeshivah students."

Yaakov caught his lip between his teeth. "Could you try to describe it?"

"It wasn't completely black. The color tended a little toward brown."

"Is that all?"

"No. I'm not positive, but I think the *kipah* was made of leather."

In the matter of yarmulkas, Yossi had stood out in his yeshivah. One morning he had appeared in the *beis midrash* wearing a large, colorful, Bukharan-style *kipah* that covered half his head. He had purchased it in the Machaneh Yehudah shuk. The other boys had gaped and giggled, and the *mashgiach* had ordered him to don his normal yarmulke at once. "You don't have to try to look different from all your friends!"

"Why not?" Yossi had challenged in apparent innocence, well aware that he was breaking one of the yeshivah's unwritten rules.

"Just because," the *mashgiach* had answered, unwilling to enter into debate with him on the subject.

Yossi had yielded in the matter of the Bukharan *kipah,* but from that day onward he had expressed his rebellion by beginning to wear a leather yarmulke.

For some reason Yaakov never understood, the *mashgiach* had pretended not to notice. Perhaps he felt it advisable to cut Yossi some slack. Now, telephone in hand, Yaakov reviewed the whole story in his mind. Had Yossi's appearance in the Bukharan *kipah* been mere chutzpah — or a desperate desire to draw attention to himself, to let his friends know he was in trouble? The silent cry of a young boy in crisis… Yaakov wasn't sure. But it was entirely possible. If anyone had known, if they had listened, could this tragedy have been averted?

Through his thoughts, he heard Koselovitch's voice. Yaakov roused himself.

"I think that's the boy we're looking for. *Baruch Hashem!*"

"Yes? You really think so?"

"I do." Yaakov paused. "Tell me, Reb Mordechai, did you see him pass near your house more than once?"

"Yes, several times."

"If I brought you a picture, would you be able to identify him?"

Mordechai Koselovitch hesitated. "Hm...I think so... That is, I'm not sure."

"I know you must be in a hurry to get to work. Just one more question?"

"All right, but please make it quick."

"At what time of day do you see them coming to that house?"

"Around dusk."

Yaakov thought a moment. "Will you be home this evening?"

"Yes. Why do you ask?"

"Because, with your permission, I'd like to visit you. You'll hear the whole story then. I'm sure it will horrify you. This is a question of *piku'ach nefesh,* Reb Mordechai — of rescuing a Jewish soul. You can be a part of this great mitzvah."

"I'm listening."

"Good. So I can come tonight?"

Despite his private misgivings, Koselovitch's answer came promptly. "By all means. If I can help, why not?"

"Thank you very much. Good-bye."

"Good-bye, and good luck."

Yaakov hung up slowly. A smile played about his lips as he went into the kitchen to prepare a cup of coffee. He took tiny sips of the scalding brew, marveling at the way the investigation had progressed. Surely Heaven itself was helping him! He had begun without a clue how to proceed. It was

Elazar's lucky encounter in south Tel Aviv that had turned the tide. That had led to what looked like a really significant clue.

Was Yossi concealed in the green house? Yaakov had no way of knowing the answer to that question. But he did know — or rather, believed with all his intuitive might — that the solution to the mystery was tied, somehow, to that house…

His hand flew up and smacked his forehead at a sudden thought. He had not asked Koselovitch one all-important question: Had he seen the yeshivah student recently — yesterday, for example? Dismayed, he asked aloud, "How could I have forgotten?"

"Forgotten what?"

He spun around in surprise. His wife stood in the doorway. It was time to prepare the children's sandwiches and snacks for school.

"Oh, nothing. Nothing." He made a weak attempt at a smile.

She came closer, studying her husband. "Is there a problem, Yankel?"

"Not at all." Taking a sip from his mug, Yaakov waved his free hand dismissively. "Why would you think that?"

Her eyes never wavered. "Tell me the truth. What's on your mind?"

"Nothing!" His face, however, told a different story.

"A problem with the bank? Or at the *kollel*, maybe?"

Yaakov stood up in some annoyance. "Rochel, I told you everything's all right, *baruch Hashem!* Why the interrogation?"

"I'm sorry. I didn't mean to make you angry."

He softened. "That's all right. I'm also sorry, for snapping at you."

Leaving his wife to her morning chores, he went into the living room, where he selected a thick volume and began to learn. Presently, one by one, his children departed for their schools and play groups, and his wife for her job. Only then did he leave his desk.

He went directly to a large, cluttered box that stood in a corner of the service porch off the kitchen. A few minutes' rooting yielded a metal file, a skeleton key and a set of screwdrivers in their special plastic case. He stored these items in the bag he would take with him tonight, on his visit to the corner of Aliyah and Selma Streets in Tel Aviv.

A profound silence fell over Zevulun's apartment after his friends had left. In his imagination, he followed each of them home. What were they thinking about him right now? What kind of opinion did they have of him after his outburst? He cringed inwardly. Why could he never manage to control himself?

He lit a cigarette and perched restlessly in an armchair at one end of the living room. It was some time before he realized that his whole body was trembling. Was it with rage — or shame? Why had he turned on his friends in that way? What, after all, had they done to him? Their only desire was to help! While he was certainly not obligated to agree to their demands, he might have declined politely. Why all the anger, and the shouting?

Was it possible that, deep down, he suspected that they were right? Had the shouting been Zevulun's desperate attempt to silence the voices that were only echoing the message of his own heart?

He did not know. Now that his fury was spent, shame crept in to take its place. Shame for the way he had treated two Jews, Torah scholars and good friends — especially Yitzchak Abramson. Every time they met, Zevulun was keenly aware of the widening spiritual gap between them. Both those men were far above him. And now, in a single moment, he had wounded them without cause.

Zevulun pulled himself out of the armchair. It was nearly 2 a.m. Yitzchak should be home in Petach Tikvah by this time. Almost of its own volition, his hand reached for the phone and dialed the Abramsons' number. He wanted to apologize to his friend before he went to bed.

At the first ring, however, he lost his nerve. Cowardly, he hung up.

Zevulun had hardly turned away from the phone when it suddenly shrilled. The sound seemed to fill every corner of the sleeping apartment. He started up in a kind of terror. Who could be calling him at this hour?

Elazar had told him about Yossi's two late-night calls to Yaakov Frankel in Jerusalem. Could — could this, too, be Yossi? He pounced on the phone. Then, remembering how he had babbled into the phone the other night, thinking he was talking to his runaway son — only to have the caller turn out to be his other son, Elazar — Zevulun adjured himself to go slowly. Cautiously, he said, "Hello? Who is this, please?" The words emerged jerkily, as his heart thumped in nervous anticipation of hearing Yossi's voice.

"Zevulun, it's me — Yitzchak," he heard instead. "Did you try to call me two minutes ago?"

Disappointment slashed through him, leaving Zevulun as deflated as a balloon. "Yes," he answered dully. "It was me."

"I knew it."

"How?"

"I know *you*, Zevulun. After we left your place, I'm sure you were angry at yourself for exploding. You wanted to reach me at once, tonight, to soften what had happened between us." A pause. "Am I wrong, Zevulun?"

Zevulun ground his teeth in chagrin, even as he was forced to admire his friend's sagacity. He rose masterfully to the occasion: "No, you're absolutely right! Congratulations, Yitzchak. I mean that."

Yitzchak ignored the implicit compliment. "Now, admit it, Zevulun: The moment you acknowledged the truth and confessed that it was you who called me just now, didn't you feel better than if you'd denied calling, and added, 'And I think I was 100 percent justified in yelling at you when you attacked me!'?"

Zevulun laughed. "Touché, Yitzchak. I really do regret ending the evening so unpleasantly... despite the fact that I still resist your efforts to force me to do things."

"And you're happy to make amends. Do you see the beauty, the power, of genuine *teshuvah*? It gives a person real contentment."

"What's this — a *mussar schmuess* from the '*mashgiach*' in the middle of the night?"

"*Mussar* comes when it has a chance of being heard," Yitzchak answered quietly. "And I think that, right now, your heart is open and listening. Don't try to put me off with this talk of '*mussar*' and '*mashgiach*.' We're two friends, trying together to clarify an important subject."

Stifling an enormous yawn, Zevulun asked, "So what's your conclusion?"

"My conclusion is that there's a chance now that you'll agree to go see the *rosh yeshivah*. Zevulun, stop fighting us and take our advice! Believe me, you'll feel better for it. It's what your soul really wants. Nothing but your pride stands in the way. But if taking our advice will make you feel as good as this phone call has, then you owe it to yourself!"

A silence fell between them. Zevulun could sense the battle raging inside him. Yitzchak's quiet but authoritative voice returned: "Well, what's your decision, Zevulun?"

He had no strength left to fight.

"I'll go up to Yerushalayim tomorrow," he whispered.

❧

Elazar woke up late the next morning. *Baruch Hashem,* he felt better than he had the previous day. His strength was beginning to return. If not for the occasional sharp pain in his head, he might have forgotten that the attack had even occurred.

His father had already left the apartment. Elazar had meant to ask him about all the shouting he had heard emanating from the living room the previous night. The noise had wakened him, but he had quickly fallen back asleep.

His mother, he realized, was not home either. He donned his *tefillin, davened* and then wandered into the kitchen for some breakfast. On the table he found a note, in his mother's handwriting:

> *Dear Elazar,*
>
> *Take whatever you want to eat. I've gone up to Jerusalem with Abba. This is an unexpected trip and we didn't want to wake you.*
>
> *Love and kisses,*
>
> *Ima*

Elazar read through the note twice. What was this all about? Where had his parents gone?

He did not have much time to speculate before the ringing of the phone cut into his thoughts.

"Hello — Yossi? It's Ilan!"

Elazar's suspicions sprang instantly to life. "This is not Yossi! It's Elazar!"

"Oops, sorry. Your voices are similar, you know that?"

Elazar regarded Ilan's "slip" with skepticism. The mention of Yossi's name, he was convinced, had been intentional. Had Ilan been in touch with his brother recently?

Elazar decided to feign ignorance. "Never mind. You're not the first person who's confused the two of us on the phone. So what's new with you, Ilan?"

"Elazar!"

"Yes?"

"We have to meet — urgently."

"I know. We've already agreed on that point."

"So, when?"

"You tell me."

"Today?"

"All right. But *not* by the Central Post Office. Once was enough!"

Ilan chuckled. "This time I'll pick you up at home. We'll drive some-place quiet."

Once again, alarm bells rang in Elazar's mind. "Okay, but some place where there are people around."

Ilan asked, "Are you afraid of me?"

"I don't know. Maybe."

"Okay. We'll go to Gan Yaakov, near the Bimah Theater. All right?"

"Fine. What time?"

"This afternoon at 5. Is that good for you?"

"Yes."

"I'll honk the horn three times and you'll come down."

"Okay."

"And, Elazar, don't tell your father. He has something against me."

"All right."

Elazar had scarcely hung up when the phone rang again. This time, it was Yaakov.

"Good morning, Elazar. How are you feeling today?"

"A lot better, *baruch Hashem*. What's new?"

"*Baruch Hashem* — many things. I've spoken with someone who saw Yossi!"

Elazar gripped the receiver tightly. "Really? Unbelievable!"

"Right now it's 99 percent certain. Tonight I hope to find out for sure."

"Can you give me any details?"

"Not right now. Not over the phone. I'll be in Tel Aviv this afternoon. We have to meet."

Elazar thought of the plans he had made with Ilan. "Does it have to be today?"

"Yes, today!"

"But I've arranged to meet Ilan."

"Cancel it!"

"I can't. I don't know where to reach him."

"I don't care. I want you to meet me on the corner of Aliyah and Selma, at the apartment of a family named Koselovitch. Five o'clock. Be there!"

Elazar found himself at a loss for words. What to do about Ilan?

Then, just before Yaakov hung up, Elazar heard him utter the heart-stopping words: "Look, Elazar. There's a chance we could see Yossi tonight!"

33

At precisely 5 o'clock, Yaakov Frankel rang the bell at the Koselovitch apartment.

The door opened. Mordechai Koselovitch, dressed in the garb of a Gerrer *chassid*, welcomed him with obvious pleasure. It seemed to Yaakov that Koselovitch was enjoying this adventure.

"Come in, come in please."

Yaakov entered a small living room and, at his host's bidding, found a seat on the sofa. Koselovitch pulled up a chair and sat facing him. "So how can I help you?"

Yaakov plunged right in. "As I told you over the phone, we're talking about a yeshivah boy who has apparently run away to join that cult across the street."

"How did such a thing happen?"

Yaakov shrugged. "Unfortunately, it happened."

"All right. The important thing now is, how can I help?"

"You told me that you see them every evening as they pass this building on their way to the house. I want to follow them."

"And then what?"

"I'll decide that then. Now, what time do they usually pass by here?"

Koselovitch glanced at his watch. It was nearly 5:30. "Let's say, between half an hour to an hour from now."

Yaakov was worried by Elazar's nonappearance. He had promised to be punctual. Had he changed his mind and kept his appointment with Ilan instead? Turning to Koselovitch, he asked, "Can I make a phone call?"

"Certainly." Koselovitch rose. "Will you have something to drink?"

"No, thank you. I'm a little on edge right now…"

He dialed. There was no answer at the Kimmerman place. Yaakov hung up and turned away, frowning. Where was Elazar?

He had his answer at 6 o'clock, when a rapid knock at the door preceded Elazar's breathless entrance. Yaakov demanded, "Where were you? Did you go meet him anyway?"

Shamefaced, Elazar nodded. "I couldn't get out of it."

"All right. You're still in time. Our little gang hasn't passed yet."

Elazar followed Yaakov into the living room, where he was introduced to Koselovitch, the latter having tactfully withdrawn for a few minutes. Elazar continued in an undertone, "Luckily, it was a short meeting. He had somewhere else to go afterwards."

"Well, did anything concrete emerge?"

"Nothing special. He denies all connection to any kind of cult. He also denies having ever met Yossi in Yerushalayim."

"Do you believe him?"

"What can I say? Not especially. Something in his manner makes me doubt his honesty in all this business. It's just a feeling I have…."

Yaakov considered this. "What I don't understand is why he wanted to meet with you at all."

"I'm just as much in the dark as you are. I had a feeling he wanted to tell me something, but changed his mind at the last minute."

"And you hinted that you might be interested in joining the cult?"

"How could I, when he denied all knowledge of the cult?"

"So, what did you get out of the meeting?"

Elazar sighed. "So far — not a thing."

Yaakov noticed that the younger man seemed troubled. Gently, he asked, "What are you thinking about, Elazar?"

Elazar groped for words. "I'm not really sure. It's just this feeling I have — a sense that Ilan wanted to tell me something but didn't have the courage…"

He was interrupted by a shout from the balcony. It was Mordechai Koselovitch. "Come out here, quickly! The crazies are coming!"

Yaakov and Elazar dashed out to the balcony. Elazar's heart thudded agonizingly. The mere possibility that he might soon set eyes on his lost brother — faint as that possibility was — made him weak in the knees. Yaakov made a sudden dash back into the living room for a pair of binoculars he had purchased upon his arrival at Tel Aviv's central bus station. He sped back, like an arrow from its bow to the balcony.

"Do you see them?" Koselovitch pointed at the spot where Emek Yizrael Street intersected Aliyah Street.

Tensely, Elazar and Yaakov followed the procession. It was a small group, marching in orderly fashion on the sidewalk in the direction of Selma Street, and comprising no more than 20 or 30 people. Their garb was typical Israeli, nothing outlandish or noteworthy. The cult members walked hand in hand, chanting. Each wrist, Elazar noted, sported a thick silver bracelet.

"That's probably the symbol of the Third Magical Eye," he surmised. From the distance it was impossible to tell for sure.

As the group came closer, it became possible to see their faces clearly from the vantage point on the balcony. Yossi was not among them. Koselovitch, watching at their side, whispered, "The religious boy, the yeshivah student, isn't here today."

Without answering, Yaakov lifted the binoculars to his eyes. In silence he scrutinized each face, as though trying to imprint it on his memory. Suddenly, Elazar grabbed his sleeve. "That's him! That's him!"

"Who?"

"Ilan!"

Yaakov leaned forward. "Which one is he?"

"That one, walking on the left side. He's wearing a brown vest. He's a little taller than the rest. I don't believe it! What a liar!"

"And this means," Yaakov said slowly, "that your suspicion that he's the guilty party has some basis now."

Elazar gripped Yaakov's arm. "Hey, look who's walking next to Ilan! It's the Canadian fellow — the one who was with him when I went to my father's office. Unbelievable!"

The group continued down the block, chanting softly as they went. From Koselovitch's balcony, it was impossible to distinguish the words above the steady hum of traffic below. They reached the narrow street where Elazar had followed the short, braceleted stranger two days before. That man was nowhere in sight today.

In short order, the group disappeared behind the iron gate.

Meanwhile, night had fallen on Aliyah Street. The street lamps cast their yellow light on the pavement and the roofs of cars. Yaakov asked his host not to turn on the living room lights, as he planned to stand vigil over the house opposite for some time longer.

As he watched, lights went on in the windows of that house. The binoculars helped him a great deal now. At first, the activity he saw seemed perfectly normal; the group appeared to be preparing to have a meal. Various cult members passed to and fro, carrying bowls, platters and silverware. Time passed. Yaakov watched the progress of the meal. It was not until about an hour after his vigil had begun that he noted the first sign of something unusual. The cult members stood up and began dancing around the table at which they had just dined.

Involuntarily, Yaakov pressed the binoculars closer to his eyes. "It's starting," he thought.

The dance was extremely odd. First a few shuffling steps, then a sudden leap into the air. Wild cries reached Yaakov through the house's open windows though, for all he strained, Yaakov could see no reason for such a tumult. No one, as far as he could discern, was being murdered. A few minutes later, everyone dropped to their knees and raised their hands heavenward. Then they stretched out on the floor and lay perfectly still.

"What do you think?" he murmured to Elazar, beside him. "What are those lunatics doing?"

"I'm no expert on lunatics. But it hurts to know that Yossi's made friends with such a group of madmen. Look at the way they're lying on the floor!"

"You don't know the half of it, Elazar. With these binoculars, I see them sticking out their tongues at each other!"

Another hour passed in this way. Several times their host called them in to drink and to partake of a tray of cakes he had placed on the table. "Make a *berachah* in my home," he begged. But each time, the two watchers put him off with the same words. "Just another few minutes, Reb Mordechai."

The minutes ran into hours. The cult performed various strange rituals, movements and dramatizations that had Yaakov fighting back nausea. Then, abruptly, the lights were doused. Within minutes, the group was outside again, marching up the street. This time there was no chanting. Various members chatted quietly as they walked toward the top of Aliyah Street, where the majority disappeared.

Only then did Yaakov and Elazar leave their post on the balcony.

Their host came forward to greet them, wearing a broad smile. "*Nu*, did you enjoy the show? And did you find your little bird?"

"No," Yaakov answered heavily. "No, we didn't find him. But at least now I know what we're up against."

Elazar was silent. His disappointment was keen, both because of Ilan's perfidy and because he felt no closer to the mystery's solution now than he had been at the start of the evening.

It was 9 o'clock. Elazar sat at the dining room table with the other two men, listening to them talk. His injured head ached faintly, and he still felt the need for more rest than usual. Presently he stood up and offered a hand, in turn, to his host and to Yaakov Frankel. "Good night. I'm going home."

Yaakov stopped in midsentence. He stared up in surprise. "Elazar, you're not going home. We have work to do tonight."

Now it was Elazar's turn to look surprised. "What kind of work?"

"There!" Yaakov pointed past the balcony. "We have to pay a visit to that house."

"*What?* You want us to enter that place? I'm scared!"

"So am I! But we have no choice. We have to find out if your brother is hidden in there. Or doesn't that interest you?"

"Of course it does. But what do you think we'll find in there?"

Yaakov shrugged. "I haven't a clue. But we have to go in. You come along with me, and Hashem will protect us both."

They parted warmly from their host, left his apartment and crossed the dark street in silence. Turning, Yaakov saw Koselovitch standing on his balcony, watching them. They passed into the narrow side street, Yaakov cautious but eager, Elazar hanging back slightly with every step. He was angry at himself for letting Yaakov drag him along against his wishes. He was afraid — really afraid — of this move. It would probably prove useless anyway. What were they doing?

"Want to change your mind?" Elazar whispered in a last, desperate attempt to turn Yaakov away from his course. They were standing in front of the rusted iron gate that held such unpleasant memories for him.

Yaakov did not deign to reply. He placed a hand on the gate and, very slowly, began to push it open.

When it stood open enough to let a man through, he entered, secure in the knowledge that no one was there. He had seen the entire group leave. The house was dark, except for the reflected light from the street lamps.

Yaakov strode forward confidently, careful not to make a sound. Elazar followed as though being towed by an invisible rope. "Where does he get his crazy confidence from?" he wondered as he fought off his own rising panic. Seconds later, they reached the green house's front door.

Yaakov pushed the door open and gestured for Elazar to follow. Closing it gently behind him, he drew a flashlight from his pocket. He played the light around the large room, shining it in turn on the walls, the ceiling, the floor. The place was empty. At one end stood a staircase leading up to the second story — where all the activity that they had observed from Koselovitch's balcony had taken place.

Yaakov did not hesitate. With unfaltering steps he made his way up the stairs. Elazar followed close behind, teeth chattering so rapidly he was sure Yaakov could hear. Yaakov's courage frightened him.

The flashlight's pale beam illuminated their way. There were a number of rooms on the second floor. None of the doors were locked. Yaakov and Elazar entered what appeared to be an office. First they spied a large metal file cabinet in the corner. Pulling open its drawers, they started to search through its contents when they noticed a large desk standing in the center of the room, laden with a variety of documents. Quickly, the two went to the desk and began sorting through the papers.

They had not been at their task very long when, all at once, they froze. Footsteps were climbing the stairs at a rapid pace. Doors opened and then shut. With one accord, Yaakov and Elazar dove behind the desk, their thudding hearts making more noise than the footsteps in the hall.

The office door was flung open, and a light went on.

34

Yaakov and Elazar lay flat on the floor behind the large desk. Fortunately, its proportions were generous enough to conceal them both. They lay motionless, breathing shallowly as they waited to see what would happen next. Elazar seethed with anger — at Yaakov ("What kind of crazy adventure has he dragged me into?") — and at himself, for lacking the spine to resist. Had it been possible, he would have stood up then and there and fled that dangerous house as fast as he could. But it was not possible. He lay still.

Yaakov's proximity was his only comfort. Elazar tugged at the older man's sleeve. Yaakov twisted around to look at him, his expression asking, "What is it? What do you want?"

"What do we do now?" Elazar whispered into his ear. He was dumbfounded by the total lack of fear he saw in Yaakov's face. What was the man made of?

"At the moment, nothing!" Yaakov whispered back. "Don't worry, Hashem will help us, you'll see. And now — quiet."

Though the words had been so low as to be nearly inaudible, their authority rang in Elazar's ears. Both men closed their eyes and concentrated all their attention on sharpening their hearing.

The man who had entered the room stood in the doorway for a long moment, eyes darting around the room as he tried to pinpoint the source of the noise he thought he had heard as he switched on the light. Apart from the desk, a metal file cabinet stood in one corner. For some reason, its drawers hung open. He remembered that they had been locked when he had last left the room. What did it mean?

At the other end of the room, not far from the desk, a heavy curtain concealed a door that led to the cult's most sacred place. Had someone penetrated that room?

The longer he stood there, the more he became convinced that something was not right. Softly, he called out, "Who's there?"

No answer.

Cautiously, he advanced a few steps and then stopped. "Is someone in the room? Hello!"

The walls threw back the echo of his words. Yaakov and Elazar huddled behind the desk, trying not to breathe, and praying that the man would leave.

He did not leave. Step by step, he moved forward — in their direction. He stopped again. Started, and then stopped. Every few minutes he called out, "Who's there?" But these calls, like the earlier ones, went unanswered.

Elazar thought he would explode with tension. His legs shook as he fought to keep them from running, running, away from this accursed place. Yaakov, sensing his young friend's terror, patted his arm and placed a warning forefinger over his lips. Elazar was not to say a word or move a muscle without his, Yaakov's, instructions. Inwardly, Elazar wept.

The man was very close to them now. Only a few short steps separated him from the desk behind which they lay hidden. They could hear their anonymous enemy's labored breaths. Who was he?

At that moment, Elazar saw his friend's eyes light up, as though he had come to a decision. Yaakov whispered, *"Now!"*

Before Elazar could fully grasp what was happening, he saw Yaakov — to his shock — shoot up from his hiding place and slam into the stranger's body. The two crashed onto the floor, with Yaakov firmly on top.

"Elazar, come quickly!" Yaakov gasped.

Elazar sprang to life.

"Grab both his hands and pull them behind him!" Yaakov ordered, pinning the other man down with the weight of his own body. Elazar did as he was told. Stooping, he seized the man's hands and yanked. Only then did he dare look into his face. The cult member appeared stupefied at the suddenness of the attack.

Elazar was no less stupefied. The man was the squat, swarthy stranger who had attacked him the other day at the entrance to this very house!

Yaakov stood up. The short man saw his chance. With a mighty heave, he twisted free of Elazar's grip and made a break for the open door. But Yaakov and Elazar were too quick for him. Flanking him on either side, they caught him and dragged him back to a chair that stood in the center of the room, close by the desk. With Elazar's hands planted firmly on his shoulders from behind and Yaakov holding on in front, the man — who was considerably older than either of them — was unable to rise.

"What are you doing here? What are you looking for?" he screamed, struggling futilely against their iron hold. He kicked out with his feet and squirmed his shoulders — to no avail. His captors were too strong for him.

Yaakov addressed him quietly, though with the authority of the victor. "We also have a few questions, sir. For instance, I'd like to know why you attacked my young friend here. What did he do to you? You nearly killed him! The doctors say that only a miracle prevented his brain from being damaged by the blow." He glared at the man. "Well? Do you have an answer for me?"

The cult member turned to look into Elazar's face, as though seeing him for the first time. "I don't even recognize him! I didn't hit anyone!"

A cynical smile touched Yaakov's lips. "Okay. Fine. You didn't hit him. I want to know if someone ordered you to prepare a trap for him. You had instructions to be near the Central Post Office at the time when he" — Yaakov pointed at Elazar — "was supposed to be meeting another cult member there. True?"

The man breathed hard, eyes darting from Yaakov to Elazar and back again. Elazar noted a strange fact: The man's eyes appeared completely unafraid.

"Excuse me, honored and completely uninvited guests. I have no idea what you're talking about."

"Then we'll tell you."

"I'm not interested in hearing."

"But *we're* interested in telling! We need a few answers."

The man flared into sudden anger. "Is that why you broke into this house like a couple of thieves?"

"Not exactly. But when there are important things to find out, you can't always be polite. We're only using the opportunity you've given us, by showing up here, to ask you a few important questions."

"Yes, but what are you looking for? Who are you?"

"If you answer our questions, you'll know what we're looking for."

The cult member tried once again to get up. Firmly, Yaakov pressed him back down. "I'm sorry, mister, not this time. *Why did you attack my friend?*"

"He tried to get into the house without permission," the man muttered sullenly. "I would've hit you, too, if you had come sniffing around our House of Eternal Peace."

"Ah, a pretty name. A house of eternal peace — where the unwary visitor is greeted with a bang on the head."

The man refused to react to his taunts. Yaakov tried another tack: "You know Ilan."

The other closed his eyes for a moment. "No."

"Interesting. Just a few hours ago, I saw him enter this house, together with a large group of your believers."

"I tell you again, I know no one named Ilan."

Yaakov breathed deeply. "I see. But I'd still like to know whether it was

Ilan who sent you to wait for my friend by the post office, in order to knock him down?"

Suddenly, the man commenced shouting again. "You're falsely accusing me — and in my own home! I'm calling the police!"

Yaakov and Elazar laughed. "That would be really interesting," Yaakov said. "You see, we've already called them. My friend here has lodged a formal complaint against this house — and against you."

He watched closely, but could see no sign of agitation in the man's face. Yaakov asked, "Do you want the police to come here now?"

The man did not respond.

Despite his confident bearing, Yaakov was growing more tense by the second. He wanted to end this interview, and the visit to this house, as quickly as possible. If any other cult members should show up at this juncture, it would be hard going for Elazar and him. He moved a little closer.

"All right, we'll put Ilan aside for now. Do you know Yossi? Yossi Kimmerman? A yeshivah boy, aged 16 or 17. And don't try to deny that he visited this place a week ago, and a week before that."

He winked at Elazar over the man's head. Elazar, taking the hint, applied additional pressure to the man's shoulders until their prisoner grunted with pain. Still, he remained silent.

It seemed to Yaakov that the man was hesitating, trying to make up his mind whether to say anything. They were, he was convinced, on the brink of learning important information about Yossi. He grabbed the man by the chin. *"Do you know him?"*

"Leave me alone! You're hurting me!"

"Do you know him?"

The cult member evaded the question. "Just you wait. Some of the others are on their way here now. Wait till you see what's going to happen to you. You've just made the mistake of your lives!"

Though Yaakov pretended to be unconcerned, his heart was filled with apprehension about just such a development. Elazar said urgently, "Reb Yaakov, let's get out of here before it's too late!"

Yaakov's smoldering glare put an end to Elazar's pleading. He hissed,

"Elazar, do you ever want to see your brother again?"

He whirled on the cult member again, demanding menacingly, "Answer me quickly, or you won't be seeing your friends again! Understand?" He punctuated the threat with a ringing slap. Aside, to Elazar, he murmured unhappily, "What choice is there? When it comes to *pidyon shevuyim*, it's sometimes necessary to do ugly things."

The man's head jerked back with the force of the slap. For the first time, he betrayed a flicker of fear.

"Tell me now — where is Yossi? Where have you hidden him, you animals? Is he still in this country? Is he abroad? *Talk!*"

Elazar, infected by Yaakov's warlike spirit, began squeezing the man's neck. He was beginning to believe that this was their golden opportunity to find out what had happened to his brother. From the swarthy stranger's reactions, he appeared to know something. Elazar echoed fiercely, "Talk, I said! Talk!"

The man felt the pressure of the young man's fingers, and heard the furious command. Still, he said not a word ...

35

Zevulun drove up the Tel Aviv-Jerusalem highway without a word. He was not pleased that his wife, in a sudden decision, had elected to accompany him on this visit to his *rosh yeshivah*. But he said nothing about the way he was feeling. There were long years of tension between Tzipporah and himself, centering on Yossi's upbringing. That tension had escalated dramatically with the tragic events of this week. Zevulun had no desire to heap coals on the flames.

What, he wondered as he navigated among the other cars speeding to Jerusalem, was she planning to do when they met the *rosh yeshivah*? Would she point an accusing finger at him, her own husband? Would she give the *rosh yeshivah* all sorts of unsavory details about his behavior toward Yossi? He fervently hoped not — the humiliation would be awful — but there was no telling what a distressed mother might say.

He stole a quick glance over at Tzipporah. She sat quite still in the passenger seat, head slightly bowed. Not once did she look at him. She was the picture of a woman wrapped up in her own thoughts, and it was not hard to guess what those thoughts were.

They passed Sha'ar Hagai. On the incline, Zevulun let out the clutch and moved into higher gear. They would reach the city limits in about 20 minutes. And then… No! He could not enter the *rosh yeshivah's* presence without first learning what Tzipporah had in mind. Fear and suspense rose up inside him, powerful as the engine bearing them along the highway.

"Tzipporah?"

She turned to face her husband. "What?"

"You know, we still haven't talked about all this."

Tzipporah did not respond. After a moment, Zevulun said with forced heartiness, "Did you say something?"

"No. I didn't say anything."

Zevulun gripped the steering wheel more firmly and neatly overtook a white Peugeot. "Really? Well, why not?" He tried to speak casually, but his nervousness was apparent in the stiffness of his voice.

Tzipporah turned away from her husband. Her eyes remained glued to the tarmac unrolling in front of them as, in a low voice, she said, "Because I think we've already said all there is to say on the subject."

"When? When have we even talked about it?"

"Everything's been said — not in words, but in actions." After a moment, she added more forcefully, "Mainly, in *your* actions!"

Zevulun bit his lip. He sought in vain for something to say. The conversation he'd begun had run into a dead end. As his Mitsubishi passed Shoresh and Beit Meir on the road leading past Telz Stone and Abu Ghosh, he groped for a different way to restart it. Unlike the other drivers, Zevulun clung to the far right side of the highway and reduced his speed. Tzipporah did turn then, to stare at him in surprise.

Zevulun slowed down even more, and then pulled over onto the shoulder of the road.

Yaakov and Elazar continued to hold down the swarthy cult member firmly in his chair, but they were frankly at a loss. Violent force might succeed in loosening the man's vocal chords, but they were *bnei Torah*, not street thugs! Even the one slap he had delivered had been traumatic for Yaakov. If only it had secured the information they so desperately needed... But the man refused to talk.

What next?

Yaakov decided to try appealing to the fellow's conscience.

"Listen," he said softly. "We're talking about my friend's younger brother. Do you know what his parents are going through right now? His father? His mother? Their home is destroyed! The parents are quarreling over the terrible thing that has happened to their son. They're on the verge of a nervous breakdown. They're not eating or sleeping."

The man struggled to rise again, but the hands holding him down were too strong for him. Contemptuously, he spat, "What does any of that have to do with me? Leave me alone! You'll regret this!"

"It has to do with you, because you know where Yossi Kimmerman is. I can see it in your eyes."

The man just glared.

"You're a Jew, aren't you? Where is your compassion? Tell us where the boy is! We won't tell a soul that you told us, if you're so afraid of your friends."

For the first time, he caught signs of hesitation in their prisoner's expression. Holding their breath, eyes riveted to the man's face, he and Elazar waited in mounting suspense.

Suddenly, he spoke. "Okay. All right. I honestly don't know where he is. It's a secret — a secret even from the people who come to this house. Only a few members know all of the cult's secrets. But I'm willing to look through the files. Maybe I'll find the information there. Let me get up."

Yaakov and Elazar exchanged a quick glance. With one accord, they released their grip on the man but remained near, one on either side. The cult member stood up, flexed his arms and walked over to the metal file cabinet. Elazar and Yaakov remained close to his side every step of the way.

The man clearly knew what he was looking for. He opened the top drawer and pulled out a green cardboard folder. This he took over to the desk, where he opened it. Yaakov and Elazar saw a pile of pale pink pages, covered with closely written lists.

"Maybe you can stand back and give me a little room," the man complained. "You're blocking the light."

Yaakov and Elazar moved slightly back. That was the chance the man had been waiting for. With diabolical speed he shot up, folder in hand, and burst through the space between his two captors, making for the door.

Yaakov was the first to gather his wits. In a second, he was racing madly after their escaped prisoner. On his way he pushed over several chairs; one of which broke as it fell. He caught up with the man near the door. A bitter struggle ensued. As Yaakov grasped his shoulders, the cult member delivered a solid punch to Yaakov's head. Yaakov's hat flew off and went skittering away. With a violent twist, the man managed to escape Yaakov's hold. He yanked open the door and pounded down the stairs. As he ran, the folder slipped from his fingers.

The man turned back to pick it up. He was too late. Yaakov, just behind, let loose with a powerful kick to the chest. The man took the rest of the stairs in an awkward slide, landing painfully on his back. Yaakov seized the green folder and ran down the stairs, Elazar at his heels.

The man, groaning on the bottom step, made a grab for Yaakov's foot as he passed. Yaakov lost his balance and swayed alarmingly. This time, it was Elazar who saved him. He stamped his foot forcefully down on the man's fingers. The cult member let out a shriek and released Yaakov's ankle. In seconds, the two yeshivah men were outside the house, running for their lives.

They dashed through the yard toward the iron gate. Yaakov fumbled at the latch, flung it open — and collided solidly with someone coming in.

Elazar rubbed his eyes in astonishment. Even in the dark, he could make out the face.

"Ilan! What are you doing here?"

Zevulun cut the motor and said quietly, "Look, Tzipporah. Not only hasn't everything been said between us about Yossi — *nothing's* been said yet. We've never talked calmly and rationally on that subject.

"You lashed out at me just now, telling me that I've said everything with my actions, even if not in so many words. Whatever faults I may have, I'm not stupid. I understood very well what you were hinting at."

Tzipporah said nothing. She twisted a handkerchief round and round in her fingers.

Zevulun continued: "I'm well aware of your complaints against me regarding Yossi. Come, let's admit that we've never talked it over the way we should have. We only fought and argued. Do you see the difference?"

Slowly, Tzipporah nodded. Yes, she did see the difference. Zevulun thought he detected the glimmer of tears at the corners of her eyes. Another dead end. Where tears step in, reason flees... He felt a flash of anger at the thought. Tears always forced him to give in, even when he had all the force of logic in the world at his back. *It's just not going to happen today*, he thought, igniting the engine.

He was in the act of twisting around to see if the road was clear before pulling into traffic, when he heard his wife's voice.

"*Nu*, why don't you go on talking?"

He took his foot off the gas pedal. A new calm descended on him. He turned to her and asked, "I thought you weren't interested in talking to me."

"I'm very interested."

Zevulun was conscious of an enormous sense of relief. Switching off the motor again, he rested his head on the steering wheel for a moment's thought. Then, without lifting his head, he began:

"Do you think this tragedy hasn't affected me? Do you honestly believe I don't think about it constantly? You seem to think that I just don't care, that I haven't been reviewing all my past behavior with Yossi! Do you think my heart is made of stone?

"What I can't stand is the way everyone's been judging me, accusing me, without ever having stood in my shoes. Almost before they hear what I have to say, they call me guilty. What do they know about what happened? On what authority do they come telling me their opinions? Did they live in our home all these years, did they see what was happening with Yossi?" He paused to catch his breath and to direct a challenging stare at his wife. "Don't you think that, on this point at least, I'm right?"

Tentatively, she nodded again.

"And now, apart from that, I feel that I have a problem. I'll tell you why. In many homes, parents hit their children and punish them no less than I have, and maybe even more. I've seen it with my own eyes more than once. But what happened to me hasn't happened to them. I'm talking about Yossi's wild behavior, his chutzpah and, finally, the last terrible thing he did: running away from home just to hurt you and me. I keep torturing myself. Why did this happen especially to me? Why do I see other sons loving their fathers anyway, while Yossi says that he… that he…hates me?"

He fell silent. He had not really intended to say what he just had. He had wanted to draw Tzipporah into conversation, to hear what she thought. Now, not knowing how to proceed, he stopped talking. There was also the very real danger that his voice would break, and it was absolutely out of the question for his wife to hear that… Into the turmoil of his thoughts came his wife's voice:

"And does it bother you, that he said he hates you?"

A long hesitation ended with a single, faltering word. "Yes."

"But you always told me that you don't even care about him!"

This time, the hesitation was shorter. "Apparently, that wasn't true."

Tentatively, she asked, "And now, this minute, do you care about him?"

Zevulun took a long, deep breath. His chest was on fire and his back ached. It was so hard to verbalize what needed to be said.

At last, he whispered, "Yes, very much. Very, very much…"

Tzipporah buried her face in her hands and began crying softly, bitterly. After a moment, Zevulun started the car and pulled back onto the highway to Jerusalem.

36

Ilan reeled with shock. Though the night was dark, he recognized Elazar's voice. For his part, Elazar was equally thunderstruck. Here was the final proof that his suspicion of Ilan had been justified: Ilan, standing at the entrance to this accursed cult house — the cult that had stolen his brother from him. The old, dormant anger stirred and awoke in him. He grabbed Ilan's shirt and shouted, "I've got you! Now I know everything!"

Ilan struggled to free himself. With both hands he pushed at Elazar, but Elazar held fast to his shirtfront. There was a sound of ripping fabric. Breathing hard, Ilan gasped, "You don't understand, you stupid fool! Let me go, do you hear?"

Elazar ignored him. "You visited Yossi at his yeshivah, didn't you? You dragged him into your senseless cult! And you think *I'm* stupid?"

"Very stupid, Elazar. I didn't visit your brother in his yeshivah and I didn't drag him into a cult, and —"

"Liar! Dirty liar!"

Yaakov stood by, listening to these interchanges without interfering. Had Elazar required his help, he would have charged in. There was no need for that yet. Elazar was still in control of the situation. It was good for him to exert himself on behalf of his missing brother. But his shouting could very well attract undue attention from neighbors and passersby. The man they had left lying inside, at the foot of the stairs, might rouse himself at any minute to renewed activity. It was even possible that the police might turn up.

"Lower your voice, Elazar," he said urgently. "Are you looking for trouble?"

"He's making me — so angry," Elazar gasped, as he continued to grapple with Ilan. He raised his voice again: "Ilan, are you trying to tell me that you're not a member of this cult? I saw you go into that house just an hour ago!"

"*Me?* Into that house?"

"Don't lie, and don't play games with me! Where is Yossi?"

"Elazar, are you crazy? When I asked to meet with you — "

"Yes, you had a good reason for seeing me. I had hinted over the phone that I was interested in joining the cult, and you wanted to see how serious I was! You won't be working for us anymore, you can be sure of that. I'm going to speak to my father. He's going to know exactly who and what you are!"

"And that will be a complete lie! You're not letting me speak!"

"What else do I need to hear from you? The facts speak for themselves. Now, where is Yossi? Quickly!"

Ilan lunged. Elazar toppled over, with Ilan still in his grip. The two rolled on the ground, grunting with pain. Neither was about to let go.

"I — don't know — where Yossi is! Get it?"

"Where is he? Tell me — right now! Or else I'll...."

"You'll — what? What can you — do to me — big shot? Trying to — scare me? Believe me, I want — to know where — Yossi is too. This is all — because we didn't — talk."

"If you have — something to say — then say it!"

"With your friend listening?"

"Yes! He knows everything!"

Shakily, the two rose to their feet, panting as if they had just finished running a marathon. Even in the dark, the gleam of furious hatred was discernible in Elazar's eyes. It was the betrayal, especially, that enraged him. His father had taken Ilan into his business and done so much for him, and look at the horrendous way Ilan had repaid him! For, despite the vigorous denials, Elazar remained convinced that Ilan was the one behind the tragedy.

Ilan took a step closer. "I would tell you everything now...."

"About Yossi?"

"Would you stop babbling? Don't get me too angry! I told you, I don't know anything about Yossi."

"I don't believe you!"

Ilan shrugged. "That's your problem, Elazar."

"So what new stories are you getting ready to tell me? Talk already!"

"Now? Are you kidding? I'm so worked up, I can hardly get a word out!" Ilan moved away. Elazar watched, certain that the other was planning to flee. But he did not follow. He had no strength left. Besides, he was pessimistic about the chances of getting any significant information out of Ilan tonight. He heard Ilan say, as he continued moving away, "I repeat: It's a pity we didn't talk. You would have understood a lot of things that you aren't capable of understanding at this point. You also would not have spoken to me the way you did."

Ilan paused, then threw back over his shoulder, "In fact, you might even have respected me."

A moment later, he had vanished into the shadows of Aliyah Street.

Elazar turned to find Yaakov at his side. "Did you see that creep?"

Yaakov answer quietly, "I saw. But he's not a creep."

"Are you trying to tell me that you *believe* that guy?!"

Yaakov hesitated. "I'm not sure I don't."

"Are you prepared to explain that?" Elazar was clearly controlling himself with difficulty.

"I listened to him carefully. I think he's telling the truth when he says he doesn't know where Yossi is."

"And why do you think that, O great detective?"

"Don't be angry at me, Elazar. It's just a feeling I have."

Elazar harbored a deep respect for Reb Yaakov, and had no desire to deepen the rift between them with the question that was on his mind. Still, it sprang irresistibly to his lips: "And you also think he didn't persuade Yossi to join this insane cult?"

Yaakov hesitated noticeably, then with a slight smile admitted "That, I'm less sure about. But for all that, I'm not excluding that possibility."

Elazar was dumbfounded. "I don't understand anything anymore."

"I'm not sure everything's clear to me, either," Yaakov said gently. "I'd be very interested in learning what he was so anxious to tell you. I had the impression — again, this is only a feeling — that it's connected to Yossi. But not in the way we think."

"Look —"

Yaakov grabbed Elazar's arm. "You know something? We're a couple of certified idiots. What are we doing, standing here right in front of the gate? That guy we left inside is liable to come charging out any time now. I don't want to have to start all over again with him. Besides, we have to hurry and check out the contents of this folder. Come on."

He pulled Elazar after him. By the pale light of the street lamp, Elazar saw that his own shirt was torn and dirty. His pants were in no better shape.

"Where are we going?" he asked. "I can't go home looking like this."

"Come with me to Yerushalayim. We'll go through the folder there. You know what they say — two heads are better than one."

Elazar found the idea to his liking. He would call home, he decided, from the Central Bus Station in Jerusalem. As they boarded bus number 400, Yaakov remarked thoughtfully, "You know what? I don't think that man back there in the house knows where Yossi is, either."

37

Zevulun slowed down at the entrance to Jerusalem. Traffic was heavy. He glanced at his wife. "Feeling a little better?" he asked gently.

He had felt utterly helpless in the face of her bitter tears. As he drove along, listening to Tzipporah's sobs, an internal courtroom in his mind listened to arguments for the prosecution and the defense of Zevulun Kimmerman. One voice accused him of avoiding, for a matter of years, holding a genuine dialogue with his wife about the serious problems that had beset their family. Then he considered the mitigating factors: the burden of his business responsibilities that intruded on all his waking hours and made concentration on anything — even, to his sorrow, his *davening* and learning — an ordeal. Images rose up before his inner eye: the many times he had come home from the office, tired and hungry, to Tzipporah's litany of the day's problems. He had been impatient and angry, a man at the end of his resources. ("Stop it already! Can't you see that I'm dying of exhaustion?" And then her voice, complaining, "You never have time to talk! You always come home from work like a caged lion. It's impossible to go on like this!" And he would shoot back, "Do you have any idea what kind of day I've just had? Have you ever had the 'pleasure' of a meeting with an obnoxious tax man, who's come to the meeting already convinced that you're a liar? Have you? What do you want from me? I'm only human!" But Tzipporah would not back down. "Come home an hour later, then. Go relax somewhere first. Just come home *sane!*")

And so, all the frustrations that had been allowed to mount and multiply because he had never found the time to really talk to her, were emerging now, on this drive to Jerusalem, in a waterfall of tears...

The Mitsubishi crawled among the other cars. Small scenes from his home life replayed themselves in Zevulun's mind. All Tzipporah had to do, at the end of the long day's work, was tell him even one little thing about Yossi's behavior, and he would never even wait to hear the end of the story. Furiously, he would fall upon his son, beat him soundly, and then send him to his room to the accompaniment of some final, caustic comments.

("Enough!" his wife would scream. "How much are you hitting him?" "You're the one to blame!" he would shout back. "The minute I walk through the door, you're driving me out of my mind with stories about Yossi. Don't tell me while I'm still on the doorstep!" And she would answer: "I just wanted to confide in someone. Why can't you understand?" "And why can't *you* understand when I come home, tired and tense, and I lose control?")

In his agitation, it was difficult to drive. Despite the slow tempo of traffic into the city, it was necessary to maneuver adroitly among the many other vehicles in front of, behind and flanking him on both sides. He remembered how, after many such domestic scenes, he would be overcome with remorse and shame. Maybe he *had* overdone the hitting. It had been his nerves reacting, without any spirit of logical parenting.

And still, he continued to defend himself. Most of what Yossi got was certainly coming to him... But maybe not? Did the results — the fact that the boy had run away from the yeshivah to who-knows-where — prove that he, Zevulun, should have behaved differently toward him? If only to prevent the besmirching of his family's good name, he should have sought alternative ways of dealing with his hyperactive and unruly son.

But how? How? How else could he have acted? Could the *rosh yeshivah* show him how? Did even he know? What if the *rosh yeshivah* told him that he was supposed to have kept quiet while Yossi teased and tormented his younger brothers and sisters for hours on end? Wasn't a father supposed to react to that? And wasn't a father supposed to do something when his "dear son" slashed the gym teacher's bicycle tires at school? Or over-turned his desk when the teacher called him lazy or stupid?

I don't know what I was supposed to do! What do they all want from me? he wondered in despair.

The traffic lights at Givat Shaul turned red just as he reached the inter-section. He glanced again at Tzipporah. Why hadn't she bothered to answer him?

"I asked if you're feeling a little better."

She dabbed at the last of her tears with the handkerchief, and lifted her eyes to look at him. She nodded.

Zevulun stifled a sigh of relief. Some half hour later, after a compli-cated journey through the streets of old Jerusalem, the two stood in front of the *rosh yeshivah's* timeworn house.

"Whew, I'm bushed. I'm going back to the dorm."

Yaakov lifted his head. "Come on, Elazar, let's not lose patience here. With Hashem's help, we've made it this far. We'll get further."

The two sat in Yaakov's modest Ramot living room, poring over the pages they'd removed from the green folder. The words and long lists made no sense to them. From the moment they had arrived from Tel Aviv — nearly an hour ago now — they'd done nothing but try to solve the se-cret of those pages. So far, all their combined ingenuity had met with failure. A stone wall.

"Let's read it all again, from the beginning," Yaakov proposed, his voice low. The rest of the family was sound asleep.

For the 20th time that night, Elazar asked, "What do you think these lists mean?"

Yaakov lifted the first sheet and read aloud, painstakingly:

1) ELPHW BSAKVTMVBEJH - SEELIS

2) BOWKSMBSIQBPN HNMDBMTNT - SEELIS

3) ZCJAULAWDEINBDK TNBOQLJMS - LIMMAT

4) HTJFM BTICBVSMPGO - LIMMAT

5) TVILJCNGPPO PDSKHIBZD - SEELIS

6) ZBBFBRLIPBW TMJFOMHOFTS - LIMMAT

Elazar stirred impatiently. "What in the world can this mean? It's nothing but gibberish."

Yaakov did not answer. He continued to read, silently this time, until he reached the bottom of the page. The list continued on the other side, and he went through that, too, with deep concentration. Elazar's nerves tingled as he watched Yaakov mouth the strange sounds. Abruptly, he stood up and began circling the small living room.

Yaakov paused in his reading to address his young friend. "Do yourself a favor and relax, Elazar!"

Without any visible decrease in his nervousness, Elazar returned to his seat. "Okay, I'll relax. But don't you think you're wasting your time? It's already 2 in the morning! This whole business is insane."

"If you're tired, Elazar, you can go to sleep. I'm going to plug away at this nonsense until I figure it out. I have a feeling it makes a lot more sense than you're giving it credit for. In fact, I believe I'm beginning to understand."

Elazar hardly hesitated. Of course he would stay up. How could he let an outsider display greater devotion to his missing brother than he himself? "What are you beginning to understand?" he asked.

Yaakov lifted his head. There had been a certain something in Elazar's voice — a scarcely veiled mockery — that grated on him. His answer was crisp. "Listen, then! I'm not sure, but it seems to me that this is a list of cult members."

"But what about all the strange 'names' on that list?" Elazar looked over Yaakov's shoulder, reading sarcastically, "ELPHW BSAKVT-MVBEJH! Ever heard of a name that sounded like that?"

Yaakov laughed. "Apparently, you're too tired to think straight. Unless I'm mistaken, these are code names. Maybe the letters are taken from some bizarre deities that the cult worships, or perhaps the real names are hidden somewhere in these letters. If the second possibility is the correct one, then there must be a secret key that would give us the real names."

"And what then?"

"Then, it seems to me, we'll have a real chance to find Yossi's name among the others."

"Are you so sure?"

Yaakov flung out his hands in a gesture that combined weariness with impatience. "Well, what do *you* think these names are? *Roshei yeshivah*? Religious Knesset members? I don't think so! Doesn't it make sense to you that the list would have something to do with the members of the cult?"

Elazar had no strength left for detective work. Even as he tried to formulate an answer, his eyelids closed of their own accord and his head slumped to one side. Before long it was pillowed on his forearms, which were folded in front of him on the table. On the other side of that table Yaakov plowed on with his list…

"Hey, look what I found!"

Elazar lifted his head to gaze bleary eyed at the other man. He had no idea how much time had elapsed since he had closed his eyes. "What?"

"I've been trying different arrangements of the letters, including skipping some of them. I think I've unraveled the secret code!"

As Elazar roused himself to look at the pages in Yaakov's hand, he found the excitement infectious. "Let's hear!"

"Look. Take the first name on the list: ELPHW BSAKVTMVBEJH. Means nothing, right? But if I erase every second letter" — Yaakov scribbled the name in block letters on a piece of scrap paper and began plying his eraser — "what are we left with? EPW BAVMBJ. Do you see? If we subtract one letter from each, for example — E becomes D, P becomes O and W becomes V, and so on, we have DOV AZULAI.

Yaakov's eyes shone with the thrill of discovery. Elazar's exhaustion disappeared suddenly, as if it had never been. "Let's try another name, before we look for Yossi's," he suggested eagerly.

"All right." Both heads bent over the list. "BOWKSMBSIQBPN HN-MDBMTNT," Yaakov read aloud. "A long name, no?" He grinned.

"And a pretty one." Elazar grinned back delightedly.

"Now, let's figure this one out. I'm erasing the O, the K, the M, and so on — every second letter. What are we left with? BWSBIBN HMBTT — subtract one letter and THERE IT IS!"

"Avraham Glass!"

The two bent in earnest over the list now, scanning it as seriously as soldiers studying an enemy's plans. It wasn't until near the very end, on the last page, that Yaakov cried softly, "Elazar, look!"

Elazar stared intently at the name Yaakov was pointing to. Slowly, he read, "ZVPTTNTLJP LWJRNJNFFPSDNCBLOE."

"Now, erase every second letter then subtract one. As Yossi's brother, I'm giving you that honor…"

The task took Elazar seconds — ZPTTJ LJNNFSNBO.

"Well, read it!" Yaakov ordered.

Elazar's heart was doing a most peculiar dance. In the silence of the night it seemed to him that he could hear it slamming into his ribs as he read, "Yossi Kimmerman!"

He closed his eyes. For a moment, the world seemed to swim. When he opened them again, the first thing he saw was Yaakov's face, radiant with triumph.

But even as he watched, Yaakov sobered. "You realize, of course, that celebration is premature at this point."

"Premature? Why?"

"Because we still haven't an inkling of where Yossi is. And besides, what is the word 'Limmat' that appears alongside his name, and the 'Seelis' that shows up by some of the others? We've still got our work cut out for us, Elazar."

Elazar nodded, eyes narrowed in concentration. "You're right. What could those words mean?"

"I haven't the faintest idea!"

38

Zevulun and his wife entered the ancient, ultra-Orthodox neighborhood and made their way to a very antiquated house. The sight of the place brought a rush of memories to Zevulun — memories of the times he had visited this house to discuss a point in learning with the *rosh yeshivah* or, if his behavior had warranted it, to listen to his gentle criticism. Those had been good days. For a brief period he had enjoyed a close relationship with the *rosh yeshivah,* and had felt that the venerable man liked him. Would that liking stand him in good stead today?

Zevulun and Tzipporah slowly climbed the outside staircase leading to the second-floor apartment. A sudden surge of emotion filled Zevulun's throat. This was his first visit in years. Why, he wondered as he raised a hand to knock at the door, hadn't he come more often? He hesitated another moment, and then knocked softly.

There was a stir inside the apartment, and then the door stood open to reveal the *rosh yeshivah* himself. He looked older and frailer than Zevulun remembered, but the light that radiated from that aged face warmed him like the healing rays of his own personal sun.

"Ah, Reb Zevulun! How good to see you once in a while," the *rosh yeshivah* said in the gentle voice Zevulun remembered so well. "And I see you've brought your wife, too. *Shalom aleichem!*"

"Hello," Zevulun responded, not missing the subtle message in the "once in a while." The genuine warmth of the elderly man's welcome did much to dissolve the lump of apprehension he had carried up the stairs with him.

"*Nu*, come in, please," the rabbi invited.

They followed him slowly into the tiny apartment. Their host led them into a minuscule dining room and urged them to sit. *Nothing has changed here*, Zevulun thought in wonder. It seemed to him that he had sat in this identical chair some 25 years earlier, as a yeshivah student. A feeling that was tantamount to envy touched him for a moment.

"The rebbetzin will be along in a minute with something for you to make a *berachah* on," the *rosh yeshivah* said, when the three were seated at the table. "When it comes to making guests welcome, she's an expert." He paused, regarding Zevulun with a smile. "Well now, Reb Zevulun, what's on your mind? I've been wondering what could have brought you from Tel Aviv so suddenly."

Zevulun took a deep breath. It had come: the moment of truth. He stole a quick glance at his wife, but did not glean any encouragement in her expressionless face. The glance, he saw, had not escaped the *rosh yeshivah*.

"I've come to ask the *rosh yeshivah* for advice."

"I see."

Zevulun gathered his courage. "I have a problem — a very serious problem. Actually…my wife and I have a problem."

The rabbi waited expectantly.

Zevulun's hands gripped the edge of the table until his knuckles turned white. "My son…that is, one of my sons…has run away."

The *rosh yeshivah* sat up straighter. A flicker of shock showed in the sunken eyes. "Run away? What do you mean? From where did he run?"

"From his yeshivah."

"He just ran away? Where to?"

The words emerged painfully. "He's disappeared. One day, he simply...disappeared. He apparently joined one of the cults that have sprung up all over the country."

The *rosh yeshivah* shook his head ponderously from side to side, as if to convey his deep distress over this news. A heavy sigh escaped him. "I don't know what it's coming to, this generation." His arms fell to his sides in a gesture of helplessness and despair.

Zevulun reached up to straighten his yarmulke. "This is a very big embarrassment for me, and a blot on my family. So far, no one knows about this except a few close friends. I'm afraid of what will happen when the story becomes public. Frankly, I'm worried about *shidduchim* for my other children."

The *rosh yeshivah* rubbed his eyes and put on his glasses. "I don't understand, Reb Zevulun. What, exactly, is your problem? Is it your son, who ran away from yeshivah, or the shame of it and your other children's *shidduchim*?"

Zevulun realized that he hadn't made himself clear. "With the *rosh yeshivah's* permission, I'll explain what I mean. Of course, the main problem is Yossi — that's my son's name — and the fact that he ran away. But I wanted to mention an additional result of what he's done: the shame for my family, and also the question of *shidduchim*. The *rosh yeshivah* knows how hard it is to find good matches in such circumstances. People don't like complicated situations."

The old eyes betrayed a certain amusement at this ingenuous "explanation." "*Oy*, Reb Zevulun, if these concerns with *shidduchim* are filling your head right now, with such a tragedy happening to your son, then you really do have a problem. How is it possible to think of anything else when your son has fallen into such hands?"

Abashed, Zevulun did not answer. Neither he nor his fellow students had ever responded when the *rosh yeshivah* scolded them. Interesting, the way old habits never die, even after the passage of so many years. Zevulun merely inclined his head slightly, to evade the *rosh yeshivah's* gaze.

He heard the soft voice speak again:

"*Nu*, in any case, what brings you here to me?"

Zevulun clasped and unclasped his hands. "I don't really know myself. My friends told me it would be a good idea to seek the *rosh yeshivah's* advice." He paused. "In the end, I listened to them and came."

The *rosh yeshivah* receded into his thoughts. Zevulun watched him, trying foolishly to read those thoughts in the lines of that venerable face. Finally giving up the exercise as futile, he glanced instead at his wife. Tzipporah sat as before, unmoving and expressionless.

The *rosh yeshivah* asked, "Do you have any idea where Yossi is now?"

"No."

"Have you gone to the police?"

"No."

"Why not?"

"I don't want publicity. I know that, *baruch Hashem*, Yossi is alive and, I hope, well. At this point I don't want to bring in the police."

"How do you know he is alive?"

"He sent me a fax from wherever he's hiding. In the fax, he informed me that he's not coming home."

After a moment, Zevulun added diffidently, "So, for the moment at least, I'm trying to keep this a secret. Because of...of the shame."

Zevulun saw that the *rosh yeshivah* did not like his use of that word in such a context. It had escaped from him before he could stop it.

The *rosh yeshivah* fell back into silence. His hand reached out to pick up a pen and tap it lightly, monotonously, on the table. "Why," he asked, "do you think the boy ran away? Did he have a hard time at yeshivah?"

At this, Tzipporah stirred for the first time. The *rosh yeshivah* noticed, too. Was she planning, Zevulun wondered uneasily, to intervene at this point?

"No. I don't think so," he answered quickly. He hesitated, then added, "Then again, what do I know?"

The *rosh yeshivah* said, "Maybe the other students bothered or made fun of him?"

"I don't know."

Another few minutes of silence. Then, "And — at home? Were there any problems for Yossi at home?"

Zevulun closed his eyes for an instant, hoping by that ploy to conceal his surprise at the direct question. He saw Tzipporah watching him.

"What do you mean, 'problems'?" he asked hurriedly. "I'd say the answer was no." Unconsciously, he raised his voice. "Certainly not! Oh, of course, I'd hit him when necessary, and shout at him, too. But that happens in every house, doesn't it? I think it does. And no one else runs away. Only my — "

He caught himself before, in his anger, his disparagement of his son could find expression in so many words. The *rosh yeshivah* smiled slightly — a pain-filled smile. He had seen what was in Zevulun's heart. The smile was warming and healing, and it held a world of understanding and patience.

"And what," he asked gently, "does the mother think?"

Addressed so suddenly, Tzipporah was taken aback. Various emotions crossed her face as she struggled to formulate an answer. The *rosh yeshivah* said again, "It would interest me very much to learn what the mother thinks in this situation."

Zevulun knew that he had grown very pale. The sudden ache in his head told him so.

39

Tzipporah was quiet for a long time, completely at a loss as to how to respond to the *rosh yeshivah's* question. Out of the corner of her eye she noted her husband's agitation and the way he was struggling to subdue it. In fact, to the undiscerning eye he appeared unmoved. He sat perfectly still in his chair, as though they were speaking of someone else and not him at all. Not even by the flicker of a muscle did he betray the inner storm of confusion that assaulted him. The *rosh yeshivah* watched the small drama play itself out before his aged and experienced eye.

Zevulun wondered whether the rabbi, by his direct question, was trying to ascertain the existence and degree of tension that existed between himself and his wife over Yossi's escapade. He waited, in an agony of impatience, for Tzipporah to speak.

Tzipporah closed her eyes for a moment. She knew she must answer soon. Scenes flashed before her eyes: the full gamut of flare-ups, quarrels and complexities that had characterized Zevulun's relationship with Yossi. Her dilemma was a difficult one. She had no desire to hurt her husband, to parade his weaknesses before his *rosh yeshivah.* That would humiliate Zevulun too much. It was also dangerous: There was no knowing the outcome of such a revelation.

At the same time, she felt incapable of unilaterally protecting her husband. Hadn't this been precisely the reason she had decided to travel up to Jerusalem with him — to see that Zevulun did not waste this visit by covering up the difficult reality that had led to this horrific problem? The only way the *rosh yeshivah* could provide advice that was truly relevant was to be apprised of a full and accurate picture of the situation.

She opened her eyes and said softly, "Yes, he used to hit Yossi… hit him hard…"

She faltered. The sounds of her breathing filled the silence. "…but he didn't mean him any harm. Zevulun only wanted…wanted…to teach him."

The *rosh yeshivah* looked very serious. It was clear that he was pondering the right words with which to answer.

"Did you ever ask him to stop hitting the boy that hard?"

Tzipporah nodded wordlessly. She felt as if any attempt to speak just then would open a floodgate of tears. She was remembering a particularly harrowing episode. It had taken place several weeks after Yossi's bar mitzvah. Zevulun had soundly beaten the boy — the reasons were forgotten by now — and then, his anger not yet spent, had informed Yossi that he was confiscating all the money he had received as bar mitzvah gifts. Her own heart, Tzipporah recalled, had constricted with pain, but she had been afraid to say a word.

Yossi had lain in his room downcast and dejected for several long hours. Then he had vanished for two days.

"Do you see what you've done?" she'd cried to her husband. "Don't you care about him?"

And Zevulun had answered shortly, "That's right, I don't care. I saw him outside on the street, not far from the house. He saw me, too. I decided not to call out to him."

The tears began to well up. It embarrassed her to cry in front of the *rosh yeshivah.* Quickly, she pulled a handkerchief from her handbag and dabbed at her eyes. Zevulun watched her, lifting a nervous hand to adjust his yarmulke but otherwise maintaining a deadpan expression. Inside, he was angry with himself for yielding, in a moment of weakness, to her desire to accompany him here.

The *rosh yeshivah* watched too, with compassion. When Tzipporah had regained some measure of control, he asked softly, "And when you'd ask him to stop, did he stop?"

Now that she had begun, she found it a little easier to continue speaking. Still, she chose her words with care, anxious not to belittle her husband in the *rosh yeshivah's* eyes. "To my sorrow, he didn't."

"Why not?"

Tzipporah shrugged. "I don't know. I really don't. But I do feel that I didn't do the right thing at those times. I should have understood that asking such a thing, at a moment when my husband was very angry, would only make things worse for Yossi. I was also a little hysterical when I'd try to stop Zevulun from hitting him — and that only made things worse. In other words, many times I may have been the one at fault, and not Zevulun."

She threw an anxious glance at her husband. Subconsciously, she was hoping that her words might placate him. But Zevulun would not meet her eyes.

The buzzing of a bee, entering through the open window, cut through the tension that had sprung up in the room. It zoomed around the heads of the three seated at the table, forcing even the *rosh yeshivah* to lift a hand and brush it away. Thoughts turned momentarily to the possibility of being stung. Tzipporah was grateful for the distraction. It gave her a chance to regain her self-control. Without being prompted this time, she addressed the *rosh yeshivah*.

"What hurts me most is not the beatings. It was impossible not to hit a boy like him, with the problems he was always making for the whole family. No, what hurt most were the insulting names Zevulun would call him. That was very hard."

The rabbi asked, "Afterwards, you would try to comfort the boy, wouldn't you?"

"Yes."

"Who did the comforting? You, or Reb Zevulun?"

Tzipporah's breath caught in her throat. The question had taken her by surprise. Recovering, she met the *rosh yeshivah's* eyes directly and answered, "I did!"

Then she hastened to soften the pronouncement by adding, "That is, I was usually the one. Sometimes he did, too."

The *rosh yeshivah* asked softly, "Really? He did, too?"

Tzipporah fell silent, eyes downcast. She had gone too far. In a way, she was glad. Her maternal instinct told her that she had managed to transmit to the *rosh yeshivah* the root of the problem, the true cause of Yossi's break from home. She stole a glance at her husband. He was staring at her angrily. Quickly, she cast her eyes down again.

That's it! she thought in a sort of sad triumph. *If he's angry, that means I've touched on the real problem, the one he's always trying to hide from. La verité blesses.* The French maxim from her school days leaped to mind. *The truth hurts.*

The *rosh yeshivah* rested his head on his hand. His eyes were fixed on Zevulun, who dared not meet his gaze. Inwardly, Zevulun seethed. His wife had humiliated him in front of his *rosh yeshivah*. And it had been a needless humiliation. What would the *rosh yeshivah* think of him now? Why had Tzipporah done it? What did she hope to gain? Would it bring Yossi back? He felt an almost overpowering urge to get up and leave.

Instead, it was the *rosh yeshivah* who rose. With a slow, measured tread, he walked out of the room and into the kitchen. A cupboard opened and closed. There was a tinkle of glasses and a rustle of paper. Then he reappeared, tray in hand. It held a bottle of juice, glasses and a plate of cookies. Zevulun stood up to take the tray from the old man's trembling hands.

"Sit, sit," the *rosh yeshivah* said quietly. "The angels didn't get up to help Avraham when he ran to get them something to eat — and Avraham Avinu was older than I am." He smiled as he placed the tray on the table. "The rebbetzin hasn't returned yet, and you are my guests. Please, make a *berachah*."

Zevulun and Tzipporah honored his request. The *rosh yeshivah* joined them, pouring himself a glass of juice. Listening to him make the blessing over his drink, slowly and with great concentration, Zevulun was catapulted back over the years, to his yeshivah days. He sipped his drink and took a cookie. The diversion was just what he had needed at that moment. It served to dissipate some of his anger. Once again, he marveled at the *rosh yeshivah's* astuteness.

The rabbi took advantage of the lull in the tension to say, "I know, Reb Zevulun, that you're angry with me for asking your wife these questions. And I —"

Zevulun said quickly, "Heaven forbid! I don't want the rav to think that!"

The *rosh yeshivah* made a dismissive gesture. "It's only natural for you to feel that way. There's no need to try and hide it. All I want is to help, and to try to guide you, if Hashem will permit me, with the right advice."

"Thank you!"

"In the portion dealing with the *ben sorrer u'moreh*," the *rosh yeshivah* said reflectively, "the disobedient son is described as 'one who does not obey his father and his mother.' The *pasuk*, Reb Zevulun, mentions the father and the mother separately. Why? And then it goes on to say, 'and his father and mother will take him' — both of them, together. Why, Reb Zevulun?"

The *rosh yeshivah* waited, as though expecting an answer. But Zevulun was in no condition to think clearly. And even had he been able to think, it was beyond his power to express himself with any clarity just then. His spirits were in turmoil.

❧

Elazar yawned. A glance at his watch told him it was already 3 a.m. His strength was failing him. His entire body craved the respite of sleep. But he was embarrassed to admit as much to Yaakov, who was still energetically flipping the pages of the green folder in an effort to find the meaning of the strange words that appeared beside the cult members' names.

"Look, Elazar. I think the words 'Limmat' and 'Seelis' are names of places."

Elazar was jerked out of a half-dream. "Huh? What'd you say?"

Yaakov raised his eyes. "Aha, I see. You were asleep!"

"No, no. Well, maybe I dozed off a minute."

"Listen, Elazar, what we need here is a little stamina. We decided to take action, so we have to act. I said, I think the words that show up next to the names of the cult members are place names."

"It's possible. Why do you think that?"

Yaakov thrust the papers at him. "It just seems that way to me. My intuition tells me that these words indicate where each of these people can be found. I know it's only a feeling, but you know what they say: If your heart tells you so, it's the truth."

Elazar tried with all his might to keep his eyes open. "Let's say you're right. Then where are these places?"

"That's what we don't know yet."

"I have an idea."

"Well?"

"I'll only tell you if you agree to stop now, and let us get some sleep."

"Agreed!"

"First thing in the morning, I'll contact Ilan. I'll patch up my quarrel with him, and present him with what we already know about him and the cult he's a part of. If he'll cooperate and supply us with the information we're still missing — fine. If not, I'll threaten him with the police."

Yaakov's look was pitying. "You really do need some sleep, Elazar."

But Elazar had turned stubborn. "I'm going to talk to him right after *davening*. Then we'll see who's asleep!"

"All right, go lie down already, here on the couch. I'll bring you blankets. And let's hope that your dreams will come up with a more feasible solution."

The next morning, after *Shacharis,* Elazar phoned his father's office.

"Hello, Varda. This is Elazar."

"Yes, good morning. How are you feeling?"

"*Baruch Hashem*, it was a real miracle. I'm up and around already. I'm calling from Yerushalayim."

"Wonderful! *Baruch Hashem*. Did you want to speak to your father? He's not in yet."

"Actually, I need to speak with Ilan. It's urgent. Find him for me, will you please?"

"Why? What happened?"

"Never mind. Just find him — please!"

Varda said slowly, "Ilan's wife just called here a few minutes ago. Ilan's flying out of the country in another hour. An unexpected trip, she said."

Elazar felt as if he had been punched in the stomach. As he gripped the receiver in one clammy hand, he heard Varda ask anxiously, "Elazar, has something happened? Why don't you answer?"

"N-no. Nothing's happened." His voice was weak.

"Elazar, you're hiding something."

Her inquisitiveness irritated him. "Can you tell me where he's going?"

"His wife says his first stop will be England, and from there he'll go on to the United States. He's due back in a week."

"I see." He hesitated. "She didn't hint...at the reasons for this sudden trip?"

Varda laughed. "No. Looks like she's also hiding something." Her voice sharpened. "Why do you need him so urgently?"

"I've got to run, Varda," Elazar said hastily. "Thank you!"

He hung up and looked at Yaakov, who stood at his shoulder. "Now I'm positive that he's linked to that cult. We scared him last night — scared him into running. What do we do now?"

A mischievous gleam lit Yaakov's eyes. "First we find out exactly what Ilan's travel plans are, and whether or not they're connected with our business. And if they are — we follow him!"

"I don't get it."

"You will, Elazar. You will."

40

The *rosh yeshivah* smiled, and moved his chair closer to Zevulun's. There was a peculiarly comforting quality in being the object of the great man's attention. Zevulun found some of the tension flowing away from him.

"I will explain it to you," the *rosh yeshivah* continued. "You must understand, Reb Zevulun, that successful child-rearing is dependent on unity between the mother and the father. Do you understand? That's what the verses in the Torah about the disobedient son come to teach us. When is it possible to decide that a child is beyond hope of rehabilitation — a lost cause? Only, as the *Gemara* in *Sanhedrin* explains, when he does those evil deeds despite the fact that his parents' voices are as one. If, despite the fact that there is complete unity between his parents, he *still* persists in behaving in that manner, then we know there is nothing more that can be done for him. Only then is the harshest penalty decreed for him.

"However, if there exist differences of opinion, even minor ones, between his mother and his father — if their voices are *not* as one — then the law changes. In that case, the son is not put to death. Why? Because in such a case, it is impossible to pin the blame solely on the son."

Zevulun shifted uncomfortably in his seat. "If I understand the rav correctly, he is putting the blame for Yossi's running away on me and my wife?"

Though he spoke quietly, with the utmost respect, inwardly Zevulun was beginning to fume. *Look, even my own rabbi — without knowing Yossi or all the facts of the case — is agreeing with my friends in laying the blame on me!* He could almost hear the silent gnashing of his teeth.

"Heaven forbid, Reb Zevulun! Where did you get such an idea? Did I intend to assign any blame by what I've just told you? Do I know enough of what went on in your home to judge? Am I familiar with how the boy behaved in the house and at school? Am I even permitted to express an opinion? Heaven forbid! Whatever made you think that, Reb Zevulun?!"

The old rabbi's agitation was real. Zevulun was first astonished, then awed. This was the quality that made the *rosh yeshivah* a truly great individual. What sensitivity! What understanding!

"I'm sorry," Zevulun whispered. If the rav had not intended to assign blame, then what was the purpose behind the lecture about the *ben sorer u'moreh* — the disobedient son?

"There is no need to apologize, Reb Zevulun. Just listen closely to what's being said. I want to help. When a difference of opinion exists between the parents, even a small difference of opinion, then the disobedient son is not held fully to blame. That's what the Torah says."

The *rosh yeshivah* paused to reflect a moment, then went on in a thoughtful tone. "Disunity between parents affects the climate in the home. It doesn't allow the children to feel fully at peace. While the parents may not actually be to blame, still one never knows what subtle factors can influence a child's heart when it is not whole and at peace."

Zevulun could not restrain himself a moment longer. "But I don't think this applies in our case at all! I don't think there's a difference of opinion between my wife and me here." He half-turned toward Tzipporah. "Right?"

She hesitated. The last thing she wanted to do was antagonize her husband further.

"Let's assume that's true," she said quietly. "That, in at least some of the incidents, we did not disagree. Okay, in most of the incidents."

The *rosh yeshivah* smiled into his beard. "All right, that's not the important point. What is important is that the Torah tells us that, in a case such as this, the child is not punished. Instead, we must search for ways to teach him."

Again, the urge to answer was an overpowering one. "Does that mean that the child is to be allowed to do whatever he wants? He can do whatever his heart pleases, and we can't even punish him?" Zevulun sounded truculent.

"Zevulun," Tzipporah hissed, "how are you talking?"

He clenched his jaw, muttering, "Sorry!"

"Reb Zevulun." The *rosh yeshivah* shook his head. "This is not good. It shows us that you are missing one vital ingredient in raising children — and that's patience! Am I correct?"

Zevulun hung his head. The *rosh yeshivah* regarded him benevolently. "Do you remember the *Gemara* in *Shabbos* 34, about the three things a person must say in his home on *erev* Shabbos as the sky grows dark?"

Zevulun nodded, while wishing miserably that he really did remember. He heard the *rosh yeshivah* quote a few words in Aramaic, then expound: "If we want our words to be listened to and accepted, we must speak them in a pleasant way, softly and serenely. That is what our Sages teach, and that is what our own lives show us."

The *rosh yeshivah* fell into a brief, ruminative silence, during which Zevulun dared not raise his head.

"Apart from that, Reb Zevulun, once again you did not listen to what I was saying, but only grasped the extreme. Where did you hear me say that we have to let a child do whatever he wants? How awful for all of us if that was the case! You also didn't hear me say that it is forbidden to hit an unruly child at certain times. Did you, now?"

At that moment, Zevulun loathed himself. In his foolish impatience, in his lack of self-control, he had laid himself bare to the *rosh yeshivah* — and he had done it in front of his wife. He felt like one of the warriors of old who, stripped of his armor, stands exposed to enemy arrows. As a *yeshivah bachur* he had been stubborn, sometimes due to nothing other than an obstinate and willful pride. He seemed to recall the *rosh yeshivah* remonstrating with him once before about this trait. Zevulun felt as though he would never dare look the old rabbi in the face again.

The *rosh yeshivah* rose and walked slowly to a bookcase, from which he extracted a *Chumash Devarim*. Then he took down a second, smaller volume whose title Zevulun could not discern from where he was sitting. The *rosh yeshivah* returned to his place at the table and flipped briefly through the *Chumash* until he found the verse he wanted.

"Ah, here it is, in *Parashas Devarim.* 'Listen among your brethren and judge righteously.'" He lifted his eyes with a heartwarming smile. "Moshe Rabbeinu asks his people to learn this valuable trait before entering *Eretz Yisrael.* Without the ability to listen to your brothers, it is impossible to judge righteously. The first principle, Reb Zevulun, is to listen! To listen means to pay attention. To pay attention is to understand. And he who understands will be able to take into consideration what the other person is trying to communicate."

His kindly gaze rested on Zevulun's attentive face. "Am I being too harsh? Here you are, a guest in my home, and I'm lecturing you! Not exactly a host's place."

"No, no," Zevulun protested.

"The word 'listen,'" the rabbi said, as though the interlude had not occurred, "is written in the present tense, as Rashi points out. What does this come to teach us? To listen — now! Not to assume ahead of time that we already know what the speaker is going to say. Not to believe that we know it all before we've heard a word, and grow impatient because 'I heard you already.' That is the first rule in human relations, Reb Zevulun. So I am asking you to listen to me closely — to really listen to what I'm saying — before…"

The *rosh yeshivah* let the sentence drift into oblivion, but not before Zevulun grasped his meaning: *"before you explode again."*

"Because," the *rosh yeshivah* continued, "I have a strong feeling that you don't know how to listen and how to pay attention. Especially not to your son."

"Why — why does the rav think that?"

"Because it seems to me that when a child starts misbehaving, it's because no one is listening to him. He wants to be paid attention to, and tries to let people know in that way. The rule of 'listen among your brethren' applies to children, too."

The *rosh yeshivah* closed the *Chumash* and rested both hands on it. "I see, Reb Zevulun, that you do not agree with me. So tell me, please: Was your son always as wild and unruly as you've described him?"

"No!"

"Well, when did it begin?"

Zevulun looked at his wife as though trying to find the answer in her face. Tzipporah searched her mind for a date onto which she could pinpoint the change in Yossi. "I think," she said, "it was at the end of the sixth grade."

Zevulun did not agree. "*I* think it was in the seventh grade."

The *rosh yeshivah* said, "It doesn't matter. The important thing is that you both agree: Yossi was not always this way. Have you ever stopped to wonder why it happened? What caused the change in his behavior?"

"No." Zevulun's answer sounded uncharacteristically uncertain.

"Why not?" the *rosh yeshivah* pressed.

Zevulun said nothing.

In all honesty, he did not know what to say.

Elazar gaped at Yaakov. "I don't understand. How do you intend to find out where Ilan's gone? And why do you want to go after him?"

Flipping through the pages of a telephone book, Yaakov tossed over his shoulder, "I don't know — yet. Up until now, Hashem has moved us ever closer to our goal. I'm sure He'll keep on helping. Ah, here, I found it!"

Elazar craned his neck to see. "Found what?"

"The number I want." Yaakov dialed it. "Good morning. Is this Worldwide Travel?... Is it possible for me to speak to Yehudah Tamiri? Thank you!"

A brief silence, then Yaakov spoke again. "Good morning, Uncle Yehudah. It's Yaakov…Yaakov Frankel, your sister's son. What's the matter, don't you recognize my voice anymore?… Wonderful! And how are you, Uncle?… Listen, I need some information on flights abroad. Can you help me?… No, I'm not planning a trip, at least not at the moment. I just want some details on someone who is traveling. When did he depart? With which airline? To which destination? Is it possible to get this information?… No? Why not?… Yes. Yes. Yes, I understand… Okay, then good-bye — and thank you. Give Aunt Yaffa my regards. 'Bye."

Yaakov hung up, disappointment apparent in the slump of his shoulders. When he turned, Elazar asked, "What's the problem?"

"The travel agency can't supply information on anyone who's left the country. They're not allowed to do that, except to aid the police, and even then only with a court order. Besides, there's no need to spend time following up with the airlines. Passport control at Ben-Gurion airport has a list of all departing travelers."

"Well, what now? Do we go to the police?"

Yaakov's answer was another pitying glance.

"Then what's our next step?" Elazar asked.

Yaakov began circling his living room, hands clasped behind his back, and brows furrowed in thought. Halfway through the fifth circuit, he stopped suddenly. "I have an idea."

"What is it?"

"Do you think your father would cooperate with us?"

Elazar said cautiously, "That depends. Come on, what are you thinking about?"

Yaakov spun around decisively. "Call your father's office immediately. If he's not there, I want to speak to his secretary."

Elazar went to the phone and did as he was told.

41

When no answer was forthcoming, the *rosh yeshivah* pressed, "Reb Zevulun, doesn't the question I asked interest you at all? Why *didn't* you ever stop to think about it?"

Still Zevulun said nothing. His *rebbi*, he saw clearly, was setting a subtle trap for him. He also knew that, sooner or later, he would have to answer the question. At the moment, however, he was frankly stymied. What to say?

No, he had never wondered why Yossi's behavior had undergone such a radical change. Could he admit as much to the *rosh yeshivah*? Zevulun stole a quick glance at his wife, as if hoping for a clue to the right answer. Then, just as quickly, he looked away. He hoped she had not read the helplessness in his eyes. He hated such moments, when his weakness stood open to his wife's scrutiny.

But Tzipporah had seen. Deliberately, she let her handkerchief fall to the ground and then bent to retrieve it — simply to spare her husband some of the pain and embarrassment she knew he was feeling. At such moments, she pitied Zevulun with all her heart.

"May I have your permission, Reb Zevulun, to tell *you* why? Why this change in Yossi happened?"

It was coming: the scolding. The *rosh yeshivah* stood ready to deliver a lecture. Zevulun steeled himself.

❧

Varda picked up the phone. "Good morning, Regev Investments."

Elazar smiled at the familiar, monotone greeting. "Hello, Regev, it's me again. Is my father in yet?"

"No, not yet."

"But he should have been there by now, shouldn't he?"

"Yes. I have no idea what's keeping him this morning."

"Varda, a friend of mine wants to talk to you." He handed the phone to Yaakov, who said heartily into the receiver, "Good morning!"

"Good morning to you," Varda said. There was a question in her voice, along with a tinge of uneasiness.

Yaakov went straight to the point. "I'm a *kollel* man who has spent some time in recent months learning with Yossi. We were pretty close, and I'm very concerned over his disappearance. To tell you the truth, we suspect that Ilan may have had something to do with that. We think he knows where Yossi is."

"*What?*" Varda was thunderstruck. "I don't believe it!"

"Forgive me, but this is not a question of belief. It's a matter of fact — or so we think. And I'll tell you something else: This sudden trip of Ilan's has us worried. Everything points to its being directly related to Yossi. We *must* know where Ilan has gone!"

"But — but I can't help you there. I already told Elazar everything I know."

"There are some other details you could help us with."

"All right. I'll try."

"Thank you! First of all, does Ilan travel often for the business?"

"Yes, certainly. We have many clients abroad."

"Hm… Who pays the airfare?"

"The office, naturally."

"But I understand that this time, the office hasn't sent him."

"No. This trip comes as a surprise to me. I still don't know how Zevulun will react to it."

"Actually, I do know. He will react unfavorably."

Varda considered this. There was a new aura of mystery surrounding a person she had thought she knew well — the familiar Ilan. Or perhaps she had been mistaken in thinking she knew him at all…

"Anyway, what can I do to help?"

"Please try to find out which travel agency he purchased his ticket from."

"I'll try."

"Thank you very much. Can I call back in an hour or two?"

"I hope I'll have something for you by then. Good-bye."

Yaakov hung up and smiled at Elazar, who asked, "What are you planning to do now?"

Yaakov rose and reached for his jacket. "Now?"

"Yes." Elazar got to his own feet.

"Right now, I'm going to learn. After all, despite every good thing we accomplish, 'The study of Torah is equivalent to them all.'"

Elazar was confused. "But didn't you just ask Varda to find out something for you?"

"Exactly. While she works on that, I can learn. We've wasted enough time already. I'd advise you to do the same."

"But what will you do when you find out from which agency Ilan is traveling?"

"We'll decide that when it happens. In the meantime…"

Yaakov opened the door and walked out of his apartment, Elazar close on his heels.

42

"ave you heard?"

Recognizing Yaakov's voice on the phone, Elazar gripped the phone tighter. "Heard what?"

"I spoke with your father's secretary again."

"Well?"

"Somehow, she managed to get information about Ilan's trip."

"*Well?*"

Yaakov enjoyed building up the suspense. "So where do you think he went?"

Elazar ground his teeth. The tension he'd been laboring under since his brother had run away, coupled with the pain of his injury and his recent nocturnal adventures at the green house, did not allow for playfulness — or patience. He spat out, "Tell me already!"

"All right, all right, I'll tell you. Ilan's gone to Switzerland!"

Yaakov doled out the information with the air of one who has sprung a great surprise. Elazar was at a loss to see why. "So what?"

"Don't you remember the letter that was in Yossi's closet at yeshivah?"

"Hey, that's right! It was from Switzerland."

"Well? What can you conclude from all this?"

"What do you mean?"

"All the strings are leading to that country. The solution to Yossi's disappearance *must* be there."

"Maybe," Elazar returned cautiously.

"You say maybe. *I* think it's a sure thing! Especially in view of the fact that Ilan tried to fool everyone into thinking he's traveling to England and the States. That's what his wife told your father's secretary! Doesn't that say anything to you?" He paused. "Well, Elazar? You know how to learn Gemara, no? Isn't it logical?"

This time, Elazar responded promptly. "You're right!" He considered the facts, then asked, "What do we do now?"

"I fly to Switzerland, of course! What else?"

"To Switzerland?! What will you do there?"

"What kind of question is that? I'll search for your brother, that's what! Didn't I tell you I'd decided to devote time, energy and thought to the mitzvah of redeeming a prisoner? Did you think I was joking?"

As had been happening more and more often over the past few days, Elazar was astonished at the *kollel* man's energy and decisiveness. *Isn't he afraid of anything?* he marveled inwardly, and not for the first time. Aloud, he asked, "So, you're really planning a trip to Switzerland?"

"Yes!"

"Do you know anyone there?"

"Nope."

"Then what will you do — just fly over there, not knowing who or where or what? It's a little crazy, no?"

"You're mistaken, my friend. It's a *lot* crazy! But such questions are irrelevant when you've set your sights on a goal — when you believe in what you're doing. The Gemara terms the person who isn't confident in what he's doing a sinner. I — in this area, at least — am confident in what I'm trying to do!"

Elazar was thinking that one over, when he heard Yaakov's voice again. "And you, Elazar, are coming with me!"

The *rosh yeshivah's* mien was sober. The smile that had never been far from the surface all through the meeting had disappeared. He closed his eyes for a few moments, fingers drumming lightly on the tabletop. Zevulun watched him anxiously. What weighty pronouncement was his *rebbi* planning to make?

"Reb Zevulun," the *rosh yeshivah* began, "it's not easy for me to tell you this, but, as your former *rebbi*, I am permitting myself to say what needs to be said. You've changed very little from your yeshivah days. The old arrogance is still there. Honor and appearances are still overly important to you — too important for a man of real understanding. That's why you don't love your son. And…"

Zevulun's head, which had been bowed, snapped up. Explosive words rose to his lips, only to retreat at a calming motion of the old man's hand. Subdued, Zevulun bent his head again in submission. Reserves of self-control that he had not known he possessed came to his aid. In resignation and acceptance he decided to bear the brunt of his *rebbi's* remarks without reacting.

"It doesn't pay for you to become angry with me, Reb Zevulun," the *rosh yeshivah* resumed. "That would only prevent you, yet again, from hearing what you need to hear. It is false pride, stemming from arrogance, that stands between you and your son. A proud person pushes everyone away — even *HaKadosh Baruch Hu*. There's certainly no room for your son in this self-created 'kingdom' of yours. Do you understand me, Reb Zevulun?"

Without waiting for an answer, he continued: "When your son doesn't obey you at once, your pride is wounded — and that's one thing you find almost impossible to forgive! If a stranger hurts your pride, you are usually forced to overlook it. After all, what can you do to such a person — beat him up? But when it comes to your own son, whom you regard as your property, you feel free to punish him. You hit him soundly, sometimes even cruelly. You convince yourself that the beating is being administered in the name of responsible child-rearing… but it's actually something else. It's revenge — against your son, who has wounded your pride and disappointed you so grievously.

"The very real considerations of child-rearing create a fog. Realize, Reb Zevulun, that there exists a very fine line between 'He who spares the rod hates his child' and hitting your child out of hatred, insult and a spirit of revenge. Remember — the prohibition against doing that applies just as well to your own flesh and blood!"

The *rosh yeshivah's* face reflected his real pain at having to speak in this vein to the man seated opposite him. Nevertheless, the tide of his words flowed on:

"The *Gemara*, in *Rosh Hashanah*, teaches that a community leader must not impose needless fear on his people. Rabbeinu Yonah, in his *Sha'arei Teshuvah*, comments that this prohibition applies equally to a man who tyrannizes his own household. This past week, a *cheder* principal came to me with a horrifying story. Listen closely! He told me about a boy who came to *cheder* with a bruised and swollen face, and trembling hands. The boy's eyes were filled with pain — and fear. He refused to tell how it had happened. However, the principal learned afterward that the boy's father had beaten him for not bringing home the best mark in the class on a *Gemara* test. That foolish father thought that he was inculcating in his son a love of Torah. In actuality, he degraded and humiliated the son, and without a doubt sowed in him the first seeds of *hatred* for learning Torah… The boy hadn't brought home the best mark in *Gemara*. He disappointed his father. The father could not take pride in his little 'gem' — and that was why the child deserved to be beaten! Is this effective child-rearing?

"You must understand, Reb Zevulun: Experience has clearly shown that children know the difference between a punishment that they deserve and one that's inflicted on them in anger and vengeance. Children have a very finely developed critical faculty, Reb Zevulun."

The *rosh yeshivah* stopped speaking and took a small sip from his glass. Zevulun seized the opportunity to do the same. His mouth felt parched as a desert.

"How do I know this about you?" the old rabbi resumed. "Simple!

You've admitted that you've never stopped to wonder why your son began misbehaving — a clear sign that you didn't really care about him. Otherwise, your heart would have been filled with questions: What happened? Why was my son a good boy until yesterday, while today he's wild and disruptive? Why, until yesterday, was Yossi a good student, and today he doesn't want to learn anymore?

"Why didn't you take the time to think, instead of heaping more and more abuse on the boy, as both you and your wife have described? What, in fact, gave you the right to degrade and humiliate him? Isn't he just as much a human being, a *tzelem Elokim,* as you are?"

Again, he stopped to take a drink. Zevulun, watching his every move, felt the *rosh yeshivah's* genuine emotion. The critical words pierced him like thorns, yet Zevulun found that his initial anger and resistance had given way to a spirit of submission. He wanted to listen. Of the *rosh yeshivah's* absolute integrity he had no doubt, and this certainty aroused in him his first genuine desire to absorb the words he was hearing, and to test himself and his actions in their light.

Zevulun knew that the *rosh yeshivah* was speaking from the purest of motives, and with real pain. His goal was clear: He wanted to help Zevulun. The knowledge melted any vestiges of hostility or resistance in Zevulun's heart. He lifted his head in a sudden, blinding awareness.

I'm not angry at the rosh yeshivah, he thought, *because the rosh yeshivah isn't angry at me. He's criticizing me out of the love he bears me. That is… that is…* Zevulun was unable to articulate the rest of the notion that had formed so unexpectedly in his mind.

The *rosh yeshivah* sensed the change in him. He saw the sudden spark in Zevulun's eye. "Did you want to say something, Reb Zevulun?"

Zevulun shook his head. No, he didn't want to say anything. Or rather, he did want to say something, but he wasn't sure what it was. Why had his earlier anger dissipated, despite the *rosh yeshivah's* harsh and humiliating scolding — a scolding, moreover, that was taking place in front of Zevulun's own wife? What was happening here? How to explain it?

He sensed that the *rosh yeshivah* was waiting for his reaction. At last he whispered, in a voice not his own, "What do I do now? How can I bring my son home?"

It was only by the force of clenching his jaw till it hurt that he kept an incipient tear from falling. A sidelong look at his wife told him that she, on her part, had no such compunction. She was weeping openly and copiously, and dabbing at her eyes with her handkerchief.

The *rosh yeshivah* stood up and once again slowly made his way to the bookshelf. Methodically he scanned the shelves until his hand fell on the volume he sought. It was a small book, bound in dark green. Returning to his place at the table, the old rabbi opened the *sefer* and began turning its pages. No more than a few seconds passed before he found what he had been looking for.

His finger on the place, he began to read aloud: "'*Kamayim hapanim l'panim, ken lev ha'adam l'adam.*' As water reflects a face to itself, so a man's heart reveals itself to another heart. Do you hear, Reb Zevulun? These are the words of Shlomo HaMelech. Now, listen to what the Gaon of Vilna has to say about them: 'Just as water shows a person the face that he presents to it — and if he twists up his face, that's what the water will reflect — so is the heart of man to man. If his heart is favorably disposed to another, then the other's heart will also be favorable to him, even if he does not know his own heart.'"

The *rosh yeshivah* closed the volume with care and rested the palms of his aged hands on it. His eyes tested Zevulun, as if to ask, "Do you understand?"

Uncharacteristically, Zevulun chose silence — to listen rather than to speak. He wanted to hear what his *rebbi* wanted to tell him, without the distraction of his own remarks. With his eyes, he signaled as much.

"Shlomo HaMelech, called the wisest of men," the *rosh yeshivah* began, in the voice he'd once used when delivering a *shiur* in his yeshivah, "wishes to teach us something wonderful about the makeup of the human being. A person's thoughts have an actual reality. Our minds impact on our surroundings — and especially on other people, those close to us and those not as close. These waves of influence have the power to change reality. If a person thinks well of someone, in some mysterious way he helps create similar positive thoughts in the other person. On the opposite side of the coin, as the Vilna Gaon explains, one who is hated only in someone's thoughts is still called 'hated.' Understand? A person is obligated to judge others favorably, so that he himself may be judged favorably. This is more than just a matter of 'tit for tat'... It's the reality that a person creates through the medium of his own thoughts!"

The *rosh yeshivah's* hand reached out and gently stroked Reb Zevulun's. The warm touch summoned forth a rush of memories. It was how the *rosh yeshivah* had conducted himself decades earlier, when he wished to comfort one of his students. It was impossible not to feel the old man's love.

"Seek merit in your son, Reb Zevulun. Search in your heart, in your thoughts, in your feelings. Try to understand what made him behave the way he did. Focus on his good points and not just the bad. Try to turn your anger and resentment away so that you can love him, your own son, who was cast in the image of G-d. If He can love us, despite all our sins and our shortcomings, we are surely obligated to treat those for whom we are responsible in the same way."

A heavy sigh escaped the *rosh yeshivah's* lips. "If you succeed, Reb Zevulun, in transforming your heart into a loving one toward your son — despite his behavior — I am certain that his heart will love you in return, wherever he is. Among the great men of Israel, there are documented cases where the sheer power of their thoughts wrought incredible changes for the good in the hearts of really evil men. Of course, it's necessary to *daven* as well — but *tefillah* alone is not enough. There must be a change of heart as well. If you achieve that, I truly believe that you will witness amazing things."

Once again, the *rosh yeshivah* stood up. Startled, Zevulun realized that the meeting was over. Hastily he rose and extended a hand. Though his smile was a trifle forced, he felt a genuine lightening of his spirit. The *rosh yeshivah* accompanied Zevulun and his wife to the door. There he paused, to add softly, "If you had really and deeply loved your son all these years, Reb Zevulun, then all the punishments you might have given him for this or that misdeed would not have destroyed his natural love for you. Despite the necessary punishments, he would have known that you loved him. May you merit seeing much *nachas* from him and from your other children, and may they all grow to be *talmidei chachamim* and G-d-fearing Jews. Have a safe trip home."

With a final smile, the *rosh yeshivah* stepped back into his modest apartment. Zevulun and Tzipporah turned homeward.

Not one word was spoken between the two during the hour-long ride to Tel Aviv.

43

The minute Yaakov had hung up with Elazar, he dialed again. In short order, he was connected to his uncle, the travel agent.

"Hi, Uncle Yehudah. It's me, again — Yaakov."

"Twice in one day," his uncle chuckled. "Looks suspicious! What brings you to call again? Are you interested in flying away somewhere, maybe?"

"How'd you guess, Uncle?"

His uncle made no effort to mask his surprise. "Are you serious? Where do you want to go? And what for? Are you collecting money for the *kollel*?"

Now it was Yaakov's turn to laugh. "That would be a logical guess, Uncle. But this time I'm talking about a whole different sort of trip."

"Where to, and for what purpose?"

"Where to, I can tell you: Switzerland. But the purpose isn't to be discussed over the phone. What I have to know, Uncle, is this: Is it possible for me to leave today?"

"Today? This is really getting interesting! Do you have a passport?"

"No."

Yehuda Tamari heaved a sigh. "Do you at least have passport photos?"

"No."

"Then how in the world do you expect to be able to travel today?"

"I don't know. That's why I'm asking you! You're the expert."

There was a moment's silence. Then his uncle's voice rang out again, clear and decisive. "Yaakov!"

"What?"

"Come to my office, please."

"All right, I'm on my way. I'm bringing a friend along."

"As far as I'm concerned, you can bring along your whole yeshivah. Is the friend planning to take this mystery trip with you?"

"Yes."

"I see. Well, first of all, go get some pictures taken. Passport pictures. You hear me?"

"Yes, yes, I heard you very well, Uncle Yehudah. See you soon…"

Zevulun did not go into the office that day. He went directly home and stayed there until the following morning. At one point that evening he tried to open a dialogue with his wife, but failed. The words emerged from his lips disjointed, mechanical, even confused. He understood that he needed time to let the unsettled emotions within him calm themselves. Tzipporah also needed time. The atmosphere was too charged for normal conversation.

He wandered into the living room and strolled aimlessly to and fro. The *rosh yeshivah's* speech sat in his mind like an undigested meal. It was hard to accept the fact that his *rebbi* had virtually placed the responsibility for Yossi's actions on his, Zevulun's, shoulders. Just as everyone else had been doing.

He stood for a long time at the window overlooking HaNeviim Street. Then, abandoning that spot, he passed to a different corner of the living room, where he had hidden a package of cigarettes, opened it and then put it down again. Finally, he paused before his large bookcase and surveyed his collection of *sefarim*. Though he had not found the time to read every volume in that extensive collection, he loved adding to it from time to time. His eye fell on a thin book. It was *Sefer Mishlei*, with the Vilna Gaon's commentary. Anger twisted in him — anger at himself, for allowing his personal connection to these precious books to lapse, day after day, year after year. With a hesitant hand, he reached for the slim volume and pulled it down.

Kamayim hapanim l'panim, ken lev ha'adam l'adam. The Vilna Gaon's words danced before his eyes: "Just as the water shows a person the face that he reveals to it… If he twists up his face, the water will reflect that."

He lifted his head, wondering: Who twisted up his face first — Yossi, or me? Of course it was Yossi! Zevulun remembered clearly the day his son had come home from school for the first time, completely wild and undisciplined, and how nothing had been able to calm him down until Zevulun had dealt with him in a manner that made his hand ache just to remember!

But maybe, he mused, maybe what the *rosh yeshivah* was trying to tell me, and what the Vilna Gaon is saying, is that I was supposed to change Yossi's "twisted face" by not allowing my own to get twisted? "If his heart is favorably inclined toward the other person," the Gaon had said, "he will be favorably inclined toward him as well." If he, Zevulun, had tried with all his might to control himself during those crucial moments — if he had succeeded in remaining "favorably inclined" toward Yossi — maybe the boy's wildness would have abated?

Was it true? Had he not witnessed the same phenomenon countless times, where the way he treated other people was the way they, in turn, treated him? If so… if so…

Agitated, he stood up. It was impossible to sit a second longer. Pain gathered in his heart, shattering his peace and hurling him from the comfort of his armchair. He did not close the *sefer*, but left it open on the armrest. Once again, he paced the length of the living room like a tormented spirit. What had he gained from his desire to "educate" his son? He had lost everything. Yossi had vanished, heaping shame on his father and his family and bringing upon himself exile and who knew what other harm. And he, Zevulun, if he understood the Gaon correctly, had had it within his power to prevent it all!

The fingers of his left hand curled into a fist. He pounded it softly into the open palm of his right, again and again. It hurt him, but at that moment he welcomed the pain.

"But what about the other things? What about 'He who spares the rod hates his son,' and 'Educate the youth according to his ways'? What of those? They're also in *Mishlei*, aren't they?"

He crossed back to the armchair and picked up the open *sefer*. "Let's see what the Vilna Gaon says about them," he murmured, flipping pages.

"Educate the youth according to his ways." His eyes flew to the Gaon's commentary. "It is impossible for a person to destroy his own nature... Educate and guide him to do mitzvos in accordance with his own destiny and his own nature; for when you force him against his nature, he will obey you for the present out of fear, but later, when your yoke is removed from his neck, he will depart from it..."

Zevulun felt something like an electric shock in the area of his heart. The Gaon had painted an accurate picture of his, Zevulun's, failure — the error of imposing his own will on Yossi's nature, through humiliation and degradation. And indeed, as that great man had predicted, Yossi had thrown off the yoke. He had run away... run away...

Zevulun sank into the armchair and covered his face with the open book, which he gripped tightly with both his hands.

"Have you brought pictures?" Yehudah Tamari asked Yaakov and Elazar the moment they walked into his office.

"Yes."

Yehudah's eyes rested on his nephew for a moment, then quickly passed on to Elazar. He discerned at once that the young man was tense, afraid and insecure, his will completely subservient to Yaakov Frankel's. Elazar dropped his eyes before the travel agent's scrutiny. What, the travel agent wondered, was going on here? What were these two yeshivah students up to, rushing with such haste to Switzerland? The business had begun to fire Yehudah's curiosity in no small measure.

"Okay." Yehudah Tamari was all business. "This whole affair seems very strange to me, Yaakov, but I won't interfere. The important point is that you won't be able to travel today, nor tomorrow. You need a passport, and even with all the connections my office has, that will take at least a day or two to arrange."

Yaakov exchanged a quick look with Elazar. "All right. If it's impossible today, can you try to have it all finished by tomorrow night?"

It was time to get busy with the bureaucratic round. A number of hours later, the two were back in the travel agency, bearing letters from their respective yeshivos as well as from the umbrella organization of yeshivos, declaring that Torah study was their profession, and that they were planning a short trip to Europe. Uncle Yehudah promised to pursue the matter vigorously.

At length, the passports were obtained. Holding his in his hand, Elazar phoned Yaakov at his home.

"Yaakov, I'm following your lead like a sheep in all this, but you must know that I won't leave the country without letting my parents know. Or rather, I won't go without their consent. I hope you understand that."

At the other end of the phone line, Yaakov clawed at his sparse beard. "That's really a problem. Your father's liable to torpedo the whole trip — a trip that I, personally, have great hopes for. What will you tell him?"

"I don't know. Maybe... Maybe you don't really need me there?"

"What are you talking about? If, with Hashem's help, we do manage to track Yossi down, he'll need to see someone from his own family! It won't work otherwise! As it is, it'll be uphill work trying to persuade him to leave that cult. And how do we know what kind of condition we'll find him in?"

"So what do we do?"

"If you're afraid to, I'll talk to your father. I'll try to convince him."

"It's hard for me to believe you'll succeed. My father can be very stubborn. Right now, he's also very nervous. And besides all that, he's angry at you!"

Yaakov considered for a moment, then said, "In any case, Elazar, let me try."

Not five minutes later, he was on the phone, saying, "Hello, Mr. Kimmerman. This is Yaakov Frankel."

Zevulun's voice was cold as steel. "Yes, good evening."

"I wanted to let you know that, thanks to the information I've managed to gather, we're on your son Yossi's trail."

"Really?" Zevulun thawed perceptibly. "Where is he?"

"I don't know the exact location, but everything points to the possibility that he's in Switzerland. At least, the leads are there that could guide us to him."

Zevulun's voice was charged with enthusiasm. "Oh, that *is* good news! Thank you very much."

There was a pause. Then Zevulun asked, "So what do we do now?"

"I hope to fly to Switzerland tomorrow, and I'm trusting in Hashem to guide me."

Zevulun was astounded. "Really? That's real devotion on your part! Why are you doing it?"

"Mr. Kimmerman, I believe we're dealing with the mitzvah of redeeming a prisoner. So how could there even be a question?"

"I understand… But still, you're a stranger."

Yaakov chuckled. "When it comes to helping a fellow Jew, there are no strangers. Doesn't it say that we're all responsible for one another?" He paused, then added abruptly, "Aside from that, I want Elazar to help me."

Zevulun's heart missed a beat. Hot words sprang to his lips: *No! Under no circumstances!* At the last instant, he stopped himself from uttering them. His *rebbi's* words rang softly in his ears. Mustering every ounce of self-control he possessed, he forced himself to ask calmly, "Why exactly do you need him? To learn with you on the way?"

Yaakov pretended to be affronted. "Mr. Kimmerman, your Yossi's life is dangling in the balance here. I — a stranger, as you correctly pointed out — am prepared to fly off to an unknown destination to do something about it. I asked my rav for advice, and after a great deal of thought he told me to go, but to take along someone from the family."

"Why?"

"Isn't that self-explanatory? If and when we succeed in locating him, I will need someone whom Yossi trusts, won't I?" He waited, then added, "And I think Elazar fits the bill."

Zevulun pondered. He had an uncomfortable sensation of control slipping through his fingers. First Yossi went off, without asking for permission. Now someone else was making decisions on Elazar's behalf… Suddenly an idea dawned, fully formed.

"Do you know what, Reb Yaakov? I'll go in Elazar's place!"

Yaakov was dumbfounded. He had not expected anything like this, and was frankly at a loss how to deal with it. The last thing he wanted was for Yossi's father to appear anywhere near the boy. That would be a sure-fire recipe for failure. As it was, the operation's success was nowhere near assured.

What to say?

44

Yaakov gripped the receiver tightly and chewed on his lower lip. He felt a need to sit down. From snippets of conversation with Elazar he had gathered that Zevulun Kimmerman was a difficult, stubborn man, an inflexible man. It was vital to handle him now with kid gloves. But what to say? How to achieve the desired result?

After a moment, Yaakov's innate self-confidence came flowing back. Zevulun was waiting for his reaction. Carefully, he said, "Look, Mr. Kimmerman, I think you understand that it's better, during these crucial days, that you stay a little bit out of the picture. Isn't that so?"

Zevulun's nerves tightened. "Why?"

Yaakov heard the angry snap of the single syllable. He searched his mind for a placating response. All he needed now was to alienate Yossi's father! There had to be some way to reach an understanding.

"Mr. Kimmerman, I believe that we're both seeking the same goal."

"Which is — what?"

"What kind of question is that? To bring Yossi home! Right?"

"Right!"

Good: They had agreed on one point. Yaakov drew encouragement from that fact, and from the speed with which it had been achieved.

"And, that being the case," he continued, "I think that each of us has to do whatever is necessary in order to achieve that goal. True?"

"True."

"In other words, whatever actions are necessary to help us locate Yossi and persuade him to come home. Yes?"

"Yes. So what part do I play?"

"Hm..." Yaakov weighed each word before speaking. "First of all, let's talk about the part I have to play, Mr. Kimmerman. I'll go to Switzerland, because Yossi feels close to me."

"What makes you say that?"

Yaakov disliked the other man's manner, which reminded him forcibly of an interrogation. Still, he had no choice but to continue. It was all part of the job.

"Simple," he replied smoothly. "In yeshivah, he would come over to me, wanting to talk."

"To talk — about learning?"

"Yes. Or rather, it started out that way. But our discussions soon spread to other areas. I sensed that the boy was living with very great tension. I saw how much he needed someone to listen to him. Just — to listen. For some time now, I've felt that Yossi has a problem. I'm a person who enjoys that kind of challenge: to try and 'open up' boys like him. And he, Yossi, sensed that."

Yaakov stopped, just long enough to review his own words and see whether there was anything in them to anger Yossi's father. Then he continued: "Apart from that, Elazar must have told you that Yossi tried to phone me one night recently, after midnight. He called *me*, not..." Yaakov bit his tongue.

Zevulun reacted at once. "You were going to say, he called you, and not me, his father?"

"No... I didn't mean that." Yaakov hesitated, then amended, "Or rather, yes... Yes, that's actually what I meant."

He tensed for the expected explosion. It did not come. Zevulun, at the other end, maintained a thunderous silence.

The truth was borne in on him all at once, with no softening of its blunt power. Yaakov Frankel had presented it to him just now in all its starkness. Zevulun's friends had been right. His *rosh yeshivah* was right. His wife was right — she who had been afraid to state openly what she carried in her heart. Yossi had been searching for a listening ear! Every vestige of his former contempt for Yaakov Frankel disappeared as if it had never been. This *kollelnik*, a stranger who had seen Yossi in the evenings at his yeshivah, had known at once what Yossi's own father had failed to grasp. And now, Zevulun was paying the full price for his failure....

Tzipporah chose that moment to step out of the kitchen and into the living room. Seeing her husband gripping the receiver with white-knuckled intensity, she was alarmed. "Zevulun, what is it? Who are you talking to?"

He roused himself as if from a dream. "No one..." He shook his head. "Actually, I'm speaking with Reb Yaakov Frankel."

Shaking her head in bewilderment, Tzipporah went into her bedroom and shut the door. Zevulun held onto the receiver, saying nothing. For his part, Yaakov was in no hurry to speak either.

Here, Zevulun thought, was an ideal opening to do what his *rebbi* had suggested — to understand Yossi, and to seek some sort of justification for his behavior. The boy had been desperate for a listening ear. Just as a baby will scream in its crib so that his mother will come and pick him up, so Yossi had teased his younger brothers and sisters. Teased them purposefully, destroyed their belongings and disrupted their lives at every turn. And was it not true that adults, Zevulun asked himself dryly, often do the same thing? Every one of us does all sorts of foolish things just to get attention. But when had it begun with Yossi, and why had it begun?

And even more to the point, why had he, Zevulun, decided to humiliate him the way he had? Zevulun probed the depths of his own soul, but found some areas that were still too murky for his understanding to shed light on.

"I'm sorry if I hurt you, Mr. Kimmerman," he heard Yaakov say softly. "Please forgive me. That wasn't my intention at all."

Yaakov could have kicked himself. It would be necessary to spend considerable time and effort to find the right words to rectify the error he had just made.... But Zevulun, to Yaakov's surprise, had turned very calm.

"No, no, don't worry about it. There's nothing to forgive. It's all right."

Yaakov was at a loss to understand the unexpected change in Zevulun's attitude, but decided not to press his luck with further questions. He was still searching for the best way to get Zevulun to change his mind about traveling to Switzerland.

"Mr. Kimmerman," he began cautiously, "I really feel uncomfortable about all — "

Zevulun interrupted. "Relax, Reb Yaakov, I'll save you the words. I'm backing down from my decision to go with you. Tell Elazar that I consent to his taking my place on this trip. Tell him to phone home. I want to give him some money, and also a few tips for someone who's traveling out of the country for the first time."

To say that Yaakov was taken aback would be to grossly understate the case. His aim had been achieved, apparently, by a slip of the tongue. How had it happened? He wished he understood. He tried expressing something of what he was feeling: "Look, Mr. Kimmerman, I — "

"Reb Yaakov, listen to me. There's no time to waste. What can I tell you? Go on your mission, and may Hashem be kind to you and guide you. Good-bye, and good-luck."

Zevulun replaced the receiver with a profound feeling of satisfaction. He had conquered his own nature. He was astonished with himself! He had never suspected that surrender would feel so wonderful.

As for Yaakov, he stood holding the silent phone for long minutes after Zevulun had hung up, his fingers squeezing it till they hurt.

Two days later, Yaakov and Elazar rose early and went to the *Kosel* to *daven Shacharis* with the sunrise *minyan*. From there, they went directly to the airport. Elazar was tense and afraid, with the beginnings of a headache. Yaakov was a little more withdrawn than usual, but otherwise evinced no sign of distress.

They entered the bustling terminal and, for the first time in their lives, stood in line at one of the El Al counters. A security official questioned them: "Are you carrying any sort of weapon? Has anyone given you a package to take on the plane? From the time you packed your bags, were they in your possession?" Then the handing over of their luggage and receipt of boarding passes, the long walk to the gate and, finally, the boarding itself.

The plane felt alien. Never before had either man been so completely surrounded by people so different from him. Two yeshivah students stepping out into the big world... From time to time, they would spot a religious Jew, and the sight lit a spark of confidence in them.

Elazar was the first to speak. "I'm asking you again, what will we do in Zurich? Where will we begin?"

The plane was lifting off. Through the window Elazar saw the Israeli coastline dipping away behind them. The sight caused him an anxious pang. Observing him, Yaakov smiled. "Do you think I wasted all of yesterday? I've been thinking about a lot of things."

"But where will we go right after landing in Zurich? We can't even speak Swiss! We don't know a soul in the whole city!"

"I told you, I haven't been wasting my time. I have a few addresses, including the address of a hotel not far from the city's main shul. So you see, I'm not going completely unprepared."

Elazar said nothing. His older friend continually surprised him. Though his fears remained, he felt a little more optimistic knowing that Yaakov had some things, at least, under control.

He relaxed in his seat, gazing out the window at the blue Mediterranean below. The sea filled every corner of the horizon. Yaakov watched his fellow passengers move up and down the narrow aisle, trying not to disturb the attendants in their breakfast service. Then he opened a *Chumash* and began looking over the weekly Torah portion. After half an hour, Elazar, too, took out a *sefer*.

At that moment, there was a commotion behind them. The argument was conducted in low tones at first, but grew louder every minute.

"Sir, please listen. It's impossible to pass here now. The aisle is too narrow." A steward, pushing his laden cart, looked harried.

"But I have to pass!"

"Excuse me, but why do you have to pass right now?"

"That's none of your business! It's about time El Al learned how to give some real service."

"But I tell you again, sir, it's impossible. You wouldn't try to do this on any other airline, not while a meal is being served!"

The passenger raised his voice still further, ignoring his fellow passengers' angry glances. "That doesn't interest me! I need to pass — now!"

As if on cue, the head steward approached the scene of the altercation. He tried to soothe the passenger, to no avail. In the cause of peace, he finally signaled his underling to back away with his cart and let the passenger through. The steward did so, and the passenger charged down the aisle to the accompaniment of glowering looks from most of the neighboring seats. His own face was flushed with anger and triumph.

Suddenly, Yaakov tugged at Elazar's sleeve. "Look!"

Elazar started. He lifted his head and glanced in the direction Yaakov had indicated. The irate passenger was passing their row.

"Do you see?" Yaakov hissed.

Elazar saw. Wrapped around the man's wrist was a bracelet featuring the Third Mystical Eye.

45

Elazar was beside himself with the knowledge that a cult member was on their flight. After a full quarter-hour, during which he maintained a stony silence, Elazar got abruptly to his feet. "Let me by, please," he said to Yaakov.

"Where are you going?" Yaakov asked in some surprise.

"I'll be right back. I want to see him."

"Who?"

"You know — the guy with the bracelet. It drives me crazy to think that the members of this secret cult are not afraid to wear their symbol openly, on their wrists."

Yaakov made a dismissive gesture. "Today? In today's upside-down world, what do they have to be afraid of? Today, when even grown people are not afraid of wearing rings on every part of their bodies? Today, when everyone dresses in any crazy fashion they want, do you think anyone cares about a bracelet? Does anyone even have an inkling that it's a cult symbol? It's just another crazy fashion! Anyway, sit down, Elazar." Yaakov nudged him backward.

Elazar didn't understand. "Why?"

"There are still two hours of flying time ahead of us before we reach Switzerland. The fellow's not going anywhere till then. There's no place to run. If you start promenading past him now, you'll make him suspicious. I know how excitable you can be. Anyone can read it in your eyes."

Abashed, Elazar sat down. "Aren't you curious to know who he is?"

"Of course I'm curious. Leave it to me. I'll check it out. We have time!"

Once again, Yaakov bent his head and began poring over his *Chumash*.

Elazar leaned back in his seat, consumed with a burning rage against Yaakov. It wasn't long before he asked, "When will you check it out?"

Without raising his head, Yaakov said, "I told you — not yet."

Elazar persisted, "But when?"

"Before we land."

"You don't think it's important for us to get a good look at his face? To see what he looks like?"

"I do think so."

"Well, why don't you get up? And if you don't want to, why stop me from doing what's necessary?"

Yaakov took a deep breath, slipped a small piece of paper into the book to mark his place, and closed the *Chumash* from which he had been learning. His smiling eyes met Elazar's tense ones. "Just what are you so worried about, Elazar?"

"I'm not worried. I just want to understand you."

"Then listen. Anyone who's a member of a cult, or a spy for some country, or a secret agent for his government, has his senses on extra-alert. He's suspicious of everyone and everything. If someone pays him a little too much attention, he smells danger. I'm sure that the man we're talking about, sitting not too far in front of us, will detect our interest in him immediately. I don't want to attract his attention."

Elazar demanded, "Will any of that change before we land?"

"A good question. However, you're overlooking a few fundamental principles here."

"What do you mean?"

"Before landing, people begin getting ready to disembark. I imagine our man is no different. His thoughts will be wandering, to whoever will be meeting him, to the place where he'll be staying. Maybe he'll be busy getting his things in order before we land. In other words, he'll be preoccupied with all sorts of little details, which will take something away from his alertness. He won't notice if I pass by, as if by chance, and glance at him." He grinned. "Apart from that, let's give him a chance to calm down from the scene he made a little while ago."

Elazar listened, but he was not relaxed. It was hard to concentrate on the *sefer* he had open before him. He was worried that Yaakov, in his overconfidence, might let slip an opportunity to facilitate Yossi's road home. Carefully, he turned back to his seatmate.

"Don't you think it's a sign from Above that he's here on the plane with us?"

"I do think so."

"Well, isn't it worth our while to stick to him?"

Yaakov smiled. "That's exactly what I intend to do. But you understand, Elazar, that he mustn't sense a thing."

Elazar was forced to agree: "True!"

The voice came clearly over the loudspeaker. "We are approaching Kloten Airport, outside Zurich. Local time is 11 o'clock. The weather in Zurich is overcast and rainy, with a temperature of 18 degrees Celsius. We will be landing in a quarter-hour's time. Please remain in your seats with your seat belts fastened until the aircraft has come to a full stop. We hope you've enjoyed the flight, and that you will join us again the next time you travel. On behalf of myself and my fellow crew members, thank you for flying El Al."

The passengers awoke to renewed life. People began to stir, to reach for their hand luggage. Ignoring the instructions to remain seated, Yaakov got up and walked slowly along the aisle toward the lavatories. He took up a position beside one of the locked doors, waited several moments and then started walking slowly back to his seat. His eyes drifted to the man with the bracelet.

Though he appeared no more than 30 or so, his black hair was already liberally threaded with gray and even white. His face was broad and not overly gentle, his lips set in a hard line. Engaged at the moment in untangling his seat belt, the man's head was bowed so Yaakov could not read the expression in his eyes. His attire, however, was plain to see: an expensive and new-looking gray suit — and the silver bracelet.

For a second, Yaakov toyed with the idea of approaching the man with some remark, solely for the sake of seeing his eyes. He quickly rejected the idea. Instead, he returned to his seat and busied himself with organizing his flight bag, ignoring Elazar's questioning look. Still disobeying orders, he did not fasten his seat belt.

The plane began to lose altitude. The passengers' eyes were glued to the windows, and the fast-rising land below. Yaakov put his head close to Elazar's and whispered, "Unfasten your seat belt. The second the plane lands, get up and follow me quickly. I want to stand directly behind that man on the way out. His face will be easy to recognize, and he didn't notice me. Understand?"

Elazar nodded, feeling a strangling sensation at his throat.

The plane was circling the airport now. Through the windows it was possible to make out the stretches of green that adorned Switzerland, the asphalt highways that intersected the green and the numerous cars that scurried along the highways like so many ants in search of food. Now the plane was flying smoothly above the runway itself. There was a bump, and a roar of brakes. Gradually, the plane slowed and rolled to a halt, and all was quiet.

Yaakov shot out of his seat before any of the others. He hurried toward the exit, Elazar puffing along behind. Both ignored the surprised looks of the other passengers. Yaakov paused beside the cult member's seat — and his eyes widened.

"Elazar, look!" he whispered, almost inaudibly. "He's gone!"

It was true. The man's seat was empty. He was not standing in the growing line of passengers at the exit. Somehow, through some inexplicable trick, the man had vanished.

For the first time since they had embarked on this mad adventure, Elazar read something in Yaakov's eyes that almost resembled fear.

46

The lengthening line of people waiting to leave the plane moved slowly, Yaakov and Elazar along with it. Their eyes darted ceaselessly right and left, searching for the man with the silver bracelet who had vanished into thin air, right under their noses. His disappearing act aroused their curiosity, apart from their natural desire to follow him in the hope that he would lead them to Yossi. How had he managed such a thing in the closed confines of the airplane?

They saw no sign of him afterwards, in the airport terminal, or in the passport control line, or at the baggage carousels. What had happened to the man?

"Well, we lost that round," Yaakov murmured in Elazar's ear, as they heaped their baggage onto a metal cart. Surrounding them on all sides was a surging sea of humanity, chattering in a bewildering assortment of languages. Neither Yaakov nor Elazar understood a word. For the first time in their lives they stood isolated among the rest, far from their homes and their yeshivos — in the heart of an alien reality. They felt truly alone, uncertain of their next step.

They intercepted many curious looks from the non-Jews around them. The two became acutely conscious of the way they stood out in their dark suits and their black hats.

"What do we do now?" Elazar asked Yaakov.

"Now? First we travel into the city, to the hotel, where we can rest a little and get organized. We can go by train or take a taxi. Which do you prefer?"

Elazar looked at him in surprise. "Where do you see a train?"

Yaakov pointed at a large sign above their heads: "You see? The Swiss are very organized. They've considered people like us, two foreigners from the Middle East who can't read their language. Next to the writing on that sign there's a picture of a train. See?"

Elazar saw.

"And the arrow near the sign is pointing in the direction we need to go. Get it?"

"I didn't notice."

"That's your problem in a nutshell. A *ben Torah* has to notice." Yaakov pointed their cart toward the automatic doors leading out of the terminal. "I think we'll go by taxi."

"Why? Why'd you decide that?"

"How do I know where we'll end up if we take the train into Zurich? If we hire a taxi, the driver will take us to the address we give him."

"Do you have the address?"

"I have — "

Yaakov broke off. For a few seconds he stared without blinking at a spectacle that was sending slow shivers up and down his spine. A short distance from them stood a group of four men. They were motionless, and regarding him and Elazar with distinctly menacing expressions. Each of the four wore a white hat and dark sunglasses that hid his eyes. Two were smoking; the other two had their arms draped casually over a cart piled high with suitcases. Yaakov whispered, "Elazar!"

"Yes? What's the matter?" Something in his companion's tone triggered sudden alarm.

"Stay calm. Look straight ahead, not in any direction."

"Okay, okay — but what's going on? What happened?"

"I think," Yaakov said slowly, "that we're being followed."

Involuntarily, Elazar clutched Yaakov's arm. "Who? Where?" His panic was total.

He could not help himself. Rapidly, he swiveled his head until he saw the small group, still standing motionless, still staring at them fixedly. Elazar recoiled. Through a fog of fear he heard Yaakov say, "Are you listening? I think the one in the middle — or rather, the second from the left — is the man who vanished on the plane."

Elazar darted another terrified glance at the group. "But — but on the plane he was wearing a gray suit."

"True. Still, something inside tells me it's him. I especially noticed his broad nose."

"Are you trying to tell me he changed his clothes in the plane, before it landed?"

"Possibly. In fact, probably. That's why we didn't notice him… But why are they staring at us like that? I'll admit, it scares me a little."

"Oh, what did we need this whole business for?" Elazar wailed softly.

"What business?"

"Coming to Switzerland! Jumping into an adventure that can end up being really dangerous! How do we know how this thing will end? I wish I was on my way home!"

Yaakov threw him a quick, cold glance. "And what about Yossi?"

Elazar abruptly fell silent. Indeed, what about Yossi?

By this time, Yaakov had recovered sufficiently to seize the initiative. He began pushing the luggage cart toward the automatic doors. "Come on," he urged Elazar quietly. "We'll walk toward the taxi stand. Take slow, even steps. We have to give an appearance of calm and confidence. Understand?"

"Yes." There was a noticeable tremor in Elazar's voice.

As they approached the door, they saw the four men begin moving purposefully toward the same exit.

"Come on, let's hurry," Elazar whispered in alarm.

"No. Just the opposite. If they really are following us, it's better that we find out here, in this busy terminal, surrounded by thousands of people. I wouldn't want to meet up with them in some distant corner out there. How do I know what they want from us?"

Walking a little more slowly, a little more deliberately than before, the two made their way toward the glass doors. Every nerve quivered with awareness of the four men following behind them. The doors slid open. Yaakov had pushed his cart halfway through when, without warning, he wheeled around and turned back into the terminal. The men in the white hats, close on their heels, nearly crashed into Yaakov's cart. One of them leaped nimbly aside to avoid a wheel.

Yaakov appeared abject. Smiling contritely, he murmured the single French word he knew: "*Pardon*" ("Excuse me").

One of the men answered: "You could say that in Hebrew." He said it in that language.

Yaakov reacted with apparent astonishment. "Ah, are you from Israel? How wonderful! Maybe you can help me find my way into the city? This is our first time in Zurich. In fact, our first time abroad."

The four regarded him impassively. They seemed unmoved both by the encounter with the two young Israelis and by Yaakov's effusiveness. None of them removed their sunglasses. Elazar shrank close to Yaakov's side, his legs nearly buckling.

One of the men spoke. "You seemed interested in me on the plane. May I ask why?"

Slowly, the man reached up and pulled off his dark glasses. Without a doubt Yaakov recognized him as the cult member who had so mysteriously vanished from their plane. The man watched him closely, and emitted a bark of laughter. "Did you think I didn't notice the way your eyes searched for me as we got off the plane?" His manner was harsh, authoritative and faintly menacing.

Yaakov gazed at him openly, and exclaimed, "Excuse me, sir, but I'm at a loss here. I don't recognize you, and I don't have the faintest idea what you're talking about! What are you accusing me of? Is it because I'm religious? That's not very nice!"

He began pushing his cart forward, as though eager to end the encounter. But the other three men barred his way. Forced to halt, Yaakov snapped, "May I know what I've done to you?"

"Yes," one of them answered silkily. "I'm willing to tell you what you've done to us."

"Well?"

"You came to Switzerland to follow us."

"I'm sorry, sir, but you're talking nonsense. Who are you people, anyway?"

"We are members of the Third Mystical Eye. Have you ever heard of it?"

Yaakov shook his head, and answered equably, "No. I've never heard such a strange name." (He had deemed it permissible to stray from the truth in these circumstances.)

The men exchanged surreptitious glances. "Really?" one of them asked. "You're saying you've never heard the name?"

"No!"

The man moved closer to Yaakov. "I sat behind you on the plane, mister. I heard everything you and your friend were talking about. I saw how you got up to check on him." He pointed at the man with the broad nose. "Next time you fly, it would be worth your while to remember to keep your voices down." He peered at Elazar, then asked Yaakov, "By the way, what's your friend so afraid of? Look at him — he's shaking!"

Yaakov shrugged. "You're scaring him."

His mind passed rapidly over their options. These men had obviously identified them. Feigning ignorance would be useless now. How to get out of this as quickly as possible?

He faced them and asked directly, "What do you want from us?"

"Right now, we want you to stay here in the terminal for the next half hour, until we're gone. We'll know if you ignore this request. Our people are all over Switzerland. We don't know who you're working for, but I'd strongly advise you to forget any ideas you might have of following or searching for us. That would be dangerous... for you."

The man directed a final glare at them, then turned again toward the automatic doors. His three companions did the same. Yaakov saw them hurry outside, where they found a black Mercedes waiting for them. In no time at all they had deposited their luggage in the capacious trunk, got into the car, slammed the doors and sped away like the wind.

"Zevulun."

Zevulun lifted his head from his *sefer*. It was the *Mishlei* with the Vilna Gaon's commentary. "Yes?"

He sat opposite his wife in the living room, reading by the soft lamplight. Tzipporah had been reading, too, until she found her thoughts wandering to her two sons — the one who had run away, and the one who had gone to hunt for him. The hour was nearing midnight.

"Why did you let Elazar go?"

"I had to."

"Why? I'm afraid."

"So am I. Don't ask me now. I had no choice."

"But why?"

"Please don't ask me that now. I'll explain another time."

She rose from the sofa and, without a word, passed into the bedroom. Zevulun closed the volume in his hand and put it down. He closed his eyes. With the fingers of one hand, he stroked his forehead lightly. Then he turned off the lamp and, in the still darkness, gave himself up to the thoughts that were whirling restlessly around his brain like a horde of hungry seagulls circling above the waves.

47

Half an hour later, Yaakov and Elazar walked through the glass doors leading out of the terminal.

Though neither confessed it, both were afraid. The unexpected encounter with the cult members had shaken them. They had followed the instructions they had been given to the letter, not budging from the spot until 30 minutes had elapsed. In the nonstop motion of the busy terminal, the two stood as frozen as statues carved of stone.

Yaakov knew he would face difficulties in Switzerland. Traveling as he had without a fixed plan, he had trusted more to Divine assistance than to any clear-cut and prearranged steps he might take in the field. He had firmly believed that, just as he had merited guidance in Tel Aviv — leading him to suspect that Yossi was here, in Switzerland — Hashem would continue to lead him along the correct path.

He still believed it. But the clash with the cult members had eaten away at his confidence. A sense of self-preservation was rapidly overtaking his desire to continue his quest, worthy as it was. However hard he tried to banish the feeling, it persisted and grew stronger.

As for Elazar, fear ruled him almost completely — all the more so when he realized how tense Yaakov had become. As they walked out of the terminal, he asked almost matter-of-factly, "Do you think we're in danger?"

Yaakov didn't answer. Without looking at his younger friend, he wheeled the luggage cart straight ahead, toward the first in the long line of waiting taxis. The driver leaned out and called, "*Gruezi wohl* ("Hello")!

Yaakov mumbled something in reply, though he hadn't understood the driver at all. Presumably the phrase was a greeting of some kind in the Swiss-German language. The driver hurried to open the trunk and placed the two suitcases inside. Next, he opened the back door for his two passengers, who found their way inside and wearily leaned back. Yaakov pulled out his wallet and extracted a slip of paper. "Hotel Goldener Brunnen, Roterstrasse 33," he enunciated carefully.

The driver inclined his head to signal his comprehension, switched on the motor and moved off into traffic. He and his passengers maintained an almost total silence throughout the 10-minute drive. The car passed through a tunnel and emerged in the city of Zurich.

Elazar forgot his fear in the newness of his surroundings. The city was different from any he had seen in Israel. Most of the buildings were old and built of heavy gray stone and liberally endowed with windows. Nearly every public square they passed boasted its own towering statue, and electric trams chugged down the broad avenues.

At length, the driver pulled up in front of a corner building and pronounced, "Hotel Goldener Brunnen."

Yaakov pulled out a purse filled with coins — Swiss francs — from his pocket and, unwisely perhaps, held them out to the driver. "Take as much as you've earned." The driver helped himself to his fare.

They entered the small hotel — and immediately heard voices speaking Hebrew in the dining room adjacent to the lobby. Elazar gasped. "I hope they're not here!"

"Who?" Yaakov asked impatiently.

"Those guys in the white hats and sunglasses. I hope they haven't chosen the same hotel."

Yaakov, a victim of the same concern, remain silent.

The reception clerk, accustomed to foreign visitors who did not speak any of the European languages, copied the information he needed from their passports and proffered a paper for Yaakov to sign. With a superior smile, the clerk handed over the keys to their room, and a bellhop helped them carry their bags up to it.

⁓

Time slipped past Zevulun, wrapped in his fog. He knew the hour was late — well past midnight — by the time he roused himself. His every thought was far from this room, warm and snug on HaNeviim Street in Tel Aviv. His mind had wandered into alien territory, to the unknown place where his sons were.

But where were they? Where was Yossi? And Elazar?

His fingers plucked nervously at the fabric of the armchair. It was a smooth fabric, slippery to the touch. It slid away from him...just as his son had done. As he had done a thousand times, he summoned up the words Elazar had spoken as they sat together tensely in his car in Jerusalem. *Yossi hates you!... Hates you!... Hates you!...* The memory had the power to pierce his heart just as the brutal truth had done the first time he had heard it.

Though the living room was wrapped in darkness, Zevulun hid his face in his hands. Even the faint yellow glow of the street lamp coming through the window disturbed him.

"If the *rosh yeshivah* is right," he mused brokenly, "then Yossi's hatred for me only lays bare my own hatred for him! 'So is the heart of a man toward another.' Do I really hate him?"

Like a film slowly playing before his inner vision, he reviewed the many clashes he had had with Yossi over the last five years. He did not want to see them, but he forced himself. On that last Friday, he had shoved Yossi with a harsh and contemptuous hand against the kitchen wall, and said disdainfully, "Go!" Had that been hatred? He had heard the slam of his son's body against the wall, but had not cared. Was that hatred?

The reel wound on. His wife screaming, "What are you doing to the boy? You could really hurt him, *chas v'chalilah!*" And himself, answering coldly, "What do I care?" Was that hatred?

Only now did he realize that the boy had heard every word of that exchange. Was it any surprise that he hated his father?

And that other time, when he had taken the whole family up to Netanya for the weekend, and decided to leave Yossi behind. Had that been a simple punishment for disruptive behavior? Why had he, Zevulun, felt something akin to satisfaction at the thought of Yossi separated from the family he so carelessly disrupted, feeling alone and rejected back in Tel Aviv? The *rosh yeshivah* had called it "revenge." Revenge against whom? Against his own flesh and blood! But was it not, in the final analysis, revenge against himself?

Zevulun shook his head back and forth. Enough! These thoughts were tormenting him, driving him insane. He could not bear the terrible memories a moment longer. For the first time in his life, he felt ashamed.

He struggled to his feet and opened the window overlooking the street. A frosty night wind blew forcefully on his face. Zevulun breathed deeply of the clear, cold air until his lungs hurt. *'As water reflects a face to a face...'*

If his *rebbi* was right (and of course he was right, just as *Mishlei* was right, and the Vilna Gaon's commentary on it), then he, Zevulun, had caused Yossi's behavior. He suddenly remembered another proverb from *Mishlei:* "A soft answer turns aside wrath." *My soft answer, Zevulun thought, had the power to turn aside Yossi's anger. In other words, I determine the other person's behavior. I have the power to arouse someone's anger — or to quench it! And if I have that power over any stranger, how much more so over my own son!*

His back to the window, Zevulun let his eyes re-adjust themselves to the darkness inside. He heard footsteps approaching the living room door. He tensed.

The door opened. A light was switched on.

In their small hotel room Elazar and Yaakov sat quietly, cut off from the rest of the world. Yaakov, feeling his exhaustion keenly, decided to rest for a while on one of the beds. Though Elazar was equally tired, he did not choose to follow suit.

"All right, so we're in Switzerland," he complained. "What next?"

He received no answer.

"*Nu*, Yaakov? What do you say?"

Yaakov twisted sharply onto his side and faced Elazar. "Listen," he said. "I'm asking you, once and for all, to change your attitude. I simply do not understand you. Don't you have even the minimum of faith in Hashem? All I hear from you, constantly, is the same whining: 'What's going to happen? What do we do now?' Haven't you seen how much we've been helped till now? Come on, expect the best this time, too! How many times a day do we have to go through this?"

Elazar was abashed. Yaakov reclined again — and then pulled himself up once more to add, "Just to calm you down, I'll tell you this. After we rest a little, we'll go to the big shul on Erika Street. I got the name and address from a Swiss yeshivah student who lives in my neighborhood. The shul is in town, not far from here. And there — with Hashem's help — we'll hear a few things that will — again, with Hashem's help — show us our next step."

They arrived at the shul late in the afternoon. Due to security precautions, outsiders were not readily accommodated. In the wake of the waves of terror that had passed through Israel and also touched Europe, the shul's front door was closed with a combination lock whose code was known only to the regular worshipers. Yaakov and Elazar stood beside the heavy door for a few minutes, at a loss, until some men coming to join the *Minchah* service came and rescued them.

The regulars saw at a glance that the newcomers hailed from Israel. "They're going to think we're here to collect funds for *tzedakah*," Yaakov thought wryly. But the congregation was gracious, with many members coming over to offer welcoming words.

When *Minchah* was over, a young man with some knowledge of Hebrew finally asked them, "What is your purpose in visiting Switzerland?"

Yaakov answered with a question of his own. "Do you live here?"

"Yes. Why do you ask?"

Yaakov pretended not to hear. "Do you learn in a *kollel*, or do you work at some profession?" he persisted.

The young man bristled. "Is this the way you always treat people who are trying to help you?"

"Not necessarily," Yaakov smiled. "But in this case, I have to find out whether the one who is willing to help is also *able* to help. Excuse me, I really do not mean that as an insult."

The Swiss man was growing curious. "Well, for the purposes of helping you, is it better if I'm a *kollelnik* or a professional?"

"A working man, in the know about the life of the city and the country."

The other smiled. "A *kollelnik* is actually no less aware of what's going on around him. But, as it happens, you have the good luck to be speaking to someone who does both. I learn in a *kollel, and* I work!"

This time, Yaakov's smile held relief. "Good! I'll tell you what I'm here for. We arrived today from Jerusalem. My friend's younger brother disappeared from his yeshivah, apparently to run off to Switzerland in the company of cult members. The cult calls itself the Third Mystical Eye. Have you ever heard of it? We've come to search for him."

The young man was taken aback. He gazed in some confusion at Yaakov and Elazar. Clearly, he wasn't at all certain whether to believe their story.

Patiently, Yaakov asked again, "Have you heard of the cult?"

"No. No, I haven't. But there are all kinds of crazies wandering around Zurich. It's very possible that these people are among them."

"Where do they congregate? In which sections of the city?"

"I don't know, exactly. We tend to stay away from those places... But let's go over to the table. Maybe some of the men learning there know something."

They knew, but they didn't know. The existence of cult members on the streets of Zurich was not news to them, but they had never thought about it much. They did not have any ideas to offer Yaakov and Elazar as to where to track down such a cult.

At that moment, the shul door opened and, like a blast of wind, a man came in. His name was Chaim.

48

haim studied the two strangers. He saw at once that they were foreigners, and that they had newly arrived in Zurich. That was written clearly on their faces and in the uncertainty in their manner.

"Hey, Chaim," one of the men by the table called out, "here's a couple of clients for you!"

Though not sure how to take this, Chaim nevertheless smiled broadly at Yaakov and Elazar. It was an ear-to-ear smile, impossible to resist. He thrust a hand at Yaakov, and in fluent Hebrew cried, "*Shalom aleichem, Yidden!* Where are you from?"

"From the '*aretz*,'" the two chorused.

"That I could tell at once," Chaim said. "What I meant was, where in Israel? From Yerushalayim? Bnei Brak?"

"Yerushalayim."

"Oh — Yerushalayim! And what's new there today? I'm up to date up till yesterday."

"Thank G–d, everything's the same. No special news."

Chaim grimaced slightly. "Apart from the usual problems, of course."

"Of course."

Chaim took a seat at the table and motioned for the other two to do the same. "Sit down! Why are you standing?"

Chaim, they learned, had been born and raised in Israel and educated in various yeshivos there. Some years earlier he had emigrated to Switzerland, where he worked at several different jobs. One of them was driving tourists around Zurich and serving as their guide. Yaakov felt instantly at ease in his presence. There was an energy and a congeniality about the man that he liked very much. His heart prompted him to forge a bond with him.

Chaim asked: "So which institution are you collecting for?"

The question amused Yaakov. "We've come to collect people, not money."

Chaim stared at them, not comprehending.

"What," Chaim asked curiously, "do you mean when you said you've come to collect people?"

The story of Yossi was quickly told. When Yaakov finished, Chaim remained sunk in thought for some time. The others at the table watched him, awaiting his reaction with interest. Abruptly, Chaim made a sweeping motion with his hands.

"Don't be angry if I'm a little skeptical about this whole story."

A red haze of anger enveloped Yaakov. With an awful quietness, he asked, "Are you calling me a liar?"

Chaim sat up. A slow smile spread over his face. "No, no. Heaven forbid! You're not lying! But maybe you're...imagining things a little. Now, don't take it personally. I'm always hearing stories about strange cults wandering around Switzerland and here in Zurich. I don't know about the rest of the world, but Switzerland seems clean to me. I travel a lot — in this city and throughout the country — and I haven't met these people. The story seems slightly exaggerated to me."

After a moment he hastened to add, in a mollifying tone, "Then again, what do I know?"

One of the men, who had been closely following this exchange, had a suggestion. "Why don't you take them on a tour of the city — the parts of it, I mean, that nice people stay away from? You know, the places where all the crazies hang out. What harm can it do? And you never know, you might actually find him — the runaway!"

Noting Chaim's hesitation, he added, "What's the problem? You'll be doing a mitzvah. That can't hurt you."

Yaakov added quietly, "Don't worry, we'll pay you for your time."

Chaim made a dismissive gesture. "That's not important now. I have to think."

It was clear that the other young men, seated before their open *Gemaras*, did not understand what it was that Chaim needed to think about at such length.

⚜

Zevulun screwed up his eyes against the sudden light that flooded the living room. His wife stood by the door, watching him with a steady gaze.

"Zevulun, do you have any idea what time it is? Why don't you go to bed?"

Zevulun cast a weary glance at his watch. The hands stood at 20 minutes to 4. The night would soon give way to dawn.

Tzipporah asked again, "Why don't you go to bed?!"

Her question hung quivering in the air. She advanced a few steps into the room. Zevulun met her challenging stare.

"Sleep," he said thoughtfully. "Sleep is a form of escape. Tonight, I don't want to escape."

She took a few more steps. "To escape — from what?"

Zevulun did not answer at once. It was hard for him to believe that she did not know what he was talking about. Perhaps her question was meant to goad him into a discussion. Or maybe she honestly did not know what he was going through.

Zevulun went to the table, pulled a chair close and sat down.

"Please sit," he invited her gently.

The phone rang early in the hotel room that Yaakov and Elazar were sharing. They awoke in confusion from a deep sleep. Yesterday — the flight from Israel, their encounter with the cult members, the fruitless discussion in shul — had exhausted them. In the first clear light of morning, the shrill ringing startled and then frightened them. Who could be calling? Who knew that they were here? Shakily, Yaakov's arm snaked out to pick up the receiver.

"Hello, Reb Frankel? This is Chaim speaking — we met last night in shul. I'm sure you remember me."

Relief washed over Yaakov. "Of course I remember."

"Well, listen. I've thought it over, and I've decided to take you around the city. I'll also introduce you to some people who might know something about the subject you're interested in. I asked a rabbi last night, and he said I should help you. He said it's a mitzvah."

"I'm glad to hear it. But let's get one thing clear from the start. We're paying all expenses."

"We'll talk about that later. From this moment on, you two are my guests. I'll be waiting in the hotel lobby in 20 minutes. I'll take you to shul and then you'll have breakfast at my house."

"But —"

"No, no, it's fine. You're coming to me. All right? Be ready."

Slowly, Yaakov hung up. He looked over at Elazar, who was sitting mournfully at the edge of his bed.

"You and your worries!" Yaakov chided. "Don't you see how Hashem is helping? That was Chaim!"

"What did he say?"

"That his rabbi told him to help us. That we're to consider ourselves his guests as long as we're in Switzerland. See? A little faith not only does-n't hurt, it also helps!"

They were in the lobby at the allotted time. Chaim was already there, waiting. On the way to shul he remarked to Yaakov, seated beside him, "You know what finally persuaded me to get involved in all this?"

"What?"

"The rabbi, it seems, knows a little about such things. He told me that cults exist here in Switzerland, too. That's the first thing. But the main thing is, he told me that we'd better be very careful. Those lu-natics can be dangerous."

Yaakov did not understand. "So?"

Chaim's eyes danced. "So, that interested me. The mitzvah — and the challenge in the mitzvah!"

Zurich was waking up as Chaim drove his guests to the big shul on Erika Street. In the back seat, Yaakov and Elazar sat silently, shoulders hunched slightly against the early-morning chill of that gray city. Or were the shivers only a foreboding of the adventures that still lay ahead?

The hour of truth was coming nearer. They both felt it. And yet, at the moment they were still encased in a thick fog. They knew nothing of Yossi's whereabouts in Switzerland — or even whether he was here at all. Their silence and their inner tension went hand in hand.

Chaim parked the car a short distance from the shul, as prescribed by law. The Swiss police were not interested in taking chances. Terrorist threats against Jewish institutions had given rise to fears of car bombs — leading, in turn, to the prohibition against parking in the synagogue's immediate vicinity.

Shacharis over, they proceeded to Chaim's house for a light breakfast. Then they were on the road again.

"Where are we going?" Elazar wanted to know.

"To find your brother," Chaim answered at once. "After all, you didn't come to Zurich to visit me!"

From Elazar's face, he sensed that he had managed somehow, in his thoughtless remark, to hurt the younger man's feelings. He hastened to add, "Please understand, Zurich is a city full of crazy people. They gather here from every corner of the globe. From what I hear, the same situation exists in just about every major city, at least on continental Europe. I'll admit, though — I didn't know our city contained the kind of lunatics you described to me last night.

"In any case, what I plan to do today is drive to the places where all sorts of these people hang out. We'll stop, keep our eyes open and investigate. Maybe, between the two of you, you'll manage to spot the one you're interested in finding. Okay?" He paused, as though struck by a sudden notion. "Do you have a picture of him?"

"No. What would we need a picture for? We'll recognize him."

"True."

Chaim turned toward the Weststrasse, which emptied after a few minutes into the expansive Mannesse Strasse. As they traveled, Yaakov softly recited his daily *Tehillim,* and held a small volume of *Mishnayos* ready in his free hand. Elazar, by contrast, was glued to the window, eager to see everything. A pretty river ran along part of their way, parallel to the road. Chaim pointed out an imposing, red-tiled building that he said was a synagogue used by Jews of German descent. Then they were at the Bahnhofplatz.

Elazar drank it all in: the broad plaza with its tall, ornamental building, and the impressive public fountain ringed with statues.

"What is this place? Where are we?" he asked.

Yaakov looked up from his *sefer,* glanced out the window and then, impatiently, at Elazar. "And if he tells you? Then you'll know?"

Elazar protested, "I'm allowed to ask, aren't I?" He retreated into an injured silence. Chaim sensed the tension between his two guests, though he was in the dark as to its source. He was anxious, however, to do what he could to mitigate it. Slowing down to allow his passengers time for a good look at the imposing central train station, he began his spiel.

"You see, Elazar, this plaza is called the Bahnhofplatz. In other words, it's the central train station in the city. A *bahnhof*, in German, is a train station; *platz* is a plaza."

Neither Elazar nor Yaakov answered. Gamely, Chaim continued: "From this station you can catch a train to any place in Switzerland. Actually, to any large city in Europe."

Still the silence stretched. Yaakov and Elazar gazed at the train station, at the fountain and at the numerous hurrying figures, hoping against hope to see something, anything, that would speed the progress of their quest.

From the train station, Chaim turned right, crossed the bridge that spanned the river and turned right again at the other side.

"See?" he said, playing the guide again. "This road, which stretches along the length of the river until it reaches Zurich's largest lake, is called Limmat Quai — or 'the shore of the Limmat,' which is the name of the river you see here."

All at once, Yaakov sat up. "Wait a minute!" he shouted. He felt as though all the blood had drained from his face.

Chaim, startled, nearly rear-ended the car in front of him. He regained control, then asked sharply, "What happened?"

Elazar was frightened, as he watched Yaakov pull his wallet out of his pocket and begin frantically rummaging through its contents. As his fingers worked, he muttered, "Where is it? Where is it?"

"Tell me what you're looking for!"

Yaakov could not be bothered to reply. He continued pawing through the contents of his wallet until his face lit up: He had found what he sought. "That's it!" he crowed.

"What's 'it'?" Elazar and Chaim asked in one voice. Chaim had pulled over and parked at the corner of a side street.

"Look, it says it right here. Limmat!"

"Where does it say that?"

"Don't you remember, Elazar — the list we found in that cult house on Aliyah Street?"

"Sure I remember!"

"Well, don't you remember that we didn't grasp the meaning of the strange words that appeared beside the names on the list?"

"I remember."

A light of triumph glowed in Yaakov's eyes. "One of those words was 'Limmat'!"

Elazar was beside himself. The tension that had been building between himself and Yaakov evaporated as though it had never been. He tried to control his excitement. "Just a second. I want to understand. Just what does this tell us?"

"Simply that we were right. Yossi must be in this country. We were right in thinking that Limmat was the name of a place in Switzerland. Look, we're standing right beside it now!"

"Does that mean that — that Yossi is somewhere close by?"

"Apparently."

As if on cue, both turned to Chaim, as though he, a native of the country, would be able to tell them precisely where on the Limmat Yossi Kimmerman was hidden....

Zevulun did not look at his wife. He could not. He knew that her eyes were fixed intently on him. The silence had stretched too long for Tzipporah's taste, but she would not be the one to break it. It was her husband's turn now. This was his hour.

At last, Zevulun raised his eyes and sought hers. A sad smile, and a shamefaced one, played about his lips — the smile of a child caught in a misdeed. Tzipporah thought she detected a new gentleness about her husband. Or was that just wishful thinking?

"Yes. That's it. There are crossroads in life, when Heaven takes away all of a man's defenses, the things he likes to hide behind and that help him escape from himself. The excuses, the lies, the logical justifications are stripped away. Then he stands face to face with the naked truth. That's it. No more running away."

He fell silent again. The first pale light of dawn crept in through the window. Tzipporah waited.

"And then, at that moment, as he faces the truth, all the detours he was used to traveling to avoid the truth — disappear! A narrow path leads only to hard reality. There is nothing to the right or the left. Nothing behind. And still, it's so hard walking ahead, straight into the truth. To do that would mean to admit that you've made a mistake. To admit that you haven't lived the life of the best that's within you. And the main thing is, everyone else would also know that you've made a mistake...."

He drew in his breath deeply, and smiled the same, abashed smile. "Here I am, philosophizing to greet the dawn, eh?"

Tzipporah smiled mechanically. "No, no, it's all right. Go on."

"It's — not easy."

From the street below came the first muted roar of early-morning traffic. The chirping of the birds made a soothing accompaniment.

"I don't know what finally made me rethink things. Maybe it was Yossi's running away, or the *mussar* I've been hearing from all of you... or the *rosh yeshivah's* words. I don't know. Maybe it's the cumulative effect of everything that's happened to me over the past few days." He met his wife's eyes squarely. "I don't know what it was. And anyway, it's not really important."

50

They strolled across the bridge that spanned the Limmat. Beneath them flowed the river's blue waters. Just as they reached the center of the bridge, a white pleasure-boat passed underneath. The white of the boat against the sparkling blue background was a sight that captured Elazar's heart, and he leaned on the parapet to watch.

Both the upper and lower decks were filled with people, presumably tourists. As the boat passed under the far side of the bridge, the faces of the individual sightseers became distinguishable. Suddenly, Elazar's hands clenched the railing. He narrowed his eyes to see better, and said in a low, trembling voice, "Yaakov, come here."

Yaakov and Chaim had continued on ahead while Elazar lingered on the bridge. They turned now, in considerable surprise and curiosity, to see what he wanted. Elazar motioned urgently for Yaakov to hurry.

"What's the matter?" Yaakov demanded, impatient at the delay.

"Come quickly! I think I see him!"

"Who?"

"Look, there, on the lower deck of that boat. There — on the left. Do you see anyone standing there?"

Yaakov squinted at the spot his friend had indicated. "I see a lot of people. I'm sorry, I don't know who you mean."

"Yaakov, the man I'm pointing to — it's Ilan!"

Yaakov sobered instantly, and peered again at the lower deck. He smiled. "You're imagining things, my friend."

"And I'm telling you I'm 99 percent sure that's Ilan!"

Yaakov had no desire to argue. "All right, have it your way. Say it is Ilan. Where does that get us?"

"It gets us pretty far. For one thing, we now know for certain that Ilan's in Switzerland. I think it would pay for us to follow him."

"How?" Yaakov lifted his palms. "Would you tell me that? Jump into the water and swim after the boat?"

Now Elazar was angry. "Today it's you who's being skeptical about what needs to be done." He appealed to Chaim. "Where does that boat dock? Where is the closest stop?"

"Let's see," Chaim said thoughtfully. "That would probably be on the shore of the lake, near the Burkliplatz."

The name meant nothing to Elazar. "How long will it take that boat to get there?"

Chaim thought a minute. "Let's say, anywhere from 10 to 15 minutes."

"Is it possible to drive to that plaza you just mentioned?"

"Sure!"

"Then maybe we should go. Maybe we'll get there before the boat does. We can plan an ambush for Ilan. What do you think, Yaakov?"

Elazar watched Yaakov anxiously. For once, he had put forth a plan of his own. Would Yaakov give it his stamp of approval?

"I'm sorry," Yaakov said. "For one thing, we're not even positive that the man you saw was Ilan. And even if it was, who knows if we'll get there before the boat? If we're too late, he'll have disappeared again. In other words, we're talking about a doubt piled upon another doubt." He shook his head decisively. "In my opinion, we have better things to do than go off on a wild-goose chase."

Elazar tried again. "But —"

"Let me finish, please," interposed Yaakov. "Apart from all that, even if it is Ilan, what do we have to gain by letting him see us watching him from the shore? It's a sure thing that he'll try to get away from us. For an instant he'll be taken by surprise, but then he'll do whatever he can to stay out of our way."

"So what do we do?" Elazar asked, resigned.

"I don't think we should run after him. It's not worth it."

"Then what?"

"I propose that we stick to our original plan. Chaim promised that we'd see some things that would interest us, right? If I understood him correctly, they'll be things that might be connected to Yossi. I say we continue with what we started out to do. Agreed?"

Elazar submitted, though not without some inner rancor. Reluctantly he let go of the parapet and threw a last look at the now-distant white boat, chugging away from him with its wake spread out behind. His heart was sore with the missed opportunity, as he saw it, of trapping Ilan.

They turned right from the bridge onto a stone-paved path. A short walk brought them to a small, elevated plaza.

"This is the Lindenhof," Chaim said. "All sorts of unconventional people like to hang out around here." He gestured for them to follow him.

As they walked on, what had been a vague hum of sound turned into voices raised in song and the beat of percussion instruments. Rounding a curve, the three found themselves facing a group of singers dressed in felt hats and South American-style ponchos and making a lot of noise with bongos and cymbals. They swayed to the monotonous rhythm of their song, while a small circle of bored-looking Swiss natives looked on. When the song ended, a few of the spectators tossed coins at the singers, and moved on.

Elazar was enjoying the spectacle of a tug-of-war between a middle-aged woman and her dog, who apparently wished to hear more of the music. She yanked at the leash, and tried pulling it after her, but the animal stood firm. Chaim remarked quietly, "All sorts of strange, foreign groups like to come to this place, singing for the sake of the donations they can get."

"And who are they?" Yaakov asked, nodding at the poncho-clad singers.

"I don't know," Chaim confessed.

Behind them, a voice murmured in Hebrew, "They're Los Paraguayos — a good Indian band from Paraguay."

Chaim stiffened, and would have turned around to see the speaker, but Yaakov pressed his arm warningly. The voice was familiar to him. Was it one of the men they had encountered in the airport terminal? Yaakov began moving away, pulling Chaim after him. Elazar was right behind.

They did not get far. At the corner of the Strahlgasse, a small street that intersected the Lindenhof, they came upon another group. These were dressed in long orange robes. A number of them had shaved heads. Bowls partially filled with Swiss francs rested at their feet. Their eyes were closed as they murmured a monotonous and incomprehensible mantra. No one seemed to be paying much attention to them.

Abruptly, Elazar pinched Yaakov's arm. "Yaakov, are you blind? Don't you see?"

For an instant, Yaakov didn't know what he meant. Then he said, "No, I'm not blind. I see. You're talking about the bracelet, aren't you? The bracelet of the Third Mystical Eye that some of them are wearing...."

Chaim exclaimed, "Really? I hardly believed your story yesterday — and here, so quickly, we've actually met some of them. Fantastic!"

"Quiet," whispered Yaakov. "Let's not attract their attention. Elazar, check each face carefully. Maybe Yossi is among them. Then we'll have to decide what to do."

"I — I'm scared."

"You must! That's what we came here for."

"Don't you remember how they threatened us at the airport?"

"We're three men, in an open area where a lot of people pass by all the time. Don't be afraid."

At that precise moment, three of the orange-robed figures opened their eyes and stared directly at Yaakov and his friends. Apparently, they had been able to pick up something of what he said, and they understood Hebrew. Without any warning, one of them broke ranks and sprinted away into one of the smaller side streets.

This time, it was Elazar who reacted first. Without stopping to think, he lunged forward and began running in pursuit.

"*Yossi!*" he screamed. "Yossi, it's me — Elazar! Stop, please, I beg you!"

The figure ran even faster, with Elazar after him and Yaakov and Chaim at his back. The chase did not last long. Other members of the orange-robed cult began running, too, with an eye to blocking the pursuers. One of them — a tall, powerfully built man — grabbed Elazar by the throat and halted him in his tracks. Two others, also tall and heavy, blocked Yaakov and Chaim's way.

The three cult members chattered in an unknown tongue, but their glowering faces and pointing fingers left no question as to their meaning. They wanted Yaakov, Elazar and Chaim to get away from there without any trouble — or delay.

They had no choice but to comply. In short order, they found themselves back at the bridge. When they had caught their breaths, Yaakov turned to Elazar. "Why did you call out 'Yossi'? Did you see him?"

"No. No, I didn't see him. But why was he running away from us? I thought it might be Yossi. With his head shaved and without his glasses, he would have looked different."

"But why did you shout like that, and get those crazy men all riled up?"

Elazar hung his head. "It just burst out. I don't know why! What do you want from me?"

Seeing the tears glistening at the corners of Elazar's eyes, Yaakov desisted.

They walked in silence back to Chaim's car. Without a word, Chaim switched on the ignition and began driving along the Limmat-Quai, intending to retrace their route back to the Banhofstrasse, where they would spend a few minutes thinking about their next move. But as he turned left toward the Banhofstrasse, Yaakov suddenly yelled, "Stop!"

Chaim slammed on the brakes. Like a shot, Yaakov was out of the car, Elazar on his heels. Yaakov crashed into a young man who was strolling along the street, grabbed his arm firmly, and cried, "We've got him! At last!"

51

lazar pounded along right behind Yaakov. With a sudden spurt of speed, he sprinted around to the man's other side and grabbed his arm. The man was completely boxed in. Stupefied, he gaped at Yaakov and Elazar, all three breathing hard with the exertion. His shock at the surprise attack gave way to a fresh astonishment as he took in their faces. Suddenly, he smiled.

The smile enraged Elazar. His anger burst out of him in a furious spate: "We've got you, Ilan! You thought you'd managed to get away from us, didn't you? You spread stories about a trip to England, to America. You see where that got you! We didn't believe what your wife said, and we've found you here, in Switzerland. Now you'd better do what we want! Understand?"

The last word was hurled at Ilan in a bellow. Several passers-by recoiled in disapproval. Lowering his voice, Elazar muttered again, "Understand, Ilan?"

"Sure I understand," Ilan answered easily. "And of course I'll do whatever you say." His manner was blatantly mocking. "That is, if you'll also do what I want. Incidentally, how did you know that I was in Switzerland?"

Yaakov snapped, "We knew. That's all that concerns you."

Ilan gazed at them curiously. The last thing he expected was to run into his boss's son and that son's friend in Zurich, on the busy Bahnhofstrasse. The last time they had met had not been under pleasant circumstances. Both Elazar and Yaakov were surprised to discover that there were no signs of fear or confusion on Ilan's face.

Ilan asked, "When did you arrive in Switzerland?"

"Two days after you did. We also caught a morning flight."

Ilan seemed taken aback. "How did you know which flight I took?"

"Never mind. We knew."

"Aha," Ilan chuckled. "You've become private detectives! Tell me, Elazar, does your father know you're here?"

"You may be surprised to hear that the answer is — yes!"

Yaakov was growing impatient. "Ilan, come to our car. We need to talk. I assume you know about what."

"By all means."

Though Ilan came with them willingly enough, the other two retained their grip on his arms. It would not be beyond him to make a sudden break for freedom. Ilan's ambivalence mystified them.

They entered the car, Ilan between them in the middle of the back seat. Chaim watched with interest, feeling a bit of apprehension. Where would this adventure end?

"Should I drive?" he asked.

"Yes," Yaakov said. "And quickly!"

The motor roared into life. "Where to?"

"You know Zurich — we don't. Take us someplace quiet."

The car started forward. Ilan seemed completely unperturbed by his abduction. The smile never left his face. Yaakov wondered whether he was such a proficient actor. There was no way to tell.

"Tell me," he opened the interrogation. "Where is Yossi?"

"I wish I knew. I can make a guess, but it's not exact."

Elazar flew into a rage. "What do you mean you don't know? Ilan, are you trying to make fools of us? Tell us where Yossi is!"

Ilan struggled to avoid the steely fingers that had suddenly gripped his arm again. In response, Elazar tightened his grasp. "You know where Yossi is! You're a member of that blasted cult!"

Ilan burst into laughter. "I'm not a member of the Third Mystical Eye. Just the opposite."

He sat back, watching the play of emotions — primarily astonishment — on the others' faces. Yaakov tried to regain the initiative: "I don't understand. If you're not a member, why did you fly off to Switzerland in such a hurry just when those other cult members arrived here?"

Now it was Ilan's turn to look astonished. "What? Who arrived? And how do you know about them, anyway?"

For the first time, Ilan betrayed agitation. Yaakov let him stew for a few minutes, then answered tranquilly, "That's our business, not yours. *Now, where is Yossi?*"

"You don't — What's your name?"

"Yaakov."

"Reb Yaakov, you don't understand. A tragedy is likely to happen any time now!"

Suspiciously, Yaakov asked, "What are you talking about? Why don't you answer my question directly? I'll ask it again: Where is Yossi?"

Ilan sucked in his breath. "And I'll tell you again: I wish I knew. I came to Switzerland to try to find the cult's hiding place, before something terrible happens."

"Ilan, I want you to stop avoiding the issue! What are you talking about?" Yaakov was fast losing patience.

Ilan looked at Yaakov, then at Elazar. "I'm asking for five minutes," he said quietly. "Let me speak without interruption, and you'll understand."

"Go on!"

"First of all, I'm not the enemy. I'm on your side!"

"Meaning what?" Elazar snapped.

Ilan threw him an angry look. "We agreed — no interruptions!"

Elazar muttered, "Sorry."

"All right. Elazar, do you remember why I wanted to meet you outside the Central Post Office in Tel Aviv? Do you remember?"

"Of course I remember! That was when you sent one of those Third Mystical Eye goons to beat me up!"

"That," Ilan shot back angrily, "is your mistake, Elazar."

"Really." Elazar's sarcasm was withering.

"Yes — really! I wanted to warn you about them, about the cult that your brother Yossi had apparently hooked up with. I myself have tried to infiltrate the cult — in a minute you'll understand why — but till now I haven't been successful."

Yaakov cut him off. "What? Not successful? But we saw you entering the green house of theirs on Aliyah Street! Why are you lying to us?"

"What? You saw me enter their house?"

"Yes!"

The word, reverberating around the car as it moved slowly down the streets of Zurich, was curt and slightly menacing.

Ilan nodded at them, a slight smile returning. "Well, congratulations."

Yaakov and Elazar exchanged a quick glance. "Ilan," Yaakov said slowly, "I'm asking you to stop playing games with us. We're not amused. We're very, very serious. So please get to the point."

"I'm more serious than either of you! You have no idea of the situation. I'm not a member of that cult. I tried to infiltrate them, in order to rescue my nephew, Yoav, a high school student from Tel Aviv who was lured into their clutches exactly the way Yossi was."

Elazar burst out, "Very interesting. But tell me, Ilan — how did that guy know I would be at the Central Post Office?"

"You remember, Elazar, the Canadian who was with me when we met in your father's office?"

"Yes."

"He's a member of the cult. In fact, he was one of its founders. Originally from Israel, he's been living abroad for some time now. He's been raking in a lot of money from the poor innocent fools he ensnares in his net. What happened is that he overheard me setting up the appointment with you, Elazar. I wasn't careful enough."

"But why didn't you show up yourself?"

"I came — but I was late. Unexpected things came up to delay me. Afterwards, I ate my heart out. I knew you'd never believe me again."

Even now, Elazar was not sure he believed him.

"Why did you bring that Canadian to my father's office? Because of Yossi?"

"No. He's a property investor. I wanted to win his trust. I wanted to get as close to him as possible, for my nephew's sake."

"And Yossi's too, right?"

"Yes, I would have tried to learn his whereabouts also."

"Did you succeed?"

"No. I didn't manage to find out where either of those boys is being kept. Let me tell you: They are all madmen!"

"So we gathered," Yaakov said dryly. "Why did you fly off to Switzerland in such a hurry?"

"I heard that the group was meeting in Switzerland. They're hounded in many countries. From bits and pieces I've managed to pick up, I believe they're plotting some atrocity so that they'll be left in peace."

"What do you mean?"

"I'm not sure, but I have reason to suspect that they're planning some sort of mass suicide. There have been cults in the past that have done such things. Never fear, the Canadian and other cult leaders won't kill themselves along with the others. They love life too much — life at the expense of the fools, like Yoav and Yossi, who follow them. They can afford to let some of them go... They know there'll be others just like them, only too willing to join."

Elazar felt his whole body begin to shake uncontrollably. It was only with great difficulty that he fought back an urge to break into sobs. The thought of what might happen to Yossi cast him into a bitter depression. Unless... Could it all be a pack of lies? Was Ilan making up the whole story just to confuse them? Elazar looked uncertainly from Ilan to Yaakov, who sat with eyes closed, deep in thought.

Meanwhile, Chaim continued to drive aimlessly through the streets of Zurich. Though he had managed to restrain himself from taking part in the discussion taking place in the back seat of his car, he had not missed a word. What sort of crazy situation had he stumbled into? The same fear that gripped his new Israeli friends seeped over him now, and made driving difficult. As he maneuvered the car through traffic, he felt as though he had stepped into an unreal and spine-tingling drama.

Elazar could not keep still a moment longer. He grabbed Ilan's shoulders with both hands, shook him and shouted, "Tell me where they are!"

Ilan bore the brunt of the attack without resistance. "I only wish I knew, Elazar. I came to Switzerland to look for them. Now that you say that the cult leaders have come here from Israel on your flight, I am deathly afraid. It means that the news I heard is true, and the plans are real!" He leaned forward urgently. "Let's work together to find them — to save them!"

For several long minutes, no one spoke. The silence was heavy with tension — an uneasy mixture of fear and doubt. Chaim, snaking in and out among the other cars and blowing his horn often, was obviously upset.

"What do we do now?" Elazar moaned. "What do we do? Where do we find them?"

"And if we knew that," Yaakov asked quietly, "could we do something about it?"

Ilan said, "I don't know. To tell you the truth, I'm fresh out of ideas. We're all in the same boat."

Another silence fell. Then Yaakov said, "Chaim, stop the car."

Chaim half-turned his head, startled. "Where —?"

"It doesn't matter where. At the first available spot, pull over."

52

With a screech of tires, the car pulled close to a side-street curb and came to a halt. Elazar and Ilan fixed their eyes on Yaakov with an air of expectancy. Chaim, twisting in his seat, did the same.

"I've stopped," he said. "Now what?"

Yaakov looked at Ilan. "Are you prepared to repeat what you just said?"

"Which part?"

"About the danger you're expecting."

Ilan stirred uneasily. "I don't have any definite knowledge. It's just a sense I have…."

"Okay, okay," Yaakov said testily. "Repeat it!"

"Why? Didn't you understand what I said?"

"I understood." Yaakov spoke from between his teeth. "I simply want you to repeat it in order to help me think. Also, you may mention some additional detail you left out before. All right?"

Ilan hesitated, then nodded in submission. "I said that I've been picking up hints that they're planning some kind of dramatic operation with a group of their members, here in Switzerland."

"What exactly did they say?"

"I told you, they spoke in hints. My sense was that they were talking about suicide — group suicide. They kept mentioning that lunatic, Koresh, in the United States, who committed suicide after the federal police attacked the ranch in Waco, Texas where he was holed up with his followers."

Elazar felt the familiar clutch of fear. "Are you sure that's what they're planning?"

Ilan's eyes traveled from Yaakov to Elazar to Chaim, and back again to Yaakov. Despite the air of confidence and cheer he was trying to exude, all three sensed an inner nervousness. Was he playing with them?

"Look, Yaakov," Ilan said, "I'll tell you again: It was only a feeling I had, but it was a strong feeling. Those men are capable of pulling this off. They know how to brainwash confused youngsters, telling them that the way to happiness lies in joining with the Mystical Third Eye — the Eye that supervises the world and draws all goodness to itself, and — "

Yaakov broke in vigorously. "Enough of that! To the point now. Do you have any idea at all where they might be located? We already saw one group in the city today, just half an hour ago. Is it possible that they all live here in Zurich, in the neighborhood of the Limmat?"

Ilan shrugged, eyes downcast. There was something about his manner that evoked Yaakov's distrust. It was hard to put his finger on exactly what it was that bothered him about Ilan and the story he told.

"Look," Ilan said, "I've made it my business to become acquainted with the group in the city. Last night I even participated in one of their ceremonies. We danced, we screamed... But there were only about 10 people there, all told." He paused, then added in visible pain, "Yossi and my nephew were not among them."

Yaakov inched closer. "Just a minute. I don't understand. They didn't so much as drop a hint about where they were going or where they live?"

"The youngsters did talk — about the mountains they were planning to visit soon. This is Switzerland, not Israel! In Israel, there are only a few tall mountains. Here, in the land of the Alps, the story is different. Go search hundreds of mountains for one group of madmen."

Yaakov didn't answer. His faith in Ilan was still incomplete. "Mountains, you say?"

"Yes. Mountains."

Yaakov considered this, then turned abruptly to Chaim. "How do you say 'mountain' in German?"

"A mountain is a 'berg.'"

"Berg?" Yaakov tasted the word, and repeated it. "Berg, berg…"

He reached into his wallet and pulled out another note. An enthusiastic light leapt into his eyes as he read it. "Look!" he said, passing the note to Elazar.

Elazar looked at the note. "Read it," Yaakov whispered. "Read it out loud."

The page was familiar to Elazar. It was the one they had taken from the green house on Aliyah Street, bearing the list of cult members.

"Read it, Elazar," Yaakov said again. "Read what it says beside Yossi's name."

Elazar read aloud: "Seelisberg." He raised his eyes. "You're right! It says 'berg'!"

Chaim's excitement showed. "It says the name of a mountain — Seelisberg!"

"Is there such a place in Switzerland?" Ilan asked.

"Definitely," Chaim confirmed. "It's about three hours away from Zurich, past Lucerne."

"And what's there?" Yaakov asked.

"It's a quiet village on the mountaintop, with an incredible view of a beautiful lake called the Vierwaldstattersee."

"Vierwald*— what?"

Patiently, Chaim repeated, "Vierwaldstattersee."

Yaakov gave up trying to pronounce it. Instead, he asked Chaim with some urgency, "What connection do you think that village might have with our business — with the cult, and Yossi?" He threw a glance at Ilan, and added, "Yes, and Ilan's nephew, too."

"I have no idea. It's not a very large village. It's surrounded by forest. The silence there is…is…" He groped for the right word, then ended lamely, "it's a silence you can *hear*, you know what I mean?"

All three nodded their heads. Yaakov commented, "Sounds like a nice place."

"Nice isn't the word," Chaim said. "The place is stunning. Once, over Pesach vacation, I took my wife and daughters there."

"So you know the place?" Yaakov asked, with rising excitement.

"Yes, certainly."

"Well, what do you say to a little trip there? What time is it?"

Chaim consulted his wristwatch. "It's 2 o'clock. But what will we do there now? Maybe we should go tomorrow."

"No. Now! What will we do there? I don't know. Maybe we'll go around in circles, maybe we'll come up against a dead end — or maybe we'll find something that will help us make some progress."

Chaim's face took on a resigned air. "Okay, I'm listening."

"Will we be back in the city in time for *Minchah?*"

"I'm not sure. But there's no problem — we can stop at the yeshivah in Lucerne."

Chaim started the engine and drove home quickly, where he stock-piled provisions for the journey. This adventure was proving even more exciting than he had anticipated!

53

"Y ou know," Zevulun said quietly to Tzipporah in the darkened living room, "ever since we came home from Yerushalayim, I've been looking through *Mishlei*. Did you know that?"

"No. I didn't know." Tzipporah was clearly curious.

"It's because of what the *rosh yeshivah* said — the things he quoted to me from that *sefer*. Especially the part he read with the Vilna Gaon's commentary. Remember?"

Tzipporah nodded. She waited, but her husband had fallen into a brooding silence. As she sat there in the dimness, tears began to collect at the corners of her eyes. Hastily, she dabbed them away with the handkerchief that she never seemed to put down these days.

"Are you crying?" Zevulun asked suddenly.

She made one more swipe with her handkerchief. "N-no. What makes you think that?"

He peered through the distance between them, trying to read her face in the gloom. At last he said, "All right, I'm sorry. I must have been mistaken." Zevulun went back to his interrupted thought. "Why am I looking through *Mishlei*? I'll admit it: I'm not sure. Maybe it was those words about one person's heart being reflected in another person's, just the way water gives back the reflection of a face. They spoke to me, those words. More than that — they created an upheaval in me! Yes, an upheaval. It's that simple. That verse is sitting on my consciousness now, like a big, heavy rock. Suddenly, I feel weak...small...helpless." He paused. "Did you understand the *rosh yeshivah's* explanation? The message he was trying to get across to me?"

Tzipporah was taken aback. What her husband was saying astonished her to no small degree. Her arrogant Zevulun was admitting his own error! He was feeling weak, small, helpless — and confessing as much to her! When, in recent years, had he ever admitted to having such feelings? The moment felt dreamlike to her, but she knew she must put aside such fancies and be with her husband. For this was his moment of truth.

She felt a deep compassion well up inside — compassion for Zevulun, from whom she'd longed to hear these very words for so many years. Strange....

"You're not answering me!" The voice cut through her thoughts. Startled, Tzipporah answered quickly, "I think I did. I think I understood what the *rosh yeshivah* was trying to say."

Zevulun sighed. The faint light of early morning filtered through the closed shutters. A bird rested on the windowsill, piped a few clear notes, then flew away. Zevulun said, "I'm not so sure you understood."

"Why do you say that?"

"Because it's a saying that must make a person feel depressed. And — I'll admit it — me more than anyone."

He stood abruptly. "I've got to get a drink...."

"Sit down," his wife ordered, getting up herself. "I'll bring it. What do you want?"

"Water. Plain water." With a grimace that was directed inwardly, at himself, he added, "Right now I don't want anything but the simplest and the purest... The truest!"

Tzipporah hurried off to the kitchen. On the way, she stopped to splash cold water onto her face. Full daylight would be upon them soon, and it wouldn't do to have Zevulun see her tear-stained face.

"Thank you." With a grateful nod, Zevulun accepted the glass of water she brought him. He sipped it slowly as he continued to speak.

"As I was saying, it's an amazing *pasuk!* Do you understand its significance, Tzipporah? What it's saying is that I — through my feelings, my thoughts and, certainly, my actions — can dictate another's attitude toward me. In other words, I have an awesome responsibility toward... toward... toward Yossi, for example."

He took a last sip and set the glass down with exaggerated care. The act served to postpone the continuation of his confession for a few seconds. Even then he sat silent, his breath coming loud and harsh in the quiet room. Tzipporah grew concerned.

"Zevulun."

"What?"

"If it's hard for you, don't continue." Instantly regretting her choice of words, she amended, "That is, continue another time."

"No, no! It's now or never...."

"Okay." Tzipporah, recognizing an overwrought man when she saw one, hastened to back down. "I understand."

Zevulun picked up the glass he had just put down. It helped to hold onto something. In a strained voice, he said, "On the day we found out that Yossi was missing, I drove up to Yerushalayim. I wanted to find out what had happened. As I drove, I was full of anger at his yeshivah. What kind of place could not hold onto its students? You entrust your son to them, and the next thing you know, he's run away! I was ready to blame his *rosh yeshivah*, his *mashgiach*, anyone at all...."

He coughed, then sighed. "And then I took Elazar for a drive. As we talked, I had the distinct impression that he was hiding something from me. I pressed him about it, until he was forced to tell me. I pressured him without mercy...the way you know I can. And in the end, he said..."

Zevulun sprang to his feet and went to the window. He threw open the shutters. Morning sunlight flooded the living room.

"The dark was getting to me," he muttered.

Tzipporah stared at him. He seemed almost like a stranger, with his sad face and the arrogance quenched from his eyes.

"And do you know what he told me?" Zevulun said.

"No, what?"

"He wanted to keep it from me, but I forced him to tell. It was about Yossi...what Yossi thought of me. Yossi had told him — told him — How do I say it? Yes, he told him that he...hated me...."

Tzipporah sat frozen. She had heard those identical words from Yossi's mouth more than once. And more than once, she had tried to bring them to Zevulun's attention. But her husband had closed his heart to her appeals. No criticism of his approach to Yossi had succeeded in getting past his heavy armor. She had despaired of ever reaching him.

Zevulun continued: "I was astounded. What was this about? Why should he hate me? Why didn't the boy realize that my attitude toward him was only a reaction to his own wild behavior, his lack of discipline? Didn't he see that it was all his own fault? At that moment, I felt angrier at him than ever."

He came back to his armchair and sank down again. "Do you understand, Tzipporah? At that moment, I felt more justified than ever. Justified in how I had treated him, if he was so ignorant of the fact that I was only doing it for his own good. There was something fundamentally wrong with the boy, though I couldn't figure out just what it was. I was very angry at his *rebbeim* in yeshivah, who hadn't managed to teach him right from wrong — to hold him on a short leash, the way I did at home...."

Tzipporah did not know how to react. She was mortally afraid of causing, through an unwise word, the stream of his confidences to dry up. Unsure how long Zevulun's unusual mood might last, she was also wary of being the unwitting cause of one of her husband's old-time "explosions." Silence was her best option. But she did not drop her eyes. They remained fixed unwaveringly on Zevulun's face, as though she were trying to read in it the changeable winds of his temperament.

"Well, the *rosh yeshivah* gave me a good slap in the face," Zevulun sighed. "Or rather, a good punch in the nose. I can't find a better way of describing the way I'm feeling right now."

Like a spirit in torment, he stood up once more, then immediately sat down again. Tzipporah sensed that Zevulun was trying desperately to put off a really difficult moment. As she watched, he gathered his courage:

"Suddenly, I understood that if Yossi hates me, that must mean that I — subconsciously, at least — must also hate him. That's what Shlomo HaMelech, in his wisdom, was telling us — and the Vilna Gaon, too. The *rosh yeshivah* directed me to the right *pasuk* at the right moment." He stopped and looked at her, a question in his eyes.

"Do you understand what the *rosh yeshivah* was essentially telling me? 'You, Zevulun Kimmerman, are responsible for your son's behavior! You, in your hidden hatred toward him (*"Not so hidden at all!"* Tzipporah thought), caused him to behave hatefully toward you.' In other words, the *rosh yeshivah* has blamed Yossi's running away on me. No — not the *rosh yeshivah*. Shlomo HaMelech."

Zevulun pressed a weary hand to his cheek. "As I was going through *Mishlei*, I came upon another *pasuk*: 'Educate a youth according to his way.' This raised a lot of questions in my mind. What does it mean? Isn't education supposed to be according to *us*, the parents and educators? Should we just let our youth do whatever they want? What, exactly, do the words 'according to his way' mean? Do you understand my questions, Tzipporah?"

She nodded.

"And then the Vilna Gaon came along and gave me my second punch in the face. Listen to what he says."

Zevulun picked up the *sefer* and flipped quickly through its pages until he reached the sixth verse in the 22nd chapter. He began to read:

"'Educate the youth according to his way' — teach him according to his destiny and his nature, and guide him to do mitzvos... But when you force him to go against his nature, he will listen to you now out of fear; but later, when your yoke is lifted from his neck, he will stray from it, because it is impossible for him to change his nature.' Do you understand, Tzipporah?"

Tzipporah hesitated, not sure what to say. Zevulun rushed on, "Do you? What he's saying, I think, is that if the boy ran away, I bear a tremendous responsibility. Because I must certainly have been trying to educate him in a way that ran counter to his own nature instead of with it. As a father, I should have tried to use his own character to best advantage — not try to break it. That's a sure recipe for failure!"

He closed his eyes. "Like my failure with Yossi."

His eyes opened, and he gave his wife a sorrowful smile. "Would you ever have believed you would hear me speak this way?"

Her heart overflowed with pity. "Zevulun, I think that's enough for today. Go *daven Shacharis* and rest a little. I can't stand seeing you like this."

"No." The emphatic negative was tempered with a gentle look. Though his voice was blurred with fatigue, it lost none of its firmness. "What I have to decide must be decided now."

Tzipporah sat up, alarmed. "What do you have to decide?"

"Rabbi Nachman of Breslov says: 'If you believe that you have the power to destroy, believe that you have the power to repair.'"

"Well? What are you saying?"

"I destroyed something. I hated — and that hatred was reflected in my son, like a face mirrored in water... So what I have to do now is love. To love without cause, unconditionally, in order to repair the hatred that has grown in his heart, wherever he is."

This time, Tzipporah could not hold back the torrent of tears that burst from her. She lowered her face into her hands and let them flow. Through the sound of her own soft sobs, she heard her husband's voice:

"I tried to train him, apparently, in a way that was contrary to his nature. Now I must learn what his nature really is. I'll need you to help me with that... You, whose opinion about Yossi I was never interested in hearing."

Zevulun fell silent. He felt terribly weak, as though a very heavy burden had been laid across his shoulders. Would he be strong enough to carry it?

Making an immense effort, he heaved himself out of his armchair and crossed to where Tzipporah was sitting. "And there's something else I have to fix."

Tzipporah lifted her wet face and gazed at him through tear-filled eyes.

"It's my fault, the Vilna Gaon says, that Yossi ran away. It's up to me to bring him home again."

His face was set and rigid, as though carved in stone. Tzipporah tried to read his facial expressions, to learn what he was planning to do. The strange light in his eyes signaled a decision born of desperation. What could it be?

54

They left Zurich a little after 2 in the afternoon.

The journey began in silence. Chaim steered the car with a sure hand southward, toward Seelisberg. Yaakov and Elazar, in the back seat, gazed out of their respective windows at the passing scenery. So — though not without some neck-craning — did Ilan, sandwiched between them. Yaakov had decided to remain where he was instead of sitting in the front passenger seat. He still was not completely sure he trusted Ilan, and did not want to offer him the opportunity to escape.

The soaring mountains and lush green forests were breathtaking. Here and there they caught a glimpse of a waterfall, cascading down from some unimaginable peak; or a lake, sparkling blue; or a river running parallel to the Autostrada for a while before veering away.

Some of the larger lakes featured boats, big and small, gliding slowly and silently to some hidden destination. The boats were white as the snows that covered the mountaintops that rose above the horizon. Elazar was particularly impressed by the graceful swans swimming elegantly along the lakeshore.

"Unbelievable!" he murmured, as though reluctant to disturb the serenity of the scene by speaking aloud. Then, like a man dunked in cold water, he remembered why he was here, in beautiful Switzerland. Not to enjoy the view, but to find Yossi. His spirits plummeted several notches.

Chaim said in a matter-of-fact way, "It is said that when Rabbi Samson Raphael Hirsch returned from visiting Switzerland he commented, 'Now I will be able to answer Hashem when He asks me: "Did you also see My Switzerland?"'"

The Israelis could well understand such a sentiment. Yaakov grinned. "After 120 years, at least there'll be one question to which I'll be able to give a positive answer! I surely have seen the wonders of Hashem's Creation."

"Just wait," Chaim promised. "When we reach the Seelisberg area you'll see more of the beauty of the Alps. Right now we're near Zug."

Yaakov remarked, "I'm not sure whether we'll be able to enjoy the view. We're here to accomplish our mission, Chaim. Or have you forgotten?"

"Of course not! A task of detective work!"

The highway, clean and in good repair, wound past Swiss towns and villages, replete with characteristic wooden houses. Most of the window sills boasted potted flowers, no more than splotches of bright color to the passengers of the speeding car.

"How long till we get there?" Yaakov asked.

"About another hour to go," Chaim answered.

"Okay. Describe the place to me, please."

"What is there to describe? It's a typical Swiss village, held fast on the cliffs of the mountain. What else can I say? When we get there, you'll see."

Yaakov said quietly, "You didn't understand what I meant. I'd like to plan ahead what we'll have to do to find out if we've reached the right place."

Chaim considered, then said with a trace of impatience, "I'm sorry, I can't help you there. I still don't know exactly what your aim is."

Yaakov laughed. "On the contrary, you're going to be the most helpful one of all! Isn't it obvious to you?"

"No."

"Chaim, you're Swiss. You speak the language. You won't arouse suspicion by the questions you'll ask."

"True. But I don't know exactly what I'm supposed to ask. Don't you think it'll look a little suspicious if you stand next to me, whispering questions into my ear?"

"Chaim, listen to me. This is serious. The minute we get there — what did you call the place again?"

"Seelisberg."

"Together with Ilan, you will have to use all your talents, to start sniffing around. Elazar and I will arouse suspicion by the way we dress. Naturally, you won't go up to the first person you meet and ask, 'Have you seen Yossi Kimmerman, who ran away with members of a cult called the Third Mystical Eye?' You'll have to operate secretively. What's so hard to understand about that?"

Nervously, Chaim pressed down on the gas pedal. The car picked up speed. "You know what could happen?"

"What?"

"I'm liable to meet up with Yossi himself, strolling through the town, and ask *him* where Yossi Kimmerman is! Are you getting my point? I don't know him!"

Yaakov said soothingly, "Don't get angry, and don't be afraid. My idea is simply for you and Ilan to wander through the town with your eyes and ears open. Converse with the natives, like a couple of tourists who happened to find themselves in an attractive village. All right?"

Chaim snorted. "I'm just wondering how far that'll get us."

A moment later, the car swerved into an exit lane and moved onto a side road. Chaim followed the road signs until he reached the shore of a large lake. He parked near the pier, where a single midsized boat was anchored.

"We've reached Brunnen," Chaim announced. "Do you see that tall mountain in the distance, on the other side of the lake?"

"Yes."

"There, on top, is Seelisberg."

Yaakov and Elazar squinted their eyes upward.. Visibility was not at its best that day, with a light mist covering the peak of the mountain. The same thought flashed into the minds of both men: Was Yossi up there?

Tearing themselves away from the view, they sat back to endure the last half hour of the ride. Chaim drove around the lake and began climbing a narrow mountain road that wound ever higher. Elazar, gripped with sudden tension, glanced over at Yaakov, who appeared impassive. Ilan was beginning to betray signs of nervous distress.

The car continued to climb until it reached the outskirts of the village. From that vantage point, the view took their breath away. Vast stretches of green, intersected by deep brown gorges, touched a horizon rimmed with snowy peaks. A modest lake was tucked into the little valley to the right of the road. To the left lay a thick wood, at the edges of which a number of cows grazed stoically.

The driver and his three passengers stepped out of the car to stretch their legs and fill their lungs with the pure mountain air. The sense of peace was profound, almost intoxicating. When the cows stirred, the bells tied around their necks tinkled, the chimes echoing sweetly in the silence.

Suddenly, Yaakov spun around and ran back to the car. "Elazar, follow me, quick!" he whispered in great excitement.

Elazar began to run, too. At the car, he gasped, "What's the matter with you?"

Yaakov didn't answer. Instead, he yanked open the door and pulled Elazar forcibly inside after him. It was only after he had closed the door and rolled up the window that he pointed toward the mountain, beyond the cows moving placidly to and fro.

Elazar followed his gaze. His agitation, when he saw what Yaakov meant him to see, nearly ruined everything …

55

lazar pressed his face to the car window, trembling. He stared up the slope of the mountain at the spot Yaakov had indicated. There, on a broad, sun-warmed rock, sat two youths wearing long orange robes. Several cows grazed lazily on the grass growing around the boys' feet. Elazar squinted, trying to ignore the growing physical discomfort of his pounding heart and throbbing temples. With difficulty — it was hard to speak past the sudden constriction in his throat — he whispered, "Yaakov, look! I think...I think that's Yossi! That one, on the left! Yes, yes, I think it's him..."

Without warning, Elazar wrenched at the handle and rolled down the window. "*Yossi!* he bellowed hysterically. "*Yo-o —*"

Before he could finish repeating the name, Yaakov lunged at him and slapped a hand over his mouth. Pressing Elazar back into the car, Yaakov rolled up the window and glared.

"What's wrong with you, Elazar? Have you gone crazy? You'll ruin everything!"

Elazar was furious. "What am I ruining?"

"Fortunately," Yaakov said, "I don't think that's Yossi. Maybe your shouts haven't caused irreparable damage. But if it *is* Yossi, and he heard your foolhardy, hysterical screams..." He shook his head.

"Instead of trying to stop me from calling, why don't you explain?" Elazar challenged rebelliously.

An inner voice cautioned Yaakov to stay calm at all costs. He sensed Elazar's growing anger and wanted to pull him back to safer territory. Both of them were a little overwhelmed by everything that had happened since they had flown off to Switzerland at such short notice. He spoke with renewed tranquility, "Calm down, Elazar. We have to have nerves of steel. This is when we really get tested. It looks like we've nearly reached our goal. So please, stay calm!"

"Excuse me, you're the one who's being nervous. You didn't let me call him. Why not?"

"Apparently, you forgot one thing. Yossi not only ran away from home and from his yeshivah. He also ran away from you."

Elazar gaped at him.

"Imagine," Yaakov elaborated, "if Yossi were to find you here, in Switzerland, and actually near his hiding place. Don't you think he'd disappear in a flash? He has made it very clear that he doesn't want to see any of us. If that happens, who knows if we would manage to find him a second time? Don't you see, Elazar?"

It began to dawn on Elazar that he might have made a mistake. He was still not fully convinced, however, and certainly not calm. His eyes kept straying to the window through which he had seen the two orange-robed youths. As he watched, he saw them rise in a leisurely fashion and begin to make their way into the woods.

"Yaakov! They're leaving!" he cried, grabbing Yaakov's arm.

Yaakov had seen it, too. Together, they watched the two figures stroll past the first thick trees at the forest's edge. Elazar's frenzied shouts had apparently fallen short of their mark.

"What's going to happen now?" Elazar fretted. When Yaakov didn't answer, he repeated, "What's going to happen?"

"Until now, have you ever known beforehand what was going to happen? What will happen will happen!"

Chaim had been ambling in the area, relishing the clear mountain air. He returned now, and glanced in some amazement at his two guests from Israel, crouched inside the car. "Why are you sitting there as if you are frozen solid? Come out, let's walk around a little."

Neither man answered. Both pairs of eyes were riveted to the boys in orange, moving ever higher and farther away. Frowning, Chaim followed their gaze.

His face cleared. "Aha, I get it! I didn't notice till just now. Those guys in orange, eh?"

Yaakov and Elazar nodded. Elazar added, "I think one of them is my brother Yossi."

Chaim grinned and clapped his hands soundlessly. The scent of adventure was strong in his nostrils. "*Nu?*" he urged. "Let's see some action!"

"That's it, exactly," Yaakov answered. "Now *you* go into action!"

Chaim took his place behind the wheel, then turned around to stare at Yaakov. "What do you mean, '*You* go into action' — emphasis on the 'you'? What about the two of you?"

"Right now," Yaakov smiled thinly, "the key is in your hand. Our success depends on you. Understand?"

"No! No, I don't understand!"

"It's so simple. I'll explain again. We're strangers here. We don't speak the language. Automatically, we become a focus of suspicion. As long as we don't ask too many questions, we can be considered just another pair of tourists. But the minute we act too interested in unusual things, we'll be suspect. Don't you agree?"

"So?"

"The solution is obvious. You have to do the work for us — sniff around, investigate and try to flush out the cult's hiding place."

Chaim closed his eyes. All at once, his taste for adventure evaporated. The job seemed difficult, too difficult for him to tackle, and yet he didn't feel he could refuse. His mind raced through various plans for escaping this unwanted mission, but none seemed cogent enough to meet with Yaakov's approval. For a moment he played with the notion of categorizing his own involvement in this mad scheme under the heading of *"piku'ach nefesh."* But Yaakov and Elazar sat quietly, watching him and waiting for his answer — which, in their opinion, could only be one thing. What to do?

At the end of a silence that stretched for several long, uncomfortable minutes, Chaim said reluctantly, "Okay, suppose I start sniffing around. Let's assume that I even manage, with Hashem's help, to ferret out that crazy cult's hideout. And let's say that I'm not too late, and that I manage to reach that hideout before they commit whatever crazy deed they're planning. Given all those assumptions, what will you do with the information? Will you be asking me next to infiltrate the cult, and to bring Yossi back here to the car?!"

Chaim had asked the question in all seriousness, and was offended when Yaakov responded with a peal of laughter. "And let's say we really do ask you to do that last thing. What would you do?"

Chaim bit his lip. "It really could be the last thing you ever ask me. Who knows if I would ever return?"

"Relax, Chaim," Yaakov said, patting his arm where it lay across the back of the front seat. "You're exaggerating. From the beginning of this thing, Elazar and I have felt that Hashem was leading us. We've seen different threads come together, and all the unexpected twists and turns that have helped us move forward to this point. Look at the way we met you — specifically you, an Israeli like us, who is also a driver who knows his way around. Do you think that was mere coincidence?

"I, personally, am absolutely convinced that we're going to succeed in this mission we have undertaken. Have a little faith, Chaim!"

A wry smile lit Chaim's face. "That's easy for you to say. Let's see *you* go off into those hills."

"You really sell me short." Yaakov spoke quietly, but his shoulders were back and his spine erect. "If it weren't for the fear of arousing suspicion, you'd soon see me in action. In fact, I'm not at all sure I won't have to step in at some point anyway."

The three were silent, each lost in thoughts of his own. Then Yaakov cleared his throat. "*Nu*, Chaim, let's get moving! At this rate, we're not going to make it to *Minchah* at the yeshivah in Lucerne."

"I only hope we'll be able to make *Shacharis* tomorrow morning in Lucerne, or in Zurich. Did you think I'd finish the job here in half an hour?"

Yaakov opted not to answer. He sensed that Chaim had already made up his mind to help them, but was still pawing and kicking like a newly broken horse. He didn't mind Chaim's attitude, as long as he helped them gather the vital information they needed. As though reading his mind, Chaim asked suddenly, "So what exactly do you want to know?"

"What do you mean? Is there such a cult in this village?"

Elazar broke in, "I think we're already convinced of that."

"You're right," Yaakov agreed. "What we want to know now is, who are they? Where do they live? Does anyone in the village know them? That sort of thing."

Chaim stepped out of the car, then leaned through the open window to whisper, "Okay, I'm going. Say *Tehillim* for my success."

"Hashem will help. Don't worry!"

Chaim moved slowly away, aiming for the first cottage. It stood, surrounded by a picket fence and bordered by flower beds, some several hundred yards from where his car was parked. Yaakov and Elazar saw Chaim walk up to the front gate. They saw him fumble with the gate latch — and then fall back. A huge Saint Bernard, barking wildly, lunged at him.

Chaim retreated at a good clip, the dog after him. The cottage door was flung open. An elderly man stood framed in the doorway, and even at a distance it was clear that he was furious. They saw his fist wave in the air as he shouted something. Then the door closed again as abruptly as it had opened.

"A bad beginning," Elazar sighed.

"A good beginning," Yaakov contradicted. "Why bad?"

"Why good?" Elazar countered.

"First of all, everything that Hashem causes to happen has to be for the good. Secondly, I've come to know Chaim a little better today. Failure only makes him more stubborn. I've noticed that."

Yaakov paused, then added, "There, do you see? He hasn't come back to the car. He's hurrying deeper into the village. I'm counting on him."

Suddenly, Elazar cried, "Where's Ilan?"

Yaakov started. Like Elazar, he had been so absorbed in the sight of the orange-clad youths on the mountain that he had forgotten to monitor Ilan's movements. Where was he?

"Yaakov, he's disappeared. He's gone!"

"You see, we didn't suspect him for nothing. In spite of everything, he's managed to slip away…"

They peered through the car windows, one on either side, straining for a glimpse of Ilan. There was nothing. It was as though the very earth had swallowed him up.

Elazar broke the silence first. "You realize, of course, what this means."

"I certainly do."

"We wanted to keep a low profile. Ha! Ilan's probably on his way to the cult this very minute, to let them know we're in the neighborhood. What a setup!"

Yaakov shook his head and echoed softly, "What a setup…"

56

Yaakov and Elazar were beginning to worry. Over an hour had elapsed since Chaim had begun climbing the ascending road into Seelisberg. They had seen no sign of him since.

"That's all we need now," Elazar said glumly, "for Chaim to be missing, too."

Yaakov did not answer.

The two were cramped and uncomfortable in the car, but dared not step out. Their eyes continuously scanned the horizon. The road on whose shoulder they were parked was deserted for a good deal of the time. Occasionally a car would pass, slowing momentarily as it neared their vehicle, and then it would speed on its way. At such moments, Yaakov and Elazar would sit stiff as statues, looking straight ahead. Their goal was to attract as little attention as possible.

"Where could he be?" Elazar finally exclaimed.

"Who, exactly," Yaakov asked, "are you asking about — Ilan, or Chaim?"

Elazar clenched his jaw. Yaakov's forced calm was beyond him. What a bizarre situation! Two Israeli yeshivah men, stranded in a car in a remote village in the Swiss Alps — men who did not speak the local language — and who had no idea of what was going to happen to them next. Could Yaakov really be as calm as he looked? It was possible, Elazar acknowledged privately, that his companion was indeed anxious and tense. If so, he hid it well.

The sky began to darken. The vast grassy expanses had lost their golden overtones. Now the sun painted only the peaks a pale lavender. Night was falling over Switzerland.

"If only he'll return with Yossi," Elazar said, as if trying to ward off his fears with the power of his words. Yaakov said nothing.

Suddenly, Yaakov stirred. "Look!" he said softly.

Elazar jumped. "Where?"

Then he saw. Through the dusk that was rapidly blurring the mountain paths, he saw a figure approaching. It was impossible to identify him. One thing, however, was clear: The approaching figure was neither Chaim nor Ilan.

His features came into focus. It was a local man, dressed in the style of the other villager they had seen that day: heavy shoes, thick red socks, and on his head a black knit cap embroidered with blue, white and red flowers. His face was muffled in a wide scarf against the night cold.

"Is he coming here, do you think?" Elazar whispered.

"I think so. Remember, stay calm!"

"But what does he want? Who could he be?"

"Patience. We'll find out soon enough."

This did nothing to relax Elazar's fears. Under his breath, he began murmuring snatches of *Tehillim* that he knew by heart.

The man's pace did not slacken as he came up to the car. With no hesitation, he went to the driver's door, opened it and slipped in behind the wheel as if it were the most natural thing in the world.

In the back seat, Yaakov and Elazar felt their hearts stop. Their stupefaction was such that they could not utter a word. Then Yaakov, recovering, leaned quickly forward and hooked his left arm around the stranger's throat.

"Who are you?" he shouted in Hebrew, as though the man could understand him. "What do you want with us? Who sent you — that blasted cult?"

In his rage, Yaakov felt like throttling the fellow. The tension that had been building up inside him with Ilan's disappearance and Chaim's delay in returning made him tighten his grip now, to the point that the man found it hard to breathe. He tried to say something, but failed. Only a few strangled squeaks emerged.

Yaakov relaxed his grip slightly. The "driver" seized the opportunity to bark, also in Hebrew, "Yaakov, don't you recognize me? It's Chaim!"

In his shock, Yaakov's arm fell away. The voice had, indeed, been Chaim's.

Massaging his throat tenderly, Chaim twisted around in his seat to face his friends. "You nearly choked me!" he chortled. "What have I done to make you want to kill me?"

Yaakov failed to see the humor. "If I had hurt you," he retorted stiffly, "it would have been your own fault — and your fault alone. We almost fainted when you walked right up to the car and got in! Didn't that occur to you when you decided to pull this stunt? And what's it all about, anyway? Do you think we drove all the way up here just to play games?"

The laughter faded from Chaim's face. He saw his mistake — a mistake that might have ended, Heaven forbid, in tragedy. "I'm really sorry. It never occurred to me that I might frighten you. I really didn't intend that."

"Yes, yes — but what's the masquerade for? Is today Purim in Seelisberg?"

Chaim removed the Swiss cap from his head and replaced it with his own. "Let me tell you what's been going on, and why I'm dressed up like this. Did you notice the way the man in that house chased me away and wouldn't answer my questions?"

"We saw."

"Well, that got me angry. I don't like failure. I told myself, 'Chaim, you didn't want to do what Yaakov asked you to do. But now, after this, you've got to succeed! You hear, Chaim? You must!' That's what I told myself."

He broke off, as though to test their reactions. When neither said a word, Chaim continued, "So I went on toward the village square. I figured I'd find some pub, have a glass of beer there and strike up an acquaintance with some of the natives — the more drunk, the better. Maybe I'd get some valuable information that way.

"As I was walking down the street, I saw, in the distance, a few guys in orange robes, like the ones we saw in Zurich. They were on the main street; then they turned off into a side street. I got excited — here was proof that we hadn't been mistaken, and that the cult was really located in this area."

Chaim sucked in a lungful of air. "But a surprise was waiting for me. An unpleasant surprise...."

"What kind of surprise?" Elazar demanded.

"Hold on, I'm getting to that. Near the group in orange I saw another man walking. He was dressed in normal clothes. And who do you think he turned out to be? Our old friend Ilan! Did you notice that he's gone?"

"We noticed, but only after you left," Elazar said.

Yaakov asked impatiently, "What did you do?"

"To tell the truth, for a minute I didn't know what to do. I smelled danger. I didn't like that guy from the minute we 'kidnapped' him from the Bahnhofstrasse in Zurich. I can't put my finger on it — something about his behavior put me off."

"But what did you do?" Yaakov persisted.

"What did I do? After I recovered from my first wave of panic, I took stock of the situation. It was clear that Ilan would report to them that we were here, in the area. Now he could recognize not only the two of you, but also me. In other words, our search for Yossi was foiled. They have been warned. I have no idea whether or not they believe in violence, but they could conceivably do us harm."

"So," Yaakov asked for the third time, "what did you do?"

"At first I wanted to advise you to return to Zurich, where we could put our heads together to think of another plan. Then I decided: No! We stay! Hashem will help.... Looking around, I saw that I was standing right outside a souvenir shop. I had a brainstorm. I went into the shop and bought myself a full Alpine costume. Then I went back into the street and found a room that I could rent. That part was easy. In my room, I switched clothes.

"And now," Chaim concluded, "we're going to the room I rented. It's vital that you two get out of sight as quickly as possible. My Swiss clothes will help me get around and find out what we want to know." He glanced at them apologetically. "Again, forgive me for the scare I gave you."

Without waiting for an answer, Chaim started the car. It began climbing the mountain road.

"Chaim, wait."

The car's speed slackened. Turning his head slightly, Chaim asked, "What is it, Yaakov?"

"Our *talleisim* and *tefillin* — we left them in Zurich!"

Chaim laughed. "It's all taken care of. Apparently, no one back in Zurich explained with just whom you were dealing when you met me! I've already phoned a good friend of mine, Eliyahu, a native-born Swiss Jew. He's on his way here with everything we need: *talleisim*, *tefillin*, food. I told him the story and asked for his help. He's eager to do what he can."

Full darkness was upon the village when they reached the room Chaim had rented for the night. Before stepping out of the car, Chaim pulled on his Swiss cap, chuckling, "You'll get to keep this as a souvenir when our rescue operation is over."

The landlady opened the door to them, and stood regarding Elazar and Yaakov uncertainly.

"These are my friends from Israel," Chaim introduced. "They want to experience — if only for a day — the lovely life of the Alps."

"Ah, a very lovely life," she affirmed, nodding vigorously. "The bathrooms are over there, to the left. Breakfast will be served between 8 and 9 in the morning."

"Thank you, but we've brought our own food."

She was confused. "But breakfast is included in the price of the room!"

"Yes, I understand," Chaim said. "But we brought food along anyway. Thanks just the same."

All at once, comprehension dawned. "Ah, I understand. Kosher! Your guests eat only kosher food."

Chaim nodded. The landlady bade them a crisp, "Good night," and left them to themselves.

A little while later, there came a soft knock at the door of their room. Chaim opened it. In the doorway stood Eliyahu, his friend from Zurich, wreathed in smiles. Yaakov studied him with interest. The newcomer was a tall man, sturdily built, and dressed in the style affected by many Europeans — except for the large black yarmulke on his head.

Chaim made the necessary introductions. "Eliyahu, are you tired?"

"Not especially. Why do you ask?"

"If you're not tired, come out with me for a little look around. We're dealing with a Jewish life here. It's important that we stay one step ahead of the game."

The two men went out. Chaim turned to his friend. "Let's take your car, Eliyahu. Mine's already been identified in this neighborhood."

They were gone a long time. Upon their return, they found Yaakov and Elazar still awake, though already in bed. Yaakov sat up. Elazar did the same.

"Well?" Yaakov demanded.

Chaim said slowly, "That Ilan of yours is apparently a dangerous fellow."

"Maybe so — but what brought you to that conclusion after your little 'night prowl'?"

"Something made me return to the village outskirts, to the place where we had parked the car earlier. I don't know why I felt that was a good idea. Anyway, we went there, and from a distance were able to see a few of those orange-robed guys standing exactly where our car had been! They were looking at a small pond near the road. Naturally, we didn't stop, but continued driving so as not to arouse suspicion.

"A few hundred meters further, we came upon a side road leading into the forest. We turned into it. After a few minutes we parked the car beside a thick tree and retraced our route. We managed to get to within a few dozen yards of the cult members. We saw three of them. It was hard to tell their ages in the dark, but my instinct told me they were young. We threw ourselves down on the ground behind some tall trees and tried not to breathe. We tried with all our might to pick up every sound we could from that direction. But for 10 whole minutes they didn't say a word; just stood and looked at the pond.

"Suddenly, one of them picked up a rock and threw it into the pond. We heard it splash. For a minute, all was silent again. And then we saw one of the orange-robed guys turn to another and say — in *Hebrew!* — 'Let's go. Maybe they were here, but they're gone now.'

"'Maybe their car's sunk,' the other one said. 'I want to give my eyes a chance to get used to the dark. Another few minutes.'

"'It's a waste of time! We won't find them!'

"'Is it possible that he was lying to us all along?'

"'I don't believe it.'"

Chaim fell silent. Yaakov asked tensely, "What happened next?"

"Nothing. We waited for them to leave the spot. We saw them cross the road and start climbing the slope of the mountain. When we couldn't hear them anymore, we hurried back to the car — and here we are."

"And you think they were searching for us?"

"What else? Why would they have been standing on the exact spot where we had parked the car today."

"Apparently, Ilan told them about us?"

"Apparently," Chaim concurred.

"And what did they want, those searchers."

"I haven't the faintest idea."

"Are they upset by the simple fact that we're here in the area?"

"That's certainly possible."

Elazar moved restlessly in his bed. "Maybe it was Yossi who was looking for us? Chaim, what did he look like?"

Chaim answered patiently, "First of all, there were three of them. Which one do you mean? Secondly, it was dark, so identifying them was very difficult. Thirdly, I've never met Yossi. You didn't even bring along a picture of him. Didn't you realize you'd need one?"

Yaakov intervened with a curt, "Elazar, have you forgotten the threats those men made in the airport? Don't you know with whom we're dealing?"

"So you're saying," Elazar replied with a bitter twist of the lips, "that we're up to our necks in trouble?"

"It looks that way," Yaakov agreed soberly.

No one in the room looked at anyone else.

57

Yaakov woke with the first light of dawn. The room was filled with the scent of freshly mown hay. He got up, washed his hands, dressed and recited the morning blessings. Then he flung open the window to inhale the cleanest, purest air he had ever breathed. Row upon row of pine trees climbed the mountainside, and the cold pale sun of dawn was already brushing their crowns with gold. The same gold lay on the grass and the steep brown roofs of the cottages which were sprinkled here and there across the green vista.

Yaakov's eyes strayed to those cottages, and stayed there. Heavy curtains covered their windows. What secrets were those houses concealing? Was one of them sheltering Yossi, that unfortunate child who had taken such foolhardy steps.

Then, as he watched, the door of one of the cottages opened. A young villager appeared in the doorway. For a moment he paused, stretching in the crisp, delightful air. Descending a short flight of wooden stairs, he disappeared behind the house. Presently he returned, herding ahead of him a couple of cows and several calves, which lowered their heads and began contentedly cropping the grass in the meadow fronting the cottage. Dew still sparkled on that grass, like tiny diamonds in the early sun. It was strange to think of Yossi in this pastoral setting, so alien to him. Yaakov squinted up at the mountain peak. It faced him at a distance of an hour's walk, or maybe two. If he had guessed right, then Yossi was very close indeed.

He did not wake his friends. It suited him to be alone just now, alone with the wakening day. A good time for thinking, for making plans — crucial plans. As he filled his lungs with clear Alpine air, he pictured himself climbing the winding paths leading up from the road to the distant peak. A relatively short walk — and yet, how far! How much distance must be covered to reach Yossi's heart... Assuming, that was, that they had succeed in locating him at all, and that he'd agree to exchange a word with them. They required quite a bit of Heavenly assistance still.

Yaakov thought about the men who had threatened them at the airport in Zurich. Though it had not been very long, in terms of days, since Yossi had left Israel, who knew what he had experienced in that time? Would the trauma lend itself to healing? That was another thing he had no way of predicting.

A sound behind him told him that one of his companions was waking. Turning, he saw that it was Elazar, who was soon standing beside him at the window.

For a moment he gazed out at the panorama in silence. Then, "What are you thinking?" Elazar asked.

"Guess."

"The same thing I'm thinking?"

"Whatever you say...."

Yaakov had no desire to allow Elazar into the fog of his own thoughts. In the last day or two, their impending confrontation with Yossi had been uppermost in his mind. Would the boy try to run away? Would they catch him by surprise? Would he demand that they leave him alone, or recognize the devotion that had brought them all the way to Switzerland on his trail? Would he see their persistence as a sign of genuine caring — or as a symptom of social discomfort at the shame he had heaped upon his family? Would he believe that anyone really cared about *him*, personally?

Many scenarios played themselves out in Yaakov's mind, only a few of them hopeful ones. Until yesterday, he had been certain that he would find the right words with which to reach Yossi. He had been sure he could prevail upon the runaway to come home. But now, as he gazed through the open window at the stupendous mountains of Seelisberg — the mountains that concealed Yossi — he felt the pangs of acute doubt. A feeling of helplessness swept over him. He felt an emotion approaching despair, as a person feels when a long and difficult effort is about to reach a climax whose outcome is uncertain. A creeping fear sapped his confidence — a fear that all his effort had been in vain. He believed that the attempt to rescue a Jewish soul had been a worthwhile one, and one that had earned him merit in the Heavenly Court even if it ultimately failed. But success, in a practical sense, had never seemed more remote.

At this precise moment, when he required all the nerve and self-assurance he could summon, Yaakov was anxious and tense, battling the despair that threatened to settle over his heart like a black and muffling cloak.

Chaim awoke to a mood of elation. Energy coursed through him, and he felt gratified at the thought that his friend, Eliyahu, had agreed to drive up here into the Alps to join in the adventure. He woke Eliyahu and urged him to hurry. A day of action lay ahead of them. There wasn't a moment to be wasted!

After *davening Shacharis* and downing a hasty meal, Chaim announced in the voice of authority: "Yaakov and Elazar, you are to stay here in the room. Do not step outside, understand? We have no way of knowing whether you are being sought in the village. Showing your faces could be dangerous. Okay?"

Yaakov and Elazar nodded, then watched the other two leave.

"Good luck!" Yaakov called softly.

"Hashem will help," Chaim said. The door closed behind him.

He and Eliyahu entered Eliyahu's car. Afraid that Ilan would be able to identify his car, Chaim had obtained the landlord's permission to park it behind the building, out of sight from the street. A drive of a few hundred yards took them off the main road and onto a dirt track leading upward, toward the forest and the mountain. They drove slowly until they reached the first cottage. Eliyahu braked. Chaim, dressed in the villager's outfit he had bought the previous day, stepped outside and began walking unhurriedly toward the cottage.

A dog barked. The chickens set up a clamorous squawking. A middle-aged villager was in his garden, digging. Upon hearing the noise, he lifted his head from his work, leaned on his shovel and eyed the young stranger approaching him.

Chaim halted a short distance from the cottage door and called, "*Gruess G-tt!*"

Suspiciously, the villager answered, "*Gruezi wohl.*"

Chaim took two steps closer, his eyes never leaving the pair of dogs growling beside their master. "A nice day," he ventured.

His tone was convivial, but the villager wasn't buying. He answered coldly, "Yes, sir, the day is nice." He hefted the weight of his shovel in his hands as his eyes traveled over Chaim, inspecting him from head to toe.

Chaim took another step forward. Apart from the bristling dogs, a few cows grazed nearby. Pointing at them, Chaim remarked, "Your cows look like good milkers, eh?"

This time, he had hit the mark. The villager visibly thawed. Setting aside his shovel, he straightened his shoulders and said with pride, "Thank you. I'm certainly proud of them." He paused, then added, "I had another two just like them."

Chaim injected his manner with friendly interest, asking, "What happened to them?"

"They vanished."

"Vanished?"

"Yes. Vanished. Disappeared," the villager amplified.

"What do you mean, 'disappeared'?"

The man waved a hand at the forested slopes above them. Chaim nodded his understanding, whereupon the villager stooped, picked up a stone and threw it angrily in the direction he had just pointed out. Both dogs set up a furious barking and raced to the spot where the stone had landed.

"It's all the government's fault!" the villager exploded.

Chaim did not answer, being unable to find the connection between a couple of straying cows and this vehement political denunciation. If truth be told, he was not really very interested. He wanted to find the opportunity to turn the conversation toward the cult and its operations. The villager continued spitting out words, sharp as daggers: "It's too liberal! Our borders are much too open! Foreigners are taking over the whole country. Tamils, Indians, Arabs, Jews!"

Chaim leaned gingerly against a pile of logs waiting for the fireplace, and asked cautiously, "Foreigners stole your cows?"

"Yes. Exactly! Or rather, I don't know if they're the ones who stole them, but the cows disappeared because of them." He pounded on his chest with both fists to illustrate his ownership. "My cows!"

"How terrible! And the police...?"

The villager waved dismissively. "Hah, the police!" He let his contempt speak for itself.

"Do you mean to tell me that foreigners have spread even up here?"

The villager nodded, apparently too overwrought to speak.

"Who are they? A gang of robbers?"

"No," the villager spat out. "A cult of madmen!"

"What are they doing in this place?"

"They claim to be looking for peace and quiet — to be close to nature."

"But they're taking away *your* peace and quiet?"

"Exactly! And — and we're afraid of them!" The villager reached for his shovel and began scooping up earth pointedly and vigorously. He wanted to return to his work. But Chaim was not yet ready to go.

"You know something? I'm from Zurich."

"Yes?"

"I'm doing a little sightseeing with a friend."

"Some lovely country around these parts, eh?"

"Very lovely. I'm curious. Where do those madmen live — the ones you just talked about."

"Don't go near them! There are some awful stories...."

"Really? What kind of stories?"

"I don't know exactly. But there's talk. Ask in some of the other cottages."

This was the last thing Chaim wanted to do. He had no desire to establish bonds with other villagers or to attract any more attention than he absolutely had to. With studied casualness he asked, "In any case, which path would I take to find them?"

The villager's face turned cold and hard. "You're too interested in them. That's suspicious!"

"Suspicious?" Chaim laughed heartily. "I just like a bit of adventure — something out of the ordinary routine. Don't worry about me."

Mollified, the man turned and pointed. "You see that path on the left? If you take that, in about a quarter-hour's time you'll reach a clearing in the woods with a few small cabins. They've built a stone wall around the cabins. But I'd advise you not to go near. They won't let you in."

Chaim shook the villager's calloused hand, saying, "It's been a pleasure chatting with you. Who knows? Maybe I'll find your missing cows up there."

Chuckling, the villager bade him a brisk farewell. Chaim returned to the car, where he instructed Eliyahu to drive straight ahead until he reached a path branching leftward. "You'll turn in there," he said.

"Did he tell you anything useful?"

"I hope so. We're going to check it out right now."

Eliyahu did as he had been told. He drove with care up a bumpy dirt track that had them bouncing unmercifully in their seats.

"Stop!" Chaim whispered.

Eliyahu slammed on the brakes. Chaim thrust out a hand to stabilize himself. Eliyahu asked, "What happened?"

"Look over there — to the right!"

Eliyahu looked.

"Do you see them?"

"Yes."

They had a nearly unimpeded view of a forest clearing. In the clearing were several youths dressed in orange robes. A few cows grazed nearby. The cult members were sitting in a circle on low boulders, conversing in low voices. One of them was piping softly on a wooden flute.

Chaim made up his mind. "Eliyahu, I'm going over to talk to them. I want you to come with me."

"Did you really think I've come all the way from Zurich just to stay in the car? Let's go!"

In very short order, Chaim was approaching the group and calling out a friendly, "*Gruess G-tt!*"

The youths nodded mutely. It was clear that they did not understand the language. Still speaking in Swiss-German, Chaim continued, "Are you from around here? I'm looking for someone named Uhmgarten. Do you know him?"

The young men, by dint of vigorous hand motions, conveyed the fact that they did not speak in his tongue. Chaim tried to overcome the language barrier: "You are from America? You speak English? Or maybe you are from France? Or England?"

To each of his questions, the youths returned a negative shake of the head. Chaim heard one of them mutter to another, in Hebrew, "What does he want from our lives?" He pretended not to understand.

"English?" he persisted. "Francais? Turkish?"

One of the cult members knew a little English. Laboriously, he stated, "We are from Israel."

Immediately, the others turned on him with shushing motions. "Why are you telling him where we're from? Don't you know that's not allowed?"

It was hard for Chaim not to betray his satisfaction with the way things were proceeding. They were definitely on the right track.

"Oh, Israel!" he exclaimed, beaming. "You speak Hebrew!" He pointed at Eliyahu. In slow English, he said, "He is my friend! He is Jewish! He also speaks Hebrew!"

Eliyahu recognized his cue. It was his turn to take part in this little drama. Having studied in Jerusalem's Mirrer Yeshivah for three years, he spoke a fairly fluent Hebrew. Moving closer to the group in orange, he launched into a hearty stream of touristlike talk: "Where are you from in Israel? Are you visiting here?"

The youths were clearly reluctant to enter into conversation with him. Undaunted, Eliyahu pressed on: "Are you too shy to tell me? Is it a secret? I'm not from Israel. I only studied there. My name's Eliyahu. I live in Zurich and came here for a little vacation in the mountains. This *goy*," he added, gesturing at Chaim, "is driving me around. And you? Who are you? Is this a summer camp for tourists?"

The youths exchanged hasty looks. They wanted to be rid of this nuisance at any price.

"Yes, we're from Israel," one of them replied at a rapid clip. "We're all from different parts of the country."

"Very nice! And what are you doing here?"

"Grazing cows."

Eliyahu looked surprised and slightly affronted. "Really? You could have gone to a kibbutz if it's cows you're interested in!"

"The peace of Switzerland — the divine peace — that's what interests us."

Eliyahu translated for his "driver." Chaim set his features into a semblance of pride in his country, chosen by these youths above any other. Eliyahu asked, "And what are your names?"

"I'm Doron," one of the youths offered. A second said, "I'm Shragi." And the third, bashful, murmured, "Dror."

The fourth did not say anything. Eliyahu glanced at him, smiling expectantly. The one who'd introduced himself as Doron stated, "He's called Yossi. He's the religious one among us — a yeshivah boy."

Yossi's eyes blazed at this spilling of his secret. Still, he did not say a word.

It was hard to play dumb in the face of this information, but Chaim made a gargantuan effort. As for Eliyahu, he hurried to turn the talk in a different direction. "So you guys just sit around watching the cows for hours on end? A little boring, isn't it?"

"It's not boring. This peace — that's what we want here."

"Oh, well, to each his own. How long will you sit here keeping the cows company?"

"We have about three more hours to go today."

With friendly parting words, Eliyahu and Chaim took their leave. They drove a little deeper into the forest, then turned around and headed back for the village. They had found what they were looking for. When they passed the clearing again, they waved at the youths. A half-hour later, they burst into the room where Yaakov and Elazar waited.

"Come quickly!" Chaim cried. "We found him!"

"Who?"

"What do you mean, who? Yossi!"

Elazar and Yaakov leaped to their feet and flew out the door. Seconds later, the four were settled in the car, traveling back up the mountain.

58

"It's your turn now, Yaakov!" Chaim exclaimed with enthusiasm. "We found him for you, and we'll bring you right to him. From that moment on, it's all yours!"

Eliyahu drove at breakneck speed. The curves of the road threw them back and forth in their seats, but no one paid this the slightest heed. Yaakov gripped the handrail on the inside of the door, feeling significantly more tense than any of the others at the upcoming scene. In an attempt to quiet his inner turmoil, he asked Chaim for details. "Speak clearly! Where did you find him? And what makes you think he'll still be there when we come?"

"He'll be there."

Yaakov nearly stopped breathing. "You mean — he's waiting for me?"

"No. He's not waiting for you. He has no idea on you are on you're way to see him. But I was given to understand, by him and his friends, that they'd be in the place where we met them for another two or three hours."

"Who are they?"

"A group of youngsters from Israel! All of them wearing the cult's orange rags. We saw them last night, at the entrance to the village. Remember?

"What are they doing up on the mountain?"

"Grazing cows! They do odd jobs for the villagers in the area, making a little money that they then turn over — or so I understood — to the cult's leaders."

A particularly steep curve swung Yaakov against the window. He steadied himself, then said, "All that doesn't really interest me. How do you know one of them is Yossi? Did he get up and announce, 'I'm Yossi Kimmerman, a yeshivah runaway?' Chaim, tell me!"

"You won't believe it, but that's nearly the way it happened. One of the other boys pointed at Yossi and told us his name — and mentioned that he was a former yeshivah student. It wasn't hard to put two and two together, and know that we had found the boy we had been looking for."

With hands that suddenly began to tremble, Elazar rolled down his window. Cool air blew into his face.

"I'm sorry," he said. "The suspense is killing me! I need a little air... Forgive me."

Yaakov felt much the same. His heart pounded, a prey to the twin demons of fear and helplessness. Though he had tried to prepare himself mentally for exactly this pivotal confrontation, it appeared all at once fraught with menace. He, who always knew how to stay calm and collected, felt his self-control slipping. The fear of saying the wrong thing to Yossi was nearly paralyzing ("If," he amended, "it really *is* Yossi.") He offered up a silent prayer: "Hashem, please open my lips...." What were the right words to use on such an unusual occasion? No, more than just unusual; it was bizarre. He imagined standing opposite the yeshivah student he had befriended, atop one of the Swiss Alps, the boy dressed in an orange-colored cassock like some kind of Buddhist monk.... Yaakov's head began to ache.

Chaim turned to Yaakov. "Yaakov, listen. They're sitting in a clearing in the forest that we'll reach in about 10 minutes. They like to philosophize

— about peace, mostly. Eternal peace, world peace, about the passage to a better and more tranquil life, a pressure-free life.... About the prison of this world, as opposed to the infinite expanse lying open to them inside the Third Mystical Eye.... But never mind these stupid details. We'll try to take the car in as close as possible. As soon as we stop, you jump out as quickly as you can. You've got to take him by surprise, so he doesn't have a chance to run away again. And then — Hashem should put the right words into your mouth. Don't worry, we'll be right behind you."

"And what about me?" Elazar asked. He was still trembling.

Neither Yaakov nor Chaim knew what to tell him. Chaim said, "That's a tough one. Look at the way you're shaking. That might work to our advantage — but maybe not. Your presence might, Heaven forbid, only make him angrier. We'll have to wait and see."

After a moment's silence, Yaakov drew a deep breath and said, "All right. Up until now we've done whatever we could. The rest is up to Him. We'll see what happens and hope for the best."

The car was near the clearing. The youths in their orange robes, recognizing it, did not appear startled or afraid. Then, to their shock, they saw it leave the dirt track and head straight toward them. There was no time to protect themselves from a possible collision — and, they quickly saw, no need. The car came to a full stop, just a few yards away from where they were sitting. The back door was nearly ripped off its hinges as Yaakov leaped out.

Now the youths did react. Three of them shrank back in alarm at this unexpected intrusion, though none ran away.

The only one who did not react at all was Yossi.

Yaakov recognized him at once, despite the odd clothing. His eyes swept the boy quickly, from head to toe. Yossi's face remained deadpan. He seemed utterly unsurprised at this sudden appearance of the *kollel* man who had befriended him and to whom he had confided, from time to time, a portion of what was in his heart. It was Yaakov who felt astonished — at Yossi's calm acceptance of his, Yaakov's, presence in Seelisberg.

Yossi gazed past Yaakov, to the car. He had a clear view of Elazar, hunched into his corner as though trying to make himself invisible.

Lowering his eyes again, Yossi picked up a few pebbles lying scattered on the rock on which he sat and began playing idly with them. Above, a fresh breeze whispered secrets to the trees, who replied with gentle waves of their branches. Yossi made no attempt to run.

Yaakov attributed Yossi's total lack of surprise to Ilan's disappearance. It had most likely been Ilan who had informed him of their presence in Switzerland. Yaakov found Yossi's calm acceptance of the situation a hopeful sign.

What to say? The other orange-clad youths sat silently, aware of the tension that underlay this meeting. Without speaking, they awaited developments. They were, Yaakov noted, quite young: no more than 17 or 18 at the most. Finally, he returned his gaze to Yossi, and whispered, "Yossi, are you surprised?"

No answer.

"Were you the one who was searching for us last night? Late last night, at the entrance to the village?"

This time, Yossi did react. He lifted his head, and a flash of surprise lit his eyes. It was a brief flash, quickly quenched.

Yaakov took a few measured steps closer to the boy, and then stopped, hesitating. Another step, and he was sitting beside him. Like Yossi, he picked up a few pebbles and let them slide through his fingers. Yossi did not move. On every side, eyes watched the drama being enacted before them. The watchers were silent.

Yaakov placed a gentle hand on Yossi's shoulder. The boy did not budge. There was no softening of his rigid posture — but neither did he shrink away. Yaakov took hope.

"Tell me, Yossi. Do you remember the night you phoned me?"

After a moment, Yossi nodded. Joy spread through Yaakov's chest. He leaned slightly closer, saying, "The second time you tried to call, someone stopped you, right?"

Another swift nod confirmed this.

"Well, here I am. What was it you wanted to tell me over the phone that second time?"

Yossi made no reply. Yaakov glanced at the boy's face, trying to read his thoughts. But the face was turned slightly downward, eyes glued to the ground. Seconds passed in silence — seconds that seemed to stretch through all eternity. One of the cows began swishing her tail noisily and continuously; another bawled aloud. An orange-robed youth stood up and went over to see what was bothering the beasts. Yossi glanced at them momentarily, then lowered his eyes again.

Yaakov was afraid of the lingering silence. Whatever spark of communication had been ignited between them must not be allowed to go out. He said, "Tell me, Yossi: Would you feel more comfortable talking to Elazar? You know he's here, too?"

Yossi nodded.

"Then you're willing to talk to him?"

A negative shake of the head.

"And me? Will you talk to me?"

No reaction.

All in all, Yaakov was satisfied. Yossi's rejection of him had been neither firm nor final. A few more soft words might be all that was needed to carry the conversation forward. If only he could find the right words! But they would not come easily. Yossi showed no inclination to open up.

Yaakov had no idea how much time had passed when the first stirrings of despair crept back into his heart. He waited a little longer, then removed his hand from Yossi's shoulder, stood up, and said quietly, "Okay, Yossi. I can't force you. If you don't want to talk to me, you don't have to. From your phone call, I understood that you were interested in telling me something. Because I feel that you are my friend, I made a supreme effort to reach you." He shrugged sadly. "It looks like my time and money were wasted."

He paused, searching Yossi's face, but found no response.

"All right," he said finally. "I'll respect your wishes and leave now."

He turned away and began walking slowly toward the car. The burden of failure weighed terribly on him. Was he not meant to rescue this Jewish child? What to do, *Ribbono shel Olam?* What to do?

Taking small, even steps, he went to the car, whose door still hung open after his explosive departure. Though he did not turn around to gauge Yossi's reaction to his leaving, his ears strained to pick up some sound from behind his back. He walked slowly, trying to stretch out the time, hoping against hope that something — some miracle — would happen. So long as he was not actually in the car, driving away, hope was still possible.

He reached the car. Chaim, Eliyahu and Elazar peered out at him anxiously. Yaakov spread his arms in a gesture of futility and called out in ringing tones: "That's it! There's nothing else to be done. We're going home."

No one said a word. Yaakov hesitated a moment longer, and then entered the car and closed the door. "Let's go," he ordered Eliyahu.

The driver turned, hesitating. "You don't want to wait around a bit longer?"

Yaakov's answer was harsh and unequivocal. "I told you, turn on the motor and move! I know exactly what I'm doing. Go — quickly! This is my last chance to reach him!"

Eliyahu shrugged, and did as he had been told. He executed a careful U-turn on the narrow dirt road, until the car was facing the direction from which it had come. The trees slid back as the car began moving forward. The car picked up speed.

As it did, a voice came from behind, shouting: "Reb Yaakov, Reb Yaakov — *wait a minute!*"

59

Athrust of joy and relief went through Yaakov with the force of an electric shock. His gamble had paid off! For all his apparent indifference, Yossi had all along been subtly broadcasting his desire to keep the channels of communication open. The signs were there: his midnight phone calls to Yaakov from his hiding place; the way he had come down to search for their car last night; and his decision not to run away at Yaakov's unexpected appearance. Yaakov had gambled that his intention to leave Yossi permanently alone — an intention he had proclaimed very publicly just before getting into the car — would elicit a response from the boy. It had been a calculated risk...but it had paid off. Yossi had capitulated. In this first battle in the war of nerves, Yaakov had won.

"Eliyahu," he said urgently, "stop the car — but slowly. He mustn't think we're too eager to talk with him."

Eliyahu brought the car to a leisurely halt, several dozen yards from the clearing. Yaakov got out and strolled back to Yossi, who was on his feet now, watching Yaakov's approach.

"You called me?" Yaakov asked, when he was close enough for Yossi to hear.

"Yes."

Yaakov was glad to hear the first word out of Yossi's mouth. The ice had been broken. Carefully, he asked, "Why?"

Yossi hesitated for a long moment. At last, he said, "I don't know."

The answer surprised Yaakov. "Maybe," he suggested, "you'll allow me to explain to you why I think you called me?"

Yossi's response was immediate. "No."

Yaakov's fingers raked his sparse beard as he considered his next move. He must step cautiously now. Every word must be selected with care. The next few minutes could determine the events that followed.

"Are you willing to sit down and try to have a discussion?"

"Yes."

They returned to the rocks they had been sitting on earlier. The other cult members, witnesses to this odd meeting between the Israeli rabbi who had suddenly descended into their midst and the "religious" member of their cult, moved away to sit near the cows. Something told them to leave Yossi and his visitor alone. From the distance of their new position, the youths threw many curious looks their way.

Yaakov started talking first. "May I ask again why you tried to call me?"

Yossi picked up a pebble and tossed it at a tree. He waited until the pebble struck its mark before replying, "I wanted to let you know that I was leaving forever."

Yaakov smiled. "Interesting! And why was that? Why was it so important that I hear that fact from you?"

For the first time, Yossi turned his head to look directly at Yaakov. Their eyes met. *His are still cold,* Yaakov noted silently, *but a little softer than they were a quarter of an hour ago.* He found that heartening.

Yossi removed his gaze from Yaakov and transferred it back to the forest. "I don't know," he said. "Or rather — maybe I do know."

"I'd be very happy to hear it."

Silence.

Yossi's breathing had become slightly labored, as though something was weighing on him. Yaakov tried to help: "If it's hard for you, you don't have to tell me. I'll overcome my curiosity."

"No, I…I want to tell you." Another silence, but this time Yaakov expected more. He was not disappointed. Yossi spoke haltingly: "Because you…you…you were the only one who related to me… listened to me."

The tremor in the boy's voice moved Yaakov deeply. He stooped to pick up a yellowed branch, his face averted to give Yossi a chance to recover. From the corner of his eye he saw Yossi bury his face in his hands.

Yaakov broke the dry branch into small pieces. Here was the "tiny" secret that had led to a tragedy of such immense proportions. The boy had been seeking something that every person should receive not as a favor, but as a matter of course: recognition. Recognition that he was a human being worthy of respect. Yaakov did not know precisely what had transpired between father and son, but he could make a good guess. Was this the moment to bring up those old wounds, in the hopes of healing them? What if such a move would have the opposite result?

He asked, "Did Elazar also not relate to you?"

"I don't want to talk about him. He was always on my father's side."

"But you can see for yourself: He came here with me. He pushed me to search for you, to fly out here after you."

Yossi's reply was a bitter snort. "Don't make me laugh. He's only afraid that my running away will hurt him when it comes to making a *shidduch*. After all, he's not like me. He's what they call a good boy. A very good boy…. He should be able to get himself a good wife, with a father-in-law who'll support him for years — and maybe even a car thrown in. Maybe even a *rosh yeshivah's* daughter! And now, I've ruined it all for him. I brought shame to the family." He turned to glare at Yaakov, challenge in his eyes.

A silence ensued, tense and emotion filled. Yaakov was not in any hurry to break it. It was Yossi's turn to talk now, until he had unloaded everything that had been preying on him for so long. Only when that was done would he be able to hear what Yaakov might say. Meanwhile, Yaakov closed his eyes and abandoned himself, for just a minute, to the magic of the forest. He let the cool, sibilant wind wash over his face and listened to the rustle of the thick green leaves. It was an oasis of calm in the heart of the emotional storm in which he had been living this past week.

Yossi said: "You know what? Maybe my brother's conscience is bothering him a little, because of all the grief he has caused me."

Yaakov seized upon this. "Ah, that sounds better."

"What do you mean?"

"I'll tell you. It's important to distinguish between the facts, and your own interpretation of those facts.

"Fact: Your brother Elazar urged me to undertake this complicated journey. In other words, to close our *Gemaras* for a time and go searching for you — even to fly off to where you were. That's a fact, right?"

Yossi listened intently, but did not answer. Yaakov repeated, "Right?"

"What?"

"What I just told you is a fact. A dry fact. Right?"

After a brief hesitation, Yossi said, "Right."

"Good. Now, you've decided to interpret that fact, in the light of what *you* are feeling. Who told you that that interpretation is the correct one?"

"What do you mean?"

"Yossi, listen closely! You've just explained to me that everything Elazar's done — his willingness to jump into this strange adventure to find you — is connected only to his own desire to make a good *shidduch*. To the fact that you've spoiled things for him. That's what you said — yes or no?"

Uncertain where Yaakov was heading with this, Yossi answered doubtfully, "Y-yes…."

"Good. Now, you noticed that I didn't respond to that allegation."

"Right."

"Because there was nothing to say. If you're caught up in a worldview that you've created for yourself, what can I do? Try to persuade you that it's not so? Impossible! But, luckily for me — or, more accurately, luckily for *you* — you added another sentence. Remember?"

"Which one?"

"You said that maybe Elazar has done what he's done because his conscience has been bothering him. Right?"

"Yes."

"And that, you have to admit, contradicts your earlier reasoning. With those words, you're essentially saying that Elazar has repented of whatever he might have done in the past — that he regrets it. Doesn't that contradict your earlier statement that he's doing it all just for the sake of a *shidduch*?"

Yossi sat deep in thought. Finally he responded. "It's possible," he conceded. "But I don't have a head right now for your philosophizing."

Yaakov risked taking gentle hold of Yossi's hand. To his delight, the boy did not pull away. "That's your mistake, Yossi! It's not philosophizing. This is real life! And you, unfortunately, are messing yours up — badly."

With a rapid motion, Yossi jerked his hand away. "Don't lecture me, please! I've made my own choice about my own life. I like it! It's peaceful. I've managed to shake off all the pressures I had at home and in yeshivah. Leave me alone!"

The frontal attack, Yaakov realized, had been a mistake. He backtracked immediately: "You're right, I shouldn't lecture. I didn't mean to. And if this is what you've chosen — well, free choice is something that belongs to everyone. It's built into the fabric of Creation." He paused. "And that even includes *wrong* choices, Yossi!"

He cleared his throat, which had become constricted with emotion. After a moment, he continued, "What I'm trying to say is that you chose the path you did because of the way you have interpreted what happened to you! But remember, Yossi — that isn't necessarily the correct interpretation. Here is a prime example. You yourself just agreed that there are two possible contradictory explanations for Elazar's action in urging me to search for you. Now, I'm asking you: Could there be a third explanation? Is it possible that you have interpreted things incorrectly in general?

All right, you have the free will to visit the Swiss Alps and go around dressed in an orange robe. Fine! But every decision has to be based on a true interpretation of what has happened to you. Otherwise, it's not really free choice at all — only a blind groping based on a raging emotion like hatred, or vengeance, or both together."

Abruptly, Yaakov stopped speaking. Yossi was watching him, listening intently. As Yaakov paused, collecting his thoughts, Yossi said quietly, "What explanation do you offer for Elazar's suddenly caring about me?"

"Why don't *you* think of one?" Yaakov challenged. "Maybe the word 'suddenly' is the basis of your mistake."

A sound behind them made them turn around. One of the other youths was approaching. "Sorry to intrude — but, Yossi, it's getting late. It's time we headed back."

"In a little while, Doron," Yossi replied impatiently.

Doron stood his ground. "That's a problem. You remember what happened to that Jamaican yesterday. We don't want problems with them. You know they're not exactly crazy about Israelis and Jews around here."

"Don't worry, I'll explain that an uncle of mine showed up unexpectedly from Israel, and I'm trying to persuade him to join us. Leave it to me. Anyway, we're only talking about a few more minutes."

Doron nodded, and walked away — though not before Yaakov noted his trepidation. He asked Yossi, "Do they punish you?"

Yossi tried to evade the question. "Never mind, let's finish our discussion. It's really getting late."

This was a problem. Under pressure of time, there was no way he would be able to convince Yossi. Yaakov gritted his teeth in frustration. He decided to risk speaking openly.

"Are you afraid? Is that why you're in such a hurry?"

Yossi was startled. He was aware that Yaakov was laying a trap for him, but the man didn't give him a chance to respond.

"I repeat," Yaakov said firmly, "from your reaction to my question, I gather that they use punishments to keep you boys in line. Maybe even physical punishment? I read somewhere that discipline is very harsh in these cults. Is it true?"

Yossi glanced uneasily from side to side, avoiding Yaakov's eyes. "Let it alone. I don't want to talk about it."

Yaakov pressed, "Why?"

"Come on, Reb Yaakov, let's finish our discussion. I really have to go."

Yaakov scrambled to his feet and stood towering over the seated boy. "Do you see? Here it is again! Facts and reality that you're interpreting in a twisted way, so that you can't really justify the step you've taken!"

Yossi got to his own feet, red faced and furious. He tried to say something, but Yaakov cut him off. "You're talking about the newfound peace in your life? About how you've escaped from all the pressures of home and yeshivah? About a life based on free choice — a problem-free existence? But what do I see?

"I see a boy who's enslaved to a cult and its masters — people he doesn't even know very well. You work for them and hand over the money you make. You're subject to threats and punishments. Or do you think I didn't understand what Doron was telling you?"

Again, Yossi tried to speak. But Yaakov had no idea how much time he had left. In just minutes, Yossi could get up and go — this time, forever. Yaakov must speak quickly, and he must speak openly, stating the truth that lay within him...and pray that Hashem have mercy on them both.

Elazar sat in the car for what seemed an eternity. He could see Yaakov and Yossi conversing, but from the distance could not make out what they were saying. Tensely he watched the play of expressions on their faces. He saw the way the talk grew progressively more animated. "Please, Hashem, let him succeed!" he prayed repeatedly. "Please…!"

It was torture to sit imprisoned in the car instead of taking part in the drama being enacted before his eyes. He had always thought that, by and large, he and Yossi got along fairly well. Why, then, did he have to detach himself now? Why was it his role to sit passively on the sidelines? He hadn't even had a chance to say "hello" to his own brother! From what Yaakov had given him to understand, Yossi was not interested in speaking with him. That hurt.

"Chaim, what do you think — should I go over and join them?"

Intent on watching Yaakov and Yossi in the clearing, Chaim did not hear the question at first.

"*Nu*, Chaim, what do you say? I asked you something!"

Chaim turned to Elazar. "What? What did you ask?"

"I asked what you thought about my going over and joining in the conversation. I'm going crazy, sitting here!"

"I don't know what to tell you," Chaim shrugged. "I don't know what your relationship with your brother is like."

"I think it's okay."

He genuinely did. At least, it was okay most of the time. True, Yossi avoided him many times, and did not want to learn with him as their father had ordered. True, Elazar had pressured him a bit, and seen to it that the *mashgiach* at Yossi's yeshivah kept his brother on a short leash. There had been some quarrels over this, and Elazar had been forced to present Yossi with some not-so-pleasant realities — realities that his brother had not enjoyed hearing. Still, all in all, Elazar thought, they had enjoyed good relations.

Apart from that, he was not at all certain that Yaakov knew what to say to his brother. Elazar had never really painted a complete picture of Yossi's character or described the full extent of Yossi's relationship with their father. Yaakov did not have the necessary background to handle what was transpiring. No, it really made more sense for him, Elazar, to go out and join them. Just to be close, and to listen, without saying a word...unless he thought it absolutely necessary, to get the talk back on track.

Elazar slid over to the door that was still wide open after Yaakov's precipitous exit. A second later, he was standing outside the car. The cool forest air surrounded him, beckoned him forward. He flexed his arms at his sides, hesitating.

It was not that he was afraid, exactly. But he did not relish the prospect of meeting the look in Yaakov's eye when he was spotted. Yaakov would certainly be angry at his intervention. Elazar began walking slowly toward the spot where the two were talking, carefully staying out of Yaakov's sight. Yossi, he was sure, would not give him away. There would be nothing in his manner to betray to Yaakov that Elazar was in the vicinity.

When he was about 10 yards away, he stopped, and leaned against a thick tree trunk whose crown climbed into the sky. Half-hidden behind the trunk, he listened to every word being spoken.

Yaakov said energetically, "Before you disappear, apparently forever, I want you to listen to what I have to say. I think it's important. Please give me that respect — if only for the sake of the way I treated you in the past and listened to you."

"Fine," Yossi answered. "On one condition: that you'll also let me say a few words in response."

Yaakov smiled. The boy was not stupid. And where there was intelligence, there was always a chance. He inclined his head. "All right."

He paused for several seconds of thought, then said, "These, Yossi, may be the last *Yiddishkeit* words you will ever hear. It's important for you to understand that, no matter how angry you are at various people at this moment, you still remain responsible for your own actions. You can never blame another person for your own behavior."

Yossi's eyes flashed fire. "So you're saying that my father was right in humiliating me and putting me down for years?"

Yaakov spoke in a deliberate, soothing tone. "I didn't say that. But first of all, Yossi, calm down. That's the only way you will be able to really hear what I'm saying. We'll talk about your father in a little while. Right now, I want to talk about you! About you, and your reaction to the way your father treated you.

"I told you, and I'll repeat, that every person is responsible for his own actions. Believe me, Cain felt insulted when Hashem wouldn't accept his offering — making Hashem, so to speak, 'to blame' for the jealousy that gnawed at Cain until he rose up and killed his brother. But did Hashem, when speaking to Cain afterwards, explain why He hadn't accepted the offering? No! Instead, He let Cain know that man, possessing free will, must stand up to the test! Do you understand? Instead of *reacting* to a new situation, he must *respond* properly to it.

"But Cain came with complaints against *Hakadosh Baruch Hu*. If the midrash hadn't told us what he said, we would never dare let such words pass our lips! Cain said, 'You, Hashem, killed my brother, because You created an evil inclination in me. You, Who watch over everything, allowed me to kill him. You are the One Who killed him, because if You had only accepted my offering, I wouldn't have envied him.' But Hashem completely discounted these arguments. I can't quote the midrash word for word; I don't have *sefarim* here with me. But you must have one there, in your cottage, no? You can look it up for yourself."

Yossi had been listening woodenly, eyes fixed on Yaakov's face. Not even in response to Yaakov's mocking witticism did he move a muscle. Yaakov had no way of knowing whether his words were penetrating or making sense to the boy. Two of the young cult members approached hesitantly.

"Yossi, excuse me, but it's really late. We have to go back."

Angrily, Yossi waved a hand at them, the way one might shoo away an irritating fly. Yaakov did not even glance their way.

"But Yossi, we can't wait any more. We're afraid of getting back too late."

Without looking at them, Yossi snapped, "Go return the cows in the meantime. Pass by here again on your way back. I'll go with you then."

Yaakov's eyes narrowed. "You're not going anywhere with them!" he decreed silently. The two others moved off and began the chore of rousing the cows from their contented stupor.

"Are you listening, Yossi? Cain blamed Hashem in exactly the same way that you're blaming your father! Cain said, in essence, 'It's Your fault that I killed Abel! You created an evil inclination in me, and jealousy. I *had* to react the way I did!' In other words, Cain was saying, 'I am not a free man with free will to determine my own actions. I merely react to what is done to me.' But *Hakadosh Baruch Hu* responds: 'No! You are a free man! You will withstand this ordeal, because I expect you to.'

"How? How does one withstand a difficult test? First of all, by seeking out the true explanation for what has happened to him. To understand why Hashem has refused your offering — that's the first step. Do you understand? Through Cain's story, Hashem is speaking to all of mankind, including Yossi, here in the mountains of Seelisberg. And He is saying: 'I am watching you, and expecting you to stand up under this ordeal.' But what do you do? You make yourself completely dependent on what your father does to you, like some kind of spiritual beggar, and run off to join a strange cult in the mountains. Who are you taking revenge on, apart from yourself?"

Yossi's face was turning steadily redder. Furiously, he tried to speak. "But my father —"

"Again your father! I've been telling you that it's time for you to take responsibility for your own actions — without any connection to what your father may have done. *That is the test.*" He paused. "Yossi, tell me this. If your father had treated you well, would you have let yourself be persuaded to run off to a cult? Answer me!"

The answer came slowly, tentatively. "No...."

"I believe that. I know you pretty well — well enough to know that you would never have embraced all this nonsense. Because you've convinced yourself that your father hates you, you've suddenly discovered the 'truth' of the Third Mystical Eye? You dress in an orange robe and graze cows on a secluded mountaintop.... Really, Yossi! You're not stupid."

Yossi said mulishly, "He does hate me."

"Let me finish!"

"No! You promised you'd listen to me!"

Yaakov sighed deeply. With a brief smile, he said, "You're right. Go on."

Yossi glanced into the forest. He saw his friends approaching again. Time pressed in on him, making him talk rapidly:

"Can you explain why he behaved that way toward me? Why did he always humiliate me in front of the whole family? Why did he give everyone the impression that I'm a worthless good-for-nothing?"

Yaakov opened his eyes wide. "Was it always that way?"

"N-no."

"Do you remember when it started?"

"Yes... I think so. I've been thinking about it a lot."

"Are you willing to tell me?"

"Yes."

"Well, I'm listening. Go on."

"I think it began in the sixth grade, or maybe the seventh. I don't remember exactly which. But I do remember the day it started, as if it happened yesterday."

"What happened?"

"I was a good student. I got good grades, even very good ones. My conduct in class was also okay. One day, some kids told on me, saying that I had been the one who spread glue on the teacher's chair. I didn't do it. The teacher, whose pants were stuck to the chair, became really angry. He punished me. When I tried to defend myself I got punished again — for being disrespectful and a liar. As if that was not enough, all this happened on the day before we got our report cards. My teacher went and changed my grade in *Gemara* from an A to a B-minus. He marked my conduct 'unacceptable.' And he also lowered my other grades.

"I came home with that rotten report card feeling very depressed. My father wasn't home. He came later, after I was in bed. He saw the report card and blew his top. Believe me, my father knows how to get mad! He woke me up and gave me a whipping. He wouldn't listen to a word I tried to say. Nothing! He hit me very hard and yelled that I'd shamed him…that I'm a zero, and I'd never make anything of myself.

"From that day on, he'd be after me for every little thing I did. That bad report card injured his pride…." Yossi ended bitterly, "And you say he doesn't hate me."

A new voice rang out behind Yossi. "And I say that's not true!"

Yossi and Yaakov whirled around in astonishment. Elazar took a few steps closer through the trees. "Why are you lying?" asked Elazar. "I heard you say just now that neither the teacher nor our father gave you a chance to deny what happened, and that this made you mad. Why not give me a chance to clarify what you said?"

Yossi hesitated. He shrugged. "Go ahead. Clarify."

Elazar came closer. Their eyes met. Elazar battled down a wild urge to hug his brother and burst into tears. Controlling himself with a mighty effort, he said, "After you ran away, Yossi, I spoke to Abba. He came to Yerushalayim to see me. It was a painful talk. I told him that you hate him, just the way he hates you. He stared at me in total surprise. He simply didn't understand what I was telling him. He asked me to repeat it. I did."

He broke off. The three were plunged into a tense silence. Yaakov said quickly, "Go on, Elazar. What happened next?"

"Abba stared at me with very strange eyes. I had never seen such a strange look. I didn't know what to expect next. I was scared…very scared. We were sitting in the car, parked on a side street in Rechavia. Suddenly, I heard him whisper, 'I? I…hate…Yossi? What kind of craziness is this? Hate him? Trying to educate a son is called hating him?'"

Yossi's friends were much nearer now. They stopped a little distance away, as though afraid to come too close, clearly hoping that Yossi would notice them and join them of his own accord. But Yossi showed no sign of even being aware of their presence. Elazar's last words had riveted him to the spot. He had to understand them more fully.

Suddenly, a shot rang out. Its echo reverberated through the forest. Above, birds set up a flapping, flying in all directions. The wind seemed to drop, as though holding its breath in expectation. The small group in the clearing stared at each other, startled and perplexed.

Another shot was fired — and then a long burst from a submachine gun…

61

Yossi's friends reacted first. "Yossi, come quickly!" Doron screamed. "It sounds like those shots were fired from the direction of our farm. Come on!"

They did not wait for his answer. Together, as though shot from a cannon, they began running uphill through the trees. Yossi, panicked, started after them, but Yaakov reached out a hand to block his way. Yossi tried to avoid the arm by dodging sideways, but Yaakov grabbed his shoulders and held them in a firm grasp.

"Yossi, you stay here! Don't go after them! Don't be stupid!"

Yossi began struggling with Yaakov, trying with furious persistence to break free of the man's steely grip. It flashed upon him suddenly that he was being imprisoned, suffocated, just as he had been for long years at home by his father. Painful images rose up, of all the times he had been forced to do what he did not want to do! A red rage mounted steadily inside him, consuming him. Like a wounded beast, he bellowed, "Leave me alone! Do you hear me? Who are you, anyway, to tell me what to do?"

But Yaakov did not desist. He squeezed Yossi's shoulder, saying, "No,

Yossi. I won't leave you alone. You're staying here! You have no idea what you're about to do. I want to save you from yourself!"

Yossi kicked him. When Yaakov was off balance, Yossi nearly managed, by a gigantic effort, to free himself from the imprisoning arms. Frustrated, he shouted, "Don't do me any favors, Reb Yaakov! Leave me alone! You just told me that I have free will to choose as I like. Well, what happened? Why are you giving yourself permission to take that away from me now? You're all the same! You just want to dictate to me how to live my life. You're trying to finish what my father started — to force me! To put me down! *Enough! Leave me alone!*"

Elazar watched the struggle, thunderstruck. He couldn't move. His heart wept as his mind flew frantically over his options. To interfere or not? Try to help Yaakov? He didn't know what to do. Paralyzed, he watched with a growing sense of helplessness.

Chaim and Eliyahu, watching through the car windows, saw the sudden confrontation and drew their own conclusions: Yaakov obviously required assistance. They burst from the car and ran toward the others in the clearing. Yaakov was still grappling with Yossi, who never stopped trying to free himself from his hold. At Chaim's approach, Yossi turned swiftly and kicked him in the shins.

"Yaakov, do you need help?" Chaim asked, massaging his shin.

"No — no," Yaakov panted. "It's all right."

The strange battle ended as abruptly as it had begun. Without any discernible reason, Yaakov relaxed his hold. He and Yossi faced each other, breathing hard. Yossi's eyes darted hatred at his erstwhile captor. Despite this, Yaakov smiled.

"You know what? You're right! You do have free will to choose. I won't bother you any longer. Do what you want. Choose as you will. Go with your friends! Go with them to the death, if that's what you think is the right choice."

Yossi, not yet fully recovered from the brief and violent struggle, stared at Yaakov. "Why are you talking that way? You're condescending to me! Why are you talking about death — just because you didn't get your way!"

Yaakov regarded him unhurriedly, a deep and newfound tranquility in his eyes. Something inside told him that, at this moment, serenity was the ammunition he needed in the battle for Yossi's soul. He spoke quietly, almost in a whisper:

"Yes, Yossi, I meant what I said. I won't explain why I used the word 'death.' I know things that you don't know. But I won't tell you about them now. I want you to choose! I repeat: Run until death, if that's your free choice."

After a short silence, he added, "If, that is, that's what you call free choice."

Yossi stood motionless. The freedom of choice that was being offered him — now, at this moment, so openly — made him feel suddenly weak. Being at liberty to choose set in motion some unseen mechanism in him, an unfamiliar mechanism: a sense of responsibility. Yaakov had pressed him into a corner. He had created a situation in which Yossi was forced to make a decision.

He was very troubled by this new sensation. He didn't know what to do with it. For the first time in his life, a strange and heavy burden weighed on his mind, his thoughts. He was confused.

His eyes went from Yaakov to Elazar. Elazar wanted to say something, to pass on their mother's message, her suffering and her pleas for Yossi's return, but Yossi's eyes were already traveling onward, to Chaim and Eliyahu. The forest was very quiet. No one said a word. Every pair of eyes was fixed, razor sharp, on Yossi. How would this confrontation end? The machine-gun fire, from somewhere farther up the mountain, was still for the moment.

Yossi found himself thinking of the same words Yaakov had said to him just a few minutes before. *You have to respond correctly to difficult situations, not just react to them.* The words revolved in his mind and would not give him peace. Why were they so important?

He could not, he realized, ignore what had just been revealed to him: how, until now, he had only been reacting to circumstances. He was enslaved to his father. Abba had beaten him without just cause — and he, Yossi, had reacted by turning wild, by throwing things, by teasing his brothers and sisters, by behaving disruptively at home and at school. And...and was his linking up with the cult and running off to Switzerland also nothing more than the reaction of an angry boy?

But what else could he have done? Did he have any choice? Didn't he think about his father every day — his father, who had destroyed his life? Was Yaakov right? Was he, Yossi, only reacting to what had been done to him?

The gunfire returned, a short burst this time, followed by a longer one. Yossi's head spun around to the source of the sound. He listened for a moment, then returned his attention to the group. Involuntarily, his eyes sought out Yaakov's.

"They're shooting again," Yaakov snapped. "What are you waiting for? Your friends are calling you! You've got it good there. You've finally found the peace you were missing at home and in yeshivah. True?"

Yaakov's tone infuriated Yossi. *Why is he starting up?* Yossi thought. *Is he doing it on purpose to get me angry, because...because he's convinced that he's right?*

That he had made a mistake in coming to Switzerland had become very clear to him from the start. The dream he had been following, and that had been promised him by the Israeli representatives of the Third Mystical Eye, had been destroyed almost immediately. He had hiked down to the village to phone Yaakov, to tell him that he had made a mistake, and to beg him for help in getting out of there. In that first conversation, however, he had lost his nerve. And when he tried again, it was already too late. One of the cult members had followed him, and caught him in the phone booth. He had grabbed the phone out of Yossi's hand and forced him to return to the mountains with him. They had been keeping a close and continual watch over him ever since.

No, he had found neither serenity nor the freedom he had sought from the suffocating pressures. The "House of Eternal Peace," as it was named, was run with iron-hard — and often degrading — discipline. In fact, Yossi felt himself imprisoned by the same bars he had tried to run away from. Only the hours he spent grazing the cows on the hillside afforded him any sense of liberty and well-being. Here, during those hours, he would lose himself in the intoxicating stillness and beauty of nature. The intermittent sound of the bells that hung around the cows' necks echoed and trembled in the pure mountain air. Together with a companion or two, he would let the sweet hours pass, relishing the respite from the burden of sadness and anger that never quite left him.

Home and yeshivah hovered always in the background of his consciousness, reminding him of his failure.

The hours of cowherding had begun as an escape from his home and his father; they had quickly turned into escape from the rigors of the so-called Farm of Serenity. The cult had succeeded in dragging him out here, a victim of clever brainwashing. But why was Yaakov so intent on reminding him of this fact, and so cynically? Why was he pouring salt on Yossi's wounds? And why do it precisely when he, Yossi, knew for the first time that he stood on the brink of a momentous decision? Surely Yaakov knew that he was making the choice that much more difficult?

Sounds of sporadic gunfire continued to reach them from the distance. Yossi's companions had long since disappeared among the trees as they fled up the path toward the farm. Yossi stood alone with his "enemies" — representatives of his father and his yeshivah. His disquiet increased with each passing second.

Yaakov moved a little further away, so as to remove any suspicion of coercion from Yossi's decision-making. He sat at the foot of a broad tree, leaned against its trunk and said mockingly, "What are you thinking about, Yossi? Did you want me to leave you alone? You've got it! Then why aren't you going? What are you waiting for? Decide! Or is something keeping you from following your friends?"

Yossi did not answer. At that moment, he loathed Yaakov with all his heart. He knew that Yaakov saw right through him, saw the doubts and hesitation that beset him. How alone he was! Inwardly, he cried, *Ima, help me! Save me!* He bit his lip to prevent the tears from falling. It hurt unbearably to remember his mother, who had seen what his father was doing to him, had known that Abba was wrong — and had not protected him.

Chaim began to feel concerned. He tugged gently at Yaakov's sleeve, but Yaakov, every nerve fastened on Yossi, noticed nothing.

"Yaakov," Chaim whispered, "let's go back to the car and get out of here. The police will be coming any minute. The Swiss police are extremely strict. We'll have plenty of explaining to do if we're found in this area. Listen to me!"

Still Yaakov paid no heed. His eyes remained trained on Yossi. The next few minutes would decide the boy's fate. He stood up, came a little closer to Yossi and said, "Maybe I can help you decide?"

His answer came immediately and with great forcefulness. "No!"

The word burst from Yossi like a lion's roar. Yaakov calmly replied, "That's right! The power to decide is in your hands alone. For the first time in your life, you're behaving in a genuinely responsible fashion."

Suddenly, an explosion of enormous magnitude rent the air. Yossi stared around wildly. The thunder of the explosion continued to echo down the mountain. Chaim, Eliyahu and Elazar gazed anxiously at Yaakov, who continued to look at no one but Yossi. The acrid scent of smoke began drifting their way, telling of a fire that had broken out somewhere higher up the mountain. Something told Yossi it was the Farm of Serenity that was burning. A feeling of utter powerlessness swept over him. What to do?

"Enough, Yaakov!" Chaim yelled. "I'm not willing to sit in jail for this! Believe me, the police are definitely on their way."

When Yaakov did not answer, Chaim bellowed, "All right, I'm getting out of here! Whoever wants to join me, fine. Whoever wants to stay here — stay! I'm not staying another minute."

Chaim and Eliyahu turned to where the car was parked and began trotting toward it, throwing anxious glances over their shoulders to see whether anyone was following. Elazar's nails were bitten down to the quick in his nervousness, but he did not budge. His growing panic was urging him to flee with the others — to put this spot, this forest and this country well behind him. But he was even more afraid of acting without Yaakov's consent. And Yaakov, it was apparent, had not yet abandoned hope in this impossible situation.

"Yossi," Yaakov said softly, approaching the paralyzed youth, "choose life, not death." He pointed up the mountain. "Up there — is death. You can hear it clearly: the end of the road for all the foolish dreamers that believed in something that isn't real."

Yossi met his eyes. Without warning, he screamed, "What are you advising me to do — go back to suffering? To humiliation? Is that what you call 'life'? Well, I don't want it!"

Elazar nearly burst into tears. He could not bear it any longer, the pain, the confusion, the suffering.

But Yaakov was pleased. He knew that the moment had come..

62

n the distance, like an echo from a different world, came the ululating wail of sirens. Chaim lifted his head in alarm, and listened attentively. The sound seemed to be coming from both police and fire-fighting vehicles. Rolls of smoke continued to swim down the mountain toward them. It became more difficult to breathe.

Through the trees, the smoke's source was clearly visible. It was the Farm of Serenity: The repeated and frightened looks Yossi cast in the fire's direction made that much obvious. Ilan, Yaakov thought, had apparently not been mistaken when he had spoken of the danger of mass suicide.

Another thought flickered through Yaakov's mind: Where *was* Ilan? But there was no time to dwell on that now. It was Yossi who required all of his, Yaakov's, concentration.

Chaim, frozen for a moment by the sound of the sirens, was galvanized into renewed activity. Running at full tilt for the car, he shouted over his shoulder, "You're crazy if you stay here!"

Yaakov bit his lip. The final moment of truth was upon them. It would be a short one — short and suspense filled. Very little time remained to try to sway Yossi's heart. The appearance of the police would end everything. At this fateful juncture, speed was of the essence....

Feeling like a tightrope walker carefully feeling his way, he stepped closer to Yossi. He would not leave the boy alone at this difficult hour, come what may. He called to Elazar, "Go to the car, and don't worry about us. We'll follow in a minute."

He glanced at Yossi, trying to gauge the effect of the word "we." He had used the word deliberately. If Yossi reacted with a furious, "What do you mean, 'we'? Who said I'm going anywhere with you?" then Yaakov would know he had lost.

But Yossi — to Yaakov's quiet satisfaction — did not react immediately. He stood staring up the mountain with glazed eyes. A sudden fear took hold of Yaakov. What a bizarre situation — and a dangerous one — he had become entangled in! What would become of them if Chaim actually drove off?

It did not matter. He had no other choice but to stay. He must bring Yossi home freely and willingly, not by force. Divine assistance had guided his steps to the Swiss Alps. The words Yossi had screamed a moment ago were, Yaakov thought, a shout of liberation. It showed that the boy knew what he had to choose, difficult as that might be for him.

And it would be very difficult. The pain and the degradation he had suffered — whether the suffering had been based on reality or on his interpretation of reality — formed a formidable barrier, and one which Yossi would not easily surmount. Yaakov spoke quickly, with a sense of time rapidly slipping away:

"No, Yossi! I have no intention of returning you to your former life — except to let you become free of it. After a full week of tasting the 'paradise' that the cult offers, and to which you have become subjugated, I think you know where your real place is. Am I right?"

Yossi did not answer. Gently, Yaakov took his hand. Yossi did not pull away. He asked again, quietly, "Am I right, Yossi?"

Yossi smiled, shamefaced, but did not say a word.

"It's okay, you've answered me. I understand."

The wail of the sirens grew closer, slicing the crystal air like a knife. Chaim became extremely agitated. He switched on the motor and the engine roared into life. But he could not find it within himself to abandon Yaakov, Elazar and Yossi in the forest, totally vulnerable in the face of the harsh Swiss legal system. The police were sure to suspect them of having a hand in the mysterious gunfire and explosions. Their simple presence, as strangers, would bring suspicion down on their heads.

Executing a swift turn, he brought the car off the dirt track and into the forest itself. He navigated between the trees until he reached a sudden sharp decline. From the bottom, the car would be hidden from the road. He leaped out and, together with Eliyahu, heaped fallen branches and leaves all over the car's roof and hood. Gasping and stumbling, he ran back up the incline, where he motioned frantically to Yaakov, Elazar and Yossi to follow him to the place of concealment. The sirens were ominously close now.

"Yossi," Yaakov said urgently, "you're in danger! I'm not trying to force you, but we have to hide! Come with me!"

Yaakov broke into a run, Elazar hard on his heels. He was afraid to look back to see what Yossi was doing.

The boy hesitated, not moving at first. He could hear the roar of the police cars as they climbed the track. They must be just around the next bend…. In less than a minute, police officers would surround him, hard and menacing. Yossi shot up and raced desperately for the hidden spot where his uninvited guests lay trembling on the ground. They scarcely breathed as they locked their collective gaze at the dirt road. It seemed to their overactive imaginations as though the trees themselves were bending forward to help hide them.

Three police cars rushed madly up the road, climbing ever higher. Two fire trucks came after them. For several minutes the scream of sirens filled the air, along with the departing thunder of the several engines. Only when the last echo had been silenced did the group sigh deeply in relief. A respite had been achieved.

Chaim spoke crisply. "We have to get out of here, and fast — before they come back down the mountain. I'd suggest we hit the road immediately."

Yaakov looked at Yossi. "Are you coming with us?"

"I don't know."

Chaim stood up, shaking dried leaves from his clothes. Eliyahu did the same. With large, sweeping motions they brushed the camouflage from the car. This time, it was clear, they were determined to go, even if it meant leaving Yaakov and the others behind. Elazar stood undecided. Yaakov got up, picked a few dead leaves off his pants, then turned soberly to Yossi.

"Yossi, listen well. I'm leaving now. I don't think I'm required to sacrifice my life to the bitter end. 'Your life comes first,' *Chazal* teach us. I'm not forcing you to come along. As I've told you again and again, the decision is in your hands. Listen well, and understand what I'm telling you now.

"If you decide to stay — that is, you continue to run away, and to react to what you think your father's done to you, and to remain imprisoned in your pain, convincing yourself that there's no place for you on this earth except in the company of madmen who are alien to you and your upbringing — then you'll always remain your father's slave! Even if you run to the ends of the earth, you'll take your anger and frustration with you, and live with them from moment to moment...."

Yossi tried to say something, but Yaakov made a silencing gesture. "Let me finish. There's no time! I've got to get into the car and leave this place."

Yossi submitted.

"On the other hand, Yossi, if you come with me now, if you decide to return to life and abandon the death that awaits you in these mountains, then you're deciding, in essence, to free yourself from this slavery to your father and what he's done to you. Your decision will be tantamount to an announcement, in your own heart, that the unpleasantness of your past will not be permitted to dictate how you live your life. *You* will decide how to live, not them! No one who's ever harmed you will be permitted to tell you how to live. You'll live the way you know you should: the life of a *ben Torah*, with all that implies. You'll do that despite the damage that may have been done to you.

"If that is your decision, you'll discover a new way of looking at what has happened to you. I'm not justifying your father's behavior toward you, not by any means. But I'm also not accepting your interpretation of why he did it. If you choose to come back and free yourself of the need to run away from him, then you'll also see things in a different light. You'll find out that he doesn't hate you, even though he made major mistakes with you. And do you know why you'll see things differently? It's because you'll see them as a free person. A person who doesn't just react to what's done to him, but rather chooses the correct response to his problems. Do you understand?"

Chaim had already turned on the motor. Yaakov motioned for Elazar to get inside. "What are you waiting for? I'll be right there. Go on!"

Elazar obeyed. With tentative steps he went to the car and was swallowed up inside. He left the door open.

Yaakov looked at Yossi again. He smiled benevolently. "It seems to me, Yossi, that I've said everything there is to say. I have no words left."

He extended a hand to Yossi, who took it in his own limp one.

"Good-bye!" Yaakov said.

Yossi didn't say a word, just looked brokenly into Yaakov's eyes, then lowered his own. Yaakov gently removed his hand from Yossi's and turned to the car, which had already begun inching slowly forward.

Just before he disappeared inside, he turned once more, to wave good-bye to Yossi. To his joy, he saw the boy walking slowly, head down, taking stumbling steps, toward the car….

The car hurtled toward the village of Seelisberg. Every person inside prayed fervently that they not encounter any police cars along the way. After nearly half an hour's traveling, they reached the outskirts of the village. Chaim parked the car at a reasonable distance from the spot where they had stayed the previous night. He stepped out of the car, letting Eliyahu take his place behind the wheel.

Another 15 minutes and he was back, in his own car this time. Eliyahu followed as Chaim drove some distance from the village, where he stopped again. This time he brought a bundle over to Eliyahu's car. It contained Chaim's clothes.

"I'd suggest," he told Yaakov, "that you tell your young man here to get rid of that orange robe immediately. Here are my clothes. I'll stay dressed as a Swiss villager" — he grinned mischievously — "and hope that my wife will recognize me when I get home."

Lucerne was an hour's drive away. They made a rest stop at the local yeshivah. Yossi declined to leave the car, but Elazar got out. He wanted to phone home without his brother's knowledge. Once he had told his story to the yeshivah administrators, they permitted him to place the call to Tel Aviv.

Elazar waited in an agony of impatience while the connection was being made. He heard the phone at the other end ring once, then again. A familiar voice answered.

"Ima, Ima, do you hear me? It's me — Elazar! I'm calling from Switzerland!"

Tzipporah, at the other end of the line, felt her heart begin a rapid, painful pounding. Cautiously, she asked, "What's new? Are you enjoying yourselves?"

"Enjoying? Ima, we found Yossi!"

Tzipporah sank into an armchair that fortunately stood nearby. Her hands shook and her vision swam. Her lips moved, forming incoherent words. Through the receiver she heard Elazar's voice: "Ima! Why aren't you answering? Did you hear me? Yossi's with us! Yes, yes — with us, here!"

Tzipporah could not utter a word. Nor could she cry. She passed a hand over her forehead, which had become suddenly cold and clammy. Finally, mustering all her strength, she managed to croak, "I heard, Elazar. *Baruch Hashem! Baruch Hashem!* Can — can I talk to him?"

"No. He doesn't know that I'm calling. He's out in the car right now. It's still hard for him, Ima. Even talking to me is hard. It's all Reb Yaakov's doing. He was incredible!"

Tzipporah leaned back in her chair, closing her eyes as an ineffable weariness overcame her. "Where did you find him?"

"Ima, that's a long story. We'll come home and tell you everything. Where's Abba?"

"Abba? Abba flew to Zurich this morning."

Elazar was thunderstruck. "What do you mean, 'flew to Zurich'? Tell me!"

Breathing deeply, Tzipporah found the strength to speak more normally. "I don't know how much you know about the way Abba's suffered since Yossi left. He tried to act outwardly calm, but inside, his conscience was killing him. And you should also know, Elazar, that he's changed. Abba has changed a lot in the past few days. So has his attitude toward Yossi."

"So what happened?"

"Abba suddenly decided to become a part of the search. He wanted Yossi to see that he doesn't hate him."

"But what did he do? How would he know where to look?"

"I don't know."

"He just flew off into the thin air? I don't get it!"

"Not exactly. He thought it was necessary for him to do something concrete to try and repair the situation. He was sure that Hashem would guide him in the right direction."

Elazar was overcome with emotion. Elation filled him at the news that his father's approach to Yossi had undergone a transformation. His first impulse was to run and tell Yossi, but he quelled it almost at once. Yossi was going to have to learn to trust his father again, and it would have to happen gradually. Elazar was afraid of saying too much, too soon.

"Ima! Can you hear me?"

"Yes, darling. I'm still here."

"In another few hours we'll be at the Goldenn Brunnen Hotel in Zurich. The address is Roterstrasse 33. How will Abba find us?"

"I hope he'll phone me, and I'll give him the address. Tell me again. What was the name of that hotel? I'm writing it down."

"Goldenn Brunnen, Roterstrasse 33."

"I have it. Meanwhile, have a safe trip to Zurich. Tell Reb Yaakov that I thank him from the bottom of my heart. And tell Yossi...tell Yossi...."

She couldn't go on. All her strength departed, leaving her weak and trembling. Elazar asked sharply, "Ima, what's wrong? Why'd you stop? What did you want me to tell Yossi?"

She bit her lower lip, and managed to whisper into the receiver, "Give Yossi…a million kisses from…his mother."

"It's too early for that, Ima. Everything's still very sensitive around here. Good-bye for now!"

"Good-bye," she whispered.

Slowly, very slowly, she replaced the receiver. Her hands came up to cover her face. And this time, the tears did come.

63

The two cars, Chaim's and Eliyahu's, left Lucerne and turned onto the highway to Zurich.

In Chaim's car, silence reigned. Yossi sat wrapped up in himself, eyes fixed for the most part on an indeterminate spot on the floor. From time to time he would lift them just long enough to survey the passing scenery, and then lower them to the floor again. The major portion of his energy went into avoiding the others' eyes. Yossi and Elazar had yet to exchange a single word.

Finally, Yaakov decided it was up to him to break the ice. There was nothing like pleasant conversation to bring about a warm and friendly atmosphere. Casually, he asked Yossi, "Are you hungry?"

Yossi shook his head.

"Thirsty? Want something to drink?"

The same negative headshake.

It was not hard for Yaakov to discern the inner tension that was plaguing the boy. Yossi was a prey to apprehensions about the unknown future.

He was doubtless nervous about renewing his acquaintance with the world he had run away from. His upcoming reunion with his parents — especially the one with his father — would stir up additional anxiety. And here was a fresh cause for concern: Would he be able to return to yeshivah? How would his friends receive him? Yaakov was keenly aware of the many challenges that awaited the runaway.

Well, Yaakov would do his share to protect him. He would not leave the job half done. After having labored and traveled to find Yossi, he would not stop here, depositing his prize into the very world that had led to his self-destructive behavior. Yaakov was confident that no one — not the boy himself, nor his father — would object to his taking Yossi under his wing.

In a quiet, gentle voice, he asked, "Did you know we had come to Seelisberg?"

Yossi nodded affirmatively.

"Was it Ilan who told you?"

Another nod.

"You mean he reached the cult's base? The farm?"

Softly, Yossi answered, "Yes."

Silence fell again. The riddle of Ilan's role in the whole affair troubled Yaakov. Unsure how to broach the questions uppermost in his mind, he ventured finally, "Was Ilan the one to convince you to join the cult?"

"No."

"Is he a cult member?"

"I don't know."

"Well, what was he doing there?"

"I don't know."

"One more question. Did he have a nephew in the cult?"

"I think so."

Yaakov's curiosity was even stronger, but he desisted. He would leave the questions for another, quieter, time. The wound was still fresh, and Yossi's turbulence and confusion still too great.

An hour and a half later saw them at the outskirts of Zurich. Dusk was spreading a purplish shadow over the city. With a sure hand, Chaim navigated the car toward Roterstrasse 33 and the Goldenn Brunnen Hotel. Yaakov was the first to emerge, signaling for Yossi to follow. This Yossi did, with an air of one resigned to his fate. The small group entered the hotel lobby, where Yaakov approached the reception desk for the keys to their room.

Suddenly, from one of the comfortable armchairs arranged around the lobby, a tall figure arose. He walked slowly, almost fearfully, in their direction. Elazar was the first to notice. His breath stopped in his throat. A single word burst from him:

"Abba!"

Yossi reacted as though he'd been scorched. Spinning around, he saw his father, looking larger than life. The blood drained away from Yossi's face as the strength drained from his body. Tremors ran up and down his legs. Watching him, Yaakov saw that the boy was close to collapse. Throwing a protective arm around Yossi's shoulders, he murmured, "Be strong, Yossi! I didn't know he was here. This comes as a surprise to me, too. But maybe it's a good thing. Be strong. I'll be with you every step of the way. Always!"

Zevulun stood watching his younger son with pain-filled eyes, his heart hammering in his chest like a set of wild drums. He could not have moved if his life had depended on it. This unexpected meeting was just too much for him.

They stood in frozen tableau for an eternity — until Zevulun finally took one small step forward. He stopped. Nobody else moved a muscle. Putting one foot in front of the other, Zevulun began walking again, still at a snail's pace. At one point he bent and placed his attache case on the floor, as though he wished to free his hands. He understood that the responsibility for taking the first step was his own. He was the father, the adult, and it was up to him to change things.

Nobody paid the slightest attention to the young desk clerk whose arm was upraised, dangling a key that Yaakov never took. He, too, sensed the incredible tension in the air, and watched the unfolding drama with mesmerized eyes.

Zevulun came closer to Yossi, who stood paralyzed. Yaakov, an arm still around the boy's shoulders, felt Yossi's muscles stiffen at his father's approach. How, he wondered apprehensively, would this surprise meeting end?

Now Zevulun was standing very close to Yossi. For several seconds, nothing happened. Then the father's hand lifted, and he placed it on his son's head. It was a gentle hand, almost a caressing one. The hand crept down to stroke Yossi's cheek. Yossi felt a shock, as if of electricity, beginning at the top of his spine and running clear down to his toes. He understood that his father was holding out the olive branch — compassion, warmth, love — everything that had been denied him so long. His heart constricted painfully with the force of his emotion. The pain was nearly unbearable....

Suddenly, he lunged forward and threw his arms around his father in a powerful hug. Zevulun returned the embrace just as powerfully. Yossi held on as though he never wanted to let go. He trembled uncontrollably, and his eyes dimmed with tears....

Yaakov was the first to recover. He signaled to Elazar, whose face was already awash with his own tears, to Chaim, who was vastly enjoying the drama, and to a fascinated Eliyahu, to leave the two alone. Without a word, the four walked to the elevator wich took them up to their room.

Elazar sank onto one of the beds and buried his face in a pillow. The other three sat silently, each thinking his own thoughts and sipping the mineral water they had found in the room's tiny refrigerator.

At last, Chaim broke the silence. "Well, what do you say? Some story, eh?"

Eliyahu replied fervently, "The main thing is that we succeeded, thank G-d."

Chaim put his glass down. "Know what I've been thinking about just now?"

"No, what?"

"Who knows how many other boys like Yossi are caught up in cults all over the world, and for the same reason? It's a crying shame!"

"Who knows," Yaakov said, "how many of them are back there in Seelisberg? What interests me now is: Who is Ilan? That's one riddle to which I would like to know the answer."

Chaim glanced at his watch. "It's 8 o'clock. The news will be on. I'd like to find out what the shooting and the explosions were all about." He stood up and turned on the bedside radio. The newscaster spoke evenly, monotonously, in Swiss-German. Neither Yaakov nor Elazar understood a word, but Chaim and Eliyahu listened attentively.

"Quiet," Chaim said in excitement. "They're starting to talk about Seelisberg! Ah...the police found close to 90 bodies on the farm. Do you hear? Ninety people dead! What a miraculous escape your Yossi had! Wait, let me listen.... They say they also found two critically wounded men, who were taken to the hospital. On the way, the police managed to question them a little. One of the injured men, an Israeli, said that he had been at the farm to try and rescue his nephew."

Elazar cried, "That must be Ilan!"

Chaim shushed him. "Let me hear! I want to continue translating for you... The injured men described what had happened at the farm. It seems that the cult's leaders announced that they had to die before being destroyed by alien invaders from outer space. Only in that way, the leaders claimed, would they merit eternal life. Most of the others, the wounded men said, agreed to commit suicide."

"Lunatics! Madmen!" Yaakov exclaimed.

"Sssh, just a minute... Not everyone agreed. So the cult leaders and their followers opened fire. They killed all those who refused to go along with them, and then killed themselves... The wounded men — both of whom died later of their injuries — said that the farm housed youngsters from countries all over the world. He listed some of them: the U.S., India, Israel, Jamaica, France, Egypt, Canada, Belgium, even two from Russia."

"Did they mention the names of the people who were killed?"

"No. But the injured men said that before the mass suicide, the cult leaders decided to burn down the whole farm."

"Go understand the minds of madmen."

Yaakov stood up and began circling the room, brooding. Chaim watched him. "What's the matter with you suddenly?"

Yaakov didn't answer.

"Tell me, what's bothering you?" Chaim tried again.

Yaakov halted. "You won't believe what's 'bothering' me."

"Well?"

"Really two things are troubling me — on the bigger picture, I know that had Yossi sought to discuss the problem with his *rebbeim* or other competent people, then things would never have escalated to the point of Yossi's running away. I wonder where things went so wrong!"

"And the second thing?"

"Ilan."

"What about Ilan?"

Yaakov came back and perched on the edge of one of the beds. "Who was Ilan? Aren't you curious?"

"Curious?" Chaim considered. "I suppose I am interested. But I wouldn't waste my energy on finding out who he was. That's the fate of a young Israeli who made a wrong turn in life. Hashem should have mercy on him."

Elazar put in, "I feel better, anyway. Ilan didn't betray us. He spoke the truth!"

"Still," Yaakov said, "I feel troubled by the whole thing. Ilan filled an important role for us — even a crucial one."

Suddenly, he leaped to his feet. "That's it! Without meaning to, I've solved the riddle!"

"Maybe you can stop speaking to *us* in riddles?" Chaim asked, exasperated. "Explain yourself!"

Beaming with the satisfaction of doubts laid to rest, Yaakov stabbed a finger in the air, and explained:

"Even back in Israel, I sensed something evasive in Ilan's behavior. Something inexplicable. His appointment with Elazar outside the Central Post Office in Tel Aviv never took place — but precisely for that reason we were able to track down the cult's headquarters on Aliyah Street. We didn't know which direction to pursue in our search for Yossi, though it was apparently somewhere abroad — and then Ilan's hasty flight to Switzerland pointed the way for us. Then, in Zurich, we had no idea where to continue our search — and stumbled upon Ilan, strolling along the Bahnhofstrasse. Without too much of a struggle, we got him to lead us to the cult's hiding place in Seelisberg. Doesn't that tell you something?"

"*Hashgachah pratis*," Eliyahu said, awed.

"Exactly! It was good to hear from Yossi that Ilan didn't convince him to join the cult. But in the practical sense, even that wouldn't have been important."

Yaakov leaned against the wall by the window and raked his fingers through his thin beard. "Listen," he said, "I'll tell you what I'm feeling at this minute. I don't know if it's right, but it's the way I feel." He drew a deep breath before continuing. "The Torah tells of Yosef, who was searching for his brothers in the fields of Dosan. It says that a 'man' met him and told him where they were. Who was that man? Nobody knows. Rashi says that it was an angel — the angel Gavriel. The Maharal says that the angel was a messenger, Hashem's messenger, whose job was to set the wheels in motion. In other words, he was there to help move the necessary events along — the events that Heaven wanted to happen.

"That was the 'man's' role in the story of Yosef and his brothers. The Torah doesn't tell us who that man was, and it's not important. What is important is the task he fulfilled. True?"

Without waiting for an answer, Yaakov hurried on. "Ilan was that 'man' for us! That holds true even if we never manage to unravel his true role in the story."

Nobody said a word. It was apparent from the quality of the silence that none of them disagreed with Yaakov's theory. Elazar stood up, facing the door.

"Where are you going?" Chaim asked.

"To Abba and Yossi."

"What's wrong?"

"Does anything have to be wrong? I'm a relative, remember?"

Yaakov interposed forcefully: "Don't go!"

"Why not?" Elazar was impatient.

"I think it's a good idea to leave them alone for now."

"Why?"

"Give them a chance to get re-acquainted with one another. Did you see the way Yossi hugged your father? Did you see what he was searching for during all those long years when they were distant from each other? And did you see how much your father also needed to be close to his son? Leave them alone, Elazar! You can only do damage by interfering now."

Elazar was not convinced. He grasped the door handle, but was stopped by Yaakov's commanding tone. "No, Elazar. Why go now? You'll have other chances. There's plenty of time."

Chaim glanced at his watch and shot to his feet. "It's late! Let's go to the shul on Erika. They'll be starting to *daven Ma'ariv* in just a few minutes!"

The four left the room and rode the elevator down to the lobby. Elazar swept the place with his eyes, searching for his father and brother. But they had gone.

Elazar was downcast. "Where could they be?"

"Relax," Yaakov comforted him. "Everything's all right. Believe me."

They arrived at the shul just as the congregation was preparing to say the *Shemoneh Esrei*. Abruptly, Chaim yanked at Elazar's sleeve.

"Look — over there! At the front of the shul!"

Elazar looked. So did Yaakov and Eliyahu.

There stood Yossi, beside Zevulun, both of them swaying gently as their lips murmured the *tefillah*. Their swaying was serene, untroubled, almost synchronized.

Yaakov and Elazar exchanged a warm glance. Then they joined the congregation in the *tefillah* and, for each of them, their prayers held an intensity and a fervor beyond any they had experienced in a long, long time.